ACROSS THE CHINA SKY

BOOKS BY
C. HOPE FLINCHBAUGH

Across the China Sky

Daughter of China

ACROSS THE CHINA SKY

A NOVEL

C. HOPE FLINCHBAUGH

BETHANY HOUSE PUBLISHERS
Minneapolis, Minnesota

Published by Bethany House Publishers
11400 Hampshire Avenue South
Bloomington, Minnesota 55438

Bethany House Publishers is a division of
Baker Publishing Group, Grand Rapids, Michigan.

Printed in the United States of America

ISBN-13:   978-0-7642-0239-1
ISBN-10:   0-7642-0239-1

Library of Congress Cataloging-in-Publication Data

Flinchbaugh, C. Hope.
    Across the China sky / C. Hope Flinchbaugh.
        p.   cm.
    ISBN-13: 978-0-7642-0239-1 (pbk.)   ISBN-10: 0-7642-0239-1 (pbk.)
    1. Christians—China—Fiction. 2. Cults—China—Fiction. 3. China—Fiction.
I. Title.

    PS3606.L56A65   2006
    813'.6—dc22   2006017379

To my father and dearest friend, Rev. Glenn Keenan,

for modeling humility and faithfulness and for always

taking time to talk to me about "important things."

Do not participate in the unfruitful deeds of darkness,

but instead even expose them . . .

THE APOSTLE PAUL

HOPE FLINCHBAUGH is a wife, mother, and freelance writer from Pennsylvania, covering the international persecuted church, revivals, and family issues for adults, teens, and children for magazines such as *Christianity Today, Charisma, Focus on the Family, World Christian, Campus Life, Brio, Breakaway, Clubhouse,* and *Clubhouse Jr.* You may contact Hope through her Web site, *www.seehope.com,* or send correspondence to:

C. Hope Flinchbaugh
Bethany House Publishers
11400 Hampshire Avenue South
Minneapolis, MN 55438

★ ✹ ★

CHAPTER

One

Chen Liko tugged at the yoke, signaling the old gray water buffalo to stop. The animal snorted and pointed his horns to the ground.

"That's the last row for today, Old Gray. Tomorrow maybe we will finish the job, eh?"

The animal raised his head up and down with pleasure as his young master rubbed him hard on the neck.

Liko pulled a handkerchief from his back pocket and wiped away the sweat that had trickled into his eyebrows. He leaned over, unhooked the lines from the yoke, and dropped the heavy wooden plow into the dark, rich soil where it would stay until the next day's work. Tired but satisfied, he slapped Old Gray on the backside with his stick.

"Back to the shed with you."

Some of the villagers were already walking back to Tanching, the large square boxes strapped to their shoulders hanging in front of them, empty now of the hundreds of young rice plants that had filled them that morning. Liko's eyes scanned the watery rice paddies in the distance, then stopped on a figure still bent over in the murky water. Kwan Mei Lin seemed tireless, thrusting green rice shoots into the mud below the water.

Liko was grateful for her presence. Any moment of the day he could search for her and draw pleasure just knowing she was next to him in the fields of Tanching, far from the awful prison life she had endured two years before.

Mei Lin stood then and waved at him. He waved back and pointed toward her family's cowshed.

The old cowshed was on the hill behind her house, and during spring planting Mei Lin often met him there to help him bed down Old Gray for the night.

The sun was setting behind him as he walked, casting a warm orange glow over the otherwise dull cement houses and chicken yards of Tanching Village. Mei Lin's house was the first one in from the sugarcane fields. He let the rope slacken as he led the water buffalo behind the Kwans' chicken house and carefully picked his path up the hill so the creature wouldn't trample the family's large vegetable garden.

He glanced behind him before going inside. Mei Lin was already at her house below the sloping garden. She would change out of her wet shoes and meet him soon.

Liko enjoyed the coolness of the little cowshed, with its familiar smells of fresh straw and grain and shafts of light that pierced through the wall's bamboo slats. He turned the large animal around, backed him into his stall, and closed the gate.

Old Gray pawed the ground, anxious to be rid of the yoke.

"In a minute, old man, in a minute."

Liko leaned over the water bucket by the wall and splashed his face and arms, washing away the day's hard work and sweat. He pulled his shirt collar up to his face and wiped it dry.

Turning, he saw Mei Lin. Her black shoulder-length hair caught the sun's rays as she stood in the doorway, holding out a long-handled rice bag in one hand—probably his dinner. She was as thin and delicate as a dove on the outside, but her spirit was as strong as Old Gray. Her smile brought a rush of warmth into his chest.

"Mei Lin!" Liko took her hand and led her inside, then took both of her hands in his. "These beautiful hands are water-logged."

Mei Lin wrinkled her nose at him and pulled her hands away. "You should see my feet. I can't wait until the water warms up. My toes are wrinkled and numb!"

"It's bad for your feet to stand in water all day."

"Now you sound like *Doctor* Chen instead of Pastor Chen," Mei Lin teased.

Liko smiled down at her and brushed the hair back from her cheek. "Perhaps you would prefer to marry Doctor Chen instead?"

"I'm planning to marry Chen Liko, not his occupation or title," she answered.

"Ah, now Ping would soundly rebuke you for your 'poisonous Western thinking,'" Liko said.

"Probably."

Liko searched her face in the darkness, glad for this time of day when they could be together. "Let's bed down Old Gray. Then we can talk."

Mei Lin gave Old Gray the bucket of clean water by the wall, leaning over the stall gate to grab the stale water bucket from the stall. She hauled the old water outside to her grandmother's garden and dumped it over the row of growing cabbages, then walked down the hill to her courtyard to refill the bucket at the courtyard pump.

Liko, meanwhile, grabbed the wooden mallet from the nail on the shed wall, then opened Old Gray's stall. He skillfully tapped the wooden pins out of the side of the yoke, and the heavy wooden under-collar shifted to the ground. Old Gray shook his sides with delight and snorted. Liko hoisted the collar and the other separate pieces onto their large wall hooks.

After returning the fresh water bucket to the wall, Mei Lin used an old cracked rice bowl to scoop fresh grain into the feeding trough. She scratched Old Gray between his horns. "Now you're earning your keep, aren't you, Old Gray?"

When she turned, Liko was smiling at her, waiting to shut the gate. "Don't I get scratched between the ears for helping?"

Mei Lin smiled. "Maybe." She dipped her hands into the water and then shook them dry.

"Ready?" Liko asked, suddenly serious. Lately Mei Lin seemed to be hiding something behind those beautiful eyes. He hoped tonight to find out what it was.

Mei Lin nodded and waited as Liko pulled the lantern down from the wall. She brushed his arm as they walked through the door together, and her stomach fluttered into her throat.

You're still a love-sick schoolgirl, Mei Lin chided herself.

Liko took her hand, and in unspoken agreement they walked behind the shed to their favorite spot. The field workers were gone now, most of them preparing evening meals.

Liko had never wanted to be a field worker, but he had replaced his father in both the field and the pulpit after Pastor Chen's death two years ago. Mei Lin was proud of the way he shouldered the responsibility for his mother and for his father's expanding church.

They were the perfect team. When it wasn't spring planting or harvest, Mei Lin spent her free afternoons evangelizing throughout Tanching. Liko taught on weekends. The Gospel was like a newly discovered stream of cool water, wending its way throughout the parched village. Everyone was eager to drink its sweetness—everyone but the cadre and Old One Tooth, the village fortune-teller.

Their small house church of Tanching was now divided into three smaller cell groups. Liko headed one group, Mei Lin's father a second, and Liko's mother the third. Their dream was to start a training school for evangelists, but they needed teaching materials.

When they came to the rice paddies just beyond the cowshed, Mei Lin and Liko slipped off their shoes and rolled up their pant legs. Leaving their shoes behind, they carefully walked across one of the slippery ridges that separated the watery rice paddies.

Liko led the way off the path and into the cold water.

"Your neighbor will have his rice planted up here by the end of the week," he said, wading in water up to his shins.

"Then we'll meet in the cowshed again, like last winter?" asked Mei Lin, her voice shivery. She rolled her pant legs a little higher above the knees.

"Maybe. Until the new rice shoots are well rooted."

Slowly they walked through the paddy, cold wet mud squishing between their toes with each step, making their way to a large rock that jutted out of the water. Mei Lin jumped easily onto the rock and then sat beside Liko on its edge, splashing the shallow water between her muddy toes until they were clean.

Mei Lin loved the view from the rock. Facing the cowshed, she could barely see the top of her house. To the far right, the sun set behind sugarcane fields and rice paddies that went on for miles, as far as they could see, up the distant mountain. On the left, the small houses, gardens, and winding paths of Tanching were alive with people watering their gardens and finishing the day's work while neighbor children congregated to play.

Liko moved up higher on the rock, and Mei Lin scooted up beside him, pulling their supper and thermoses out of her rice bag.

"I fried lotus roots last night."

She handed him steamed vegetables, fried lotus roots, and a vegetable and egg spring roll.

"You take good care of this farmer, don't you."

"I try." She laid their rice bowls, chopsticks, and food items on top of the bag. "And you're only a temporary farmer."

Liko hunched forward, resting his elbows on his knees. "I've been wondering about that today . . . wondering if I'm a temporary farmer or a temporary preacher."

"You're a temporary farmer," said Mei Lin confidently. "And a full-time preacher, with great potential to be a doctor."

Liko smiled. "And, don't forget, a future husband." He took her hands in his. "Let's pray. God, we thank you for another day of good blessings and good work," he said sincerely.

"And thank you for giving Fu Yatou your favor with Cadre Fang," said Mei Lin.

"Yes, Lord," agreed Liko. "We ask for Fu Yatou's identity card to be issued this summer so that she can go to school next fall. And we ask you to free Mei Lin's time from the house so that she will once again be able to do your missionary work in the village."

Mei Lin hesitated. She hadn't told Liko about the new opportunity that had come her way.

The rice paddies climbing the hills in the distance caught her attention. Their watery glaze reflected the dazzling reds and yellows of the setting sun. "Lord God, we ask you for strength to continue to climb to the top of the hill you've put before us, to do your work with joy."

"Please show us the way you want us to go, Lord," Liko prayed earnestly. "And thank you for the rain that has brought us this food to fill our bodies."

Both of them waited for a moment in silence.

"Amen," said Liko.

"Amen," said Mei Lin.

"I'll be glad when we can pray together in our own house and sit at our own table." Liko scooped his vegetables on top of his rice. "Two more years seems like forever."

Mei Lin allowed her thoughts to slip into the future when she would have her own home to care for and meals to cook for Liko every day. "You will be twenty-two before we know it," she said. "Then we will marry, and you will come in from the fields and I will sauté chicken and tomatoes with mushroom dumplings. And we will eat rice that we harvested ourselves. And Father and Amah and your mother will come for supper on Friday evenings."

Liko's eyes twinkled. "Just like the old days when your mother and my father were alive."

"Perhaps they will invite us for tea and—"

"And then our child will roll down the hill in a race to the bottom!" Liko laughed.

Mei Lin bit her lower lip and said nothing.

"I like to dream with you, Mei Lin."

Liko had unknowingly touched her deepest well of sadness. Even Amah hadn't guessed, because Mei Lin carefully pretended to use the menstrual pads she bought at market each month. The truth was that the torture and starvation she had endured in Shanghai Prison had robbed her of her most precious gift to Liko and Father—her body no longer had the capacity to bear a child.

But Mei Lin didn't want to think about her own child just now. There were other children on her heart tonight.

"Liko, there's something I want to talk to you about."

"What's that?"

"I received a letter from Mother Su in Shanghai," she said. "Remember how Pastor Wong helped her husband get out of prison?"

"How is Sun Tao doing? Has he recovered from nearly starving to death?"

"Much better," said Mei Lin. She smiled and looked up into Liko's face. "Mother Su wants me to come and see her this summer, only for a couple of months. I'd be back in time to help with the harvest."

"But ... I thought you would want to evangelize here, in Tanching."

"We have three house churches now in Tanching. There are plenty of evangelists here."

"Shanghai is a big city," said Liko.

"Well, I wouldn't be going to evangelize. At least not primarily." A smile crept across Mei Lin's face. "Mother Su and her husband are rescuing orphans. They can't change the state-run orphanage, so they have started one of their own."

"An orphanage? Really? An orphanage run by Christians?"

"Yes," answered Mei Lin. "Sun Tao works driving a taxi during the day, and their daughter works, too. Mother Su is only working part time in the factory so she can dedicate more of her time to the orphans. But she needs help."

Liko ran his hand through his hair. "That's incredible. Is it legal?"

"I don't know. But when I think of what Fu Yatou went through, I'm ready to help. Do you remember the stories?"

Liko smiled. "You haven't let me forget them."

Mei Lin had met Fu Yatou in a park in Shanghai, soon after her release from prison. The child was nine years old, though she looked much younger, and was living on the streets after escaping from an orphanage. With the help of some other Christians, Mei Lin had brought the little girl home to Tanching.

"Well, if the state-run orphanages don't improve, perhaps the best solution is to start privately owned orphanages run by Christians. I'm not sure what Mother Su has found out, but I want to help her. It will be a good experience. And I think it's the right thing to do, Liko. I can feel it—in here." She pointed at her heart.

Liko was quiet for a few moments. "Mei Lin, I . . . I'd be lying if I said I wanted you to go. It's so soon after Shanghai Prison, and . . ."

Mei Lin could read his thoughts. "And so soon after your father's death?"

Liko quietly stood and stuffed his hands deep into his pockets. "Sometimes I wrestle with the absolute cruelty of it. My father's only crime was his faith in Jesus, and what a high price he paid."

Mei Lin stared up at Liko's tall frame, silhouetted against the darkening sky. His father, like her mother, died as a martyr for his beliefs. He seldom spoke of his father's death at the hands of communist prison guards.

Liko looked stricken. "The Public Security Bureau could find out what you're doing. They sent Sun Tao to prison just for driving others around to help orphans. How can I possibly release you to such wolves?"

"You'll never release me to the wolves," Mei Lin whispered.

She stood and reached up to touch his cheek. "Release me to God, Chen Liko. Release me to the Good Shepherd."

Liko stared across the deepening horizon. "It will be difficult to run the churches without you," he finally said. "When will you go?"

"In two weeks. I want to help Father finish the spring planting first."

"And how long will you be gone?"

"About ten weeks."

Liko was quiet.

"Do you want some time to pray about it? I don't have to decide today."

Liko shook his head. "No. This is so close to your dream, Mei Lin. I can feel it, too. In here." He tapped his heart and then put his arms around her. "I will miss you. In fact, I miss you already."

Mei Lin squeezed him tightly. "Thank you. Thank you for understanding."

He buried his face in her hair. "Come back to me, Mei Lin."

Mei Lin closed her eyes. "I will. I love you, Liko."

*   ✱ *

CHAPTER
Two

Kwan So finished the last row. He lifted his *cao mao*, pulled the handkerchief out of his pocket, and wiped his brow. It was too hot to plow the fields at midday. He propped the plow handle on his shoulder and rubbed his calloused hands. It was the moment he'd waited for since April—the spring planting of the rice was finished.

So walked toward his house, pulling his plow upside down behind him. His great-grandfather had built the house more than 150 years ago. His grandfather added the fishpond, and his own father built the chicken house. Although he hadn't told anyone else, he wanted to add another bedroom, perhaps two, to the house this year.

One bedroom had never really been enough. Even when Mei Lin was a baby, the house was crowded. Now Fu Yatou slept in the pantry, his mother and Mei Lin in the bedroom, and he was still on the couch in the front room near the wood stove.

He put his plow in the corner of the chicken house, then went into the courtyard to take off his muddy boots. After washing his face and hands at the pump, he went inside where it was cool and dark. The smell of fried fish from lunch lingered in the kitchen. He walked through the kitchen to the pantry door on the right.

"Amah," he called to his mother. "Amah, I'm home."

He poked his head into the bedroom door against the back

wall. Mei Lin was off collecting used clothing for the Shanghai orphans. Fu Yatou wouldn't come home from baby-sitting until dinnertime. And Amah was gone, too. He smiled. His timing couldn't have been better.

So went back into the pantry and shut the door behind him. He walked past Yatou's cot and, picking up a hammer from the top shelf, pried open a floor plank at the back of the room. He laid aside the board and knelt over the hole.

Amah and Mei Lin knew of the secret place in the front room where they hid their Bible and his wife's notebooks, but only So knew of this second hiding place. He reached into the hole and lifted out a wooden box, blowing the dust off the top. He touched the edges of the box with his finger.

Kwan So didn't go to his wife's grave site to mourn. He always came here—to the box of memories. He knew that when he lifted the lid he would touch the past. But his heart had to be ready. The last time he had looked in here was when he was waiting for Mei Lin to return from Shanghai Prison.

Carefully he pried the edges open. Shan Zu's wedding ring lay in the little jeweled box Amah bought for her to keep her ring in during planting and harvest. He took it out and ran his finger around the circle, inside and out. Memories were in that circle. Memories of laughter and affection. Memories of faithfulness in life's most wicked moments.

So followed his heart to the first night he had kissed her, to the evening tea parties she hosted, to the laughter and beauty his wife brought to this house. A picture was tucked in the bottom of the box—Shan Zu when she was pregnant with their child. In his memory, his hand touched the roundness of her belly. Tears sprang to his eyes. Mei Lin was so much like her.

He laid aside a few books and a baby blanket wrapped in a rice bag. There it was, folded inside the blanket. He took out the scarf, bunched it up in his hands, and buried his face in it, yearning for Shan Zu's fragrance again. To feel something that was hers, to draw strength from her at this time when their daughter was venturing out, away from them.

"Oh, Shan Zu, I wish you were here," he said softly. "Mei Lin needs you." He choked back a sob. "I need you." He wiped his tears away. "God, give me strength to go on without her. It's been fourteen years, but I miss her still. And I know that something is troubling Mei Lin's heart. I don't know if it's something that happened in prison or an inner struggle that she feels she can't talk to me about, but this is something old Baba can't fix. She needs her mother, but Shan Zu is with you now. Help me to raise our child, please. In Jesus' name."

So heaved a jagged sigh. He repacked the box of memories, keeping the scarf under his arm. He'd waited all these years for the right time. If Mei Lin couldn't have her mother, then he would at least make sure she had something that belonged to her.

Mei Lin sat on the low bench poking a long stick into the fire under the stove. It wouldn't take much fuel to warm the simple lunch. She pulled the large wok from the wall where it hung among Amah's collection of cooking utensils.

While she waited for the pan to get hot, Mei Lin looked back at her father. He was sitting in his usual chair, leaning back with his hands behind his head while resting his feet on a little bench in front of him. It was a rare opportunity to talk to him without Amah or Fu Yatou in the room.

"Tell me, Father, do you approve of your future son-in-law?" she asked, her eyes dancing.

Without shifting his position in the chair, Father answered, "Ah, I lose a daughter, and you want me to approve of the man who takes her away from me?"

Mei Lin grinned. She dumped the noodles and cabbage into the wok, added a dash of freshly minced onion, and then pulled a chair up in front of her father's chair. "Baba, you will gain a son, I promise you."

Father smiled. "Baba, is it? I haven't heard you call me that in a long time, Mei Lin."

Mei Lin pulled her chair side by side to her father's. He squeezed her closer with his arm.

"I remember when you were a little girl. Your mother put your hair in one long braid in the back. Sometimes she would tie a red ribbon on the end."

"Oh, I remember that. Ping envied my red ribbon and pestered her mother until she bought her one just like it. Then we wore our hair the same way when we had tea."

Father kissed the top of her head, just as he used to when she was a little girl. Mei Lin sat quietly beside him, unwilling to interrupt this quiet moment.

After a few moments, Father cleared his throat. "Mei Lin?"

"Yes, Father?"

"Do you still remember your mother?"

She bit her lip. She did not want to disappoint him, but Mother had died when Mei Lin was only six.

"It's hard to remember now," she answered carefully. "Pictures of Mother have faded into pictures of Amah."

Father sighed. "That is only natural, I suppose. Your amah has taken care of you since you were very young."

"I remember Mother used to lie on the cot beside the stove, right where you sleep now. I remember feeling scared because she was so sick."

"Is that all?" he asked.

Mei Lin smiled. "Well, I do remember that when Ping came over, Mother would do our hair with those red ribbons. She even made us matching dresses once, remember?"

Father chuckled. "You and Ping squealed when she showed them to you. Everyone said you looked like twins."

Mei Lin giggled. "We were so proud. We showed off to all the other girls in our class and tried to convince them that we really were sisters. I started to believe it myself."

"I wish we could have given you a sister or brother," said Kwan So. He sighed again.

"Are you all right, Baba?"

"Oh, I was just wondering what you remembered."

"Do you still miss her?" she asked quietly.

Mei Lin was shocked to see the tears that sprang to her father's eyes. She tried to cheer him. "I also remember when Liko and his family came for afternoon tea, and we would roll down the hill on our bellies, racing to the bottom! Mother always wore a pretty dress."

Father's eyes twinkled. "And do you and Liko plan to visit us after you're married?"

"Oh yes," Mei Lin answered. "You know that we will."

"You give me much to look forward to, daughter. And will my grandchild race down the hill on his belly?"

"Father," she scolded playfully, caught off guard.

Mei Lin stood up and went to the stove. Absently, she took the turner from its hook on the wall and stirred the noodles into the pan.

What would he think if I told him the truth?

Mei Lin bit her lip, fighting tears that tried to mock her strength. To forgive the prison guards and warden for the merciless beatings and starvation in the prison was much easier than forgiving them every day for her fruitless body.

What would Liko say if he knew? Would he still want to marry me?

Father longs for a grandchild.

Everyone in my neighborhood will say I am cursed—maybe even cursed by the gods! People may not want anything to do with the God who made the earth and skies if they see I cannot bear a child.

"Where's little Fu?" asked Father, interrupting her thoughts.

"She's helping Sung Ping with the baby again," Mei Lin answered. "Ping says she doesn't know what she'd do without her."

"Does the cadre know you're leaving tomorrow for Shanghai?"

"Ping told him I was going away for a while to visit friends.

He really doesn't know anything."

"He doesn't *want* to know anything," Father added. "Cadre Fang will probably be relieved that the authorities will not come around to ask about you anymore."

"I still can't believe he found an identity card for Fu." Mei Lin stirred the fire under the stove with her stick, covering the flames with ashes so that it would go out easily.

"Amah!" Father called. "Mei Lin has lunch ready."

"For whatever reason, I think the cadre actually likes our Fu Yatou," said Mei Lin as she set out the small rice bowls and chopsticks.

"He likes the help his wife is getting," said Amah, coming out of the bedroom with her arms piled high with laundry.

Mei Lin pulled out a chair, and Amah slowly shuffled to the table and sat down.

"Ping has given Fu too many gifts already," said Mei Lin. "In fact, I had to talk to Fu and tell her it would be sin to love the baby only to win the cadre's favor."

Father smiled. "After the card comes, I will be the only man my age in Tanching with two daughters."

Mei Lin brought the rice and cabbage to the table, then poured the tea.

Together they held hands while Father prayed. Then Mei Lin scooped the rice into the bowls.

"Mei Lin, I have invited my house church for tea this evening."

"Father!" exclaimed Mei Lin. "So many people for tea?"

Father smiled. "Well, our numbers are growing. But the Huangs aren't able to come, so there will only be about forty of us, plus Ping and Cadre Fang. It would be rude to leave them out. Don't worry, we'll all fit in the courtyard easily enough."

Amah, who was about to put rice into her mouth, stopped in midair and put her chopsticks down.

"Surely you aren't going to have a prayer meeting with the cadre here?" Mei Lin asked incredulously.

"No, we'll have tea. A lot of tea and a little prayer after the cadre leaves." Father's eyes were smiling.

"Father, what are you up to?"

"I think it's perfectly normal to have a tea with my friends in celebration before I send my daughter off to visit friends in Shanghai."

"Really?" asked Mei Lin. She jumped up out of her seat and threw her arms around his neck. "Oh, thank you, Father!"

Father nodded at her, obviously pleased with himself. "It will be my pleasure."

"I'll fill the thermoses again right after lunch," said Mei Lin. She sat down, but her appetite was lost at the thought of so many people coming to the house that very night.

"I'll fill the thermoses," Amah offered grumpily. "I may as well get used to doing all the work around here. I'll be all alone by tomorrow."

"Amah, Fu Yatou will come home to help you," said Mei Lin.

She had not told her grandmother that she would be helping a secretly run orphanage in Shanghai. It would only give Amah more to fret about.

"I'll be home early for dinner," said Father, and he tweaked his daughter's nose as he sipped the last of his tea and brushed past her. "We'll have tea at seven."

Amah didn't mention Shanghai again. The rest of the afternoon was filled with preparation for the tea. Mei Lin watched with amusement as Amah gingerly swept the courtyard, scoured the floors, and scattered their few benches around.

Amah can take care of herself, she thought.

"Where will we put fifty people?" Amah muttered as she poured the hot water into the thermoses. "It's a good thing we have plenty of tea."

"I'm sure everyone will bring their own benches," said Mei Lin. "And we can serve hot water if we run out."

"We'll have enough," Amah insisted. "My tea garden did exceptionally well last year."

After they cleaned the courtyard for the party, Amah disappeared into her bedroom. Mei Lin boiled water for rice and cut the vegetables she'd bought at the market the day before. The stove fires never went out all afternoon, heating water and then dinner and then more water. Mei Lin's thoughts turned to Liko. He'd probably known about the tea before she did.

Even though her hands were busy, her heart felt strangely lonely for him. She opened the courtyard gate to welcome more air into the warm house, then stirred mushrooms into the vegetables until they were evenly softened. Making Liko's favorite dish helped her to feel better. She poured her brown sauce over the vegetables, simmering and softening until they were fully cooked, then scooped some into a bowl.

"I'm going to help Liko bed down Old Gray," she called to her grandmother. "I'll be back in time for supper."

"Don't be out late," Amah ordered. "We have company tonight."

"I'll be back in half an hour." Mei Lin walked out of the courtyard, then up the hill to the cowshed.

"Liko?" she called into the darkness of the shed.

"I'm over here, getting the harness off," he called back. "How did you know I would be here this early?"

"Father told me about the tea," she said. "I'm sure you and your mother were invited."

Mei Lin made her way toward the *tap tap tap* of the harness pins, guessing her pathway through the darkness until her eyes adjusted.

"So, your father told you." He hung the harness on the wall, then splashed water over his head, running his hands through his short black hair. "We don't have time to go to the big rock tonight, do we?"

Mei Lin hung her head. She had hoped to spend her last night alone with Liko, but she could never spoil Father's party.

"I have to be back soon to help with supper and the tea," she answered. "I made your favorite dish."

He took the sack of food and laid it aside. "I'll eat later." He took her hands in his, holding them to his cheek.

A rush of warmth went through her belly, and she leaned over and kissed his cheek.

"Mei Lin, can you squeeze in a walk with me after the party tonight? Do you think your father would mind?"

Her stomach fluttered, standing so close to Liko. "Not at all. I hope to say my good-byes to Father tomorrow morning."

Liko turned to stare out the open doorway at the rice paddies. "The fields are nearly planted now. I can finish the rest by next week sometime. I'll need to keep busy, you know."

"I washed most of the bedding today. Yesterday I cleaned out the chicken coop and weeded the garden. I have to wash my hair before the party tonight."

"Are you sure you'll have time to take a walk?" Though his voice was strong, his eyes were pleading.

Mei Lin knew she would need to get up before dawn to accomplish everything, but she longed to spend time with Liko before she left.

"Yes, let's do it!"

Liko drew her close and then, just as quickly, took her shoulders and held her at arm's length. "I need to go home and get a bath before this great party."

"Right now?"

"Well, maybe we can spend ten more minutes," said Liko. "Where shall we go?"

"Right here," said Mei Lin, pointing to the doorway.

Liko threw an empty feed sack onto the dirt floor by the inside wall, and the two of them sat side by side. Mei Lin snuggled closer, laying her head on his chest. Liko bent his head over hers, lifting her hair to his face. She listened to the gentle rhythm of his heart, and he drank in the smell of her hair. And for ten minutes their hearts exchanged love that transcended words.

* ✱ *

CHAPTER
Three

It was the perfect evening for a party. The half-moon hung low
in the sky, and silver stars twinkled smiles on the celebration.
Amah had outdone herself. Festive lanterns decorated with
freshly picked flowers hung on clotheslines and doorways, their
soft light reflecting on the floors she and Mei Lin had scrubbed
clean. Wash buckets, chicken cages, and brooms were all dis-
creetly put away to make room for benches carried in on the
shoulders of friends.

The courtyard was brimming with villagers holding teacups,
mingling around trays of freshly steamed corn *jiaozi*, one of
Father's favorite dumplings. Amah had even gathered flowers to
decorate the few small tea tables and lovely fine porcelain teapots
she borrowed from neighbors. She was particularly proud of her
Lu Shan Yunwu tea, the finest green tea in Jiangxi Province,
according to her. Father often teased that she should name it
Tanching Yunwu tea.

Mei Lin poured hot tea into fine porcelain cups for her old
friend Ping and her husband the cadre, then extended her arms
to baby Han. "May I?" she asked.

Ping looked at her husband.

"Of course," he answered. "You probably won't recognize
him when you return."

Mei Lin held the baby's head close to her chest, his silky

black hair tickling her chin. "You're right. And he probably won't remember me at all."

"We wish you well, Mei Lin," said Ping.

The cadre nodded his approval. "Fu will certainly have her identity card by this summer. Your father wants to send her to school this fall."

Mei Lin looked at Ping's husband. She was glad that he was married and not chasing her anymore, yet she couldn't help feeling sadness for Ping. She wasn't the happy young friend Mei Lin had grown up with.

"Thank you, Cadre, for helping Fu obtain her identity card," said Mei Lin. "We couldn't have adopted her without your help."

The cadre smiled, his mustache twitching.

"May I take Han to show Father?" asked Mei Lin. She drank in the baby's sweet, milky smell and welcomed the soft hands that patted her shoulders.

Every eye turned toward baby Han as she carried him across the room. A baby was a wonderful attraction in any gathering.

Father had an easy way with children. He left his conversation to talk to Han, and the baby reached out and grabbed his nose, to the delight of the guests nearby.

"May I have him now?" Fu Yatou was at Father's elbow, her arms out for her prized baby. Han eagerly jumped toward her, squealing with happiness.

"That's my boy," she said. "Now I'm going to take you to see the rest of my family." She bounced off toward Amah.

Father went back to his conversation, and Mei Lin made her way to Liko, who had just come in with his mother.

"Welcome, Mrs. Chen. I'm so glad you could come tonight."

"This is a night of celebration," Mrs. Chen answered. Then she looked at her son. "Celebration and sadness."

Mei Lin looked at Liko. A smile turned up the corners of his mouth, but his eyes revealed his hidden sorrow. She felt a twinge of guilt. "Ten weeks will go quickly," she said. "It's not forever."

"Of course, Mei Lin," Mrs. Chen replied. "We will miss

you." She stole a glance at her son. "But we will be cheering for you."

Cheer was a code word for *pray,* and Mei Lin knew that Mrs. Chen would indeed be praying for her as she helped Mother Su with the orphans.

She turned toward the sound of laughter and saw a slender young woman with long thick hair standing near the doorway, chatting comfortably with Ping and some other old friends from high school days.

"Who's the new girl?"

Just then the girl left the doorway and walked toward Amah. The beautiful newcomer brought second glances and murmurs of attention as she passed through the courtyard.

"That's Law Jade," Liko answered. "She's a second cousin to the Laws from Mother's 'club.' It's odd—the Laws said they only met her this summer."

Mei Lin's eyebrow arched. "Really?"

"Jade told Mother that she has some *guanxi* in Singapore that may be a help to our clubs."

"What connections?" Mei Lin asked. She wanted to ask if the girl was married or at least engaged. Then she chided herself for the pang of jealousy that had crept into her heart.

"Jade just started," said Mrs. Chen. "I don't know what *guanxi* she has, but she really seems to enjoy our friendship. She said she knows Dad."

Mei Lin smiled inwardly at Mrs. Chen's veiled reference to Father God. At the same time, she wondered how this Jade had tiptoed into Tanching Village without her realizing it. Was she so caught up in her own life that she failed to see what was happening in Liko's family? Even her future mother-in-law seemed to be drawn to the girl.

Mei Lin tried to shrug off the annoying thoughts. Her father had planned a night of happiness and celebration for her, and darkness had no place here.

"Come on, Mei Lin," said Mrs. Chen. "I'll introduce you."

Mrs. Chen led Mei Lin by the hand through the crowded courtyard. Mei Lin was surprised to find that Jade was even more beautiful up close.

"I understand this party is because you are leaving," Jade said. "I'm sorry we won't be able to get to know each other."

"Will you only be here for the summer?"

"Yes. I'm staying with my cousin. I hear you're going to Shanghai. You have friends there?"

Just then Kwan So stood in the center of the courtyard and called everyone's attention, and Mei Lin breathed a sigh of relief.

"Friends and neighbors," Father announced. "I have invited you here tonight to honor my daughter, Kwan Mei Lin, who will be going on a trip for the next couple of months to visit friends and relatives."

A murmur of approval swept through the group.

"She's always been independent and headstrong, much like her mother."

A ripple of warm laughter went over the courtyard. Mei Lin's mother was honored and revered by the house church Christians in Tanching as the first evangelist ever sent out from their village.

"She is also very beautiful, like her mother. Come here, Mei Lin."

Mei Lin felt her face growing warm as she walked toward her father. Every eye was upon her as Father handed her a gift enclosed in a small rice bag.

"Not very colorful wrapping," he said sheepishly.

Mei Lin's heart warmed. She reached into the bag and pulled out a soft, silky material.

"Oh!" cried Mrs. Chen.

"Kwan So!" Amah gasped at the same time.

Mei Lin's spine tingled. What was this mystery cloth that arrested the attention of the two most important women in her life?

"Father?"

Kwan So straightened his back and smiled. He took the cloth

from his daughter and ran his hands over it until he held one end of the material in each hand. Then he flung the middle toward the sky, over her head, creating a banner over her. The night air caught the thin material and waved it above her as though the air itself knew the secret of the cloth and participated willingly in revealing it.

Father flung it two more times toward the heavens, and Mei Lin tilted her chin and watched her father perform with the wind. The scarf curled in the sway of the breeze, then landed silently on the back of her head and slid down across her shoulders. It was airy and light, but to Mei Lin it seemed to bring another world to her shoulders.

Father broke the silence. "An invisible red thread connects those who are destined to meet, regardless of time, place, or circumstance."

Amah's crackly voice joined Father's. "The thread may stretch or tangle but never break."

"Ahhhhhhh." Collective sighs of agreement with the ancient Chinese saying went up from the small group.

"This—" Father's voice was tight, as if he would choke. "This is a gift to you from your mother and me."

"Mother?" *How could this be a gift from Mother?*

Mei Lin saw tears in her father's eyes. A lump formed in her throat, and she quickly looked down at the material in her hands. She touched the solid ivory center, tracing her fingers to a light green leafy vine embroidered on each side. The vines deepened in color until they were a dark green cup holding beautiful red lotus blossoms at each end. She ran her hands from the center to the end of the scarf, fingering the fine red threads that encased the lotus blossoms in the cloth.

Her fingers flashed pictures in front of her, memories of her mother before she was taken away, sitting in Amah's rocker, embroidering cloth and sewing little dresses. Mei Lin put a lotus petal to her cheek and was transported to her childhood, where it was dark outside and her head lay on her mother's shoulder, her cheek resting on this scarf, as they walked through the woods.

Tears sprang to her eyes, "Mother!" she cried. "I remember, Father!" She turned to Amah. "Amah! I remember! It's Mother's scarf!"

Women dabbed their eyes, and men coughed away the lumps in their throats.

Kwan So grabbed his daughter's forearms and squeezed them, then stood behind her and addressed their friends. "Thank you for honoring Mei Lin and me by coming tonight. Some of you remember Mei Lin's mother. If you would like to honor Shan Zu, please share your memories with us before you leave tonight."

Someone touched Mei Lin's shoulder, and she turned around to greet their next-door neighbor, Mrs. Lang.

"Mei Lin, soon after we were married, I developed pneumonia in my lungs, and eventually I couldn't go anywhere. Your mother brought a meal for us every evening after she put you in bed. Your amah sent medicinal teas.

"While she cleaned my kitchen, Shan Zu told me about her faith in God. I wish I had listened back then. I waited too long. When I saw you come home two years ago, so skinny from prison, I remembered when your mother came home. Oh, she looked so awful. When you came home, it made me think again about everything she told me, until finally—" Mrs. Lang looked around and spotted the cadre. "Finally I joined the club."

Mei Lin squeezed her hand. "Thank you, Mrs. Lang. I didn't know Mother helped you so long ago. And I'm so glad you joined the club."

Mei Lin was surprised as one person after another came to share fond memories of her mother. An elderly woman from Liko's house church said that Shan Zu had prayed for her and she was healed of cancer.

A woman in her forties put ten yuan into her hand and told her she went to school with Shan Zu. She hesitated a moment, then leaned close to Mei Lin's ear. "Everyone thought your mother was crazy when she kept you. They said she should wait for a boy to take care of her in her old age. But now I see your mother's wisdom. You look just like her, and you carry her spirit, too. I can tell your father is proud."

Mei Lin barely had time to think about that before Cadre Fang approached her.

"Mei Lin, I was a teenager when your mother died. I remember that she tied ribbons into your hair and took you to market with her. She was a good wife to Kwan So and a good mother to you."

His mustache twitched, and Mei Lin could feel a rebuke coming. He looked around their courtyard and house. "It's a shame she gave up all of this—for nothing."

Mei Lin's cheeks burned. "My mother died for a cause. Her death has returned life to our village."

The cadre leaned closer to her face until she felt his breath on her cheek. "I can make you the leader of Tanching's first Three Self Church. Then you will have the freedom to preach and you won't need to worry about prison."

Mei Lin stepped back. "Thank you for your kind offer, Cadre Fang," she said politely. "However, as a Three Self Pastor, I would be permitted to speak once a week, and my sermons must be approved by the government. I wouldn't be allowed to pass out literature or pray for the sick or evangelize. Worse, none of the children in our village would be allowed to attend. How could I agree to such a thing?"

"I can see you are growing more like your mother every day," he said. "Don't let me find out where you are going, Mei Lin. I don't want to know."

Mei Lin couldn't tell if the cadre was threatening her or trying to protect her. "I will go where my heart leads me," she finally answered.

Just then Amah and Fu approached them. "Mei Lin, Fu and I have something for you, too."

Fu Yatou handed her a package.

Mei Lin unfolded the brown paper, turning it over in her hand until a shiny metal object appeared.

"A compass," said Amah.

Mei Lin smiled at her grandmother. "Amah, are you afraid your stubborn granddaughter will lose her way in the big city?"

Everyone laughed, and the conversation with the cadre was totally forgotten in a gush of well-wishes. A few guests slipped red envelopes of money into Mei Lin's hand before they left, grand gifts of love during springtime planting when money was low. Mei Lin promised in her heart that every fen would be used for the orphans.

Fathers shouldered wooden benches they'd brought, and mothers gathered their children as they left the tea for their homes. In the end, only Mrs. Chen and Liko stayed behind to help Amah clean up.

Mei Lin followed her father into the kitchen. "Father? You kept the scarf all this time?"

"Not even Amah knew I had it," he answered. "Sometimes I pulled it out and touched it, just to remember your mother. I wanted you to have it when you grew up. It seemed like tonight was the right time."

Mei Lin walked toward him, the scarf lightly stirring about her shoulders as she hugged him. "Father, thank you."

"It's from both of us, Mei Lin."

She touched the scarf again. "Thank you, Mother," she whispered. "I'll always remember."

"These threads are easily seen," Father said softly, touching the fabric. "But the invisible red thread will always connect the three of us."

"It's already helped me to remember things," said Mei Lin. "I remember laying my cheek against the scarf as Mother carried me. But it was dark. Why were we walking through the woods?"

Father smiled. "We were going to the DuYan house church meetings, remember? Your mother was often asked to teach there. She loved to take you with her."

"I'd think that a little girl would be in the way."

Father sat down at a chair by the table and motioned Mei Lin to sit across from him. "Well, I offered to keep you, and sometimes I did. But your mother usually wanted you to go with her. She loved you and wanted you near her. But mostly, she wanted you to love Jesus as much as she did."

Mei Lin studied her father's face. She liked the way it softened when he talked about Shan Zu.

"And did I?"

He looked up. "Did you what?"

"Did I love Jesus when I was a little girl?"

Kwan So chuckled. "Yes, you did. You and your mother used to sing about Jesus in the rocking chair at night after the lights were off. You sang until Amah yelled out and told you to stop."

"What did we sing?"

"Oh, the same songs we sing now, I guess. I don't remember." Father stared wistfully outside the open door into the courtyard, where the others were still cleaning up. "Your mother brought music and laughter and tea parties and Jesus into my life. She was an incredible woman."

"Thank you, Father," said Mei Lin. "I won't forget."

Father squeezed her hand. "Go along. I understand you have an appointment with Liko?"

"You don't mind?"

Father smiled. "He asked permission to whisk you away on your last night. Now go."

Mei Lin grabbed her jacket off the wall hook. Carefully she tucked her mother's scarf under its collar, letting the loose ends dangle in front of her. She wondered how many times Mother had walked hand in hand with Father while wearing this scarf.

Liko saw her enter the courtyard. "Ready?" he asked, one hand extended to her and the other holding a lantern.

Mei Lin put her hand into his and let him lead her past Amah's fine cabbages and tea plants, up the hill, beyond the cowshed to the rice paddies. The night air was cool.

Hand in hand they waded out to the big rock in the center of the Langs' field. There they sat and said their good-byes under the gaze of the moon and the kisses of Tanching starlight.

CHAPTER

Four

Mei Lin's eyes searched the Shanghai train station. People everywhere were waving to passengers.

"Mei Lin!"

She swung around. "Mother Su! I didn't see you back there!"

Mother Su threw her arms around Mei Lin. "I can't believe you're here!"

Mei Lin hugged her friend. The first time they met, Mother Su had been selling cigarettes outside Shanghai Prison. She was the first person Mei Lin talked to after she was released, and the first person outside the prison whom Mei Lin led to Christ.

"Let's sit down over there," Mother Su said. "No one is using the benches now that the train has arrived."

Mei Lin followed Mother Su to the bench near the exit door of the train. "Where is Chang?" she asked.

"My daughter is at work. She said to tell you she will see you this evening."

"I was so glad when I heard that Tao was released from prison," said Mei Lin. "And even happier when you wrote to say he is working again."

"Our lives will be changed forever because of you, Mei Lin. You gave him great hope in prison. He says that you cleaned his floor and his heart all at the same time! And look at you! You are so beautiful. Your amah has fattened you right up!"

Mei Lin would have felt embarrassed if anyone but Mother Su had said that.

"Now I've got you! Stupid railroad rats." The conductor stomped down the exit stairs of the train, grasping a boy in each hand. "I'm taking you straight to that guard over there. Then you'll find out—"

"Those boys are mine!" cried Mother Su. She sprang from the bench and ran toward the conductor.

"What?"

"They are my boys," she repeated. "Now, boys, did you lose your tickets? I told you to hang on to them! You can't come to see your aunt without tickets!"

The boys' grimy faces were glazed over with shock. Their hair was long and dirty and their pants were dirtier, with holes in the knees. The older one had only one good eye.

"What?" said the conductor again. "Who are you? These boys are railroad rats. They don't belong to anybody."

"They belong to me," said Mother Su. She pulled a wad of money out of her pocketbook. "Here, this should compensate you for the tickets they lost."

The conductor looked at the money, still not loosening his grip on the boys.

"Well, all right. I don't know what you want with these rats, but if you want them, you can have them."

Mother Su smiled. She handed the money to the conductor and took the boys' hands. "Come, boys. Aren't you going to say hello to Cousin Mei Lin?"

"Hello," said Mei Lin, stepping right into her role. "How was your trip?"

"Uh, fine, miss," said the younger one. He looked back at the conductor, whose eyes followed them, still narrowed with suspicion.

"Why don't you help Mei Lin with her bag?" Mother Su asked.

The older boy took Mei Lin's bag, and Mother Su reached

down and hugged him. She whispered, "I really do have a home where you both can stay. You can sleep in a warm bed tonight and eat steamed rice, vegetables, and beef for supper. How would you like that?"

The younger boy looked at the older, then blurted, "I'd like that a lot, miss."

Mother Su took his hand, then turned to the other boy. "And what about you? Would you like that, too?"

"I don't know," he said. He looked toward the back of the train station.

"Are there others?" asked Mother Su.

"No," he answered quickly. "No others."

"Well, maybe you can introduce them to me later," said Mother Su. She led them all through the exit door. "Maybe after dinner this evening. We'll have to get to know one another first."

"Miss, are you really gonna feed us beef and rice?"

"Yes, I am," answered Mother Su. "And you'll sleep in your own bed, too. My name is Deng Su. Everyone calls me Mother Su. I have more boys and girls just like you."

They walked out of the train station and onto the sidewalk. In the glaring afternoon sun Mei Lin took a closer look at the older boy. Although the wound in his eye looked like it happened some time ago, she could tell it needed medical attention.

"Taxi!" Mother Su called.

A red taxi pulled up.

"No, that one," said Mother Su, pointing to a second taxi behind the first.

"Look, lady, I was here first," said the first cab driver, leaning out the window.

"I'm sorry, but I asked that one to wait for me," said Mother Su.

The first driver shrugged and pulled away.

Mother Su climbed into the back with the boys. "You sit up front, Mei Lin."

The cab driver jumped out and put Mei Lin's bag into the

trunk, then hopped back into the front seat and pulled out into a barrage of traffic. Mei Lin was pleased to be back in Shanghai. Tanching rarely saw a car, and it was a secret thrill for her to look out of the window and see buses and red taxicabs dodging in and out of traffic.

"It's wonderful to be back," she called to Mother Su. She looked back and smiled at the younger boy, who was nestled up against Mother Su's side. The older one was staring out of the window, scratching the side of his face.

"Dear lady, you are a *guiren,*" said the driver.

Mei Lin looked at the driver. *Is he talking to me? Why would he call me a saintly person?*

Then she gasped. "Are you? Are you—"

The driver smiled, revealing front teeth that were partially knocked out at an angle, right to left. "I am Sun Tao. Welcome back to Shanghai, Mei Lin."

Sun Tao certainly knew his way around Shanghai. He easily wove in and out of buses and taxis, making so many turns Mei Lin wondered if she'd ever find her way around the city. As he drove, Tao told the story of his release from prison.

"I couldn't believe it when the guard came and walked me out, just like that," he said, snapping his fingers. "That day, I knew it wasn't a dream when you came to clean my floor in prison and told me about Jesus. I knew that it really happened."

"Brother Tom arranged it," said Mother Su. "I've never met a man with more *guanxi.* His connections in America and inside the prison helped to get Tao released. He has become one of our closest friends. Our lives have changed a great deal since you came to Shanghai."

Mei Lin sighed, resting her head on the back of her seat. "Back then, my dream was to study to become a teacher at Shanghai University. Instead, I landed in the same prison they put my mother in years earlier."

Tao looked surprised. "Your mother survived Shanghai Prison No. 14?"

Mei Lin looked over at him, tears glistening in her eyes. "She was released, but by that time her body was so tortured that she did not recover. She died when I was six years old."

"I am truly sorry to hear that. And your father? He is a Christian, too?"

"Yes. He's a house church pastor in Tanching."

"Ah, he must be proud of you," said Tao.

"I think he's missing my mother a lot right now," said Mei Lin. She turned around to talk to Mother Su and saw tears running down her friend's cheeks.

"Mother Su, what's wrong?"

"Oh, I can't help but think about it. Your mother didn't survive prison, and Tao did. Here you are without a mother, and my Chang has both of her parents alive and well."

The older boy looked at Mother Su, then at Mei Lin. For the first time, Mei Lin saw his face soften.

"It is not easy being an orphan," she said. "But Jesus has a special place in His heart for orphans. He wants people to take care of them, not chase them away and call them names."

The boy turned his head to stare out the window again, his hand to his face.

Mother Su started digging in her purse. "Here, take these," she said, offering them packets of crackers.

The boys opened them eagerly and devoured two of them in seconds, stuffing the rest into their pockets.

Mei Lin looked at Mother Su. "You are a wonderful mother," she said. "Chang should be proud to have you—to have you both."

By the time they arrived at the orphanage, the sun had set and darkness enveloped them. Tao pulled into an alley, made a few turns, and stopped.

"We're here," said Mother Su. "Boys, I have quite a few children. Some of them are from the train station. Others . . . others

41

we found on the street. My helpers will be feeding them supper right about now. Are you still hungry?"

"I am," said the younger boy.

"What is your name?"

The younger boy kept looking at the older one, who refused to talk. Mother Su exchanged glances with Mei Lin.

"Some of the children in our big home didn't know their names when they came to us, or didn't want to tell us. They chose to take new names when they arrived. Would you like that?"

Again, the younger boy looked at the older, till the older one nodded, then looked into Mother Su's face with just a glimmer of trust in his eyes.

"So we decided that the children in our home can choose a name after a person in the Bible," she explained. "The Bible is a holy book. Which of you would like to be named Philip?"

"I would!" said the younger boy.

"Then Philip it is," said Mother Su. "Mei Lin, I would like you to meet Philip, the newest member of our children's home."

Mei Lin caught the twinkle in Mother Su's eye and replied, "I am honored to meet you, young Philip."

"In the Bible, Philip and Nathaniel were friends. Would you like to be called Nathaniel?"

The older boy didn't smile. "I don't care," he said.

Mother Su introduced the boys to each other, and the matter was settled.

"I am pleased to meet you both," she said. "Can one of you carry Mei Lin's bags for her? Tao has to finish his taxi run."

Nathaniel got out of the car and started walking backward in the darkness, pulling away from the group. Mei Lin came and put her arm around him, but he shrugged away from her.

"Nathaniel, what is it?" she asked. "Mother Su won't hurt you."

Mother Su was digging in her purse again. "Nathaniel, here are the keys to the gate. Will you open it for us? You may hold the keys to the gate while we look around. If you want to leave, you can leave. If you want to stay, you can stay. Is that fair?"

Nathaniel backed away a little farther.

"Come, Nathaniel," said Mother Su. "Open the gate for us. Philip, will you help Mei Lin with her bag?"

Philip followed Tao to the trunk and took the bag without saying a word.

Tao jumped back in the taxi and pulled away without turning on his headlights, then disappeared around the corner.

CHAPTER

Five

Let's go," said Mother Su. "I'm sure Cook Chu has saved us some supper."

The word *supper* seemed to jar Nathaniel out of his backward shuffle. He and Philip followed Mother Su down the alley. Mei Lin walked behind them, just in case Philip changed his mind about staying and took off with her bag!

They approached a large iron gate connected to an even taller fence. Mother Su showed Nathaniel how to unlock the gate. It was like a giant black iron wall that creaked as it opened widely for them to walk inside.

"This is the textile factory," said Mother Su, pointing to a long gray building on the right. "We've only been here two months, but I've come to know the owners there, and they are very kind to us. Sometimes they drop rice bags filled with groceries out of their windows or leave gifts for the children by the gate."

"It's good they favor you," said Mei Lin, "or you could be in a lot of trouble."

"The police know that we have a private orphanage. So far they haven't reported us for not registering with the state."

She turned to the boys. "This building is where you will sleep tonight. The other children are eating in the schoolroom right now. Come in and see." She opened the door to the large bunkhouse.

A long, low table at the wall across from the door held many cups with a toothbrush sticking out of each. On the left and right were bunk beds, each with a blanket folded at the bottom and a pillow at the top.

"This will be your bed," said Mother Su, patting the bunk bed in the far left corner of the room. "You boys can decide who sleeps on the top or bottom. I'll have Cook Chu get you a blanket and pillow after supper. Our boys sleep here, and the girls sleep in the room next door. Boys and girls aren't to go into one another's rooms."

Philip sighed. "That's good."

Mei Lin stifled a giggle.

"Are you hungry, Mei Lin? Chang is preparing something for us at home, but we can eat here if you'd like."

"I'm fine," said Mei Lin. "Let's wait for Chang's cooking."

Mother Su led them across the courtyard toward a long building that was perpendicular to the bunkhouse.

"The building straight ahead is the staff house. That's where you'll be staying, Mei Lin. To the left is our kitchen."

When Mei Lin stepped up onto the porch, she saw that it extended the length of the building and was partially covered from the roofs of the bunkhouse and staff house. About ten yards down the covered porch walkway, a woman was stooped over a pot, stirring something inside. The pot sat over a little burner.

"Where did you get a stove like that?" Mei Lin asked.

"Guanxi," said Mother Su, her eyes dancing.

"Brother Tom?"

"Yes. It's a small outdoor burner. Someone gave it to him, and he gave it to us."

"And you cook for how many children on that small stove?"

"Eight children and two staff members, besides me. Ten children now, if Philip and Nathaniel decide to join us."

Mother Su looked back at Nathaniel. His knuckles were

white, still gripping the large key in his hand. She smiled at him. "Come on, let me introduce you to Cook Chu."

Cook Chu had wire-rimmed glasses and short hair that she kept back with a scarf. Her long apron showed telltale signs of a full day of labor.

Mei Lin extended her hand. "I am pleased to meet you, Cook Chu."

"Ah, you are the Mei Lin we have all heard about." Cook Chu raised one eyebrow. "Is it true that you spread the Gospel on your hands and knees scrubbing floors in Shanghai Prison?"

Mei Lin looked at the floor. "It really wasn't so glorious," she said softly. "I was starved and exhausted most of the time. But Jesus told me it was to be my ministry."

Cook Chu turned back to stir her pot. "All the same, many souls were won in that prison. I am honored to meet you."

"Thank you. I'm glad to meet you, as well. You have a big family to feed here."

Cook Chu laughed. "And as you have already observed, Mother Su will see to it that it grows bigger." She smiled at Nathaniel and Philip.

Right beside Cook Chu's porch kitchen was a door that led to the staff room. Mother Su showed Mei Lin the nurse's bed on one side of a wooden partition about eight feet tall, and the bed on the other side where Cook Chu slept. There were two dressers and one cabinet that held a few medical supplies.

"Nurse Bo comes here on the weekends and cooks and helps with any medical problems," said Mother Su. "Cook Chu gets the weekends off. She still sleeps here, but she doesn't have responsibility for the children during those days. We hope you might like to come home with us on weekends this summer."

Mei Lin smiled. "Thank you for your kind offer. I would think you had enough of me in your house two years ago!"

"Never. God sent you to my husband and then to me. You made us feel special."

"Well, I would like to spend some time with you this summer," said Mei Lin. "And maybe I will spend some time with the children on the weekends, too?"

Mother Su had a look of satisfaction on her face. "Good. We don't want to wear you out! Now come, meet the children."

She led them into the schoolroom. Eight dark-haired children looked up from their desks. They were just finishing their dinner.

Mother Su introduced Philip and Nathaniel to the group and seated them in two desks near the windows along the far wall. Cook Chu brought the boys steaming bowls piled high with fried rice and dumplings. They plunged in, ignoring their chopsticks. Mother Su didn't say anything, so Mei Lin didn't, either.

In front of the classroom were a long chalkboard, a wooden podium, and a larger desk and chair in the corner, where the teacher most likely sat.

Mei Lin watched Mother Su walk among the children, calling them by name and hugging them. A few smiled shyly at her; others looked down at their food and pretended she wasn't there. Some of them resisted Mother Su's open affection, but Mei Lin could tell they were pleased that it was offered nonetheless.

Their clothing was clean but mostly worn thin at the knees and elbows. Mei Lin couldn't imagine providing baths for so many children, much less doing their laundry and feeding them. No wonder Mother Su was requesting her help!

Two of the youngest children broke away from their seats to run to Mother Su and hug her.

"Hello, David. Hello, Jonathan. How are you?"

Mother Su sat in one of the children's low chairs and drew one of the little boys closer. "I looked for your sister today at the train station, Jonathan. I didn't find her, but I did find Philip and Nathaniel. Maybe after supper we can ask them if they've seen her, okay?"

Jonathan put his fingers in his mouth, making his lower lip stick out. "Okay."

Meanwhile, the newly christened Nathaniel and Philip didn't hesitate to push more food into their mouths. Mei Lin saw

Nathaniel eat one dumpling and stuff two more into his pocket. She wondered if she should stop him, but Mother Su signaled her not to say anything.

Mother Su instructed the children to wash and dry their bowls and return them to the table near their bunks. The children filed out of the room, and Philip and Nathaniel followed after them.

Mother Su and Mei Lin followed the children to the bunk-house.

"When the orphans first come, they usually eat a bundle and save some for later. Remember how Yatou did that?"

Mei Lin nodded. "Now Fu Yatou has learned better manners. Amah made sure of that."

"Yes, and these boys will learn, as well. But they aren't used to relying on anyone but themselves. We can't take that independence from them right away, or they'll get scared of us and run away."

"I understand," said Mei Lin. They reached the bunkhouse door. "Where will I be sleeping?"

"I will set up a bunk for you in the nurse and cook's room tomorrow night. But tonight my Chang wants to see you."

Mei Lin smiled. "And I want to see her."

She remembered how cold Sun Chang had been to her when she first brought little Fu Yatou to their apartment. Chang was afraid that the PSB would find the runaway orphan there and arrest her and her mother. Back then, Chang wanted nothing to do with being a Christian.

"How does she feel about the orphanage?" asked Mei Lin.

Mother Su smiled. "Chang visits here on weekends and helps with the laundry and plays with the children. When she can, she buys little things for them."

"Oh, that reminds me. I brought treats for the children."

"When we go back to the classroom, I will introduce you to the children, and you may give them your gifts."

Fifteen minutes later the children were seated back at their desks. Mother Su stood at the front of the room.

"Children, my friend Miss Mei Lin has come from far away in the southern province of Jiangxi." She pointed to the map of China that hung on the wall. "Miss Mei Lin lives *here*. And we are right *here*. She lives far away, doesn't she?"

A few nodded their heads.

"I know that some of you are used to calling your teachers 'professor' or 'auntie' or 'uncle.' However, I want you to address your new teacher as Miss Mei Lin. Can you clap for Miss Mei Lin?"

The children applauded, and a few of the rowdy ones in the front row made grunting noises and banged their chairs.

Mei Lin unzipped her black bag. "How many of you like school?" she asked.

Most of the hands went up.

"I brought you something to use in school." She pulled out three packs of paper and brand-new pencils. "There are enough pencils for everyone."

Squeals of delight went up from the children. They quickly opened the tops of their desks and shoved their few sheets of paper and one pencil inside. One little boy in the back used the pencils as drumsticks, while another raced them across the floor.

The three girls in the class sat beside one another in the back row. Mei Lin handed each of the girls a pencil and then showed them how to draw a lotus blossom on the paper. Lydia, the girl in the middle, worked hard at forming the petals and even included ripples in the water around the flower.

"That's beautiful, Lydia!" said Mei Lin.

Lydia's face was plain, like an unopened package. But when she smiled, her eyes shone, and Mei Lin thought she could see right down into her soul.

"How old are you, Lydia?"

"I'm nine. At least, that's what Mother Su figured out."

Mei Lin understood. Most orphans didn't know when they

were born. Fu didn't even have a name at first. She simply called herself "girl"—*Yatou*.

"You are a good artist for a nine-year-old. Maybe we can draw together sometime, all of us?"

The girls smiled, and Mei Lin commented on each picture, encouraging them.

Mei Lin returned to the front of the room, where her bag lay open on the teacher's desk. She pulled out the candy, and squeals of delight went up from all over. Several boys rushed out of their seats toward her.

Mother Su raised her hand. "Now, let's show Miss Mei Lin our good manners. No one will be left out. Miss Mei Lin?"

"The people at my church in Jiangxi Province gave me money so I could buy you the paper and pencils and candy," said Mei Lin. "So these gifts are from all of us."

She went around the room and passed out the candy, but to her surprise only one child began to eat it.

"You may eat it," she said. "You don't have to wait."

They stared back at her. She watched two of them slide the candy off of their desks and into their pockets.

"Or you may save it for later," she said. She would work to win their trust. Then they wouldn't be afraid of losing anything.

"Let's sing a song for Miss Mei Lin, shall we?" said Mother Su. She clapped her hands three times, and the children began to sing:

O Lord, I praise you
Because you have chosen me
In the midst of the crowd
It was you who found me.

The children sang the little chorus over and over again until Mei Lin memorized the words and joined them. She clapped for them afterward, and the children giggled with excitement.

After Mother Su taught the children a Bible story, they stayed in their seats until they were called up by name. She called

Nathaniel and Philip first, and Cook Chu came in and led them out. Mei Lin was sure that the cook had prepared a bath for them.

One by one, Mother Su called the rest of the children up front to her chair. She spent time with each child, holding or hugging them. Mei Lin followed her example, starting with the three girls in the back.

She called Priscilla first. Priscilla was taller than the other girls but seemed much more insecure and wouldn't look Mei Lin in the eye. Mei Lin squeezed her hand. "We're going to be great friends," she whispered.

Priscilla looked back at Lydia as if for approval.

"We'll *all* be great friends," said Mei Lin.

Priscilla headed toward the bunkhouse, and Mei Lin called Elizabeth forward. "Are you glad we'll have school tomorrow?"

Elizabeth shrugged her shoulders and looked down.

"I'm looking forward to having you as a student," said Mei Lin.

Elizabeth looked up at Mei Lin. "Good night," she said.

Lydia was last. She warmed to her instantly, so Mei Lin kissed her on the cheek and watched her walk out the door. At first glance, the orphans looked like a normal classroom of children. But speaking to them individually, she could tell that they needed a great deal of love and healing.

"It was good to have you with us tonight," said Mother Su after the children had all left. "They do need to be tucked into bed with hugs and kisses and personal attention. It's just so hard with only a cook and a part-time nurse. There is much to do."

"How do you pay your staff?" asked Mei Lin as she helped Mother Su push in chairs and straighten the room.

"Cook Chu is a volunteer from our church. We give Nurse Bo her room and board and a small amount of spending money. We have to rely on God to help Tao make enough money to pay her. The orphanage was his idea, you know. He works twelve-hour days to keep it running."

"Oh my," said Mei Lin. "That's a long day."

"Yes, but we are happy."

"And all of this has come about in two months?"

"Yes, it's hard to believe, but it's true."

The building, Mother Su explained, actually belonged to a church member whose father used to own a business painting porcelain tea sets, figurines, and trinkets before the Revolution. It had been abandoned for many years.

Mother Su checked her watch. "Tao is planning to pick us up at nine."

They checked on the children one more time, stopping at Nathaniel and Philip's bunk last.

"Your hair is still wet," Mei Lin said to Philip, and she rubbed it a little with her hands to dry it. He pulled his blanket up to his eyes, and Mei Lin smiled.

"I like you, Mr. Philip," she said. "And I think you and I are going to like it here."

Mother Su spoke to Nathaniel. "Nathaniel, there is a little girl at the Shanghai train station. Do you know her?"

Nathaniel shook his head and looked away. His wounded eye looked infected.

"We'll have the nurse look at your eye this weekend. She's very gentle and she may be able to get that eye healed up for you."

Nathaniel still would not respond. He clenched the key tightly in his fist. Mother Su put her hand over his, and he tensed.

"You just keep that key until you're ready to stay," said Mother Su. "I have another one. We're all free here, Nathaniel. Free to stay, free to leave. But I do hope you will stay with us. We will talk more later on." She patted his hand and turned to the rest of the boys in their beds.

"I want all of you to remember your first night here. You needed people to be kind to you, remember? I want everyone to show kindness to Philip and Nathaniel this evening. Cook Chu will be in her room if you need anything. Adam, I want you to be the room monitor this evening. Will you look out for these boys?"

"Sure," said Adam. He was the biggest boy and one who was making the most of rolling pencils earlier.

A few of the other boys laughed and pulled the blankets over their heads.

"Kindness," said Mother Su. "Let's repeat our three rules. Ready?"

Everyone said the rules together: "Love God. Love each other. Love yourself."

"Wonderful," said Mother Su. "Good night, boys."

Mother Su suggested that Mei Lin go through the same routine with the girls. The girls had four bunk beds in their room but chose to share one bunk bed between the three of them. Lydia slept on the bottom with Priscilla, and Elizabeth slept on the top by herself.

Mei Lin hugged each of them one more time, repeated the three rules, and quietly shut the door. "It's hard to leave them in there. They're so little."

"I know," said Mother Su. "We need more volunteers to help us. But two months ago all three of those girls didn't have a bed. They were fending for themselves."

Mother Su motioned her toward the staff room, where they said good night to Cook Chu. She then led the way back to the alley to meet her husband.

"We found Priscilla living behind the garbage cans in the back of a restaurant. Poor thing—it was early April and she was so cold. She had lived with her grandmother, who died last winter, and she had no one to care for her."

"How awful," said Mei Lin. "And Elizabeth—she makes eye contact, but she seems so sad."

Mother Su let them through the gate and then relocked it. "Elizabeth is more high functioning socially and emotionally than the other two girls. She is very polite but stays to herself all the time. We found her at the bus station on her way to nowhere."

"And Lydia?"

"I haven't quite figured out what happened to Lydia. We found her at the train station. We didn't know she was a girl until we gave her a bath!"

Mother Su led them to the same spot where Tao had dropped them off hours before. "Her hair was much shorter, and she had all the boys fooled at the train station. It was her way of surviving. She has scars on her hands but won't tell us how she got them. Maybe she doesn't remember, I don't know. Many of these children don't trust adults because adults have hurt them. I'm hoping, since you're so young, that some of our children will find it easier to trust you."

CHAPTER

Lise

Liko dropped the yoke from Old Gray before putting him in the stall. The creature shook its sides and nuzzled the bottom of the gate, looking for the water bucket in the darkness. Liko picked up a dry rag and wiped down the animal's sweaty sides. It was good that his spring planting would be over by lunchtime tomorrow. Old Gray was getting old, and he wouldn't endure pulling the plow in the summer heat.

"Hello, Liko."

Liko swung around to see the silhouette of a young woman. His heart nearly leaped from his chest. *Mei Lin?*

"I knew I'd find you here."

"Jade—hello," Liko answered, trying to hide his disappointment. It was the third time she had tried to talk to him this week. "This isn't a very good place to meet. This is the Kwans' cowshed. Besides, it's dark in here."

"Then I'll have to stand where you can see me." She stepped inside the cowshed and stood so that the few rays of sunlight that came through the bamboo walls highlighted her tight blouse. "I needed to talk to you—alone."

Liko hung up the rag and leaned over the water bucket to wash his face and arms.

"You can wait for me at my house," he answered. "Mother

should be home by now. I'm sure she'd enjoy talking to you until I get there."

"I can wait," answered Jade, tucking a loose strand of hair behind her ear. "We can walk there together."

Liko wondered if it was her bold approach or her persistence in speaking to him that bothered him more. Most of his church members made appointments or came during evening tea. But Jade was from the city and seemed to abide by a different set of rules.

He picked up the buckets and dumped all of the old water over Amah's garden. He hoped Jade would leave while he hauled water from their pump, but he knew she was still there. No one was home at the Kwans', and he was glad for that. It would be hard to explain the beautiful city girl waiting for him in their cowshed.

Under Jade's watchful eye, Liko dumped grain into Old Gray's trough and then hung the harness on the wall.

"Let's go," he said.

The two of them walked down the path beside Amah's garden, between the houses to the main road that ran behind the row of houses.

"I enjoyed your sermon on Saturday night," Jade began. "You have quite a way with words."

"Thank you," Liko answered. "Is that what you wanted to talk about?"

"Sort of. I'm just trying to find a way that I can help you."

"Help me?"

"Well, help the house church," she said quickly.

"I see. Did you talk to my mother about it?" Liko chided himself for being so difficult, but Jade made him nervous. "We depend on God for whatever we need."

Jade threw her long hair behind her shoulders. "I thought perhaps you would like to offer some professional training to your comrades."

"What sort of training?" asked Liko. There wasn't a seminary for hundreds of miles around.

"My cousin is the General Secretary of the Haggai Institute in Singapore. Have you heard of it?"

"Oh yes. Pastor Wong speaks highly of the Haggai Institute. A few very fortunate leaders of the house church movement have trained there, although it's difficult to get passports out of China these days."

Jade smiled. "My cousin comes to China sometimes to do business. He's planning to travel to Beijing next week and then on to Nanchang."

"That's nearby," said Liko. "And you plan to visit him?"

"Actually, he wants to visit me."

"Here?" Liko could hardly believe a businessman from Singapore would come this far into rural China to visit.

Jade laughed. "Tanching isn't so bad! My cousin is from Jiangxi Province originally. He lives in Singapore now, but aside from his work at the Institute, he runs a successful business in Beijing. This business is a good way to get him in and out of the country so that he can visit alumni to see how they are doing in the churches. He wants to help house church pastors in this province study at the Haggai Institute."

This conversation was getting more interesting by the moment. Since his father was publicly shamed because of his leadership in the house church, Liko's chances for going to medical school were greatly diminished. He was satisfied to be a house church pastor now, but secretly he'd longed for a higher education. To be trained in the Scriptures at the prestigious Haggai Institute was an unbelievable opportunity.

"I don't know." He didn't want to reveal his excitement to Jade just yet. "It sounds wonderful. But I can't imagine that the government will give all of us visas to leave the country."

"Jin already thought of that," she answered. "He's done this before. He can get you visas by telling the government that it is a business trip and he is employing all of you. Of course, you'll need to give us background information and tell us how many of you there are."

Liko could hardly believe his ears. There were three house churches in Tanching now, and eight that were connected to Pastor Zhang's church in DuYan. Every leader would benefit from training at the Institute.

"I can talk to Mei Lin's father, Pastor Kwan," Liko replied. "And I would want to contact Pastor Zhang, as well. We are all connected, you know, so it's a decision we should make together."

"Jin is coming in two weeks," said Jade. "I know that's not much notice, but hopefully you can come to a decision by then."

Liko raked his hand through his hair. "I can't imagine the honor of learning at this institute. Pastor Wong may want to be involved."

"Pastor Wong would be most welcome," said Jade. "He has many house churches, doesn't he?"

They turned up the path that led between the houses.

Liko looked at Jade. "Why are you doing this? You just met us this summer. And I thought you weren't a Christian before."

"I wasn't," Jade answered defensively. "But your mother convinced me that this is the right way. I wrote to Jin and told him about my conversion. I knew he was a Christian, but I never knew he was involved with the Haggai Institute. He's really quite a remarkable man. After all you and your mother have done for me, I wanted to do something for you."

Liko looked around to see if any neighbors were outside. "Let's talk about this when we are inside with my mother."

Usually Liko watered the garden before going inside. Today it didn't seem that important. He unlatched the courtyard gate. "Mother!"

Jade followed him inside. The Chens' courtyard had a few benches scattered about and a water pump in the center. Most of the other furnishings had been burned in the fire by the PSB shortly after Liko's father was arrested two years ago.

Liko sat down on one of the benches and pulled off his muddy boots as Jade poked her head inside the doorway of his home.

"I love all the windows," said Jade. "It's so light in here!"

"Father had put extra windows in the house as a wedding gift to my mother years ago. Two windows would not do! Father told everyone that he wanted the double wedding blessing hung on more windows than anyone else in Tanching. Mother said their house became well known as the double double blessing house."

Liko smiled to himself. His parents were truly blessed twice over. He would never forget the love in Father's eyes when he looked at his mother. He hoped that he and Mei Lin would share the same deep love.

His boots finally off, he walked inside the house in his stocking feet. "Mother!"

"I'm coming," a voice answered from behind him.

Liko swung around. His mother walked in the gate, carrying her market basket full of groceries. Jade rushed toward her to help her carry a few of the heavier items.

"Hello, Jade," she said warmly, extending her free hand. "It's good to see you. Please do come inside and sit down. I'll put these away and be right with you."

"Thank you, Mrs. Chen." She followed the older woman inside. "You look so happy today."

Mother laughed. "I am happy. I just talked to Ping, the cadre's wife. Do you remember her?"

"Yes, she has a beautiful baby."

"Yes, well, Ping said she wants to come to our house church meeting on Saturday. Isn't that wonderful, Liko?"

"That's great," Liko answered. "Just be careful. The cadre may not approve of his wife coming to secret church meetings."

"Yes, I thought of that. But Jesus welcomes every person who comes to Him, including the wife of the cadre. How can I not do the same?"

"You surely know how to solicit converts, Mrs. Chen," said

Jade, her eyes smiling in approval. "Sung Ping probably couldn't keep herself away. You are quite the persuasive one, and I find that admirable."

Mother stopped in her tracks. "Why, Jade, I didn't coerce Ping into coming. She asked all on her own."

An odd look passed over Jade's face. "Of course."

Liko leaned back in his chair. Jade sometimes bewildered him. She worshiped God enthusiastically during the meetings, just like the others. She was zealous. But for what? Did she think Christians in Tanching should conduct themselves like those she was acquainted with in the city? Perhaps it was because she was a new Christian.

"God himself gives us the choice to receive or reject Him," Liko explained quietly. "We may present that choice to others. But it would be wrong to push people to convert."

"Yes, I'm sure you're right," Jade said quickly. "I . . . I'm amazed at how quickly your churches are growing, that's all."

"Mother, Jade has a proposition that I thought you should hear," said Liko. "I'll let her tell you about it while I wash up."

When Liko returned from scrubbing his face and arms at the pump, the two women were deep in conversation.

"Liko," said his mother, "this would be the opportunity of a lifetime. Your father told me that some of the pastors from the South China Faith Churches were trained at the Haggai Institute."

"I hope you are able to come," said Jade. "Jin said he will need each of you to write a résumé describing your office in the church, your family condition, church status, and a request to learn at the Institute."

"I think we should at least consider Jade's offer," said Liko. "I'll talk to Pastor Zhang this weekend."

Jade stood up. "You won't be disappointed, I'm sure. The reputation of the Haggai Institute speaks for itself."

"Indeed, it does," said Mother. "Thank you, Jade, for your part in this."

Jade smiled. "I'm glad to help. You've both done so much to

make me feel welcome. I should be thanking you. Oh—there is one more thing. Should you decide to study at the Institute, you will need to include your addresses, cell phone numbers of the pastors, and a picture of yourself with a copy of your government identification card. That way the leaders at the Institute will be able to make a decision about your acceptance."

"Why so much personal information?" asked Liko.

"Cults," answered Jade. "The Institute doesn't want cults to infiltrate their student body."

"I'll let them know," said Liko. He watched his mother escort Jade to the gate.

———————

Mei Lin followed Mother Su and Sun Tao up the stairs to the third floor, where they removed their shoes outside the door marked 311.

"I can smell the fried rice out here!" Mei Lin exclaimed.

As Mother Su opened the door, Mei Lin felt a rush of memories go through her. The apartment was laid out just as before, except a few more furnishings were added, a sign of Tao's financial help in the home.

"Mei Lin!" Chang wiped her hands on a towel and ran across the kitchen, through the living room, to the front door. "I can't believe it's you!"

Mei Lin laughed as she squeezed Chang's hands. "How are you, Chang?"

Chang pulled her close. "Here's a warm family hug to make up for all my meanness when you were here two years ago."

"Oh, now, you weren't so mean," said Mei Lin. "You were just looking out for the welfare of your mother and father, that's all."

Chang let go of Mei Lin and studied her at arm's length, still hanging on to her hands. "Mei Lin, you—you're beautiful!"

Mei Lin laughed. "I was so scrawny when I came to you the first time," she said. "I looked like a half-plucked chicken!"

"A soaking wet half-plucked chicken!" said Chang.

Everyone laughed at that. Tao took Mei Lin's bag, and she quickly used the bathroom and washed for supper. She paused just a moment to examine her image in front of the same mirror that had horrified her two years ago.

You have fattened up a bit, she told herself.

"Supper is ready," Chang called from the kitchen.

They sat down, and Sun Tao extended his hands to his wife and daughter. The four of them formed a circle of prayer around the small kitchen table.

"We give thanks tonight to the One who made the earth and skies," said Tao. "We are grateful for the crops of the field and especially for our friend Mei Lin, who has come to share our burden this summer. We ask you to show us all your dream for the children of Shanghai. In Jesus' name."

"Amen," said Chang.

"Amen," echoed Mother Su and Mei Lin.

"What do you think of the orphanage?" asked Chang.

"We picked up two more children at the train station today," said Mother Su. "So Mei Lin saw firsthand where some of our children come from."

Mei Lin nodded. "The children show so much promise. But I am surprised at one thing."

"Oh? What's that?" asked Tao.

"No babies," said Mei Lin. "I expected to see babies." She thought with some embarrassment of the baby bottles and boxes of powdered formula she had purchased and carefully packed in her suitcase.

Mother Su answered, "Tao wants to see babies, too!"

"You would think that one daughter wasn't enough for Baba," said Chang.

Her eyes twinkled, and Mei Lin felt a pang of homesickness for her own baba, who was also willing to take in one more daughter.

"We will need more staff to take in babies," explained

Mother Su. "We have barely enough staff to feed and train the older children now. School is out for the summer, but the orphans you met this evening haven't been in school for a while. I think a few of them have missed it altogether. I know you wanted to be a teacher, and that's exactly what we need right now."

Mei Lin picked up the fried vegetables with her chopsticks. "But isn't this why you were arrested in the first place, Tao? You knew too much about the Shanghai Orphanage?"

Mother Su and Tao exchanged glances.

"We know that our mission is very dangerous," said Mother Su. "But after talking with Brother Tom, we have all agreed that this is the work that God wants us to do for Him."

"Right now there are approximately twenty to thirty *thousand* taxicabs running without government approval in Shanghai," said Tao. "There are even more illegal cabs in Beijing."

"Ah, so you are one of many," said Mei Lin. "Why are so many drivers avoiding the authorities?"

"Money," said Tao. "Most of us can make more money by establishing our own taxi operations or driving independently. We find regular customers in the outlying areas where the buses don't run. Some pick up at the airports and remote railway stations. I am an independent driver for a different reason—I want to help the orphans. I am careful to avoid picking up customers in the areas normally frequented by government officials."

"Don't the police check up on you? The county cadre still visits DuYan to see if I'm engaged in passing out seditious literature."

"Yes, they do come by," said Tao. "I put in applications at jobs here and there so they know I am looking for work. But no one will hire an ex-prisoner—including the government-approved taxi service."

"Are you usually the one who finds the orphans?" asked Mei Lin.

"Usually. Sometimes Chang tells me about an orphan she hears about at work or, like today, I take my wife to the railway station or the bus station, and Deng Su will see an orphan there. We bring them to the orphanage and give them their basic necessities. We want to do more, but—"

"You need help."

Tao sighed. "Yes, and it is difficult to find help we can trust. Most of the church members work to support themselves. Thank God we found Cook Chu. She is a widow and is willing to work there for room and board. Of course, we pay her extra when we can."

"Tell her about the babies, Baba," said Chang.

Tao put down his chopsticks and folded his hands in front of him. "We have found babies, Mei Lin," he said. "One outside a department store and another at the train station at the same time we found Lydia. And we have done our best to find Christian homes for them. Our church passes the word along from one person to another until we find a family not directly connected to our church that will take them. If they adopt illegally and are found out, it could jeopardize the entire orphanage. Everyone knows it won't be long until the babies will be found out, and the adopting parents will lose everything they own in order to keep the child. It's a terrible problem, but I don't know what else to do."

"A new baby does better if it can attach to one caregiver," added Mother Su. "That's almost impossible in an orphanage."

"Yes, I learned that in school," said Mei Lin. "Basic trust is established in the first eighteen months of a child's life."

Mother Su's eyes brightened. "That's right! So we are trying to keep the babies in Christian homes for the first eighteen months at least. We'd like to keep them in homes until they are of school age and then transfer them to the orphanage."

Mei Lin pushed food around on her plate with her chopsticks, separating the vegetables from the chicken and then mixing them again. "Children weren't meant to be raised in institutions," she finally said. "God meant for them to be raised in families. And with the older ones there are so many other things to consider—

the trauma, abuse, abandonment, and disruptions in care that they've experienced over the years."

Mei Lin felt Mother Su staring at her.

"Mei Lin, you have studied all this since your father adopted Yatou, haven't you?"

"Yes. Fu Yatou was reason enough for me to research orphan adoptions. But the sights and smells of the orphanage in WuMa spurred me to look up alternatives to state-run orphanages. Remember her friend Zhu, who died there? He was lame, but he died of malnutrition."

"Do you think the caretakers are using the funds on themselves?" asked Tao.

Mei Lin looked in his eyes and nodded. "And Fu Yatou tells us that the Shanghai Orphanage wasn't any better. Pastor Wong says that there are cleaner and more caring institutions in China, but I haven't seen them."

"So you were already thinking about orphans before Mother sent you the letter?" asked Chang.

"Oh yes. Liko tells me that I talk about orphans constantly." Mei Lin smiled at the thought of Liko. "But he doesn't really mind. Perhaps he will be a doctor in an orphanage one day."

"And you will be the teacher," said Mother Su. She reached over and squeezed Mei Lin's hand.

CHAPTER

Seven

It was seven o'clock in the morning when Mei Lin pulled her bag from the back of the taxi and shut the trunk.

"This is the key to the gate," said Mother Su, "and this is the key to the classroom. This one is to the room you will share with the nurse and Cook Chu. Be sure to lock the door when you aren't in the room. The older boys have been known to steal medicine from the cabinets."

"Whatever for?"

"Money. They are used to stealing in order to survive."

Mei Lin shook her head. "Pray for me, Mother Su. I've never heard of disorderly students. Where I come from, everyone does what they are told."

Mother Su laughed. "Don't be nervous, Mei Lin. You are here to teach. We don't expect you to change their behaviors."

Mei Lin stood in front of the iron gate, her keys in hand, and silently prayed. *Jesus, help me to be a teacher like you were.*

Bang! Bang! Bang!

Mei Lin looked down to see David and Jonathan on the other side of the gate.

"Hello, boys! Why are you banging?"

"Come in!" cried Jonathan.

"Come in!" David echoed.

Mei Lin opened the gate, and Jonathan took off running,

giggling at his game, David in pursuit. She could smell the rice *congee* cooking on the porch. Most schools played music on the loudspeaker until morning exercises. Mei Lin guessed that this school either couldn't afford the music box or didn't want to draw attention to the orphanage. Maybe both.

Lydia stood outside the girls' bunkhouse, smiling shyly as Mei Lin approached.

"Ni hao, Lydia!" Mei Lin greeted her.

"Ni hao, kind teacher," Lydia answered.

Mei Lin gently placed her hand on Lydia's head as she passed her. "I'll see you later," she said softly.

Mei Lin greeted Cook Chu, who was working on breakfast on the outside porch, then opened the staff room with her key. She pulled her chart out of her bag. Last night she put the names of all the children on a behavior chart. Ping's aunt had given her red flag and red flower stickers that she planned to use on the chart to encourage the children to listen. She had also saved the rulers for today. The students would have to draw their own squares on the new paper before she taught them the characters.

Bang! Bang! Bang!

Mei Lin opened the door a crack and peeked outside.

"Ni hao," said Jonathan. He smacked his hands together and repeated his greeting over and over. *"Ni hao, ni hao, ni hao!"*

David mimicked Jonathan until Mei Lin laughed and joined with them in their clapping. *"Ni hao, ni hao, ni hao* to you, Jonathan! *Ni hao, ni hao, ni hao* to you, David!"

The boys giggled again and ran away. Mei Lin stole a glance at Cook Chu, who looked up at her and smiled.

"David always follows Jonathan, whatever he does. They are always together."

"Then let us hope that Jonathan likes school," answered Mei Lin.

At seven-thirty Mei Lin joined the children for rice *congee.* Cook Chu ordered them to wash and dry their bowls and spoons afterward and report back in ten minutes. The children quickly obeyed, then lined up in the courtyard.

"I do not teach them," said Cook Chu, "but I have made sure that they do their calisthenics every morning for half an hour after breakfast. Then we read a Bible story."

"Wonderful," said Mei Lin. "Will you continue with this in the mornings? It will give me time to work with individual students who may need extra help."

Cook Chu was happy to oblige.

Mei Lin bounced up the three stairs to the classroom and unlocked the door. She felt a swell of emotion rise in her throat. Here she was, actually living her dream of being a teacher. She looked at the blackboard, wishing she could have gone to Shanghai University first. She laid her materials on the teacher's desk in the front corner, then opened the blinds on the far wall. She sat in a chair in the back of the room, just to see how it would feel to be a student in her class. Then she slipped from the chair and onto her knees.

"Lord Jesus, thank you for letting me teach. I feel as though you are handing me my dream, but I know I am not qualified. I need your guidance. Please show me how to teach these children, who are probably at many different levels of learning. Thank you."

There was something empowering about standing at the front of the classroom. Of course, it was easy to feel commanding when there was no one to command! But an empty classroom was a place to dream, prepare, and hope.

"The children are our future." That's what her political science teacher always said. Although she didn't agree with all of his party doctrine, he was a dreamer and he loved his students. And although he was a high school professor, Mei Lin hoped to copy some of his good qualities in her own teaching.

By the time the children filed into her room, her chart was hung and each desk had pencil and paper on top of it.

Mei Lin taught her class the counting song. They learned the song quickly, but writing the numerals didn't come as fast.

"Very good, class!" said Mei Lin after they finished the song. "We will practice this every day this week until we learn our numbers by singing and clapping together."

She picked up a piece of chalk and started to write on the board. "Now, some of us know how to count to ten in Chinese."

A few of the students giggled. Mei Lin looked over her shoulder.

"Is it funny to count? Really?" She turned around and leaned over her desk, watching Mark, Paul, and Adam, the three boys who didn't want to sing earlier. "What if you have five pounds of rice and you go to the neighbor who agrees to pay you? Or what if you have a bottle of aspirin to sell? What will happen if you don't know how to count?"

Paul's face suddenly grew serious, and he raised his hand. "They might cheat me," he said.

Paul stole medicine, thought Mei Lin, *yet he doesn't want to be cheated out of one fen!*

"Let's begin by counting from one to ten. I will write the numbers as you say them. Ready? *Yee, uhr, sahn, suh, woo, lyo, chee, bah, jo, shur.*"

Mei Lin wrote the characters in a column on the board. "The number four is the hardest to write," she said. "But if you think of it as a funny hat inside a window, you will remember how to draw it."

Lydia was engrossed in the lesson, her dark eyes twinkling back at Mei Lin. Priscilla followed Lydia's interest, but Elizabeth stared out the window. Mei Lin resisted the urge to call on her. She wanted to give all of the students time to adjust to this new routine.

"Let's have Nathaniel, Philip, Paul, Adam, and Mark come to the front."

Philip was eager to come, but Nathaniel's little face turned red, and Mei Lin immediately regretted calling on him. Quickly she pulled out her box of chalk. "Nathaniel, will you pass out the chalk to the boys? Then I'd like you to open the windows in here. It's getting stuffy."

Relief washed over his face. "Yes, Miss Mei Lin."

"I want the rest of you to write your numerals on your paper. Lay your pencil on your desk when you are finished so I can see your work. Don't worry if you cannot write your numbers immediately. It takes time and practice."

Elizabeth wrote her numbers easily and laid her pencil down before David and Jonathan finished number *uhr*.

Mei Lin stopped at Elizabeth's desk. "You went to school before, Elizabeth?"

Elizabeth looked at her paper and nodded. "Yes, Miss Mei Lin."

"At what grade did you stop?"

"Second. I was going into third when I . . ." Elizabeth looked at the others around her.

Mei Lin gently touched her hand. "Why don't you talk to me about your other school later on—maybe during lunch."

Elizabeth bit her lower lip. "Okay."

Mei Lin quickly wrote some addition problems on Elizabeth's paper and then moved on to watch the others. She pretended not to notice that the three older boys were struggling at the board, but she did keep her eye on Philip, who seemed enthralled with the chalk and the marks he could make. She quietly walked around the room, encouraging each child.

"Good work, boys," she finally said. None of them had completed the numbers. "Erase your work, and you may return to your seats to write your numbers on your paper."

Mei Lin hovered over David's and Jonathan's desks, helping them to form their characters. "Girls, you may go to the board now to write your numbers."

Elizabeth finished first. Mei Lin was quite impressed. The girl's characters were every bit as good as her own. She wondered where Elizabeth came from and why she was orphaned.

By the time recess was called, Mei Lin knew that all of her

students except Elizabeth would need to begin with basic math skills. Most of them knew how to count orally, but none except Elizabeth were able to draw the numerals.

The children quietly filed out of the room, reached the bottom step, and ran wildly across the courtyard. The boys kicked a cloth ball around the yard. Mei Lin watched as Cook Chu set up a snack table with cookies and cups of water. While the children played, Mei Lin created math sheets and made flash cards of the numerals from one to twenty. For the smaller children, she drew pictures of chopsticks, birds, fish, and other creatures to see if the children could match the numerals to the number of objects.

The children lined up single file outside the classroom door, red cheeked and sweating. Mei Lin called Cook Chu and asked her to prepare one more drink of water. The children sat at their desks and sipped from cups as Mei Lin went over the numerals one more time.

After drilling the numbers orally, she asked them questions. "How many girls are in our class?"

Philip's hand went up.

"Philip—stand up and tell us how many girls are in our class."

"*Suh,* including you, Miss Mei Lin."

She wanted to hug him. "Good job, Philip!"

The children responded well to the oral drills. By eleven-thirty, Mei Lin had Elizabeth brushing up on her subtraction and the others associating the Mandarin characters with the numerals.

Even though Nathaniel had opened all the windows, the air in the room was hot and stuffy. At noon, Mei Lin had the children line up at the door.

"Let's pray over our lunch," she said. She offered a prayer and then touched the top of every head, quietly praying a prayer of blessing over each child as they filed out into the courtyard.

"Miss Mei Lin?" Philip was last in line, and he stopped in front of her.

"Yes, Philip?"

"I want to see the picture of China again," he said in a low whisper.

Mei Lin touched his face. "You mean the map that Mother Su showed us?"

Philip nodded.

"What if I can find a map of the whole world? Would you like that?"

Philip nodded, then broke into a big grin and wiggled his tooth. "Look!"

Mei Lin bent over. "Why, Philip, it looks like you're growing up! Everyone knows that when boys grow up they lose their baby teeth."

Philip skipped down the stairs, and Mei Lin followed him out to the courtyard.

"I've never seen them so quiet!" exclaimed Cook Chu. "They filed out here quiet as fish in a pond. How did you do it?"

Mei Lin smiled. "They are a great class," she said loudly enough for all of the children to hear. Then she drew closer to Cook Chu. "Where is Nathaniel?" she whispered.

Cook Chu sighed. "He takes his food and runs away to hide it. He's still in a survival mind-set."

"Did he tell you anything when you registered him last night?"

Cook Chu wiped her hands on her apron. "He said he ran away from an orphanage. He wouldn't tell me which one."

"Hmmm. His eye needs attention."

"Nurse Bo will look in on us this evening," said Cook Chu.

"Good. We already prayed over lunch—they are yours until one o'clock!"

Cook Chu handed Mei Lin her lunch and tin cup of water. "Go into the staff room," she said. "It's cooler in there."

"Thank you," replied Mei Lin. "I need to meet with Elizabeth first. Is it okay if we talk in the staff room? Are there rules against that?"

Cook Chu was drenched in sweat from standing over the

stove to cook their noodles. She smiled and pushed her steamed glasses closer to her eyes. "Our rules are love God, love others, and love yourself."

"Those are wonderful rules," said Mei Lin.

Sun Tao had stopped in earlier to put up another partition in the staff room. Now there were medicine cabinets in the front of the room with a small bed for the nurse. A second panel served as a wall behind the cabinets. Behind the panel was Cook Chu's bed and dresser, and then another partition with Mei Lin's cot and dresser behind it. It was small and barely private, but Mei Lin didn't mind. She was used to sleeping with Amah all of her life.

Mei Lin called to Elizabeth, and the girl walked with her past the partitions to her bed at the back of the room. The two of them sat comfortably on her cot.

"Elizabeth, you are doing very well in your studies," said Mei Lin. "Did you like your other school?"

Elizabeth sipped her water but left her noodles untouched. "I don't remember much," she replied. "That was two years ago when I was seven."

"Do you know your birthday?"

"Yes. October 23."

Mei Lin repositioned herself on the cot. "Elizabeth, can you tell me how you left the school and came here?"

Elizabeth snorted a little laugh.

"What's so funny?"

"Well, I didn't exactly leave school and come here."

"A lot happened in between?"

Elizabeth looked straight ahead. "My mother died in a car accident two years ago." She spoke without emotion, as though she were reciting something for history class. "My father didn't want me, so after a while I left home and tried to get a bus ticket. Only, I didn't have enough money, so Mother Su found me and brought me here. I plan to get money for a bus ticket someday, and then I will leave."

"Do you miss your mother?" asked Mei Lin. A tear slid down her cheek as she thought about her own mother's death.

"Who?" asked Elizabeth.

"Your mama. Do you miss her?"

"Oh."

Mei Lin waited for an answer that never came. She wanted to offer comfort or counsel, but Elizabeth's heart was like a steel wall.

Just then the door banged loudly three times. Mei Lin jumped a little.

"It's just David and Jonathan," declared Elizabeth. "They always bang on doors."

"Really?"

"Yes. And if you don't go answer it, they'll try to sneak in here and steal whatever is in your garbage can."

"The garbage can? That's not good. I wouldn't want them to open a medicine bottle and drink it. They could hurt themselves."

"That's how they used to eat before they came here."

Elizabeth sounded like a nine-year-old adult.

"Yes, but they have food now," said Mei Lin.

"Mother Su says don't yell at them about it," said Elizabeth. "Mother Su is nice."

"Yes, she is nice."

Suddenly the door creaked open. Mei Lin put her finger to her lips. She heard the boys' little feet shuffle across the floor. Then the garbage can clunked over. Mei Lin sneaked around the corner and stood behind them, arms crossed, and watched as they sorted through all the garbage. Paper went back in the can, and any food or metal scrap went into their pockets.

David found a half-eaten pack of crackers, and Jonathan grabbed them out of his hands. "Mine!" he said.

"Mine!" said David.

Then Jonathan stuffed a couple of crackers into his pocket and popped the last one into his mouth.

"I'm not going with you no more," said David. He stood up and shoved a used string of dental floss into his pocket.

Mei Lin felt a smile creep across her face. "Why are you boys stealing garbage?"

Both of them froze in place. David gasped. "We didn't do nothing," he said.

"We take what people don't want," said Jonathan. "Leave David alone."

Mei Lin stood still, with Elizabeth at her side. "Boys, if you ask me I will give you the rest of my crackers. I'll even give you some dental floss that isn't used."

"Some what?" asked Jonathan.

"Never mind," said Mei Lin. She walked toward the boys, and they backed up like two tiger cubs who'd been cornered in a cave. David put his hands in front of his face as though he was afraid she would hit him.

Mei Lin stopped. "Oh, David, I would never hurt you. I love you. I love both of you. If you are hungry, I'll give you food. If you want string, ask for it. I'll give you some."

Neither boy moved. Mei Lin wasn't sure what to do, so she prayed out loud. "Jesus, please show David and Jonathan that we love them and we won't hurt them."

Suddenly she knew what to do. "Okay, boys. Should you come into people's rooms when they aren't there and take their garbage?"

Jonathan shook his head no, and David imitated him.

"Okay, then, here's what I'm going to do. Every time I catch you in my room without permission, you have to let me hug you for a long time."

Jonathan gulped. "What do you mean?"

"Come here," said Mei Lin.

Jonathan finally stood up, but David whimpered, his hands to his face in a defensive position.

"You know how Mother Su holds you at night before she goes to bed? Whenever you come into my room without asking and I find out about it, then you have to give me a hug like you give Mother Su. Agreed?"

Jonathan looked back at David. Mei Lin looked back at Elizabeth. She was smiling.

"Agreed," said Jonathan.

"Okay, then, let's start now," said Mei Lin. She sat down in the chair by the medicine cabinet, and Jonathan walked toward her hesitantly. She reached her arms out toward him. "I love you, Jonathan," she said. She drew him to her, and it was like hugging a stone. "Uh-oh. You have to hug back, remember?"

Mei Lin heard a low-sounding wail come out of Jonathan.

"It's okay," she said. She drew him into a hug and held on. He was still hard like a stone, but the longer she held him, the more she felt the emotion welling up inside of him.

"David, come on," said Mei Lin. "I want to hug you, too."

It took David a few minutes to finally get close to Jonathan and Mei Lin. When he finally drew near, Mei Lin took him into her arms. David still whimpered, but Mei Lin could feel his resistance lessening. She knew that this was why she had come. If she could bring this kind of love—the freeing kind of love—to just one child, it was worth the trip to Shanghai.

CHAPTER

Eight

Late on Sunday afternoon, Liko ducked into the entrance behind the woodpile inside Pastor Zhang's home in DuYan, his mother and Mei Lin's father following behind him. As the dark tunnel gave way to light ahead, Liko was surprised to find a large number of people gathered for the meeting.

"Chen Liko! Kwan So, Mrs. Chen!" Pastor Zhang greeted them. "It's good to see all of you. How rare it is for all of us to gather together."

Mother extended her hand to Pastor Zhang and greeted him. "Will your mother be joining us, as well?"

"Yes, Mother will join us as soon as the way is clear."

"Very good. I wanted her wisdom and prayer in this meeting."

While Mrs. Chen mingled with the other women, Kwan So gripped Zhang Liang's hand. "It's wonderful to see you, Pastor Zhang."

"And you, Pastor Kwan. Have you heard from Mei Lin?"

"No," replied Kwan So. "I suppose it's too soon to hear from her. Amah looks for the mail every day. She is growing anxious."

"And this young man? Is he anxious, as well?"

Liko smiled. "August can't come soon enough for me. But Mei Lin's heart is tied to doing orphanage work. I think she will come home satisfied and full of ideas that will help orphans."

Liko looked around the room again. "Tell me, Pastor Zhang, are all of these people pastors?"

"We have forty-four so far. I called Pastor Wong on his cell phone. There are about twenty-five pastors here that he sent to us from the northeastern part of the province. I'm told that each of these men and women oversees at least fifty house churches."

"Amazing," said Liko. "And the others?"

"Word spread quickly," said Pastor Zhang, grinning. "I am loosely connected with the others here in southern Jiangxi. Most of these have spent anywhere from two to thirty years in prison for their faith."

The room, which was usually packed with the familiar faces of local church members, was today filled with China's greatest heroes—courageous men and women who were willing to suffer for Jesus Christ. For the first time, Liko realized the vast number of Christians who could be impacted by this very meeting. He hoped to serve them well.

The meeting assembled and, after an opening prayer, Liko explained to all of them what Jade had told him the week before. Then he opened up the meeting for questions.

"I am Brother Wei, from Pastor Wong's house church network," said a man in the third row. "I am wondering—if all of us go to the Institute, who will be here to help the churches?"

"Good question," replied Pastor Zhang. "Many of our close assistants are now pastors. Liko?"

"I think that if you feel your churches would be jeopardized by your absence, then you should stay. But if you have a close assistant or someone else you feel could benefit from the Institute, you could send them in your place. That way every house church network will benefit from this opportunity."

A murmur of approval went up from the group.

"I would like to say something," said Mrs. Zhang. She was sitting on a bench beside her mother-in-law near the entrance of the cave. "One of the problems we have in our DuYan churches is the lack of regular theological training. This seems like an answer to that problem."

"I agree," said Pastor Wei. "Some of the churches in our network were started very quickly through evangelism. Some of the pastors were saved only three months when they began to lead their churches. They don't even know any of the Old Testament stories, but we have no choice but to use them. There are so few Bibles and even fewer Bible teachers. With an inadequate biblical foundation, the weaker churches may succumb to heresies that are spreading in China today."

A man in the second row stood up. His hair was disheveled, and he looked as though he'd not slept for three days. "I am Brother Jim. I walked most of the way here yesterday and today from the northern part of the Jiangxi Province. In our area there are cults that are actively disturbing the churches. These cults seem to be everywhere. I agree with Sister Zhang. Regular theological training would give us an answer to that problem."

Liko spoke up. "Once we have been trained, we can teach our house churches what we have learned at the Institute. Perhaps we will be able to return to open similar seminaries to train the new Christians to teach their people and to send out evangelists."

"When will the training begin?" asked Pastor Zhang.

"I'm not sure," answered Liko. "But Law Jin, the General Secretary of the Haggai Institute, will be in Tanching—that's where I live—the end of this week. We should have our paper work together by then if we plan to participate."

Liko noticed that Pastor Zhang's mother had been very quiet throughout the meeting, and it troubled him. "Mother Zhang, do you have any thoughts to share on this venture?"

Mother Zhang's dark eyes sparkled through wrinkled slits. Her hair was pulled back in a white bun with feathery wisps coming loose around the edges. As the elder in the room, her presence was honored.

"It is admirable to seek a stronger foundation in the Word of God, so I prayed and fasted this week over your decision today. I have heard nothing from heaven, nothing from my Bible reading. I think that it would be wise to fast and pray this week before we answer."

"I agree," said Liko. "Only, we must begin our paper work right away, or we won't be ready in two weeks. What do you suggest, Pastor Zhang?"

"I think you are both right. We will fast and pray this week and do paper work, as well. Liko, will you explain again what is needed?"

"For those of you who traveled far from here, we will help you in any way that we can," said Liko. "Each of you will need to write a résumé describing your office in the church, your family condition and church status, and a request to learn at the Haggai Institute in Singapore. You also need to include your addresses, any cell phone numbers of the pastors, and a picture of yourself with a copy of your government identification card. That way the leaders at the Institute will be able to make a decision about your acceptance into the Institute and contact you later."

The rest of the meeting was a flurry of paper and pens, questions and answers.

Chen Li Na watched her son as the pastors crowded around him, many of them taking notes as Liko answered their questions. Liko was taller than his father, but he carried his demeanor and easy smile. Li Na smiled when she saw her son raise his hand in the air and point upward, his hand slightly tilted—the image of Baio flashed before her in that moment, and the memory made her husband seem close to her again. Liko was very much like him, and she wondered what Baio would say if he could see their son now, leading pastors into training that would impact most of the house churches in Jiangxi Province.

"I wish to speak to the two of you."

Li Na turned to see Mother Zhang and Kwan So in front of her. "Me?"

"Yes, Mrs. Chen. You and Pastor Kwan."

"Come, sit here, Mother Zhang," said Kwan So.

Mother Zhang sat back down in her chair near the tunnel entrance. Mrs. Chen and So each pulled a stool up close to her.

"What is it, Mother Zhang?" asked So.

Li Na looked from Mei Lin's father to Mother Zhang, unsure what this was all about.

"Last night I had a dream."

"Tell us your dream, Mother," said Li Na.

"Yes, tell us."

Mother Zhang folded her hands in her lap and closed her eyes. Li Na thought she looked like an elder before the brilliant throne in heaven.

"The dream was short," she said. "I saw Kwan So standing in calm water, knee deep. The water suddenly became dangerously high, and waves from every direction flew over him, nearly knocking him down. The sky was dark and stormy, and Kwan So grew weary with fighting the waves." She opened her eyes and turned toward Li Na. "And you, Mrs. Chen," she said, pointing. "You suddenly emerged from underneath the same troubled water. As soon as you came up out of the waves, I saw a hand reach out to you and take you out of the troubled water."

"Just a hand?" asked So.

"It was a large hand. I don't know, but I think it may have been God's hand."

"Then what happened?" asked Li Na.

"Mrs. Chen, after you were taken out of the water, you turned around and extended your hand to pull Kwan So to safety. Then I woke up."

Li Na shuddered slightly. "You were fasting yesterday?"

Old Mother Zhang nodded. "I would not have considered it worth telling had I not been seeking God in prayer and fasting. I will tell you that as I read my Bible yesterday, the Lord directed me to read the dreams of Joseph, Mary's husband, and the dreams of Paul. It seems that both of these men heeded warnings given to them in dreams from heaven."

"Do you think this is a warning to us?" asked Kwan So. "Is the troubled water telling us that the Public Security Bureau will find out about our trip to Singapore?"

"For now, God has hidden the full meaning of the dream," said Mother Zhang. She took one of their hands in each of hers. "I believe that this dream will be revealed later—at a time when you need it the most. God will show you."

Li Na squeezed Mother Zhang's hand. She was so full of faith and love and godly wisdom. "Thank you, Mother Zhang. I will remember what you've told us."

"As will I," said So.

Li Na smiled into the old woman's face. "I am so thankful for your prayers and for sharing the things that God shows you in Scripture and in prayer. I hope to be very much like you one day."

Mother Zhang laughed at that. "Oh, you are far too beautiful to wind up old and wrinkled like me!"

Li Na patted Mother Zhang's hand. "I'll take your wrinkles if your intimacy with Jesus comes with them."

Mother Zhang was called then to talk to one of the pastors. Li Na watched her, but her mind went back to the dream. It seemed it was a warning of danger. For the second time, she wondered if she should join the others in the Institute training.

CHAPTER

Nine

The first week flew by quickly. Every day Mei Lin entered the classroom the same way she had the first day. She opened the blinds on the far wall and then sat in a student's chair in the back of the room. Every day it was the chair of a different student, and every day she prayed that she would know how that student felt as he or she sat in her class. After meditating for a few minutes, she routinely slipped from the chair and onto her knees. When she got up, she could feel heaven smiling down on her.

On Friday morning she sat at Lydia's desk and prayed for her. Despite the scars on her hands, Lydia drew beautiful artwork— yet her handwriting was terrible. Mei Lin tried to get her to make her characters in the little squares on her paper, but Lydia's hand stiffened, and she tried so hard and performed so terribly that Mei Lin hated to ask her to pick up her pencil. She barely drew her numbers correctly. Mei Lin sat and meditated, praying quietly for Lydia today.

By the time she stood up, she knew that today she would ask Lydia what had happened to her hands.

As in most classrooms in China, Mei Lin's personal education was built on foundations of rote memorization with little room for creativity. One of the ideas that her political science professor explained to her class in high school was a new educational movement in China that allowed children to explore their own individuality. This could be accomplished through assignments that let them express their own creativity and encouraged them to find their individual talents. Although Mei Lin's schooling was very formal and rigid, she tried to combine the rote memorization method with more creative projects to work on.

That afternoon, she was pleased to present the class with the job of drawing a map of China. "I want you to use whatever colors you would like. You may hold your paper up and down or sideways. Make the boundaries as close to the original map as possible. But inside the map you may highlight China's mountains, rivers, and deserts, or you may draw the boundaries for our provinces and list the capitals. Some of you may be more interested in drawing small animals on your map to show animals that are unique to our country, such as the cormorant birds on the Li River or the panda bear."

The children sat still for a long time. No one moved, and Mei Lin wondered if she had explained the assignment clearly. She sat down at her desk with a pile of papers in front of her to correct. She started working and then looked up. Still no one moved.

"You may begin," she said. "Choose any color you like. Decorate your map any way that you would like. All I ask is that you do your best to draw the boundaries around China. Your map may be large or small."

Lydia was the first to act. She pulled out her new set of crayons and got to work. One by one, the other children dared to venture into the new assignment.

The minutes formed an hour. Mei Lin corrected her last paper and looked up at the children. Priscilla was just putting away her materials, but Lydia was still fully engrossed. Now was her chance.

Mei Lin stood up and announced, "Class, you are dismissed for the day as soon as you finish your map of China. Put your crayons inside your desk, but leave the map on top of your desk. I will collect them later."

The students quickly shuffled out of the room, Jonathan and

David scurrying ahead of everyone else. Nathaniel walked past her, a satisfied look on his face.

"Nathaniel, your eye looks much better," she said softly so no one else could hear her.

"Nurse Bo put medicine on it."

"Wonderful. You are a good student, Nathaniel. Keep working hard."

"Yes, Miss Mei Lin."

Mei Lin watched David and Jonathan to see if they would run to the staff house and knock on the door. Even the little boys decided to join a game of kickball, and Elizabeth and Priscilla hung around the front door of the classroom waiting for Lydia.

"Girls, why don't you go play with the jump ropes?" said Mei Lin. "Lydia will be out in a little while."

Elizabeth and Priscilla rarely played alone together, and Mei Lin was pleased when they followed her advice. She turned her attention to Lydia.

"Lydia, your map is beautiful," said Mei Lin. And in truth it was. She somehow captured the bordering Korean Peninsula and the South China Sea in striking symmetry to the map on the board. She mixed her crayon colors so that the sea looked as though it moved over the paper.

Lydia smiled up at her. "You will hang it up?"

"Certainly," said Mei Lin. "I will hang up the flags from yesterday, too. The paint dried overnight."

Mei Lin crouched down beside Lydia and took her hands into her own. "How can you draw so beautifully when your hands are scarred like this?" she whispered. "Does it hurt to draw?"

Lydia withdrew her hands. She bit her lower lip and looked at the floor.

"Lydia, it's okay," said Mei Lin. "God made these hands." She took them back into her own hands again. "God made your hands to hug Mother Su before bed at night. He made them to help Priscilla find the right page in her spelling book. God gave you a great talent to draw beautiful pictures. Will you tell me what happened?"

Lydia sighed. "The stick," she finally said.

"The stick?" asked Mei Lin. "Someone hit you with a stick?"

"'Do—it—RIGHT—Lydia!'" she said. *"Bam, bam, bam."* Lydia slammed her left fist into her right one, imitating the stick hitting her hand.

"Oh no!" cried Mei Lin. "Who told you that? What did they want you to do?"

"The auntie at the orph—uh, the teacher I had before."

"Why?" Mei Lin asked. "What did she want you to do?"

Lydia sighed deeply and wrung her little hands. "I couldn't make the characters on the tablet," she finally admitted. "It's like Priscilla."

"Priscilla?" asked Mei Lin.

"Priscilla wet the bed at night, but they took away the ladder, and she was on the top bed. Every morning she wet the bed. She couldn't get down to go to the bathroom. And every day they took away her food. Or sometimes they beat her and locked her in the dark closet."

Lydia looked into her eyes, and Mei Lin felt she could see into the girl's soul. "That's horrible," she whispered, her voice tight with emotion.

"Priscilla's scared at night," said Lydia. "So I let her sleep with me."

"And what about you?" asked Mei Lin. "What are you scared of?"

Lydia's eyes welled up with tears. "I can't write," she said, her voice cracking. "I try . . . I just can't write!"

Lydia pulled Priscilla's empty chair close to Lydia's and sat beside her. "You know, Lydia, if you never learn to write, that really isn't so terrible."

"What?" she asked.

"There are other things in life besides forming proper Mandarin characters inside tiny squares on a tablet."

Lydia looked straight ahead and sat up in her chair. "I am an idiot, an imbecile! Everyone can write. I cannot write because my parents were dim-witted and brainless. Father and Mother were anti-revolutionaries. They deserved to die."

Mei Lin felt waves of shock going through her. "Is that what you really think?" she asked.

"I think what I am told," said Lydia. Her voice was icy.

"I am your teacher now," said Mei Lin. "Let me tell you what to think!"

Inside she was boiling angry at the teacher who crippled this child's hands and damaged her basic trust in her biological parents.

"You are beautiful, especially when you smile. You are very bright, and you excel in art. Your mother and father did not agree with the Communist Party, but that does not mean they deserved to die. In fact, your parents probably loved you, and maybe they even loved God."

Lydia gasped.

"I didn't know your parents. But they didn't deserve to die because they didn't agree with the Communist Party."

There. She had said the words. But how could she push them into this child's heart? How could she untangle the dark cords created between her mind and heart by unfeeling orphanage teachers?

"Lydia, I'm so angry at your teacher for doing this."

Lydia looked at Mei Lin, bewilderment etched across her little face. Mei Lin felt hot tears forming in her own eyes. "But I have to forgive her," said Mei Lin.

Mei Lin tilted her face to the ceiling and prayed. "Father, I'm angry at Lydia's orphanage teacher. She hurt Lydia's hands, and she hurt her heart. Please take away my anger."

Mei Lin felt a sob escape her throat, and tears brimmed and splashed over her cheeks. They were tears of compassion for this precious little girl. She continued. "Jesus, I want to hate this teacher. But right now, because you tell me to love, I forgive her."

Mei Lin wiped her face with the back of her hand. "Lydia, now I want you to pray. Will you do that?"

"If I can," said Lydia.

"Here, say this—say, 'Jesus, I want to hate my teacher.'"

Lydia repeated, "Jesus, I want to hate my teacher."

"What was her name?" asked Mei Lin.

"Auntie Feng," said Lydia.

"Okay, then say this. Say, 'Jesus, Auntie Feng was mean to me. She was wrong to hit my hands.'"

Lydia repeated Mei Lin's prayer.

"And, Jesus," said Mei Lin. "She was wicked to say bad things about my parents."

Lydia's eyes widened. "She was wicked?" asked Lydia. "*I'm* wicked."

No! Mei Lin wanted to shout, but she held her tongue. "Honey, if Jesus were standing right here beside you, would He tell you that you are an idiot and an imbecile and your parents deserved to die?"

The little girl's eyes filled with tears. "No."

"Would Jesus tell you that you are a wicked girl?"

"I don't think so," said Lydia.

"I don't think so, either," Mei Lin agreed. "Whom did Auntie Feng love? Did Auntie Feng love God? Did she love you or the other students? Or the Communist Party?"

"I don't know," said Lydia. "I guess she loved the party."

Mei Lin felt the desire for freedom pounding in her own heart. At that moment, nothing mattered to her more than Lydia's freedom from a belief system drilled into her by a deceived orphanage staff.

"She was thinking of the party, and she said wrong things and behaved wickedly when she hit your hands. Let's pray for her now."

"Okay."

"Jesus, Auntie Feng was wicked to say mean things about my parents."

This time Lydia repeated the prayer, and there was a surge of confidence in her voice.

"But I forgive Auntie Feng for being mean."

Lydia repeated the prayer.

"And I forgive her for hitting my hands and hurting them."

Mei Lin thought about her own scars, hidden deep inside her womb. And once more, she forgave her persecutors for her barrenness.

"Amen."

"Amen."

Mei Lin took Lydia's scarred hand into her own. "You know, honey, when Auntie Feng said those terrible things to you, it hurt your heart, didn't it?"

Lydia nodded.

"Then I'll pray for your heart to be healed," said Mei Lin. "Jesus, I ask you to heal the scars inside of Lydia's heart. And thank you for giving her a special love for Priscilla. Help her and Elizabeth and Priscilla to become kind and happy friends. In Jesus' name."

Mei Lin gathered Lydia into her arms and held her. Just like the others, Lydia was stiff and unyielding at first. Then Mei Lin began to rock her back and forth. "I just know your mother loved you," said Mei Lin. "And I'll bet your baba was proud of his baby girl."

Lydia shook with dry sobs. Mei Lin kept rocking her, holding her, speaking life over her. After some time, Mei Lin felt Lydia's fingers grip the back of her shirt. She wasn't sure how it happened, but she felt sure that something was healed inside of this little girl.

Mei Lin was hanging up the students' paintings of the Chinese flag when Mother Su walked into the room.

"Oh, look at all this color!" she said. "Now, this is what a school should look like—red flags and maps of China hanging from the walls, and the chalkboard full of numerals."

Mei Lin looked over her shoulder. "You like it?"

"Oh yes. Here, let me help you clean up." Mother Su set to work picking up scraps of paper from the floor.

Mei Lin taped the last map to the wall and turned to clean off her desk. "Did you receive any letters for me?"

"Not yet," said Mother Su. "Perhaps they are waiting to hear from you first?"

"Maybe. I sent a letter on Wednesday."

"Oh, they will write soon. Are you ready to go?"

"Go?"

Mother Su grinned. "It's Friday. Tao insists that we take you out for dinner tonight. He says it's the least we can do after all you've done for us."

"Out for dinner?" How exciting! Mei Lin had only gone to tea with friends and neighbors in Tanching—never to a restaurant. "Doesn't Tao have to work?"

"He's taking a few hours off," said Mother Su. "Let's go."

CHAPTER

Ten

"Mother!" Liko called. "They're here!"

Chen Li Na arranged the grapes and sectioned apples on a tray and carried it to the courtyard while Liko opened the gate.

Jade was holding on to her cousin's arm, smiling. Law Jin wasn't much taller than Jade, but he was dressed in a business suit and carried a briefcase, which made him look rich by Tanching standards.

Li Na watched them, her heart still unsure. Who would manage three house churches in Tanching if they all went to the Institute? Was it Mother Zhang's dream that made her doubt? Or Liko's youthful exuberance?

Kwan So walked in behind Jade and Jin, and the group gathered around the courtyard table to talk.

"Law Jin, this is Chen Liko, head of the house churches in Tanching."

Jin extended his hand, and Liko shook it cordially. "I'm pleased to meet you, Mr. Law. This is Kwan So, my future father-in-law, and this is my mother, Chen Li Na. Kwan So, Mother, this is Jade's cousin, Mr. Law Jin."

"Please, just call me Jin."

Li Na made sure that So and Jin had the better chairs, then served tea to her guests. She watched the way in which Jin held his teacup, then put it to his lips with an air of nobility. His hair was combed in small spikes on top of his head, a style Mei Lin said was popular in Shanghai. Although he was small in frame, he was decidedly handsome, and he carried himself as though he were a doctor or lawyer from Beijing.

"Jade tells me you are quite a successful businessman," said Liko as he seated himself on the bench without a back.

"Ah, well, I needed to have a good excuse to come into China so often," Jin answered. "My real business is helping the house churches. On the side, I am a salesman for a small enterprise that pays me to sell their latest cell phones to new service companies in China. Right now we work in three provinces, but we hope to expand our business."

"It must be lucrative, to keep you traveling so much," said Kwan So.

"Yes, we will need to expand our company and hire more sales representatives. At least, that's what we will tell the government when we apply for your visas."

Li Na seated herself beside her son, her hands caressing her warm teacup. "And your company—it hires men *and* women?"

"Oh yes," replied Jin. "We couldn't leave out the women. China wouldn't have it!" He reached over and took her hand. "And the more beautiful, like yourself, the better."

Li Na flinched and quickly withdrew her hand. *How can overseas people be so open with members of the opposite sex?*

Liko spoke up, saving her from further embarrassment. "In Tanching we are not so open with our comments—or our gestures."

Li Na shot her son a grateful smile.

Jin sat back and folded his arms, seemingly unruffled by their response.

"Although I do agree my mother is quite beautiful, what does beauty have to do with phone sales?"

Jin leaned forward and toyed with his teacup, running his finger around the rim. "Well, beauty can enhance the sale of anything, I suppose. But the big bosses say that beautiful women are more . . . persuasive, shall we say, when it comes to selling."

"Then perhaps we need to leave our women behind when we go to Singapore," said Kwan So. "I do not want to put them in uncomfortable positions."

"No, no," Jin said quickly. "You don't understand. I actually hire only three people, and I've already chosen them from the northern provinces. Which brings me to a problem with the passports."

"Problem?" asked Liko. "We sent you all the passports and ID card photos. Didn't you receive them?"

"Yes, of course," Jin answered. "The Institute had a board meeting. They are concerned about the amount of time it will take for us to process so many passports and airline tickets. You want to be home in time for the fall harvest, true?"

"What are you suggesting?" asked Kwan So.

Jin quickly glanced at Jade, then reached for his briefcase. "First of all, here is some material I brought to introduce you to the history of the Haggai Institute."

Li Na flipped through the catalogue. The building itself stood like a monument to God—something that would not happen here in China. She lingered over the back section, perusing the courses offered.

Liko found the same section. "Are any of these courses electives, or do we all take the same classes?"

"The first-semester courses are the same," Jin replied. "The second semester you may take two electives."

"Which two electives would you take?" Jade asked Liko, leaning over his book.

Liko quickly paged through the back of the book. "I don't know. They all look so good."

"Yes, well, praise the Lord. As I said, the Institute is concerned that we will not be able to process so many passports. So they have suggested sending teachers from the Institute to Jiangxi Province. This plan would also be less expensive."

"Where would we go?" asked Li Na. "We can't meet in the

open in China as you do in Singapore."

"Here's how it works. There are too many of you to put in one house, so they would like to divide your pastors into about six groups. Each group can hear the teacher in one house, then two weeks later switch to the next house, where they will get twelve straight days of the second course, and so on. This way, everyone can be taught without raising too much suspicion."

"A brilliant idea," said Jade. "Don't you think so, Liko? If we start the first weekend in July, we will have eight weeks of solid teaching. That way your pastors will have the first four courses completed by September. Then perhaps we can run a winter teaching."

"What about food?" asked Li Na. "There will be so many for one family to feed."

"Everyone is asked to bring three hundred yuan, if possible," said Jin. "We will divide the money into six, and that should be sufficient for food."

So sat back and shook his head. "Our pastors do not have that kind of money."

"We know this," said Jin. "I have friends—shall we say, business acquaintances? They have offered to sponsor your pastors for the Institute. They will donate two hundred yuan if the poorer pastors can bring in one hundred."

Liko sighed. "I don't want to put pressure on our church members to pay this kind of money."

"I will help you," Jade said quickly. "I can sponsor all three of you."

"You have that much money to help all three of us?"

Jade looked at Jin. "Yes. I have that much money. Really, it's not so much compared to all you've done for me."

"Where would we meet?" asked So.

"Train stations," replied Jin. "We will meet next weekend— it will give us an early start so we can get you home in time for harvest. Do you think you can have your pastors ready by then?"

"There were forty-four pastors at the meeting," said Kwan

So. "I don't know if all of them will be able to attend."

"No matter," said Jin. "We will have teachers available and break up the groups by region and by number. But the Haggai Institute did request that we train *pastors* this time, not laymen. They are particularly interested in pastors who influence larger groups of house churches. They can spread the teaching to more house church networks that way."

So stared into his teacup. Li Na thought he looked uneasy.

"Please, tell the poorest pastors we will try to help them financially," said Jin. "Don't let anyone stay away because of money. We will do our best to house and feed them and train them. It's a . . . a personal request from the board at the Haggai Institute."

Li Na looked at the front of the book at the doctrinal beliefs of the Haggai Institute, then ran her finger again over the list of courses. "Your father dreamed of such an opportunity, Liko. He would have jumped at the chance for formal training."

So sighed. "Yes, Mei Lin's mother would have jumped at this opportunity, too." Then he laughed a little. "In fact, they probably would have asked her to teach at the Institute after they heard the fire in her message."

Liko smiled at Jin. "My father and Kwan Shan Zu were forerunners of the Gospel in Jiangxi. They left a legacy to all of us, and we want to make them proud."

Li Na wiped her eyes, then picked up the tray and took it inside. "Should I go help her?" she heard Jade inquire.

"No," said Liko. "She still misses Father. I'm sure she wants to be alone."

In the house, Li Na's hands trembled, and she nearly dropped the tray onto the table. She gripped the edge and quietly prayed for strength. The whole plan sounded so wonderful, so full of possibility and promise. Why, then, did she feel like crying? She longed to talk to Mother Zhang. A good dose of her spiritual wisdom was just what she needed. She wiped her eyes and returned to the courtyard.

Jin was scooting back his chair. "It's settled, then," he said. "Did Jade tell you? We will need one more signature, the signature of the pastor who oversees most of the churches in this province."

Liko looked at Kwan So. "We are a loosely connected group of churches who serve one another. Why do you want this signature?"

"The Institute wants to be sure that you are operating under proper authority. It's important that the most influential leaders in this province know of the Institute's willingness to help them. They also want to be sure that the leaders meet with their approval. Of course, you may take one of the brochures to show this pastor—uh, what is his name?"

Liko hesitated.

"Ah, just bring the signature and contact information with you when we meet at the train station. I'm sure next weekend will give you enough time." Jin glanced at his watch. "Jade, I believe we promised our aunt that we'd be home by eight o'clock?"

Li Na sat down while Liko walked their guests to the courtyard gate. "Have you heard from Mei Lin?" she asked Kwan So.

"No, not a word. Has Liko?"

Liko returned and joined them. "Nothing. It's only been a week, but I miss her so much."

"Well, it looks like we'll both be busier than we dreamed this summer," said Kwan So.

"Did you finish planting your vegetable garden yet?" asked Liko.

"By Wednesday, I think," answered Kwan So. "I'm a bit behind this year after helping the neighbors."

"I finished earlier this week," said Liko, "so I'm free. I'll go to DuYan and explain the arrangements to Pastor Zhang." He reached for his mother's hand. "Are you all right, Mother?"

Li Na nodded. "I cannot explain it. I felt . . . I felt awkward telling a complete stranger about your father."

"That is how I feel around Jade. She is very outspoken and open with her comments to me, as well. I thought it was from her city environment. Perhaps it was her family?"

Li Na smiled. "I like Jade. She has a childlike quality that endears her to me. Kwan So, what do you think about the arrangements for the schooling?"

Kwan So was staring at his hands, which embraced an empty teacup. "I'm not sure I can leave Amah so long," he said. "What's more, I don't know if I can leave our house churches for so long. I don't think all three of us can go. Perhaps I should stay home."

The three of them sat for some time, lost in thought. The sun was slipping closer to the horizon, and the golden light reflected off the eastern wall of the courtyard.

Li Na was the first to speak. "I think that I will be the one to stay home."

"No, Mother!" cried Liko. "Father would want you to go. You must go."

"I am not comfortable with the thought of going, Liko. I know it is a fine opportunity for everyone. I just don't think I'm supposed to do this."

So leaned across the table. "Are you saying this because he said you were beautiful?"

Kwan So's voice was so caring, so sincere, that Li Na did not feel embarrassed. "No. I thought about it all week long. I've fasted and prayed, and—Liko, what is that look on your face?"

Liko squirmed and looked like a child caught in a misdeed.

"I . . . I must admit I feel a bit of a sting in my heart right now. I've been so taken with preparations of the passports and ID cards, I neglected to take so much as a day to fast and pray about the journey."

Li Na didn't reprimand him in front of Kwan So, but she did raise an eyebrow to show her displeasure.

"Do you know what you're to do yet, Mother?"

"I haven't heard a voice or seen a Scripture," she answered

slowly. "It's in here." She tapped at her heart. "The churches will need someone to lead them. And Amah will need someone to check in on her. It will give us a chance to plan the wedding. Kwan So, I think you should go."

So tapped his fingers on the table in front of him. "My next-door neighbor, Mr. Lang, can watch over the house churches. He's been a Christian for two years, and I know I can trust him. As for Amah, I can ask Mrs. Lang to look in on her." So leaned over the table toward her. "You must go, Li Na," he whispered softly. "Your husband would be proud."

A current of warmth went through Li Na's stomach. She was accustomed to helping everyone else. It had been a long time since someone had looked out for her welfare. Kwan So's heartfelt wisdom was exactly what she needed. He was right—Chen Baio would be proud. She would go.

★ ✱ ★

CHAPTER

Eleven

Mei Lin rode in the back of the taxi with Mother Su. Two years ago her last tour of Shanghai's Old Town was taken on a bicycle with Fu Yatou riding on the back. It was wonderful to see modern-day Shanghai from the cab.

"Look!" said Mei Lin. "That's the third time I've seen a poster of a magnolia."

"The magnolia is the city flower," said Chang from the front seat. She tilted her head back and recited, "'The magnolia is in full blossom in early spring and before the Clear and Bright Festival, which usually falls on April 5. The flower has large white petals, and its eye always looks toward the sky. Therefore, the flower symbolizes the pioneering and enterprising spirit of the city.'"

"Good recitation, Chang," said Mei Lin with a smile.

"'The gold triangle over there is the city emblem,'" Chang continued. "'The triangle emblem has a picture of a white magnolia flower, a large junk, and a propeller. The propeller symbolizes the continuous advancement of the city. The large junk, one of the oldest vessels in Shanghai's harbor, represents the long history and bright future of the port. And the large junk is set against a white magnolia flower blossoming in the early spring.'"

"So you still remember all this from school?" asked Mei Lin. "Perhaps you should come to my class one day next week and teach us about Shanghai culture and history."

"Really?"

"Yes," said Mei Lin. "Those poor children don't want to know about Tanching history!"

Chang laughed. "Oh, I do need to rescue them from that lesson, don't I? But I can't come until late afternoon, after work."

"That's fine. You will be our special speaker. The children will love it!"

"Do you want Cantonese food?" Tao asked over his shoulder. "Sun Ya Cantonese Restaurant is good. Or the San Xiang Mansion has braised pickled pigs' feet, in Hunan style—a Shanghai specialty."

Mei Lin looked at Mother Su. "Is he serious?"

Mother Su laughed. "It's very good, really! Tell her, Tao."

"Before my prison term, I often transported government officials from one place to the other." He laughed. "The mark of a good taxi driver is his ability to drive rich people to rich places. Tonight, we are rich!"

"Baba is like a professional tour guide of Shanghai's finest restaurants, hotels, and tourist attractions!" said Chang.

Mei Lin enjoyed this family's lighthearted exchanges. And Shanghai was truly enchanting.

"You may choose from eight styles of food in our restaurants," Tao continued. "Shanghai concentrates the specialty dishes of the whole country into one city. I can take you to a Sichuan restaurant for some hot taste rice crust. Or we can go try Xincheng's Sichuan three-in-one mashed dish. Or, if you prefer, they serve Yangzhou lion-head-shaped meatballs at Laobanzhai."

"What about Shanghai City Restaurant?" said Chang. "Mother likes their seafood, and I wanted to try the steamed deer's paw."

Tao looked in his rearview mirror. "What do you say, Mama?"

"Shanghai City sounds perfect," said Mother Su. "Do you like seafood, Mei Lin? They have poultry, too."

Mei Lin smiled. "I am hungry for dumplings."

"Oh, then you will have Shengian, the Shanghai fried dumplings," said Tao. "Chang, you've made the right choice."

Tao made a quick U-turn and zoomed in and out of traffic and pedestrians. He handed the cell phone to Chang. "Call and make reservations."

While Chang made her phone call, Mei Lin rolled her window down and felt the hot air against her face, tickling her sweaty neck as it lifted her hair. The occasional wave of exhaust vapors burned her nostrils, but she ignored that and indulged herself in feeling the wind.

"This is fun!" she said to Mother Su. "Fu Yatou would love this!" She didn't want to tell Mother Su that this was the first time she had ever ridden so fast with her head out of the window. She felt like a child, windblown and free.

Freedom was a delicious word. Mei Lin felt as if she could taste its meaning in the wind . . . being free to go to the university to earn her degree . . . or to openly carry the New Testament, now hidden in her back pocket. But she could hardly imagine what it would be like to have the freedom to conceive a child.

A surge of grief washed over her, stealing her freedom wind. The rough prison warden kicked the fertility out of her two years ago, and today, one more time, she remembered and she had to forgive him again. Her thoughts turned toward Liko.

Where was Liko's freedom? Didn't Liko have the freedom to choose? What if she couldn't give him a child? He told her he didn't care if they had a son or daughter, but how much would he care if he knew that they couldn't have either? A picture of Jade skittered through her mind, and she tried to push it back out again. Jade was certainly beautiful, and a new and eager Christian girl who had Mrs. Chen's approval. Perhaps Liko would do better with her.

The fumes from the city buses and cars choked at her throat, and she finally put her head back inside.

"You don't like my air-conditioner?" asked Tao, grinning at

her in the rearview mirror. "Oh! Here we are."

Mei Lin knew immediately that she did not own a piece of clothing that would have suited this fine restaurant. Chang wore her American jeans and high-heeled sandals with a breezy blue chiffon summer top.

"What's the matter, Mei Lin?" asked Mother Su as they got out of the car.

"Oh, this is a beautiful place," said Mei Lin. "I feel so plain. I . . . I didn't know it was so elegant."

"Ah, we will need to put a bag over your head just to keep the young men away tonight," said Mother Su. "Let's wait over there."

Mother Su slid her arm through Mei Lin's, and the two of them walked to the front entrance and waited for Tao and Chang to park the taxi.

It seemed both natural and terrifying to receive the older woman's motherly affection. Mei Lin had hugged many children all week long. Tonight her role was reversed.

Mother Su never moved her arm. She patted Mei Lin's hand. "What's on your mind, Mei Lin?"

Mei Lin shrugged. "The children, I guess. Each one is so special, and their backgrounds are so diverse."

"Yes, the children are in need. But what about you? What are your needs?"

"What do you mean?"

"You seem to be preoccupied most of the time—as though there is something on your mind. Are things all right with you and Liko?"

Mei Lin felt a rush of heat on the back of her neck. "We are all right," she said. "He encouraged me to come to Shanghai. He knows how important it is to me to help orphans in WuMa, a city in northern Jiangxi Province. Both of us hope that I'll gain experience here with you that I'll be able to take back to the orphans in my province."

"Ah, a worthy goal," said Mother Su. "I won't press you anymore, dear. But I fell asleep praying for you last night. You seem restless or worried. Then I had a dream."

"Tell me," said Mei Lin. "Tell me your dream. Was I in it?"

"Yes, you were in it."

"Look. Here come the others."

Mother Su patted her hand. "Perhaps we can talk about this later. After dinner."

It was dark by the time they headed home. Tao and Chang chatted amiably about gourmet dining and food prices. Mei Lin was glad for the opportunity to ride in the back with Mother Su and ask about her dream.

"In the dream, I saw you standing in a valley. There was a bear in front of you," said Mother Su. "You seemed fine for a moment, but suddenly the bear stood up and made an awful noise. It startled you, and you began to run. You ran up a mountain and the bear chased you. You climbed a tree and seemed safe for a little while. In the dream, an evil woman riding on a dragon approached the tree from behind you. You didn't see her because you were watching for the bear. Suddenly the bear was coming toward you, and the woman on the dragon attacked at the same time. You climbed as high as you could in the tree while trying to hold both of them back with your bare hands."

"A rather fruitless effort, don't you think?"

"Yes," replied Mother Su. "But even as I prayed for you last night, I found myself asking God to help you find peace for whatever is troubling you."

"Am I that transparent?"

"I don't think Chang has noticed. She hasn't said anything."

Mei Lin grew quiet. The bear probably stood for her infertility. She could never talk to Amah about it. Amah was proud that she had had five children in the '50s and '60s—the perfect number of children before the one-child policy. Two of them died during the Cultural Revolution, and one ran away and was never heard from again, leaving Father and Aunt Te alone with Amah.

To Amah, infertility was a sign that a woman was cursed by the gods. To make matters worse, Amah still had not verbally acknowledged her faith in Christ. Mei Lin's infertility would be the perfect excuse for Amah to refuse to associate with Christianity. She'd probably light incense or offer food to the ancestors again.

Mei Lin felt sick inside, thinking about it.

"Have you prayed about it?" asked Mother Su, interrupting Mei Lin's thoughts. "You are always the keen one for hearing God speak to your heart."

Mei Lin exhaled slowly, trying to let the tension go out of her body. "Yes, I've prayed. But there's so much confusion around this situation. I really don't know what to do."

"Well, I think God gave me that dream so I would pray for you and be here for you if you ever need to talk."

Mei Lin looked at Mother Su. For the first time since she first touched the scarf at the party, she missed her mother. Mei Lin wondered if her own mother would have seen through her troubled heart. She wondered if she would have been sharp with her like Amah or gentle like Mother Su.

"You are so kind," said Mei Lin. "I'm not even your daughter. I don't want to trouble you with my concerns."

Mother Su sat up, adjusting herself so she could turn sideways and face Mei Lin.

"Mei Lin, your obedience in prison saved my husband. When you left prison, you walked across the street and stopped to help me—even though you knew that you could be thrown back into prison for witnessing so quickly. If it weren't for you, none of us would know Jesus. My husband would be dead or suffering in jail. Then when you told us that your mother died from injuries she sustained in prison, it broke my heart. I feel that God wants me to help you. That perhaps your stay in Shanghai will benefit you as much as it will the orphans."

Tao turned into the alley, and Mei Lin quickly rummaged for her keys.

"Thank you for coming with us," said Chang. "We love having you back again, Mei Lin."

"Thank you for inviting me," said Mei Lin. "And for buying dinner, Sun Tao, and letting me be a part of your family. You are all so wonderful."

"We are honored to have you, Mei Lin," said Tao as he pulled to a stop in front of the orphanage gate. "Mother Su and I wish that all of China's daughters could feel the happiness of Jesus like you and my daughter, Chang."

Mei Lin laughed. "Then we should pray for China's sons that they would know Jesus, too."

"Now you're talking," said Chang. "China's daughters need to marry China's sons, don't we? Speaking of marriage, does Liko have any Christian friends?"

"None in Tanching," said Mei Lin. "But I know a few Christian guys in DuYan."

Chang laughed. "Oh, Mei Lin, you always take me so seriously. I'd never move from Shanghai."

"Never?" Mother Su asked.

"Well, I never want to. I'll put it that way."

Mei Lin said nothing. Sometimes she felt like a *tu-bao-dz*, a country bumpkin around Chang. She wondered if she'd ever get used to her banter. She opened her door and stepped outside.

"Thanks again," she said. "It was a wonderful evening."

"Shall I walk you inside?" asked Mother Su.

"No, I have the keys here. You go on." She stepped back and waved as she watched the headlights go up the alley and make a sharp left turn. Then she walked to the gate and stopped for a moment, jingling her key this way and that to make it fit into the hole.

Suddenly she heard footsteps.

Mei Lin shivered. In Tanching no one would be out at this time of night. She turned and looked up the alley. Under the streetlight at the corner, a woman quickly shuffled past the garbage cans that lined that part of the alley. She was stooped over, and there was a large bag in her hand.

Mei Lin turned back to the gate.

Crash!

The woman had fallen at the corner. Mei Lin hesitated. Then she wrapped the key ring snugly around her middle finger and ran to help. By the time she got there, the woman was on her hands and knees, struggling to get up.

"Here, let me help you."

"I'm fine," the old woman snapped. "Mind your own business."

Something about the woman's demeanor did not scare her at all.

"Well, that's a fine thank-you," said Mei Lin, her arms crossed.

The woman gaped at her in surprise. "So you have a tongue in that mouth of yours, do you?"

"Yes, and you're in a predicament and I daresay need my help," said Mei Lin. "Here, take my hand."

"What do you know?" grumbled the old woman. However, she grasped Mei Lin's hand and pulled. Mei Lin put her hand underneath the woman's arm and lifted her to her feet. She had a tiny frame and stood easily.

After the woman was steady, Mei Lin bent over and picked up her bag. "Here, don't forget your bag."

The old woman snatched the empty bag out of Mei Lin's hands and hobbled away.

"You're welcome," Mei Lin called behind her. Then she felt guilty for yelling. She adjusted her pocketbook on her shoulder and watched the woman until she disappeared into the darkness.

Mei Lin turned to go, then stopped to listen.

Unmistakable. There was a cry coming from the alley the old woman had first come from.

Mei Lin walked toward the sound. The cry was sporadic, and she walked a few steps, then waited until she heard it again. It sounded like a wounded animal.

"Where are you?" Mei Lin asked into the night. No answer.

She stopped and waited again, listening, her hand still gripping her keys.

There. Now the cry was more distinguishable. Oh, it was a pitiful, painful sound.

"Where are you?" Mei Lin asked again.

This time the cry was throaty and full.

CHAPTER
Twelve

Mei Lin quickly threaded her way through dozens of metal garbage cans, the realization thumping in her chest. The cry had come from a baby.

She lifted one lid, then another. She began wildly pulling off lids, tossing them behind her. They were making an awful racket, but she didn't care. She had to find the baby.

The baby's voice was getting hoarse. Perhaps the clanging lids were terrifying the poor child. Quietly she lifted one of the three lids left. No baby. She stopped in front of the can nearest the wall.

"It's okay, honey," she said softly. She placed her hand on the metal lid and pulled, but it was jammed tightly onto the can.

She slid her keys into her pants pocket and pulled harder. One yank, then another. Mei Lin took a deep breath and lifted the lid. The most pitiful sound she had ever heard pierced the darkness.

There, in a bath towel, lay a baby on top of putrid old food and used bottles.

Mei Lin gasped. "Oh! Oh, Jesus! Oh, Jesus!"

Mei Lin lifted the infant's little head and put her hand underneath the neck, the way she'd seen Ping pick up Han when he was first born. She carefully cradled its bottom, then lifted the little package to her breast, its blanket still intact.

The baby was screaming now, and Mei Lin looked around. She was alone. People rarely came to this part of the alley except to throw away garbage. She let the lids lie where they had fallen and carefully picked her way around the debris. Suddenly a car turned down the alley toward the orphanage. Mei Lin held the baby tightly against her and walked quickly to the gate.

It took a moment to maneuver the keys, her pocketbook, and the baby. After what seemed like hours she opened the gate, went inside, and turned and locked it again.

"Shhhhhhh," she said. "You'll wake up my students with all that noise."

Mei Lin quickly stepped across the courtyard and opened the staff house door. Suddenly the ceiling lightbulb went on.

"What's going on?" Poor Nurse Bo was shielding her eyes against the light. "Is that a baby?"

Mei Lin had been hoping to meet Nurse Bo this weekend, but not like this!

She jiggled the little one to try to calm it down. "Oh, this isn't a very good way to introduce myself, Nurse Bo. You won't believe this. I can't believe it."

Mei Lin took the baby to her little room in the back and laid her on the bed. She turned on the dresser lamp, then pulled back the baby's blanket. She gave a cry and covered her nose.

The baby's fists and legs shook, startled at her outburst. Mei Lin immediately regretted shouting, but she had expected to see a pink-cheeked, dark-haired baby. Instead, this child was caked with what looked like dried blood all over its stomach and legs. Its head was caked with dried scabby matter.

Mei Lin felt bile come up in her throat. A dark red glob of wet slime with a long gray rope lay beside the baby.

"Oh!" she cried. "What is that?"

Nurse Bo, who had been right at Mei Lin's shoulder, was running to the medical cabinets.

"It's the placenta, Mei Lin," she said. "The afterbirth from the mother. And the umbilical cord. Whoever gave birth to the

114

baby just wrapped everything in that towel. Where did you find it?"

Mei Lin's hand trembled as she covered the baby again, overwhelmed by the horror of the whole situation. "You won't believe it," she answered. "In the garbage. Oh, God help us. Who throws newborn babies into the garbage?"

"Doctors and midwives throw second- or third-born babies into the garbage," Nurse Bo said, still rummaging in the cabinets. "Sometimes mothers and fathers throw them away."

"I thought they changed the one-child policy," said Mei Lin. "At least in the big cities."

"Ha! It's a new rule for the rich. The parents lose all their savings and must supply the child's entire education."

Nurse Bo scurried back to the bed as quickly as she had left, carrying a pile of clean sheets and a medical bag.

"Quickly, Mei Lin. Go boil some water and clean out the yellow basin so there are no germs inside. Look, Mei Lin. It's a girl! We'll need to clean her up right away."

"Ye-es," Mei Lin replied weakly. She had seen enough. "Now I know why God called me to be a schoolteacher," she mumbled as she went for the water.

Her stomach was still churning as she put the water on the little stove on the porch and cleaned out the basin. She stuck her head back inside the staff room door. The baby had stopped crying. "Do you want the basin water to be all boiling water?" she called.

"No, just hot. You'd better start two pots of water. And bring me an old rice bag, will you?"

Mei Lin quickly added another pot to the stove and found the rice bag.

When she got there, Nurse Bo was putting her gloved fingers up the baby's nose. What a howl!

"She doesn't like that," said Mei Lin.

"I can't believe that she survived without anyone cleaning out her nose and mouth," said Nurse Bo. She looked up at Mei

Lin and smiled. "My guess is she came out howling and spitting—and anything lodged in there flew out!"

"She is a screamer, isn't she?"

Nurse Bo grabbed a scalpel and clean sheet. "Okay, if you're squeamish, you'd better step out for a minute."

"Thanks for the warning," said Mei Lin. "I'll check the water."

Mei Lin quickly shut the door, expecting the baby to scream at any moment. *Whatever is Nurse Bo going to do with that knife?*

She mixed the boiling water with a bit of the cold water, then carried the basin to the door. When she stepped back inside, there was no howling.

"Is it safe?" she called.

"Safe and sound. Is the water ready?"

"Right here," said Mei Lin. "How is she?"

"Sleeping," said Nurse Bo. "Look at her. She's sucking on her fist."

There was a plastic clip on the baby's belly button. It looked painful.

"Where's the other stuff?" asked Mei Lin. "The placenta. And the rope."

Nurse Bo laughed as she dipped a clean cloth into the water. "When the baby is born, the umbilical cord runs from its belly button to the placenta inside the mother. The placenta comes out after the baby. I had to cut the cord. I put an antiseptic right here to keep it clean."

"It looks painful," said Mei Lin. "Does it hurt?"

"No more than getting your fingernails cut," said Nurse Bo. "Do you want to help me clean her up?"

Mei Lin took a clean cloth from the pile on the bed and dipped it into the water. While the baby contented herself sucking her little fist, Mei Lin took her free hand and wiped over it.

"It's not coming off," said Mei Lin.

Nurse Bo sat back on the bed a little. "You're right. I think we're going to need to immerse her. I didn't want to do that right after cutting the cord. I guess I should have waited to do that until after we bathed her."

Mei Lin cringed. "I'm thankful you got rid of it," she said. "Is the water too hot?"

Nurse Bo nodded. "Can you clean out another bucket and dump half of this into it? Then add a little cold water and we'll bathe her. Save some warm water in a thermos so we can at least give her water to drink later on. And you'd better bring both basins back here. I think she's going to need a clean rinse when we're finished."

When Mei Lin returned, the baby was awake and looking around.

"Okay, let's do it," said Nurse Bo. "Put the basin on your dresser."

The baby jerked a little as Nurse Bo lowered her into the water. "Okay, let's soak her for a minute and then try to clean her up again."

Her little face, still caked with a hard, cheesy substance, scrunched up, and Mei Lin touched her cheek. "It's okay, sweetheart," she said quietly. "We'll take good care of you. Tell us, what is your name? We know your birthday, don't we."

Mei Lin put the baby's fist around her pointer finger and lowered it into the water. "We're going to have to clean those hands if you're going to be sucking on them so much!"

"You are so maternal," said Nurse Bo.

"Me?" asked Mei Lin. "I nearly fainted when I saw her. I feel like an idiot."

"Being maternal doesn't mean you like to look at afterbirth," said Nurse Bo. "It means you know how to relate to a child. See how she calms down each time you talk to her?"

Tears glistened in Mei Lin's eyes. "Do you think so?" *This may be as close to a newborn baby as I'll ever get,* she thought.

The baby's little body squirmed in the water, but she seemed to like it. She moved her little arms and legs in jerky rhythms.

"Here, you hold her now and let me work on cleaning her up," said Nurse Bo.

Mei Lin's hands trembled slightly as she cradled the baby's neck and bottom. Nurse Bo didn't seem to notice. She skillfully rinsed the top of the baby's head until the paste softened and finally loosened and rinsed off.

"Look at that," said Mei Lin. "Now we see a little bit of black hair. Just look at you!"

The baby's eyes went sideways toward the sound of Mei Lin's voice. "We see you," said Mei Lin. "We're going to take care of this baby girl."

"I wish I had some formula," said Nurse Bo. "I don't know where to find it this time of night."

Mei Lin smiled. "I know exactly where to find it," she said. "I brought a suitcase full of baby blankets, diapers, bottles, and even a few boxes of powdered formula with me."

Nurse Bo smiled wide. "Ah, what they tell me about you is true, Mei Lin. You are a *guiren*."

"Oh no," said Mei Lin. "People from my village helped me buy these things. My amah even made a couple of blankets."

"Like an angel from heaven," said Nurse Bo. "That's what everyone says."

Mei Lin felt warm inside. She had felt like a *tu-bao-dz* when she came to the orphanage with blankets and bottles, only to find no babies here.

"Okay, turn her over," said Nurse Bo. "I have to wash her back."

"Turn her over?" asked Mei Lin. "You mean, without dropping her? She's so slippery."

"Here. Let her rest her head and neck right here on your forearm. Good. Now hold her thigh right here."

Mei Lin watched with interest. This sweet child seemed to emerge more from an eggshell than a womb! All of the blood and cheesy stuff was melting away, and a wet little bundle of life was emerging.

"Okay, you hold her, and I'll switch tubs," said Nurse Bo. "We need to wash her one more time in clean water. Oooh, this first tub is foul."

Mei Lin hadn't noticed. Her eyes were on the baby now. Carefully she lifted her as Nurse Bo took away one tub and slid the other one underneath. The baby scrunched up her eyes again and cried. Mei Lin felt the water with her elbow and then gently laid the baby into it. Her crying stopped when she was immersed in the clean, warm water.

"Oh, she has chill bumps," said Mei Lin.

After the second washing, the baby even smelled clean. Nurse Bo wrapped the towel around her, and Mei Lin took her into her arms and dried each finger, fold, and crease.

The baby let out a single cry. *"Waaah."*

"Oh, you're talking to me now, are you?" asked Mei Lin. "Are you telling me you're hungry?"

"Where's your suitcase?" asked Nurse Bo.

"Over there, under the bed."

Nurse Bo laid the suitcase on the floor and unzipped it. "Wow, there's enough in here for ten babies."

Mei Lin smiled. "Exactly. I thought there would be babies here, so I brought supplies. I felt silly when I got here and there were only schoolchildren."

"Ha! That little one you're holding doesn't look like she's ready to draw her characters on Monday!"

"Waaah!"

Mei Lin was amused at the difference in her cry now. Before, she was frightened and confused. Now Mei Lin was sure she was simply hungry.

Nurse Bo quickly mixed the leftover warm water from the thermos with the powdered formula. She shook the bottle and brought it over to Mei Lin. "Here, this should be just right."

"Shouldn't we diaper her first?"

"Oh yes! Right!"

Nurse Bo grabbed a triangular cloth diaper and pins.

The baby's hair was still wet, so Mei Lin rubbed her little head with one of Nurse Bo's dry cloths. She grabbed the soft blanket that Amah had made and wrapped her snugly inside. When she finished, only the little face was sticking out.

While Nurse Bo held her, Mei Lin moved her pillow and propped it up at the head of her bed. After she was sitting comfortably, Nurse Bo handed her the baby.

"Here we go," said Mei Lin. "What's this, little one? Are you hungry?"

The baby had a hard time getting her mouth around the nipple. She struggled, reaching with her tongue.

"Waaaah!"

"Oh, now you're mad!" said Mei Lin. "Listen to her, Bo!"

"Try squeezing a little bit out of the nipple so she knows what's there."

Mei Lin did as Nurse Bo said. At first the baby didn't respond, but after a few more attempts, she was ready to try the bottle again. This time she latched on and drank voraciously.

"Is it coming out too fast?"

Nurse Bo looked at the bottle. "No, I think that's about right. She's just a hungry little gal. You know, you will need to hold her on your shoulder and burp her after she drinks every ounce— at first you may need to burp her every half an ounce."

Nurse Bo cleaned up the room while Mei Lin fed the baby. She burped easily the first time but took a little longer the second time because she kept crying for more. Mei Lin looked into her sweet little face.

"We don't know, sweetheart," said Mei Lin. "Maybe your mama did want you, but someone took you away. Do you know what? I want you. You are precious to Jesus. Do you know He loves you?"

While the baby sucked, Mei Lin touched her flat little nose and ran her finger along the arch of her eyebrow. Now that she'd hatched out of all the blood and afterbirth, she was truly a beautiful child.

By the time Nurse Bo had put everything away, the baby was sleeping.

"I've been sitting here thinking about a bed," said Mei Lin. "Can I borrow your table out front?"

"Certainly."

Bo held the baby while Mei Lin placed the low table close to her bed. She pulled out her bottom drawer and emptied its contents onto her bed. Then she took several baby blankets and placed them uniformly into the empty drawer, then laid the drawer on the table.

"What do you think?"

"Perfect," said Nurse Bo. She covered her mouth with a yawn. "We'd better get some sleep," she said. "We may get quite a few hours. I think she's played out."

"Show me how to make the bottle," Mei Lin requested. "I'm not sure how much formula to add to the water."

"There's still enough water here for a few more bottles," said Nurse Bo. "I'll measure the powder into a couple of bottles. Then you just need to get up and add water and shake it."

"Thank you," said Mei Lin. She took the baby back into her arms. Nurse Bo measured the powder, then kissed the baby good night.

"You've been such a dear," said Mei Lin. "Thank you for jumping in to help tonight."

Nurse Bo smiled. "Are you kidding? This was probably the most exciting nursing night of my life!" She laughed and walked to the front door and turned off the main light.

"Good night," she called to Mei Lin.

"Good night," Mei Lin whispered into the darkness. She didn't want to waken the little one she held so close to her heart. Mei Lin sat with her back to the headboard again, cherishing the few minutes with this beautiful newborn baby.

"Jesus, thank you for helping me find her." She giggled. "I wonder if you had an angel trip that old woman just so I'd find this sweet little thing."

★ ✱ ★

C H A P T E R

Thirteen

The orphanage had its own church meeting on Sunday mornings. Mother Su taught that morning, but Mei Lin's attention was focused on the new baby. She cried a little at the beginning but settled down into her nap after Mei Lin fed her.

Afterward they met in Mei Lin's room to talk about her.

"What are you going to name her?" asked Mother Su as she poured them cups of tea. "She needs a name. You know how Yatou felt about being called *girl* all the time."

Mei Lin smiled at the memory. "I don't know. I just call her 'sweetheart.' This drawer is actually big for her, isn't it? Does she look hot to you?"

July in Shanghai was sweltering, something Mei Lin was trying to get used to.

She pulled the little socks off the baby's feet and laid them on her bed. The baby looked like a ray of sunshine in the darling little yellow pants and sleeveless shirt—an outfit that Ping had given her before she left.

Mei Lin watched as the baby turned her eyes toward her when she talked. As usual, she was working to get her little thumb into her mouth.

"Waaah!"

Mei Lin and Mother Su laughed. "Look at her, Mother Su!

Her greatest accomplishment in life is getting that thumb into her mouth."

Mother Su pulled her chair closer to the little drawer cradle, scraping the floor. "She is so beautiful. We need to come up with a name so we can register her here at the orphanage."

"But you won't register her with the state?"

"No, not yet, anyway. The state may be responsible for her being thrown into the trash can."

"Shh-shh," said Mei Lin playfully. She put her hands over the baby's ears. "She's listening."

"She recognizes your voice, Mei Lin. Look at her."

Mei Lin took the infant's little hand and helped her get it to her mouth. She fought ferociously to keep it there, sucking and jerking until it finally popped out again.

Mei Lin was beginning to fall into rhythm with the baby's needs. She ate every two to three hours. She almost always needed a diaper change ten minutes later.

Nurse Bo said that she was doing well to feed her only once at night, so Mei Lin could rest. She was tired, but the adrenaline of having a new baby to care for kept her energy high. The only thing that was missing was Liko. She wanted to watch him with a new baby. He didn't pay much attention to Ping's baby, but then, he and the cadre weren't best friends, either.

"I think we should name her Mei Lin," said Mother Su.

"Mei Lin?"

"Why not? We can name her after you if we want."

Mei Lin kissed the baby's foot. "I would be honored, but it may become confusing around here with two Mei Lins."

"Hmmm. Perhaps you're right."

"What about Mei Bo? Since I found her, and Nurse Bo is helping me care for her."

Mother Su clapped her hands together. "Mei Bo it is! Oh, what a wonderful name."

"And we'll call her Little Mei for short," said Mei Lin. "Just so no one gets confused. How does that sound?"

"Perfect," said Mother Su. "It's a name to be proud of."

"Anybody here?" called a voice.

"That's Chang," said Mother Su. "We're back here with baby Mei Bo!"

Chang appeared around the corner. "Father's here," she said. "Can I invite him in? He didn't want to barge into the girls' staff house unannounced."

"Sure," said Mei Lin.

Chang left and shortly returned with Sun Tao. His face lit up as soon as he saw the baby.

"Oh, look at her!" he exclaimed. "And you look like a little mama, Mei Lin!"

Mei Lin felt a knife twist inside her, but she smiled at Sun, covering her thoughts. "Here," she said. "Do you want to hold her?"

"Oh yes!" Tao picked up the baby and held her against his shoulder. "I'll take her for a little walk, okay? Oh, this reminds me of holding my Chang. Isn't she sweet, Mother?"

"She is," said Mother Su, smiling at her doting husband.

Tao left, and Chang sat on the bed beside Mei Lin.

"What are you going to do with her?"

"What do you mean? We're going to take care of her."

"But what about school?" asked Chang. "You have to teach tomorrow."

"I know," said Mei Lin. Deep in her heart, she didn't want to hand Little Mei to anyone else. She looked up at Mother Su, a thousand questions running through her mind. *Who will take care of her tomorrow? What about after I leave? Who will care for her then? How can I leave her tomorrow, or any other tomorrow? Who will love her?*

"What is her sleep schedule?" Mother Su asked quietly.

Mei Lin sighed, trying to rid herself of her heavy thoughts. "So far, she's awake for about an hour two times a day. Other than that, she eats every two hours and goes right back to sleep."

"I watched you holding her through church this morning," said Chang. "You're a natural."

"She's due for another nap now, isn't she?" asked Mother Su.

Mei Lin looked at her watch. "Probably. It's hard to say. I'm pretty new at this, you know."

Mother Su patted Mei Lin's hand. "And you're doing beautifully, dear. What if I ask Cook Chu to watch her for the first hour of class, from eight-thirty to nine-thirty? Then she'll probably sleep, and Cook Chu can keep the window open to listen for her."

Mei Lin bit her lower lip. She wanted to be with the baby when she woke up after her nap. "Okay," she finally answered. "But why don't we dismiss the class for lunch a little earlier, at eleven-thirty? Then Cook Chu can feed the children, and I'll feed the baby when she wakes up."

"Sounds tiring to me," said Chang. "Teaching all morning and feeding and diapering a newborn. When are you going to eat?"

Mei Lin shrugged her shoulders. "I found time to eat this weekend. My drawer will do for a bed for a while, but we'll need more powdered formula soon. There's a lot to think about. What do you think?"

Mei Lin wanted Mother Su's approval. The orphanage was her responsibility, and Mei Lin didn't want to usurp her authority.

"We will make sure you have the formula and clothing for Little Mei," said Mother Su as she got up from her chair. "Don't worry about that. As far as the schedule, I think you can give it a try. I'll talk to Cook Chu and see what she thinks about the arrangement. Nurse Bo has already agreed to help you on weekends, but she told me today that she hasn't had much to do—you've taken care of our Little Mei on your own for the most part."

Mei Lin yawned. "I think I'll feed her, and we'll both take a nap," she said. "Are you sure Nurse Bo is used to handling the students on her own every weekend?"

"Every weekend," said Mother Su. "She told me she's glad for your company."

"Wait until Cook Chu sees Little Mei tomorrow," said Mei Lin. "Won't she be surprised!"

———

Liko pressed his forehead against the pane of glass next to him, watching the manicured ponds of shining waters sparkle over tiny green sprouts of rice that could barely be seen. A man guided a water buffalo and plow across the last rows of a field, his long stick tapping and prodding the large creature. The farther north they went, the more *cao mao* hats he saw bent over trays of rice shoots. Workers waded in water up to their ankles, bobbing up and down in long rows as they thrust the plants into the water.

The rhythmic chatter and chortle of the train had rocked his mother to sleep behind him. He wondered how she slept with so many people brushing by her and the noisy game of mah-jongg going on inside the sleeping compartment across the aisle. The single aisle seats were uncomfortable at best, and again he wished he could have afforded a sleeping compartment for his mother. She was exhausted from preparing for their departure so quickly. He still couldn't believe everyone was ready and on a train in six days. Each group was meeting at a different location, with everyone traveling today. Kwan So and Pastor Zhang and his wife were traveling with Liko and his mother.

Liko couldn't sleep if he tried. He didn't want to miss a thing. He hadn't ridden in a train since he was fifteen, when Father took him to see the medical college in Nanchang. Liko closed his eyes and tried to relive the memory. It wasn't hot, like today. It was November, and the harvest was over. Father sold some of their furniture and ten of their chickens in order to pay for the trip. They drank soda from straws and ate noodles Mother had made the day before.

That was only five years ago, but it felt like a lifetime. All of his dreams for becoming a doctor were gone now. Gone with Father, another sacrifice made for the work of heaven. He wanted to remember. He wanted to feel close to his father again.

"Would you like something?"

Liko looked up. A stewardess pushed a metal cart full of items to buy, everything from dried noodles to yo-yos. She quickly demonstrated to the passengers around him that the new yo-yo defied gravity and entertained youngsters.

"No, thank you," he said.

After collecting the money from someone who purchased a glass thermos, the stewardess moved ahead, and another one came behind her.

"Hot water?" she offered. "Hot water, anyone?"

Liko smiled at her and shook his head, then looked out the window again. He couldn't believe this opportunity for greater theological training had come into his hands so quickly. There were ten pastors from the DuYan/Tanching area and twenty-four from the regions farther north. The enthusiasm was so high that Pastor Wong had sent his friend Brother Tom to DuYan with money for all ten of the DuYan and Tanching pastors. God had met every need so far. Liko wondered which class they would take first.

He ran his hand along the side pocket of his pants and felt Mei Lin's letter. It came just before he left, and nothing could have lifted his spirits more! He couldn't read his Bible openly on the train, but no one would fault him for reading a letter. Liko opened it carefully and read the words from the girl who made his heart come alive.

"Mother."

Chen Li Na felt a gentle shaking on her shoulder.

"Wake up. We're here."

She rubbed her forehead and eyes, covering a yawn as she looked out of her window. "We are in Qing Bei? So soon?"

The train wheezed and screeched, slowing as it neared its destination. Several people scrambled to use the rest room before it stopped completely.

"Yes. You stay seated. I will grab our bags from the top."

As soon as the train came to a complete stop, a line of passengers fell into the aisle. Li Na watched her son easily hoist four bags from the top rack. Liko was taller than both of his parents and very handsome, but she attributed his kindness to the example he had seen in his father. She knew that he missed Chen Baio, and she longed to reach out to their son in his grief. She hoped that Mei Lin would fill some of the void left in his heart these past two years.

Her thoughts turned to their marriage. It was expected that the newly married couple would live with the groom's parents for at least the first year. But what then? They could stay with her, but if they chose to buy their own house, she would be alone for the first time in her life.

Jesus, help us, she prayed silently. *Heal the ache inside of our hearts. Fill the emptiness we both feel without Baio.*

"Stay right behind me," said Liko. He carried her larger bag and she carried her school supplies.

"Liko, I need to use the rest room."

"Can you wait to use the one at the train station?" Liko asked.

"I'll wait," she answered.

Outside, the train yard was a bustle of activity. Liko waited outside the brick building while she went inside. She rounded the corner to find that there was no door on the bathroom! When she stepped to the side at just the right angle, she could see two women squatting side by side. Surely the bathrooms were private!

Li Na ventured through the open doorway and around a small partition. There were five holes in the floor, three of them crowned with women squatting over top of them.

Having no choice, she chose the hole nearest to the back wall, far away from the view of the outside. She pulled paper out of her bag and squatted.

Moments later she joined Liko.

"There are no doors in there!" she exclaimed. "Women just stand side by side over open holes in the cement floors. I never heard of such a thing."

Liko seemed amused. "So you ran out of there as fast as you went inside?"

"No, I had no choice. But there aren't even doors to the outside of the rest room!"

"Perhaps the old ways of Tanching are better?" asked Liko with a teasing smile.

"Perhaps we could teach them modesty," she answered. "Have you spotted the others?"

"Over there—they just got off the train."

Their group walked through the inside of the dark train station and back outside again to the main road in front. A small cream-colored van pulled up to the curb.

Li Na was surprised to see that Law Jin was driving. *I thought he was busy with his cell phone business.* And Pastor Wong was sitting in the passenger seat!

"Pastor Wong!" exclaimed Kwan So. "I had no idea you would be here!"

Pastor Wong jumped out of the van. "Kwan So, Zhang Liang, it's wonderful to see you on such a happy occasion. Chen Liko," he said, hugging the younger man. "Have you heard from Mei Lin?"

"Yes, I—"

"Hey!" Jin called to them from inside. "Let's exchange our greetings in the van. We're gathering attention out here."

Li Na looked around. No one seemed to be watching. But this was a strange city, and perhaps she should be thankful for Jin's watchful eye.

"Jin!" Liko exclaimed.

"Great to see you, Liko!" said Jin. "I was assigned to your

group. Well, I asked to be assigned to your group! Come on, all of you get in."

Li Na let Liko take her large bag. She kept her smaller one with her and climbed into the middle seat with Mrs. Zhang. A rush of excitement went down the nape of her neck. It was thrilling to travel together with such great men and women of God!

The men piled the luggage inside the back hatch, then climbed through the side door into the back of the van.

"No, no, you go up front," said Pastor Zhang when he saw Pastor Wong trying to climb in the back. "We will be fine back here."

The van pulled away from the curb, and the passengers quickly engaged in conversation.

"I feel very much like a schoolgirl again," Mrs. Zhang whispered to Li Na. "I can't remember feeling this eager to learn in years."

Li Na squeezed her hand, smiling as though she, too, could burst. "I know. The most exciting thing will be returning home to teach what we learned. Everyone back home will benefit. And we'll get a chance to know one another better."

"My husband has talked about starting a seminary in DuYan."

"What a wonderful idea. Would you host it in your back room? That cave really is a grand hiding spot."

"Yes, it is—although it's rather stuffy and dark without any windows. We thought the Tanching and DuYan Christians might merge. Then all of us could take turns teaching."

The whole group relaxed in spirited discussion of how to spread the teachings from the Institute throughout the vast South China Faith Churches network.

CHAPTER

Fourteen

The van stopped, and Jin turned around to face his passengers. "We'll stop here to eat and refresh ourselves, and go on to our destination after nightfall. It is safer to travel under the cover of darkness. It will be a long drive, so stretch while you have the opportunity. Don't forget to use code language inside. We don't want to raise anyone's suspicions. If anyone asks, we are old friends meeting for a reunion."

Li Na looked out of her window. The last time she'd eaten at a restaurant was in DuYan with her husband five years before. Baio had saved money from the harvest and waited until their anniversary to surprise her. He sat across from her, ordered the food, and gently held both of her hands in his. He had leaned over the table and whispered, "Li Na, I want to look at you today. I want to look into your eyes until I see your heart."

Li Na quickly wiped tears from the corners of her eyes.

"Mrs. Chen, are you all right?" asked Jin. She didn't notice that he had tipped the rearview mirror up and was watching her.

She nodded. "This is a fine restaurant, Mr. Law. Thank you."

It was a rare treasure to spend time and leisure with one another. Pastor Wong led a house church movement that numbered more than twenty-five million people over six different provinces. Secretly, Li Na wondered if the Haggai Institute shouldn't sit down and listen to Pastor Wong. She was amazed that even this seasoned general was hungry for more of God's Word.

The group gathered around a large round table, each one seated in a comfortable chair. Mrs. Zhang seated herself between her husband and Li Na.

Jin ordered and paid for an extravagant meal of Peking duck stuffed with delicacies, pork fried rice, stir-fried vegetables with noodles, and fried winter bamboo shoots, a Jiangxi specialty that was said to curb obesity. Peking Duck was China's finest food—the same thing her husband ordered for their anniversary meal five years ago. The entire meal was served in large bowls and placed on a round revolving tray in the center of the table.

Li Na scooped rice into her saucer, then added the Peking duck first and a scoop of stir-fried vegetables. The skin was brown and crispy, and her first bite with the fine chopsticks triggered more memories. She listened only halfway to the conversation going on around the table—safe talk about the upcoming Olympics and the weather change from southern to northern Jiangxi. She stared into her bowl and allowed herself to remember Baio's face, his touch, the exhilaration on his countenance whenever he preached.

Once, when she was particularly exasperated with Liko for jumping off the furniture when he was little, Baio came home to find her scolding him. She had made Liko sit in a chair. When she turned around, there was Baio standing at the door, his arms crossed and a grin across his face.

"Tiger father begets tiger son," he said. Then he ran after her and chased her around the table and into the bedroom. Little Liko thought it was great fun. Baio had caught her and swung her around, then tilted his head back and laughed. Oh, but he could laugh!

Other pictures flashed in front of her now. Pictures from her nightmares only a year before of fists punching him, a board smashing out his front teeth until they fell, white stones mingled with blood falling to the floor. She dropped her fork.

"Mother!" said Liko. "Are you all right?"

She felt Mrs. Zhang's hand on her shoulder. "Mrs. Chen, perhaps we should visit the rest room together?"

Shaken, Li Na nodded. "Yes, that would be good."

"What is the matter?" Mrs. Zhang asked as soon as they were alone.

Li Na stood with her back to the wall, leaning against its coolness for comfort. "I'm sorry. I just—" Unexpectedly, she burst into tears. "I am suddenly remembering Chen Baio today. The last time I was in a restaurant we were together. We ordered Peking duck—"

She sobbed, brokenhearted and aching with fresh memories. "I pictured us laughing together, and the next moment—the next moment boards smashing his face."

Mrs. Zhang pulled her friend into an embrace. "Oh, sister, dear sister. How awful for you."

"I'm so sorry," said Li Na. "I haven't felt like this in months. I haven't even cried for months. I don't know what's the matter with me today."

Mrs. Zhang stood back at arm's length. "Mrs. Chen, perhaps it is the insecurity of this new adventure without him. And then eating here and ordering the food made the longing return. It's not a shame to miss your husband."

Her voice dropped to a whisper. "It is a beautiful thing to long for his company again. But remember this, you honor his memory when you hold to the good pictures and the meaningful words. He would not want you to imagine the torture. It would break his heart. Remember the good, sister."

Li Na nodded and blew her nose in the toilet paper Mrs. Zhang handed to her. "It's so silly of me, after all this time. I am sorry to make a scene. I thought I was over the pictures of torture."

Mrs. Zhang leaned close to her ear. "I will pray for you now. I don't care if we are in the restaurant. Lord Jesus, please heal my sister's heart. Help her to remember the good. In Jesus' name,

I break the spirit of torment that wants to grip her soul right now. I loose healing of the heart and the soothing Balm of Gilead into every wounded place. Please bring the good pictures of Chen Baio back into her mind now, in Jesus' name."

Li Na blew her nose once more and used the rest room. When she came out to wash her hands, Mrs. Zhang was still waiting for her.

"You are a true friend, Mrs. Zhang," she whispered as they walked out the door together.

"Please, call me Jun Lee."

Li Na truly felt lighter inside as she returned to the table. Liko shot her a puzzled look, but she was glad he didn't question her openly again. The meal was complete with dessert, Qing Bei's finest fried walnut- and cashew-filled tarts.

By the end of the meal the sun was setting, and the group climbed back into the van. Li Na sat next to the window again, surprised to find it securely blackened by dark curtains that were stretched tightly from the top to the bottom and could not be forced open.

"What is this?" she asked Jun Lee.

"It looks as though we're in hiding. Obviously Jin fixed the windows while we were preparing to leave the restaurant."

A murmur of questioning went up from the front to the back.

"A precaution," said Jin. "Pastor Wong, perhaps you can sit in the middle with the women?"

"Why are the windows blackened, Mr. Law?" asked Pastor Wong. "It is dark outside. No one can see us."

Jin closed his door, looked around to be sure all windows were closed, and then turned so that everyone could hear him. "I've been instructed by the leaders of the Haggai Institute to transport you to a smaller city about two hours away. After we arrive, the curtains can come off, but we must keep them up for now to avoid detection. If the Public Security Bureau sees a large group of us leaving together or spies such a large group of people in the van, they may be suspicious. The less they can see of all of you, the better. There were two Christians arrested in Qing Bei last week. Everyone is nervous."

With that said, Jin turned around in his seat and started the engine. Pastor Zhang and Pastor Wong switched seats, placing Pastor Zhang next to his wife. Li Na scooted as close as she could to the side of the van to give them room. She placed her hand on the cool metal siding underneath the window. At least Jin kept the front windows open, or the heat would have been unbearable.

Li Na propped her school bag onto her shoulder and leaned sideways into the wall of the van. She fell asleep until the bumps in the dirt road outside Qing Bei wakened her.

"You slept well?" whispered Jun Lee.

Li Na smiled sleepily. "Very well, thank you. Where are we?"

"Jin said we have about twenty more minutes to go."

Li Na looked out of the front window. "Why, it's pitch black!" she exclaimed. Then she whispered, "How does Jin know where he is going?"

"I don't know," answered Jun Lee. "We've been traveling off and on without the headlights since we left the city." She put her hand over her mouth to catch a yawn. "I'm ready to go to bed."

"I hope I will be able to sleep tonight," said Li Na. "I never take naps during the day. I guess traveling makes one weary."

"Yes," her friend agreed. "And you have an added weariness—the weariness of the heart."

Li Na couldn't see Zhang Jun Lee's eyes in the darkness, but she could hear the tenderness in her voice.

"Perhaps it is the change in routine," she said softly. "I have not cried like that in over a year. It was very improper to do so in the restaurant—I hope you'll forgive me."

Jun Lee leaned toward her and whispered, "It was a very proper Christian response, Li Na. Don't worry about crying in public. Remember, Jesus wept."

Li Na smiled at that. Jesus certainly didn't behave like a

Chinese man. But then, her husband used to say that he didn't behave like most Jews, either. *"He watched His Father in times of prayer,"* Baio used to say. *"And whatever He saw the Father do in heaven, Jesus brought that down to earth."* He must have seen the Father cry. He must have known that heaven cried over Jerusalem.

"We're here," said Jin. He turned left, and the headlights revealed a long dirt driveway with a small house at the end of it. A light shone in one window.

"You are free to speak here," said Jin. "This family is related to one of the board members of the Haggai Institute. They are Christians who have taken the courses you're about to take, only they went to Singapore. You can bring your suitcases. We'll bunk down here for the night."

Li Na followed her friends out of the van, glad to stand and stretch her legs.

"One more thing," said Jin. He was standing outside the van door helping them out. "There is a church in our society that is not so stable. We fear they are infiltrating our cell phone system here. Please do not make any phone calls."

Li Na knew that the only person possibly carrying a cell phone was Pastor Wong, and she watched for his reaction to this news. Pastor Wong needed to carry a cell phone. He was responsible for a network of thirty million Christians and thousands of house church pastors.

"Surely you mean only for tonight," said Pastor Wong. "I cannot stay out of touch permanently."

Jin picked up one of the bags, and Liko, his arms loaded, followed him inside. "I'll explain more inside," Jin called back. "The principal of the school is expecting us. He especially wants to meet you, Pastor Wong."

Li Na waited behind the others so she could get her larger bag.

"I'll take that," said Kwan So. He hoisted her bag off the back of the van and stood to face her. Li Na could see the outline of his broad shoulders in the dark.

"I'll come back for my bags later," he said.

"Thank you, So."

"Li Na, I will pray for you while we are on this trip. Please do not hesitate to come to me if you have any . . . concerns."

"I'm sorry to worry everyone with my outburst in the restaurant. I really should have controlled myself."

So held out his arm. "Let me walk with you," he said. "It's difficult to see where to step."

Li Na gratefully took his arm. She was beginning to wonder if this trip was such a good idea after all. One moment she felt giddy with excitement to learn and the next moment ready to burst into tears—and she wasn't sure why. Maybe it was renewed grief over her losses. She felt out of character and out of place. After Baio died, she evangelized, led one of the house churches, and worked hard to help the new converts. She liked being strong, confident, and secure. Today she felt weak, confused, and vulnerable. She trembled just a little, and So put his arm around her shoulders.

"Do you want to talk now?" he asked.

She and Kwan So had been friends since childhood. Their families had meals together many Sundays when their children were young. Kwan So was like a rock—stable and strong—and right now she was glad to lean on him. He stopped outside the doorway and waited.

"I am used to traveling with Chen Baio." That's not what she meant to say. She tried again. "I mean, I know he would have enjoyed this journey. He liked to travel and, as you know, his dream was to go one day to a seminary like this. We didn't get to travel much and—So, I'm sorry. I can't seem to find words. Inside I am excited one moment and confused the next. I can't seem to shake this feeling, this despair in the pit of my stomach."

"Did you have it before we left Tanching?" he asked.

She thought about that for a moment. "I'm not sure."

"Maybe since Jin took your hand and called you beautiful?"

Li Na gasped, shocked by his honesty. "Kwan So!"

So set down the suitcases on the porch. The door moved.

"Are you all right out here?" It was Pastor Zhang.

"Yes, Brother," replied So. "We will join you in a moment."

Li Na saw Pastor Zhang smile inside the light of the doorway. "Very good. Take your time."

"Jin's remark was out of line," Kwan So said softly. "Even if city people are more open with their remarks, a Christian man should not speak that way to a woman he just met."

Li Na allowed Kwan So's words to sink into her mind. It only took moments for his comment to reach her heart. "So," she said softly. "You are right."

"A woman, especially a Christian woman, is deserving of honor. If Liko did not have this for Mei Lin, I would not have consented to their engagement."

"His father taught him how to honor," Li Na answered.

"Yes, and if Chen Baio were here, he would teach Jin how to honor you, as well."

Li Na laughed out loud. "You are a bold man, Kwan So! And you are right. Chen Baio would stand up for me."

So glanced inside the house. "Jin may have asked to be assigned to our group so that he could be closer to you. I don't want to judge his heart, but I think his sudden appearance today shocked you and made you long for Baio to shield you."

Li Na looked back at the van, remembering. "You know, the very first thing that Jin said today was that we were gathering attention by greeting one another outside the van at the train station. But I looked around and saw other travelers greeting friends and family. I thought perhaps he was overreacting and then chided myself for doubting his words."

"I will do my best to shield you from Jin," said So. "I think we will need to be bold with him, but he seems quite interested in his business and this school. Still, I am glad that Pastor Wong is traveling with us. I'm sure he will try to help us handle any situations that arise."

For the first time since the day she met Jin, Li Na felt safe. The fog of confusion lifted, and she could see everything more clearly. "I don't know what to say."

"I am sure that Baio would have done the same for any sister in the church who felt threatened by an outsider."

Li Na thought about that. "Yes, you are right." Then she laughed. "And my stomach is feeling much better now!"

He smiled. "That's a good start, Li Na." He looked down at the suitcases. "Are we ready?"

"We're ready."

Inside, the rest of the group was already gathered around a low table with Bibles and empty teacups on top. An electric fan blew on the group at the table, and a second fan blew on the woman near the stove. Li Na was astounded—she'd never seen a house with two fans before.

"Starting school already?" asked So, setting down the suitcases.

"We are waiting for the tea water to boil," said Pastor Zhang. "Come, join us."

While So returned to the van to get the rest of the luggage, Li Na looked about the room. The old farmhouse was larger than any she'd been inside of before. The dining room adjoined the large kitchen to the left. The kitchen walls were bare except for a few utensils hanging above the stove. The open wall behind the kitchen table jutted out just enough to show a larger room with chairs scattered about and a chalkboard on the wall—probably the room where they held classes. Several closed doors apparently led to the bedrooms.

The front door swung open, and Li Na turned to hold it.

"Where shall I put these?" asked So.

"We have three guest rooms," said Jin. "We thought we would put the ladies in the room over there, and the rest of us can settle down in the others."

Li Na picked up her luggage and walked toward the room on her far right. There was no light inside, so she laid her suitcases next to Zhang Jun Lee's. She was glad she wouldn't spend the night alone but wondered how her friend felt about being separated from her husband in this strange place.

She rejoined the others and scooted her chair up to the table beside Jun Lee.

"Here comes the tea," said Jin. "Yan, I'd like to introduce you to Jiangxi Province's finest Christian pastors and leaders—Pastor Wong San Ming, leader of South China Faith Churches with more than thirty million Christians. And these are some of his friends who lead churches in rural Jiangxi, Pastor Zhang Liang and his wife, Jun Lee, of DuYan Village. The others are from Tanching. There is Chen Liko and his mother, Chen Li Na, and their friend Kwan So. I would like to introduce you all to Wen Quon and his wife, Yan. The Wens hold house church meetings here and are sometimes called upon to help with the Haggai Institute. They also donated money to help some of your pastors go to the Institute this month."

"Thank you for having us," said Pastor Zhang, shaking Wen Quon's hand. "We are all eager to start the classes. Will you be teaching?"

The Wens looked at each other and then at Jin.

Jin cleared his throat. "We are waiting for the teachers to arrive tomorrow," he said. "Until then, we have much we can talk about."

Li Na saw Jun Lee put her hand to her mouth. "Perhaps Mrs. Zhang and I can leave you gentlemen to talk?" she asked.

Jun Lee shot her a grateful smile.

"Certainly," answered Jin. "Mrs. Wen? Can you show the women the bathroom?"

Li Na and Jun Lee followed Mrs. Wen through the large classroom to the back of the house. Suddenly Liko was at her side.

"Mother," said Liko, "what was wrong—at the restaurant?"

Li Na waited until Mrs. Wen and Mrs. Zhang walked farther ahead.

"I'm sorry to worry you, Liko. I'm fine now. It's just that—well, I was missing your father. The last time I dined in a restaurant, it was our anniversary."

Liko put his arms around her and hugged her tightly. "I was thinking about him today, too, Mama. My last train ride was with him. Remember when he took me to see the medical college?"

Li Na nodded, then cupped her hand around his face. "You are just like him, Chen Liko. You've made me proud. And Father, too. I know it." She tapped her heart. "In here."

"Do you still think you should have stayed home?" asked Liko.

His eyebrows were scrunched together, and she rubbed them playfully. "I think I'm going to stay right here and keep an eye on you."

Liko smiled at her. "I'll see you in the morning."

"Good night, son. Tomorrow is a new day."

CHAPTER

Fifteen

Chen Li Na watched her son return to the table, then quickly joined Mrs. Wen and Mrs. Zhang. The two women were walking back inside from the courtyard.

"The bathroom is right here, by the courtyard," said Mrs. Wen. "The light switch is on the wall to your right."

"Go ahead, Mrs. Zhang," said Li Na. "I can wait."

Mrs. Wen folded her arms and looked out into the darkness of the courtyard. Li Na followed her gaze, enjoying the warm breeze that played at her hair.

"The courtyard is quite large," said Mrs. Wen. "If the weather permits, perhaps we can enjoy breakfast there tomorrow morning."

"That would be nice," said Li Na. "Do you have a basin where we can wash?"

Mrs. Wen smiled and shook her head. "There is a sink and a bathtub in the bathroom. Usually we suggest that half of the group bathe one night and the other group the next. In between, we use the sink. It's a good thing we have a live spring up here on the mountain. So far we have only run out of water once, and that was during the drought of '97."

Li Na was surprised to learn that they were on a mountain—a detail she must have missed while sleeping. "We darkened our windows coming up here. How close are your neighbors?" she asked.

"Oh, we have neighbors down the road a mile or so. They're elderly, and we take them meals now and then and check up on them."

Just then Jun Lee came out of the bathroom, and Li Na took her place. The bathroom was small but functional. It was unusual to see a sink, toilet, and tub all together in one place. Mei Lin had told her that the apartments in Shanghai were like this.

Afterward, the three women walked back to the kitchen together.

Suddenly Mrs. Zhang stopped short. "Liang!" she screamed.

"Jun Lee!" cried Li Na.

Pastor Zhang sprang to his feet and rushed to his wife's side. "What's wrong?"

Everyone turned toward the door where she was looking.

"There was a man peeking in that window," she said. "As soon as he saw me, he darted away. Did you see it, Li Na?"

"I saw something move by the door after you screamed. Are you all right?"

Mrs. Wen went to the door and locked it. "I'm sure it's old Mr. Gao. He's from the residents' committee, and he's a busybody. That's why we put him in our guesthouse."

"You have a guesthouse, too?" asked Li Na. She was amazed at the properties and appliances this couple had.

"Yes, but it's in the woods down the road from here. We like our privacy. I'll have Quon check in on him before we go to bed."

Li Na looked at Jun Lee. "Perhaps we should lock our door?"

"That won't be necessary, I'm sure," answered Mrs. Wen. "Mr. Gao wouldn't hurt a flea. He's just nosy."

"Then I will bid you all good night," said Li Na.

Jin spoke up. "Before you sisters turn in for the night, I wanted to collect the money from everyone so we can divide it up for the room and board. I already have the teaching money, of course, but we'll need to give money to the Wens so they can buy food and prepare for the week."

"Of course," answered Li Na. She immediately pulled her money out of her purse.

"I'll need to make a copy of your ID cards, too," said Jin as he collected the money. "I'll get them back to you tomorrow evening sometime."

It felt odd to hand over all her money and her ID card, but the others were doing the same.

"I want my cell phone returned in the morning," said Pastor Wong. "I must make some calls."

"Certainly," answered Jin. "Perhaps I can take you higher on the mountain; the frequency is bad here for some reason."

Pastor Wong smiled. "We are truly out in the country here, aren't we? Liko, perhaps you'd like to go with us? I may be able to find out how Mei Lin is doing."

It warmed Li Na's heart to see her son's face brighten when Mei Lin's name was mentioned. "I can't imagine talking to her from here," he said. "It would be wonderful."

"Mrs. Chen, Mrs. Zhang, let us know if there is anything else you will need," said Jin. He looked at his gold watch. "I'm a bit concerned that our guests still aren't here. They were to arrive before us. Since we'll need to give them time to rest tomorrow, you may sleep as long as you wish in the morning."

"Very well," answered Li Na.

"Good night, Mrs. Chen," said Kwan So.

"Good night, Mother," said Liko.

She smiled at both of them. "Good night."

Jun Lee followed her to the bedroom. Shortly after they turned off the lights, Jun Lee fell asleep, but Li Na lay in bed wondering what tomorrow would hold for them.

She felt uncomfortable hearing one Christian calling another names like "busybody" and wondered if Mr. Gao was really harmless. She chided herself for judging the Wens just because they had money. *Money itself isn't wicked; it's the love of money that is the root of all evil.*

Li Na wasn't used to being so uneasy at every turn, and, for the second time that day, she wished she had stayed home.

Despite Jin's offer to sleep in, Li Na wakened at sunrise. It was her habit to waken at the first light of morning and read Scripture and pray. She quickly put on her slacks, buttoned up her short-sleeved shirt, and slipped into her loafers. Grabbing her toiletry bag and Bible, she tiptoed out of the room, never waking Jun Lee.

After freshening up in the bathroom, Li Na quietly stepped out into the courtyard. The sunrise splashed against the sky over the mountain. A reddish tint reflected from the cement walls, extending its glow to the Wens' exquisite outdoor metal furniture. Li Na ventured past the two tables and chairs, drinking in the cool, dewy scent of the first morning air. The dark purple haze of morning gathered on the left and the right, framing a deep red exhibit of God's glory. Streaks of bright orange zigzagged amidst the red.

Li Na's home in Tanching was nestled in a small valley surrounded by bamboo hills to the east, so the sunrise was not as visible. The backyard sloped upward and appeared to end at a ridge some ten meters beyond the house.

Quietly she unlatched the iron courtyard gate and ventured a little farther. A current of pleasure rippled down her spine. Li Na clutched her Bible and walked the incline until she reached the knob of the hill. The sky's purple haze was turning to a lighter blue. The hill dipped low in front of her and, at the bottom of the hill, a lake shimmered in the morning breeze, reflecting the fiery red and orange of the sky above it.

Li Na could see a small line of houses, like a string of pink pearls, many miles down in the valley. Beyond the valley, mountains jutted up from the earth, pointing to the sunrise.

"Father, this place is so beautiful," she whispered. It was pure grandeur, and she felt she'd never seen anything so wonderful. It seemed . . . holy.

The morning light gathered around her, and she found a rock embedded into the edge of the hill that was large enough to sit on. The cool breeze gently turned the pages of her Bible, stopping in the book of Matthew. Two verses nearly jumped off the page. *How can one enter a strong man's house and plunder his goods, unless he first binds the strong man? And then he will plunder his house. He who is not with Me is against Me, and he who does not gather with Me scatters abroad.*

Li Na ran her fingers over the Mandarin characters and read them again. She felt as though all the fish from the lake below were swimming in her stomach. The voice of the Holy Spirit was as still as the beat of a butterfly's wing, but it was there. And she knew. Something was wrong.

Li Na tried to put her finger on it, to bring some light to all the confusion in her soul. She could not find the words, but the fish in her belly kept flipping, swimming, faster and faster.

We must leave this place now. I need to tell the others.

She was about to stand up to leave when other thoughts swarmed around her.

I am one small house church pastor. Who am I to warn someone like Pastor Wong, who oversees thirty million Christians? Will he believe me? Who am I to give such a warning? Is the PSB coming, or is it something else?

She drank in strength from the sunrise, now dissolving into a pink mist on the horizon. *I have to tell them.* She held her Bible to her chest and stood up to go inside.

"You are up early."

The swimming fish suddenly turned into horses stampeding through her middle. Jin's unseen presence behind her was both shocking and beguiling, like that of a jeweled snake in her garden.

"Yes," she replied. She turned away from his handsome face and looked intently into the sunrise. *Jesus, this man makes me nervous. Please protect me. Give me strength.*

It felt as though her thoughts were shouting through her skin, *Get out! Get out now!* She hoped Jin couldn't hear them screaming at her. She was reminded of the night when Chen Baio held the house church meeting despite her misgivings about the PSB's investigations earlier that week. Baio was captured and beaten that night. It was the last time she saw him.

"May I sit with you?" asked Jin.

Her hand trembled, and she hid it behind her Bible. "You are welcome to sit here," she replied. "I am finished—I was about to go inside."

Jin caught her by the arm, and a streak of terror went through her middle.

"Why are you afraid?" he asked. "Is it the memories of your husband that have shaken you?"

Li Na gently pulled her arm away. "Perhaps," she answered. She couldn't move fast enough. She walked down the hill toward the courtyard gate, hoping he wouldn't follow. Nervously, she tried to unlatch the gate, but her fingers fumbled. The horses were still stampeding.

"Let me help you," he said. She could feel his warm breath on the back of her neck as his fingers softly closed over hers. "You turn it to the left, like this, and then down. That's right. Pull down hard."

The horses wouldn't let her say a word in return. They galloped forward, and it was all she could do not to break into a run.

"Kwan So!" Relief rushed over her.

Kwan So had just come out of the bathroom. He looked past her, and as soon as he saw Jin, he walked with resolve toward Li Na. They met at the table nearest the house.

"What is it, Li Na?" asked So. "What happened?"

Jin was busying himself with something at the gate, and Li Na took the opportunity to speak to her friend.

"Something is dreadfully wrong," she whispered. "My stomach was full of fish flipping about this morning. Now—" She glanced over at Jin. "Now the fish have turned to horses stampeding over my heart."

"Did he assault you?"

Li Na shook her head. "No. I don't know what it is, but I think we are supposed to leave."

There. She had said it.

"I will insist upon taking you back to the train station," said So. "The Wens have a van. They can drive, and I will accompany you."

He didn't understand her warning; she could see it in his eyes. "Kwan So, it's not just me I'm concerned about." Jin was coming, and she needed to say it quickly. "It's all of us. I feel sure we should leave."

"The teachers did not come last night," So said.

Jin stopped at their table and drew out a chair to sit down.

"Jin!" Mrs. Wen stood just inside the kitchen, motioning.

"Excuse me," he said and walked toward Mrs. Wen.

As soon as Jin was far enough away, Li Na continued. "I had these same feelings the night Baio was arrested." She turned the pages of her Bible to Matthew 12. "This morning as I watched the sunrise, I read this Scripture. I believe it is God's message to us today." She read the verses aloud.

So leaned across the table. "I don't know what Pastor Wong will say about this. He was so excited yesterday in the van."

He studied her face, but she did not feel uncomfortable. She had nothing to hide from Kwan So.

"I believe you, Li Na," he said at last. "Let's tell Pastor Wong and Pastor Zhang."

She felt her eyes brim with tears. "Thank you, So. Thank you for believing me."

"You've never given me any cause not to believe you," he said.

Suddenly Jin came running into the courtyard. "Chen Li Na, Kwan So! The state is issuing a crackdown on the house churches. Our teachers have sent word. They were followed and are hiding in another place. We'll have to scatter!" He ran back inside, shouting the same directions to the others.

Li Na felt Kwan So's arm on hers, but she barely noticed. Jin's last words echoed inside of her: *"We'll have to scatter."*

No—no, we can't scatter. "He who does not gather with me scatters abroad."

"Let's go," said So.

The whole room was a fury of movement, everyone packing and stacking their bags in the dining area.

Li Na broke away from So to get her toiletry bag from the bathroom.

Jun Lee was still dressing when she walked into their bedroom. "Li Na, what is it? What is happening?"

Li Na grabbed her suitcase and threw her few belongings from the night before inside. "Jin said that the state is cracking down on the house churches in this area," she answered. "The teachers never made it here last night. Jin said we must scatter and hide in other places."

Terror was etched across Jun Lee's face. What a terrible way to wake up in the morning.

Li Na looked at her friend. Tears welled in her eyes, and she pushed them away with the back of her hand. "Jun Lee, this morning, before Jin gave us the alarm, God spoke to my heart. He told me that everyone should leave this place. And He gave me two verses in Matthew."

"What does the Scripture say?" asked Jun Lee as she threw her items into her suitcase.

"It says that the one who does not gather with Christ scatters abroad."

Jun Lee looked confused. "I don't understand, sister. You say we're supposed to leave, but the verse says not to scatter. Yet Jin tells us to scatter."

The horses were stampeding again, running in terror, until Li Na wished they would jump out of her chest and take her back to Tanching.

"I don't know," she answered. "I think we should leave, but we should stay together. I think we should all go home."

"Home?" asked Jun Lee.

"Come, let's tell the men," said Li Na. She knew that Jun Lee didn't understand, but she told her all that she could possibly say and ran back to the dining room. She ran to her son and put her suitcases beside his.

Liko embraced her. "Mama, you stay with me," he said.

"Liko, we should all go home," she said.

"Home?" he repeated. "Jin said if we all split up we should be relatively safe. After all, it's not a crime to visit friends from other villages, is it? We just need to make our groups smaller. It makes perfect sense."

"Liko, I don't know what to do," said Li Na. "I just know we shouldn't scatter like this." She was growing to hate the very word. In fact, if she could name an enemy at this moment, it would be the word *scatter*.

Then she added, "Read Matthew 12:29 and 30."

"Mother, why do you always throw doubt on good things when they happen?"

She felt her son's exasperation, which was bordering on scorn. Determined not to allow an offense to rise between them, she simply said, "I told your father the same thing the night they came to arrest him. Don't you remember? I told him we should all go home."

Liko's face sobered. "I remember."

Jun Lee pulled her suitcases beside them. "I think your mother is hearing a warning from heaven, Chen Liko," she said. "I think we should listen."

Jin came bounding out of the bedroom near the stove. "Where is Pastor Wong?"

"In the bathroom," answered Liko.

"Okay, I think we have it now," said Jin. "Pastor Wong and Chen Liko will go in the red van. Mrs. Zhang and Mrs. Chen will go back to the white van, and Pastor Zhang and Kwan So will remain here."

"Here?" asked Pastor Zhang. "I thought there was a danger in remaining here."

"There is a danger in *all* of us remaining here," said Jin. "You and Kwan So can tell the PSB you are here to do some fishing and visit with the Wens. The PSB will think that is reasonable. The rest of you must immediately get to the vans."

Kwan So stepped forward. "Pastor Wong, I think we need to go home."

"Go home?" cried Liko. "Why does everyone think we should go home? Don't you want to study anymore?"

Li Na knew her son well enough to realize that Liko's heart was set on this schooling. He wasn't going to allow a PSB raid to take it from him.

"Liko," she said, touching his shoulder, "Kwan So is right. We need to return home."

"Jin, I would like my identity card, please," said So. "And my money. I want to go home."

Just then Mrs. Wen ran into the room. "Run quickly! The neighbors called, and the PSB just passed their house in a police van!"

"Women, go to the white van," Jin ordered. "Liko and Pastor Wong, to the red van."

Li Na saw Pastor Zhang's face. He looked positively stunned.

"I am sorry to separate you and your wife," said Jin. "But for Mrs. Chen's sake I see no other way."

"Of course," he answered. He briefly hugged his wife and helped her to the van outside.

"This is madness," said So. "You are all moving out of fear without clear direction from God."

Liko didn't hear Kwan So. He was outside at the white van where he threw his mother's bags into the back and then ran back inside to get her.

"Mother, come," said Liko.

"In a moment, Liko," she replied. She wanted to see what transpired inside. And she knew the answer was not to scatter. Especially not now.

Jin was scrambling to get his things. He said, "Kwan So, you and Pastor Zhang need to grab my fishing rods and nets. They're hanging out in the courtyard. Go down to the lake behind the courtyard and sit there and fish. If the PSB asks for our visitors, we will tell them you are fishing and are here to visit Zhang's second cousin, Wen Quon. Will you remember that story?"

"Yes," answered Pastor Zhang. "But my identity card—"

"I'll copy them and get them back to you in a few days," said Jin. "I didn't expect the PSB to hunt us down like this."

"I don't like it," said So. "I want my card now. I think we should leave together and we should all go home."

"I wish we had time to devise a better plan," said Jin, rushing by So's words with a plan of his own. "I'll be in touch," he called over his shoulder. "Liko, help your mother."

Li Na allowed Liko to lead her past Jin, who was talking to Mrs. Wen, to the white van. At least, she thought with some small relief, Mrs. Wen would drive them to their next destination, and Jin would be out of her life.

She barely had her seat belt hooked when she saw Mrs. Wen jump into the red van. Just as quickly, Jin threw his suitcases into the white van and jumped into the driver's seat. Li Na gasped and started to unbuckle her belt, determined not to go anywhere with Jin, but he turned on the ignition and threw the van into reverse.

Jun Lee screamed as they both flew forward.

"Hold on, sisters, we need to leave quickly," Jin shouted.

Li Na grabbed the back of the seat in front of her and held on tightly.

He pointed the car up the hill away from the house and put it in drive. Li Na turned around to see Liko waving to her from the red van. So ran toward them from the house, signaling with his hands to stop.

"Law Jin, Kwan So is waving to us to come back," she said.

She tried to make her voice sound calm, but inside a thousand horses stampeded through her heart, and she could not tame them.

Jin sped off, and within seconds dust clouded her view of Liko, So, and the house.

Jun Lee grabbed Li Na's hand. "Let's ask him to take us home," she whispered.

Li Na nodded.

"Mr. Law," said Jun Lee. "Mrs. Chen and I have discussed this and we feel that, after we've hidden for a while, we would like to return to the train station. We want to go home."

Jin looked back at them in his rearview mirror. "Right now we must escape the PSB," he said. "Pull the curtains closed."

Jun Lee got up to obey, but Li Na leaped up beside her and whispered, "Be sure to leave a crack open so we can see where we are going."

"But Jin said—"

Li Na put her finger to her lips. "I know."

She went to the back and tried to see if the red van was following them. She was glad that Liko was with Pastor Wong, but she wished that their parting words had been more agreeable.

She saw the house in the distance, and then Jin turned right. There was nothing now but woods and dust.

CHAPTER

Sixteen

Liko rode silently in the back of the red van, peeking through the drawn curtains. He wished that he and his mother had left on happier terms, but he was thrilled that Jin had paired him off with Pastor Wong. He could think of nothing more stimulating to his spiritual walk than to spend time with the highest leader of the house church network in Southern China. In fact, he felt it would prove to be just as valuable as the courses themselves.

As they rode farther into the mountain area, Pastor Wong studied his Bible and took notes in the middle seat. Liko thought of a few questions he wanted to ask Pastor Wong later and wrote them down.

Mei Lin was on his heart today, and he wondered where she was and if she needed anything. He prayed for her, covering every need he could possibly think of. He smiled, imagining her face when he told her how he had spent his time when she was gone. He had written her a brief letter about it before they left yesterday, but she would truly be surprised when she found out about the train ride and the sudden adventure this morning.

Today was Friday, and he wondered if they would start school on a Friday. He felt a twinge of disappointment at not being able to begin right away, but at least everyone had escaped before the PSB arrived.

The van veered to the left and pulled onto a bumpy dirt road.

"We're going to stay at this little house for the first few days," said Mrs. Wen. "There's a teacher here that Jin wanted you to hear. The house is small, but the people are wonderful. We'll start school after lunch."

Liko and Pastor Wong exchanged glances.

"It's finally beginning," said Liko. His disappointment evaporated into a wellspring of hope.

"Are you excited?" asked Pastor Wong. His eyes were twinkling, and there was a tease behind his smile.

"Is it that obvious?"

Pastor Wong laughed. "There's nothing wrong with being excited. You look like you're going to jump right out of that seat at any moment."

"I might jump out of this seat if the bumps get any bigger."

The van hit a large bump just then, and they both flew and hit their heads lightly on the ceiling.

They passed a row of small houses that lined the road, then turned down a short driveway. The one-story concrete house was probably half the size of the one they had just left. In fact, it reminded Liko of his own home in Tanching.

While Mrs. Wen talked to someone, they collected their bags and walked through the courtyard. A dark, colorful rooster was perched on a windowsill, watching them. Chickens scattered toward the outside walls as they walked through the center of the courtyard and into the house. They stepped right into the small kitchen, where two women were cutting food at the counter. The little room smelled like wild onion and fried rice. The women kept their messy hands over the counter and looked over their shoulders to greet them.

Liko grinned. They were young teenagers. Their hair was cut exactly the same length, just above the collar, and they looked remarkably alike. "Hello. I am Chen Liko, and this is Pastor Wong."

"I am Yin," said the first.

"I am Yen," said the second. "We are pleased to meet you."

"Are you twins?" asked Liko.

The two girls looked at each other and laughed. "No, but we are cousins," the first one answered. They looked as though they were barely fifteen.

"Pleased to meet you, cousins," said Pastor Wong. "May we help you?"

Liko saw the surprise register on their faces.

"Oh no. You are guests. Please sit down. Lunch will be ready in about half an hour."

Liko was surprised, too. It was unusual for an important man like Wong San Ming to offer help with kitchen work.

"Your food smells wonderful," said Pastor Wong.

Yen smiled, obviously pleased.

"Do you need water?"

The girls looked at each other. "Yes," replied Yen with a bewildered look on her face.

Pastor Wong picked up the two water basins and went out to the courtyard.

Liko cleared his throat. Obviously, he should be thinking more about serving than being served, too. "Um, may I do something to help you?"

Yin wiped her hands on a towel. "Do you want to see your rooms?"

"Okay." He picked up Pastor Wong's bags and followed Yin back out into the courtyard. She directed him to one of two doors on the left side.

"Your bedroom is in here," she said. She opened the door on the right. "If you need anything else, let us know."

"Thank you. This is fine."

Yin left, and Liko looked around. There were two beds in the narrow room, with a nightstand between. There was a chair at the end of each bed but no dressers or desks.

Liko put Pastor Wong's suitcases on the bed on the left and sat down on the other. He liked this place better than the fancier house with two fans and a bathroom. It felt more like home.

After Yin and Yen served them a delicious lunch, Liko and Pastor Wong met in the courtyard with their new teacher, Mr. Kong. He was a short man with balding hair and wire-rimmed glasses that sat on the end of his nose.

As soon as class began, Liko knew that this short man had very big intelligence. It was incredible to sit in the courtyard and open their Bibles together. Two years ago, he didn't even own a Bible. Today, he was studying it with two prestigious teachers. They paged through prophecies listed in the Old Testament and then turned to the verses in the New Testament where the prophecies were fulfilled.

Liko took careful notes inside his Bible, listing the New Testament verse reference beside the text of the Old Testament prophecy. By the end of class his hand hurt, but his head was full.

After class, Pastor Wong stayed to talk more with Teacher Kong. Liko felt a little disappointed. Pastor Wong was always busy serving people or talking to them.

He left the courtyard and peeked into the kitchen. "Hey, what smells so good in here?"

The young women giggled, then quickly covered their mouths as though they were embarrassed to show their smiles. Liko liked them. They were childlike and had hearts to serve— both qualities that were valuable in God's eyes.

"I will get you some water," he said.

They protested, but Liko grabbed the basins. One was empty and the other mostly empty. He dumped the remainder of the water into the basin they were using to do dishes and went outside to draw water. Teacher Kong was still engaged in conversation with Pastor Wong.

"I understand your concerns," Liko heard the teacher say. "You have had a harrowing morning, and I'm sure you still feel a bit jittery. Perhaps we should take the evening off?"

"No, we should stay on schedule," said Pastor Wong. He

shook the teacher's hand. "Thank you for taking the time to explain your views."

Liko worked the pump handle. He could tell that Teacher Kong enjoyed speaking. His face seemed bright, and there was an air of excitement about him that matched Liko's heart, which flew like a kite in a perfect breeze.

He was living out a dream that his own father shared with him years ago—to become grounded in the Word of God so that the churches would grow and not be easily influenced by sects and cults. So many churches were teaching confusing doctrines because they had few Bibles or no Bibles to read.

The others will be pleased that I introduced them to this institute, he thought. *And who knows what the impact will be after we go home and teach what we have learned? Perhaps we will send teachers to the villages to evangelize. There may be as many as ten new churches started by next year.*

The basins were full, and he carried them inside one at a time.

———

Li Na made sure the cracks were not visible from the front, but from their vantage point they could see a little bit outside.

"Where are we going?" asked Jun Lee.

"There's a family who lives about three hours from here," Law Jin answered. "We should be safe there."

"Will Pastor Wong and Liko join us there?"

Jin shook his head, obviously annoyed with the question. "We will send the teachers around house to house so that you can learn two by two. After the warning this morning, I think it's better this way. We can't teach the Institute courses to the people of Jiangxi Province if you're all in jail."

Li Na felt sick inside. Kwan So and Liko were separated from her, and she was left alone with Jin and Jun Lee and whatever teachers finally came to teach them. *I'm holding on to you, Father,* she prayed silently.

Li Na reached for her Bible as though she were reaching for a gun to defend herself. She was glad they had escaped the PSB, but she knew they should not have scattered. She opened the pages and parted the window curtain enough to read. She saw Jin look at her through the rearview mirror, but he didn't say anything. Jun Lee followed her example.

After the first half hour, Jin seemed to recover from his fear of the PSB and slowed the van to a more reasonable speed. For the next three hours, the two women sat with heads bowed over their Bibles, sneaking glances of their journey through the cracks in the curtains. Li Na wrote down details about landmarks and how long it was since the last turn.

They turned left onto a dirt road. There were potholes everywhere, and Jin zigzagged the van to try to avoid them. After fifteen minutes of dust and bumps, they came to a small driveway that led to a lonely looking two-story building. A few chickens scattered in front of the van as they pulled in. Li Na pulled back the curtains on the side near the door. The cement building was cracked and the roof leaned a little, in obvious need of repair. The windows on both floors were painted with dark green oil paint. Li Na wondered if Jin's friends planned to teach in the darkness.

The two women pulled their suitcases from the back of the van and followed Jin into the house.

A tall man greeted them at the doorway. "Hello, Jin," he said, shaking his hand. "And these are your pastor friends?"

"Hello, Teacher Liu," said Jin. "I'm surprised you're here so quickly."

"I traveled all night to get here. You did want to start on Friday?"

"Well, yes, but the students are being taken to new locations now." He turned to the women. "Sisters, this is Liu Shun Ting, one of Haggai Institute's finest professors."

Perhaps it was his dark shiny suit, but Mr. Liu reminded Li Na of a well-polished shoe, the kind the PSB wore when they raided meetings. He didn't look as though he'd been traveling all night. His blue tie hung perfectly, and his black shock of hair looked oiled and neatly pasted into place. Although he was taller than Jin, he wasn't nearly as handsome.

Jin led them inside. The house smelled musty, as though it hadn't been used in a while.

"Let me get you some tea," he offered, explaining to his friend that they hadn't had time to eat breakfast before leaving.

"There are fresh eggs and spring onions on the counter," said Mr. Liu. "Grandma Zhou will fix them for you."

Li Na looked around. At first it was dark and difficult to see, as there were no electric lights, but after a few minutes her eyes adjusted. The kitchen was small, and there was no chalkboard or open space as there was at the Wens' house. An old woman was bent over the windowsill, pouring water over beautiful leafy green plants.

"Your plants are very beautiful," said Li Na. The woman did not answer, so she repeated her comment with more volume.

"I'm not deaf," the old woman said.

Li Na blinked. The woman's back was facing her, but the woman and her plants faded from view, and right behind the woman Li Na saw the tail of a dragon. *Swish swish.* The tail was huge, larger than the woman, and it whipped back and forth in a fury.

Li Na shuddered. Her country saw the dragon as a sign of good fortune, but her Bible depicted the dragon as an embodiment of Satan.

Jun Lee spoke then. "Where is the bathroom?"

"Outside," the old woman replied, never bothering to look at her.

"The bathroom is behind the house," Jin said. "I'm sorry the accommodations aren't as nice as the Wens'. The upstairs is a little better."

Jun Lee and Li Na walked back outside, quietly closing the door behind them. There was a small cement landing and then dirt. They walked around to the back of the house to look for the outhouse. The backyard was overgrown with weeds with a narrow dirt path cut through the middle.

"I don't suppose they have toilet paper," said Jun Lee.

Li Na handed her some from her pocket. "Did you try the rest rooms at the train station?" she asked.

Jun Lee shook her head no.

Li Na smiled and shared her experience. "Liko laughed at me, but I was so glad I had some toilet paper in my pocketbook. I've been carrying it in my pockets ever since!"

Jun Lee laughed, and her voice eased the tension inside of Li Na. "I'll have to remember that," she said. "Thank you. After you."

Li Na stepped inside, then turned around and went back outside to catch her breath. "It's awful."

"Try again," said Jun Lee. "Hold your nose when you go in and then breathe into your shirt."

Li Na hesitated, took a gulp of air, and quickly went inside. In a moment she flew back out the door, gasping for air. "We must find another place," she said. "Certainly a tree would serve us better."

Jun Lee flew out of the door a few seconds later, and it was decided. They would build a new outhouse.

Without telling anyone their plans, the women gathered long bamboo sticks, twisting the green ones until they finally broke and gathering dead tan ones from the ground. They walked about twenty meters behind the old outhouse till they found four trees that weren't exactly even but close enough to form the four corners of their new building. They slid one long bamboo pole through the Y in two low tree branches, then used a vine to tie another horizontal pole about three feet below the first one. They placed all the other bamboo poles in a line, leaning them on the first two horizontal poles. The first wall went up in about ten minutes.

"What is this about Matthew 12?" asked Jun Lee as they

worked. "Tell me what God said to you this morning."

Li Na leaned on the bamboo poles in her hands and stood still for a minute. "He warned me against being scattered. That's all I know. And within ten minutes, Jin went flying through the Wens' house telling us we had to scatter. He even used that word. I read the verses again and again while we were in the van; let's see if I can repeat them. 'How can one enter a strong man's house and plunder his goods, unless he first binds the strong man? And then he will plunder his house. He who is not with Me is against Me, and he who does not gather with Me scatters abroad.'"

Just then Jin came out. "What are you doing? We really do have bedrooms for you inside," he teased.

Jun Lee laughed. "Mrs. Chen and I have decided we need two bathrooms. That one is for the gentlemen," she said, pointing to the old smelly outhouse. "This one is for the women."

"I apologize for these primitive conditions," he said.

His face fell momentarily, and Li Na wondered if he truly did care.

"Coming here was a last-minute decision. I didn't know where else to take you on such short notice."

Jin's silver necklace danced under the sun, accenting his broad neck and shoulders. Li Na looked away, remembering her thought that morning about his being a jeweled snake.

"I will help you," he offered. He hung his neat business shirt on a nearby tree branch and worked in his sleeveless T-shirt. Within half an hour they had four walls.

Li Na wiped the sweat from her brow. "Now," she said, breathing hard, "all we need is a roof."

"Oh," said Jun Lee. "Perhaps tomorrow we'll build a roof."

"I agree," said Jin. "Besides, I'm thirsty. Let's get some tea."

The three of them washed their hands with the pitcher of water, soap, basin, and towel that sat outside the front door. After tea, Mr. Liu explained that there were four rooms upstairs—one for the men, two for the women, and the fourth for teaching.

They looked into the teaching room first. It had a chalkboard on the left wall and two windows on each of the other walls. Of course, the windows were all painted with dark green oil paint, so the room was dark and foreboding. Li Na was anxious to see if their bedrooms were as gloomy.

"The dark windows give us more time to escape," Mr. Liu explained. "Should the PSB come to raid us, you have two options. You can jump out of the window here—" He pointed to the window facing the back of the house in the teaching room. "There is a branch right here, and you can try to go down the tree that way. Or . . ." He walked over to the wall between the teaching room and the women's room. "You can hide here." He slid the panel of the wall to the right.

Jun Lee gasped. "Why didn't we think of this, Mrs. Chen? If we had a sliding panel like this one, old Mother Zhang wouldn't need to continually stack wood after we've all gone inside our secret house church."

"Is there a panel on the other side?" asked Li Na. "Is there a panel in our room?"

Mr. Liu shook his head. "We never got around to putting one in. But most of your time will be spent here, in the teaching room."

Li Na relaxed a little. The fact that Mr. Liu was showing her methods of escape made her feel a bit more secure. Of course, the new toilet facilities they just built helped, too! Next they went into the bedroom.

"Why did you divide the room into two small bedrooms?" Li Na asked. There was a wall and a door with a bolt on the outside of each small room. There was barely enough room inside each cubicle for a bed and dresser.

Mr. Liu smiled. "We've found that using smaller spaces like this works better for the study environment," he said. "Sometimes one roommate wants to stay up and study, and it disturbs the other roommate. So we made this."

Li Na was glad that the bedrooms were clean and the beds

sturdy. In fact, the bed was wider than any she'd ever slept in before.

"Why are there bolts on the doors?" asked Jun Lee.

"Ah, the idiots put the doors on backward," he said. Then he and Jin looked at each other and laughed, as though sharing some private joke. "But the doors work well from the inside, and you can visit with each other whenever you like."

"I smell the omelets," said Jin. "Let's eat lunch. I'm starving."

The old woman served them without speaking. Jin explained that she was a farm woman they'd hired to cook and clean the house whenever they needed to use it. He seemed to trust her, but Li Na felt uneasy around her.

After lunch, they gathered in the teaching room on the second floor, Bibles and notebooks in hand.

"Isn't this exciting?" said Jun Lee. "I can't believe we're actually starting!"

Li Na felt that she had only dampened everyone's spirits with her warnings so far, but the fish were still swimming inside. There was nothing she could do now but join Jun Lee in the teaching room.

Mr. Liu's class was called "The Harmony of the Gospels." He taught eloquently on the timeline of the life of Jesus and how the four Gospels fit perfectly together. This was a new approach to the life of Jesus, and, within the hour, Li Na let down her guard and drank in the teaching.

That evening, after supper, she sat in her bed and studied Mr. Liu's notes. Although it was light outside, no light came through the green painted window. She had to light the small lantern on her nightstand to see.

She was so grateful for the timeline Mr. Liu gave them, and she studied the events closely. She noticed that the statement Jesus made in Matthew 12 was repeated again by Luke in chapter 11. In a separate account, John also talked about sheep being scattered. She read John 10 one more time.

After hearing Brother Liu's wonderful teaching that afternoon, Li Na felt much calmer. She wondered if she had judged Law Jin too harshly. She laid her Bible and notes on the nightstand to the right side of her bed and put out the light. Then she lay quietly in the shadows, praying for Liko, Kwan So, and Mei Lin. She prayed for strength for all of them and that they would all remain hidden from the PSB until they were united again in their homes.

CHAPTER

Seventeen

Mei Lin's hand wrote Mandarin strokes on the board, but her mind was on Little Mei. She had worked hard all week to keep the baby's umbilical cord clean with alcohol, but she wondered if she had done enough. Little Mei hadn't slept well the night before, and she felt warm. At least it was Friday—Nurse Bo would be back this weekend to check on her.

In the classroom, Mei Lin was having some success at encouraging Lydia to actually draw her characters. She delighted in showing her the meanings of the strokes and how they actually drew pictures of the words she spoke. David and Jonathan were warming up to her. She had caught them twice that week in the staff garbage can, and both times she held them for a long time. When Mother Su couldn't come one evening, the children seemed satisfied to receive Mei Lin's affection before bedtime. She also taught them through Little Mei that every life was important to God.

Priscilla was totally enamored with the baby and plunged her very soul into helping Mei Lin care for her. At first, Mei Lin felt like her time with Little Mei was invaded. But as the week wore on and her sleep was more and more sporadic, she was glad to have Priscilla at her side, offering to help in any way she could.

Elizabeth was the one who worried her. Academically, she met what was required, but she didn't seem interested in her studies. Several times a day, Mei Lin saw her staring out of the window, engulfed in another world.

Mei Lin wrote the last character on the chalkboard and looked at her watch.

"Children, I want you to copy your characters neatly into the squares on your tablet. When you are finished, bring them to my desk, and you may be dismissed early for lunch."

A ripple of excitement swept over the room. The weather was too hot to stay outside for long, but the children still relished playing the games Mei Lin had brought with her. They usually gathered in their bunkhouse, where it was cool, and sat on the floor to play. Mei Lin knew that each child deserved to have his or her own family, and the orphanage could never give them that kind of care. Still, she felt satisfied that she was giving each one of them her very best.

Elizabeth was the first to come to the desk. She laid her paper at the corner. "May I be dismissed?" she asked politely.

"Certainly." Then Mei Lin leaned over her desk. "Elizabeth, I want to talk to you today during lunch, okay?"

Elizabeth looked down. "Yes, Miss Mei Lin."

"Good. I'll come and get you, and we'll talk in my room again."

Elizabeth turned and left quietly. Mei Lin sighed. "Priscilla!"

Priscilla quickly came to the desk.

"Are you almost finished with your characters?"

"Yes, Miss Mei Lin."

"Priscilla, I want you to help me care for Little Mei at lunch-time, okay?"

A large smile broke out over the girl's face. "Yes, Miss Mei Lin. What do you want me to do?"

"While I am talking to Elizabeth, I want you to hold Little Mei and feed her if she is hungry, or just watch her for me." Mei Lin thought she saw Priscilla shiver. She took her hand. "You do love her, don't you?"

"Yes, I do. She doesn't have anybody to care for her except us."

Mei Lin smiled. "That's right, Priscilla. She probably thinks you are her big sister. I'll call you when I need you, all right?"

By eleven-thirty, everyone but Lydia was finished. Mei Lin walked to her desk and looked over her shoulder at the paper.

"Why, look at that," said Mei Lin. "It says 'lamb.' You are a fine artist, Lydia."

Lydia looked up. "It took me a while."

"That's all right. You'll write it so often that soon you'll draw the characters without thinking about it. I'm really proud of you, Lydia. You are doing your best, and I see a lot of improvement."

"I'm still not finished."

"I know," answered Mei Lin. "I want you to put your paper on my desk anyway. On Monday I will have you do the same characters again. I want you to draw all of these characters until you can do it with your eyes shut."

Lydia giggled. "I can hardly do it with them open, Miss Mei Lin."

"But you will. Put the paper on the desk and go on outside."

After Lydia went out the door, Mei Lin reached under her desk and pulled out a shiny new blue ball. She went outside.

"Boys, I want you to come here, please," she called. Mei Lin stood on the steps at the doorway, hiding the ball behind her back. All of the boys lined up in front of her as though they were about to file back into the classroom. That is, all of the boys except David and Jonathan. They were busy running from the gate to the doors of the dorm and back to the staff room. Mei Lin hoped they wouldn't wake up Little Mei before she had the chance to get there.

"Boys, you are all getting along this week. Paul and Mark have been good leaders at recess. Thank you, boys, for letting everyone play your rock game with you. You even included Philip, although he's the youngest and new at the game. Adam, you were a great dorm monitor this week. I haven't had one peep out of your bedroom all week after lights-out. Good job."

Each boy was beaming, except for Nathaniel. "Nathaniel, you are looking stronger and healthier every day. I think you've grown an inch since you came here. I'm proud of you for taking care of yourself."

Nathaniel wouldn't look at her, but she thought she reached him. She knew he wanted to look bigger like the older boys.

"I have a gift for all of you. You have been so good that I wanted to reward you. Here."

She pulled the bright blue ball from behind her back.

"Ohhhh," said many voices together.

Mei Lin smiled, and the boys' eyes sparkled back at her.

"The ball belongs to all of you," she said. "Because you are all doing such a wonderful job." She threw it into the courtyard. "Go get it!"

All of the boys took off, squealing with delight. Even Nathaniel forgot himself and ran toward the ball. "You have to share!" Mei Lin called after them.

She quickly locked the school door so David and Jonathan wouldn't steal the trash, then walked to the staff house.

"How is she?" she called to Cook Chu.

Cook Chu looked up from her noodles at Mei Lin, her face red and glistening with sweat. "She's waiting for you!"

Mei Lin heard a commotion behind her. All of the children were running toward the gate, so she followed them.

"Sun Tao!" exclaimed Mei Lin. "How good to see you!"

"Look what we got!" said Adam. "You want to play?"

Tao was grinning, the bright sun reflecting off his bald head. "Oh yes," he said. "I stopped by just to play with you for an hour."

Mei Lin clasped her hands together. "Oh, thank you, Tao," she said. "They just got this ball, and I want them to share."

"No problem," said Tao. "Watch this." He kicked the ball to the other side of the courtyard.

The boys oohed and ahhed at his skill and squealed when Tao raced them across the yard to kick it again.

Mei Lin laughed. Even David and Jonathan got in the game! The boys drank Tao's attention as eagerly as Little Mei drank her formula.

"Priscilla, Elizabeth, can you help me?" she called.

"Priscilla's already with the baby," said Cook Chu. "She told me you wanted her to help you this afternoon."

Lydia and Elizabeth emerged from their dorm and joined Mei Lin at the staff porch.

"Cook Chu, can you use help from Lydia, or shall I take her inside with me?" asked Mei Lin.

"Oh, I could use another pair of hands," said Cook Chu. "Tell you what, Lydia. If you help me with getting lunch ready, I'll let you use my new paintbrush. I bought the small one we talked about. What do you think?"

"Oh yes, Cook Chu! I'll help you! How small is it? Did you buy paint, too?"

Mei Lin smiled and stepped inside the staff room door. She heard humming as soon as she and Elizabeth stepped inside. They walked to the back of the room where Priscilla sat in the chair near the drawer bed, humming an old Chinese lullaby. Little Mei was studying her own little hands in front of her, fussing every few seconds.

"Ah, Little Mei is telling us she's ready to eat," said Mei Lin. "Priscilla, would you like to learn how to mix the formula?"

Mei Lin showed her how to mix the formula while Elizabeth waited for them on Mei Lin's bed. "Now, Priscilla, I want to talk to Elizabeth. Do you think you could feed Little Mei in your dorm?"

"Oh yes, Miss Mei Lin! Could I?"

Mei Lin laughed. "Yes, you may. I'll walk you over."

Mei Lin savored her moments with Little Mei as she carried her to Priscilla's dorm and settled Priscilla on the lower bunk.

"It's cooler in here than in the staff room," said Mei Lin. She kissed the soft top of Little Mei's head and handed her to Priscilla, who held her easily as she sat with her back to the wall.

"Just remember to burp her every two ounces," said Mei Lin. "She drank all six ounces this morning."

"I'll be careful," said Priscilla. "Thank you."

"I know you love her," said Mei Lin. "And I love her, too. I thank Jesus for sending you to us so you can help me take care of her."

Priscilla didn't take her eyes off Little Mei, but a grin formed across her face.

"I'll be back," said Mei Lin. "Just play with her when you're finished, okay?"

After Cook Chu promised to keep an eye on Priscilla and Little Mei, Mei Lin went back to her room to talk to Elizabeth. She stopped to get two bowls of noodles and two cups of cool water on a tray before going inside.

Mei Lin tidied up her room a bit while she talked to Elizabeth, who sat on the side of bed. The girl moved the noodles around inside her bowl, not really eating.

"Do you have any brothers or sisters?" asked Mei Lin.

Elizabeth looked with wonder at her teacher. "No—don't you know about the one-child policy?"

Mei Lin smiled. "Of course. I just wondered if you had ever watched a baby before. Priscilla really enjoys taking care of Little Mei."

Elizabeth studied her for a minute. "I used to help my mama watch her cousin's baby. But she made me take a nap every afternoon with them, and I didn't like that."

"Most children don't like taking naps," said Mei Lin. "Although it's better than having to work all day on a farm or in a coal mine."

Elizabeth nodded. She didn't say anything for a while, and Mei Lin sat on the bed across from her and folded a basket of clean diapers. Elizabeth put her bowl of noodles on the dresser.

"I had a good mama," the little girl finally said. Tears gathered in the corners of her eyes, and she looked out Mei Lin's window at the side of her bed.

"What did she look like?"

Elizabeth looked at Mei Lin for a moment, then she dug her hand into her pants pocket. "Here, this is her picture." She held it in her hands as though it could break.

The photograph was well worn, and Mei Lin wondered that it hadn't been lost or torn by now.

"Oh, she is quite beautiful," said Mei Lin. "I think if you wore your hair in bangs like that you would look just like her."

Elizabeth sat up. "Do you think so?"

"Oh yes," said Mei Lin. "Although, I'll know better once I see you smile. Your mother looks quite happy here."

"She was happy," said Elizabeth. "We were all happy."

She grew quiet again, and Mei Lin carefully laid the photograph on the bed. She opened her large suitcase and dug around until she found a plastic bag that she'd used to carry the bowl of noodles on the train. "Maybe you could keep the photograph in here until we find a wallet for you?"

Elizabeth's eyes shone. "Yes, that would be good. I'm always afraid it will get wet on days when it rains. But I have to keep it in my pocket."

"Of course you do," said Mei Lin. She handed her the plastic bag, and Elizabeth carefully slid the photo inside. "What happened to your mama?" Mei Lin asked gently.

"Mama died when I was in second grade. A bad car accident. I . . . I think Father was with her. He wouldn't tell me what happened."

Mei Lin felt a lump form in her throat. She went to her smaller bag and pulled out her scarf. "See this? My mama wore this scarf when she went on long walks to another village to tell people about Jesus."

"Your mama is a Christian?"

"Yes. But she's with Jesus now. She died when I was six."

Elizabeth didn't look up. She touched the scarf as though it were sacred, handling it the same way she handled her photograph. "Do you still miss her?"

"Yes, sometimes," answered Mei Lin. "My father just gave me this scarf last week. He said there's an invisible red thread, just like the red threads around this lotus blossom. And that invisible red thread will connect me to him and to Mother no matter where I go."

Two large tears slipped down Elizabeth's face. "Was your father nice to you after your mother died?"

Mei Lin nodded. "I lived with him and my amah. What about you?"

Elizabeth looked down at the cot and shook her head. "My papa got real mad at me," she said. "He drank from a bottle every night and he—he said it was all my fault."

Mei Lin lifted Elizabeth's face upward until their eyes met. "Did he do mean things, too?" she asked softly.

Elizabeth's lower lip trembled. "Yes."

"Did he hit you?"

She nodded.

"Is that why you ran away?"

"Sort of," answered Elizabeth.

"Sort of?"

"He said he hated me. He told me to get out. I reminded him too much of Mama. It's all my fault." Elizabeth heaved a dry sob, and Mei Lin gathered her close in her arms.

"It's okay, little one. And it's not your fault."

"Yes, it is," cried Elizabeth. "Father said so. Now I'm gone, so he can't hate me anymore."

"Elizabeth," said Mei Lin, her cheek close to the little girl's hair. "It's not your fault that your mother died. In fact, maybe it was your father's fault. Maybe he felt so bad about your mom dying that he blamed you."

Elizabeth looked confused.

Mei Lin handed her a bit of toilet paper rolled up. "Blow your nose," she said. "Adults can do stupid things sometimes. I don't know what happened, but maybe your dad was drinking. Maybe he was drunk, and it was his fault that your mother was killed in the accident."

Elizabeth looked thunderstruck. "Why? Why would he kill Mama? I thought he loved her."

"Honey, I don't know that that's what happened. But people who drink don't usually *try* to go out and have accidents. Alcohol makes them lose control of themselves. They can't see right or think right and they can't even walk right. People who drink and then drive cause accidents."

"Oh," said Elizabeth.

"Honey, can you forgive your father for blaming you when it wasn't your fault?"

Elizabeth wiped her nose again. "I think so. Why did he say it was my fault?"

"Oh, he wanted to blame somebody," said Mei Lin. "Your father was wrong in the way he treated you, but I think inside he was truly sad that your mother was killed. And whatever happened, I'm sure it was an accident. But now you need to forgive your father for saying all those mean things and for hitting you in anger."

Elizabeth bowed her head. "I'm not angry. I want to forgive him."

"I know," said Mei Lin. "Just say this. 'Jesus, I forgive my father for saying mean things.'"

Elizabeth repeated the prayer, and Mei Lin continued. "I forgive him for doing mean things, too."

"Jesus, I forgive him for hurting my mother and maybe for killing her in the accident. I miss her, Jesus. Can't you bring her back?"

Mei Lin remained quiet while Elizabeth shared her heart.

"I forgive my father for hitting me and saying all those mean things about getting rid of me. Please—I miss my mama. I miss Amah. Please help me."

Mei Lin pulled Elizabeth close to her again. "Jesus, thank you for listening to Elizabeth's prayers. You've given her the power to forgive, and that is such a big thing. Please do help Elizabeth. In Jesus' name." She held Elizabeth closer. "You know, Elizabeth, Jesus is sad, too."

"He is?" asked Elizabeth.

"Sure He is," answered Mei Lin. "Jesus doesn't plan for people to die when they're young. The Bible says that the godly person should live and grow old and see their great-grandchildren. Only, Satan hates people. And sometimes sin or Satan gets into people's hearts, and they get tempted to do bad things that hurt other people."

Elizabeth just sat there, and Mei Lin could tell she didn't understand. "Elizabeth, do you have an aunt or uncle?"

"No aunts or uncles," said Elizabeth. "Mama was the only child."

"You mentioned Amah. Do you still have a grandmother?"

Elizabeth sniffed, and Mei Lin handed her a tissue.

"I have three grandparents. My father's parents live outside Shanghai somewhere. I can't remember where. But my other grandmother lives in Shanghai."

"Was she kind, like your mama?" asked Mei Lin.

"Sometimes. She got mad at my dad a lot."

"I see," said Mei Lin. "Have you tried to find her?"

Elizabeth looked startled. "Do you think we could?" she said. "I want to talk to her so much!"

"We can try," said Mei Lin. "But until then, I want to work with you on your schooling. Your grandmother will be proud to know that you are still working hard. And you know, I think you are a very intelligent girl."

Elizabeth grinned and rolled her red eyes. "Mama always said that, too."

"Come on, eat your noodles," said Mei Lin. "And tell me your grandmother's name and her address, if you remember it. I'll talk to Mother Su about finding her."

CHAPTER

Eighteen

Kwan So and Zhang Liang put their fishing lines into the lake. The sky was bright blue and cloudless, but So's heart was troubled. He didn't particularly like fishing, but he was glad for the opportunity to talk to Liang. The meetings were so closely scheduled the day before that they hadn't had a moment to talk to each other.

"What do you think about the teaching?" asked So.

"It's hard to discern," said Liang. "Did you know that the second day, the principal asked me to write a letter to all of the pastors who met in my house in DuYan?"

"All thirty-four of us? What did the letter say?"

"Well, he said that it would be good to make sure that the pastors were secure and that they knew we are all doing well. So I wrote a letter and encouraged them to be submissive to the interim leaders for the next two months and build relationships with them."

"I didn't know," said So.

"I am still not feeling settled here," said Liang, "but I feel better after talking to my wife last night. She said everything was all right with her and Chen Li Na."

"Did you give her my message?"

"Yes, and she said she would tell Mrs. Chen that you asked about her. Are you still concerned for her?"

"Very concerned," answered Kwan So. "I didn't like the way Jin planned it, so that he took the women and Mrs. Wen took the men."

Liang rubbed his heel into the dirt on the bank of the lake. "That's not the way we would do it in our house church, is it?"

"No. And we shouldn't have let the women go alone—especially after Mrs. Chen's warning not to scatter."

"I don't like what happened, either, but Jin acted so quickly," replied Liang. "I was stunned."

"I'm afraid Liko was disappointed with his mother," said So. "He had his heart set on the Haggai Institute. I'm still not sure why Mrs. Chen feels this warning in her heart. The PSB danger is past, and everything seems fine. But I trust Mrs. Chen. I know that she would not openly criticize the Institute unless God gave her a clear warning."

The men spent their lunch hour lifting their concerns to heaven.

Later that evening, Kwan So heard a knock on his door. "Come in," he said and laid down his Bible.

A young woman opened the door. "Hello, I'm Shuang."

"I'm pleased to meet you, Shuang," said So. "Where did you come from?"

"I arrived an hour ago with your new teachers," she said. "Mr. Wen wanted me to drop in and talk to you. He thought maybe you could help me."

The woman appeared to be in her thirties. She was quite beautiful and very Western, dressed in jeans and a pale pink blouse. Her shoulder-length hair flipped up on the sides, and she wore a pair of American sneakers.

"What do you help with?" So asked.

"I am trying to understand Christianity," she said. "May I sit here?" She pointed to the chair beside the door.

"Why don't we talk out at the dining room table?" So replied, getting up.

She turned and looked out at the table. "There are others out there," she said. "I wanted to talk to you alone."

"The courtyard, then?"

"Yes, the courtyard would be good."

He followed her outside. It was eight o'clock and the sun had not set, but the air was cooler than midday, and a breeze floated up to them from the lake below the hill. They sat at the table inside the gate.

"What is going on?" asked So.

"My husband said he was a Christian," Shuang said. "He went to America on a business trip, and I found out he took a mistress there." She looked toward the gate and was silent for a moment.

"The Bible tells Christians to be true to their husbands and wives."

"I called his apartment one night, and she was there," said Shuang. "I don't have any family to turn to. I'm an orphan."

So immediately thought of Fu Yatou and wondered how she was doing at home with Amah. He wondered if this woman's story was anything like her awful tale of rigid caretakers who left children to die of starvation.

"I have adopted an orphan," he said. "Her name is Fu Yatou. She is home now taking care of my mother."

"Fu Yatou? Blessing Girl?" said Shuang. "What an unusual name. I like it. How did you find her?"

So briefly explained her story. It felt good to talk about his younger daughter. He truly missed her. "How is it that you were orphaned?" he asked.

"My father went to Singapore before the Cultural Revolution. After it began, he was not able to come home. So he married again in Singapore. My mother and I struggled together through life. She worked to pay my way through college, but just after I graduated, she died.

"I decided to try to find my father in Singapore. He and his new wife received me, and I got a job there working as his assistant. But only three months later, my father and stepmother died in an airplane crash."

"When was that?" asked So.

Shuang smiled. "Do you wish to find out my age?"

"Oh no," he said. "I was just wondering how long you have been grieving. You've lost so many loved ones in such a short time."

"I was twenty-five when I found my father in Singapore," she said. "Since then I have been alone. My father left me a large sum of money, but what is that when you have no one to share it with?"

So nodded his agreement. "When did you meet your husband?"

"We met six years ago at a business convention in Singapore. I have run my father's computer business since his death." She smiled sheepishly. "My husband proposed to me on the second date."

She sighed. "Now he has someone else in America, and I am left all alone again. Mr. Wen told me you are a trustworthy Christian man. I did not even know that you had an orphaned daughter. I was wondering if—well, if you would consider being my brother?"

So dropped his head down for a moment and smiled. The thought of what Amah would say if he came home with such an announcement tickled him down to his toenails. He managed to erase his grin and lifted his head.

"Jesus said that all who believe in Him belong to His family. We are all brothers and sisters."

"Yes, my husband used to tell me that."

Kwan So sobered. He realized how deeply this girl must be hurting and how dangerously close she was to throwing away her faith because of her husband's infidelity.

"Jesus said that no matter where we go, He will be with us always. I'll be right back."

He returned to the table with his Bible in his hands. "Psalm

23 tells us that even when we walk through the dark valley of death and loss, we should not be afraid. God promises to be with us."

Shuang reached across the table and took his hand, and So's spine tingled.

How can these overseas people be so open?

"Thank you," she said. "You've given me much to think about."

Not knowing how else to retrieve his hand, he pulled it back and looked at his watch. "I need to study some more before going to sleep. It was good to meet you, Shuang."

"I'm pleased to meet you, as well, Kwan So. May I talk to you again sometime?"

So smiled. "Certainly. Take care." He got up and closed his Bible.

Shuang patted his hand. "You have strong hands," she said. "You work in the fields, don't you?"

He looked down at her and nodded, then pulled his hands to himself.

"I worked in the field with my mother when I was a child. I can look at your hands and tell that you know how to plow. Your church doesn't give enough to support you?"

So pushed his chair in. "Our churches in Tanching are poor. But we are very happy."

Shuang stood up and pushed in her chair. "We'll talk again, Kwan So. I want to find out more about your church in Tanching. You have helped me tonight. Perhaps there is something I can do for you."

"I don't expect payment, Shuang," said So. "The family of Jesus helps one another—no charge."

Shuang laughed. "I like your Jesus, Kwan So."

Zhang Liang came out of the bathroom just then.

"Liang!" So called. "Would you like to go down to the lake?"

"Why not?"

So unlatched the gate, and the two men walked over the ridge at the end of the yard and down the hill to the lakeside.

So had enjoyed Liang's friendship the last several days. During their time together, So watched his face beam with happiness, whether in the classroom or eating a meal together. Being with Liang made him realize how cheerless he was inside, and he hoped that some of this man's joy would rub off on him.

It wasn't that he had a difficult life. For the most part, he was truly happy. But standing beside Liang, he realized that he had slipped into a rather somber lifestyle of work and ministry, basically letting those routines run his life.

"Jun Lee and I walk like this together nearly every evening," said Liang. "If we try to talk inside the house, someone comes to us with church business, or Jun Lee gets caught up in the housework and cooking. If we didn't take walks, I wonder if we would communicate at all."

Whenever Liang talked about his wife, So felt a tug of grief inside. Right now it was for Mei Lin he grieved.

"Perhaps that is what I should do with Mei Lin," said So. "There is something troubling her, but she doesn't seem to want to talk about it. I haven't tried to pry it out of her—women like to do that, you know."

Liang nodded and chuckled a little.

"I feel like she needs her mother," So continued. "And Amah—well, Amah just isn't the close mothering type. She does her best."

Liang gave him a friendly slap on the back. "Have you thought about marrying again?"

So looked over at his friend. "No. After Shan Zu—I can't imagine living with anyone else."

Liang stopped for a moment near the water's edge. "Kwan So, it is possible to love two women in one lifetime. That does not diminish your love for Shan Zu, but it enlarges your heart to love again."

So didn't answer, and Liang seemed to respect his silence.

Mei Lin had encouraged him for the last few years to remarry, but he never considered it seriously.

He picked up a flat, pointed stone and threw it low, skipping it across the water. It barely splashed until the end when it finally sank with a *ker-plop*. The water shimmered, forming expanding round targets wherever the stone touched. Beyond the lake, the land sloped into a large valley of wheat that gently stirred in the breeze, rolling through valleys to the forest below. Pines, maples, and bamboo hedged a small village in the distance. The sun was sinking over the horizon behind the house, wrapping every stalk of wheat in a golden haze.

They walked for a while without talking. So had something else on his mind.

"Didn't you say that the women here know Pastor Wong?" he asked.

"Yes," answered Liang. "He's known them for the last year or so and has a relationship with the churches they attend."

"Shuang, the new arrival, worries me."

"What do you mean?"

"She came to my room to talk this evening. I directed her to the courtyard and talked to her there."

"Yes, it is a problem," said Liang. "The second woman, Ke, tried to get my attention, as well. Perhaps we should address it. I'm not sure how. The women may be offended by it."

"Yes, perhaps," said So. "Let's pray about it."

"And we must pray for Jun Lee and Li Na," said Liang. "I don't like being separated like this for so long."

Just then a honking noise sounded in the distance. Shielding his eyes against the sun, So searched the skies and saw a flock of ducks heading toward them.

"Look," he said. "I think we're infringing on their watering hole."

The ducks were in formation, gliding around the pond, waiting for them to leave so they could land. A few braver ones floated down to the opposite side of the small lake, yelling in duck language to the others.

So gave Liang a friendly slap on the shoulder. "It appears we aren't welcome here anymore," he said. "Let's go."

———

The women spent the next week in continuous study of the harmony of the Gospels. Li Na and Jun Lee began to relax around their teachers, and even the old woman, Grandma Zhou, seemed a little more cheerful.

Jun Lee was able to speak to her husband the third day after the PSB threat was over.

"Kwan So sends his greetings to you, Mrs. Chen," she said as she handed the cell phone to Jin. "He said that the PSB were there and they believed the story that they were only visiting their cousin Quon."

"I'm glad we got out of there as quickly as we did," said Jin. "It could have been dangerous for such a large group to be spotted in their home."

"Don't they wonder about the chalkboard?" asked Li Na.

"Ah," said Jin. "The wall where the chalkboard hangs can be flipped over in three seconds. It's one of the hiding mechanisms we built into the house."

"You built that house?"

"Well, the Wens asked for my help. I tried to give them some good advice on making it accessible to teaching groups but also equipping it with a few hiding mechanisms that would help in a moment's notice. The chalkboard is just one of the things."

"What else did you suggest?" asked Jun Lee.

"You want to know my secrets, do you?" he teased. "Well, I'll tell you just one more. There is a low panel door that runs partly underneath the chalkboard in the teaching room. We keep our teaching materials there unless we're using them. It's large enough to hide two people if they lie side by side."

"That is amazing," said Jun Lee. "I'll have to tell my husband these ideas."

"I'm feeling a bit confined today," Li Na said suddenly. She looked at Jun Lee. "Would you like to take a walk this evening before class starts?"

Jun Lee smiled. "I think the air will do us both good."

Jin looked a bit nervous.

"Something wrong?" asked Jun Lee.

"I suppose not," he answered, and then he cleared his throat. "Perhaps I'm too protective. I don't want the PSB to find us here."

"We'll stay off the main road," said Jun Lee. "Won't we, Li Na? We'll be back in an hour."

Li Na was glad that Jun Lee was so relaxed. It seemed to set Jin at ease. Something was nagging her again. Something Mr. Liu had said that afternoon during the teaching. She needed to walk and clear her head.

The two friends walked through the woods behind the outhouses and found a trail that looked like an old unused road that led deeper into the bamboo. When Li Na was sure they weren't being followed, she said, "Jun Lee, did you hear what Mr. Liu said this afternoon about Jesus?"

"You heard that, too? Something about God the Father being reincarnated when Jesus was born. What did that mean?"

"I don't know," said Li Na. "I wanted to check with you to see if you wrote down the Scriptures he used to back it up."

"There weren't any Scriptures that I heard," replied Jun Lee. "Li Na, are you still as nervous as you were at first? I am enjoying the teaching on the harmony of the Gospels."

Li Na sighed. "They've done their best to make us feel comfortable, that's for sure. I like the timeline on the life of Jesus. It helps me put things together. But twice now they have mentioned reincarnation."

Jun Lee grabbed her friend's arm and pulled her to a stop.

"Li Na. This is what your mind is saying. What does your heart say now?"

Li Na hesitated. "The fish are swimming in my stomach again, Jun Lee." She looked around, not wanting to be overheard. "Let's continue walking."

The women walked deeper into the woods, following the old path behind the outhouse, and Li Na told Jun Lee everything that Jin had said to her. "So told me that a Christian man would not make advances like Jin made, even if he were from the city."

"I didn't know—well, I did notice he paid special attention to how you were doing. But I thought that was because of what happened in the restaurant. Did he really take your hand and say his business looked for beautiful women like you?"

"Yes."

"Li Na, that is not proper for any Chinese. In fact, most Chinese people I know would find that dishonoring."

"It came as such a surprise, and I tried to pass it off because Jin and Jade are both from the city. But Liko stood up for me. I was quite proud of him. He told Jin, 'In Tanching we are not so open with our comments—or our gestures.'"

"Good for Liko. That is a son who will take care of you in your old age."

Li Na smiled. "Liko is a good boy. Jin hasn't made advances since we came here. I'm glad, but I catch him watching me sometimes, and it makes me nervous. If I hadn't talked to So, I would still be wondering why I was so upset. But I know that So was right. And he told me to lean on him for protection. Now—"

"I do not like being this far out in these woods with two men I didn't know a month ago," said Jun Lee. "I trust Kwan So's judgment. And now that I know Jin made advances toward you, I think your fish are swimming for a reason."

"And you?" asked Li Na. "How do you feel in your heart?"

Jun Lee sighed. "I miss my husband and my family. Sometimes I think it is homesickness that is gnawing at me. But my heart is telling me something else is wrong. I am having trouble sleeping at night, and when I do fall asleep I wake up with night-mares. I pray and pray until I fall asleep again. Last night I slept with the light on."

"Let's meditate on the Scripture that I received early in the morning just before Jin sounded the alarm about the PSB."

"Oh yes, that is using wisdom," said Jun Lee. "We must go back to the last time we know the Holy Spirit spoke to us. Tell me again what the Scripture said."

"Matthew 12:29 and 30," said Li Na. "'How can one enter a strong man's house and plunder his goods, unless he first binds the strong man? And then he will plunder his house. He who is not with Me is against Me, and he who does not gather with Me scatters abroad.'"

"Oh my, and here we are with two strong men," said Jun Lee. "I mean, I know the Bible is talking about demons, but—sister, perhaps we should leave. I am sure they will cooperate and take us home if we ask."

Li Na smiled, realizing that it was the first time she'd really smiled from her heart since they ran from the PSB.

* ✱ *

CHAPTER

Nineteen

It only took Mother Su a week to find Elizabeth's grandmother. She was thrilled to know that her granddaughter was alive and healthy and was anxious to see her again. Mother Su set up a reunion for the two of them for the following Monday.

The transformation in Elizabeth was amazing. There was a spark of hope in her eye and a skip in her step. She was enthusiastic in class, and Mei Lin was able to teach her twice as much as she had in the previous two weeks.

Two days before the two of them would reunite, Mei Lin prayed that Elizabeth would not be disappointed. Mother Su said that the grandmother wanted to take custody from the father, but what if she lost? What if Elizabeth had to return to her drunken father?

She thought about each of her students. Each had his or her own struggle, but Mei Lin enjoyed teaching every one of them. Still, nothing thrilled her soul as much as taking care of Little Mei, in spite of getting up to feed her three times a night. At least she could nap with Little Mei on weekend afternoons.

That Saturday, following their afternoon nap, she got Little Mei ready for church. The baby liked her baths, so Mei Lin covered her umbilical cord to keep it dry and let her splash about in the shallow water of the basin, making the dresser as wet as she liked. She placed a dry towel across her shoulder and carefully lifted the tiny slippery body to her chest.

"Oh, Be-be! Now you'll be cooled off this afternoon while everyone else is hot," said Mei Lin. She wiped her forehead. She hoped to get a bath herself before Mother Su's family came to take her to the meeting. It was the same house church she visited two years ago, and Pastor Wong was scheduled to speak. She hadn't seen Brother Tom or Pastor Wong for a long time.

Mei Lin laid Little Mei on the bed and dried her with the towel, admiring the baby's wavy black hair. "Ah, you look like a princess. Let me kiss the feet of the princess."

Mei Lin lifted the baby's tiny feet to her lips and kissed them. Then she blew on them until Little Mei squirmed. "I'll kiss them again!" she teased. Mei Lin kissed her feet again and blew on them, making loud noises. She fastened the diaper with pins, careful to fold it underneath the black knot on her belly button. She dipped a cotton ball in alcohol and carefully cleaned the umbilical cord. Little Mei squirmed a little but really didn't seem to mind.

Finally Mei Lin slipped the sweet little pink dress over the baby's head. "You look like a little lotus blossom! Look at those pretty flowers on Be-be's dress! Oh, are you the beautiful little garden today!"

Little Mei blew little bubbles and kicked her legs, the perfect picture of contentment. Mei Lin put the tiny socks in her purse. She'd save them for tonight—it was too hot to put anything on her feet right now.

The door opened. "Mei Lin, Mother Su and Sun Tao are here for you."

Already! "Tell them I'll be right there," Mei Lin called.

She brought Little Mei out to greet them. Chang was drawing a circle with chalk in the center of the courtyard floor, and all the children were gathered excitedly around her.

"Oh, look at this beautiful baby!" said Tao and immediately took Little Mei into his arms.

Mother Su was fanning her face with a paper. "Mei Lin, we brought you a fan."

"A fan? Really?"

"Yes," said Tao. "I feel guilty riding around in air-conditioning all day while you girls suffer here without even a fan to cool you. Here, Mother, take Little Mei. I'll hook it up for them."

"Oh, well, plug it in near Nurse Bo tonight," said Mei Lin. "Since Little Mei and I will be sleeping at your house."

"Oh, I brought you two fans," said Tao.

Nurse Bo was working at the little porch kitchen, and Mei Lin went to tell her. She looked so hot Mei Lin wished she could put a fan out on the porch for her.

Nurse Bo wiped her hands off on her apron and came to the door of their room, where Tao had plugged in the first fan. "Oh my!" she exclaimed. She sat down on her bed in the cool of their room, and Tao turned the fan toward her.

"Oh, this is truly a gift from heaven."

Mei Lin laughed. "Now you will have a fan to block out the sound when Little Mei cries. So you will be cool *and* sleep through the night!"

Nurse Bo smiled and lifted her hair off of her neck. "This is truly wonderful. Thank you, Tao."

"You are welcome. One of the ladies at the church helped me find a good price. And watch this."

Tao added cords to the fan and took it outside, where he set it right in front of the kitchen.

Nurse Bo put her hands on her hips and laughed. "Now I have seen everything, Sun Tao! Fanning the outside!"

Mother Su handed each of them a bottle.

"What's this?" asked Mei Lin.

"Soda," said Mother Su. "Drink it. It will cool you off."

"Thank you," she said. "What a perfect gift."

"Are you ready to go?"

Mei Lin shook her head. "I wanted to take a bath—I didn't realize you would be so early."

"I remember what it's like, trying to watch a baby and still prepare for things. We came early to bring the fans and to help with Little Mei. You take your time. Tao will keep Little Mei for you in the boys' dorm where it's cool."

Nurse Bo called the children for supper and they came running, excitedly talking about the ball game that Chang showed them. They lined up for dinner, and Mother Su and Chang helped give out the food and clean the pots and utensils.

Mei Lin quickly prepared a cool bath in her bedroom and laid out her clothing for the evening. It was a luxury to take a bath with a fan running. She added to the treat by twisting the cap off of her soda and drinking half of it all at once. Mei Lin washed her hair and immersed her head until she felt the heat leave her body. For the first time that day, she felt cool and comfortable.

She dressed quickly, dumped the basin in the backyard, and then prepared the baby's bag with spare bottles, diapers, washcloths, and clothing. She hoped that Nurse Bo had remembered to put on a pot of boiling water for the thermos. She'd need to keep the bottles going in church! She picked up the bag and went out on the porch to find the others.

"You look refreshed," said Chang. "I feel like a fried dumpling in this heat—even in the shade—and we've only been here an hour."

"It has been hot," Mei Lin admitted. "We are so grateful for the fans. May I use mine in the classroom during the day?"

"Certainly," said Tao. He was holding Little Mei under the shade of the porch, and she seemed quite comfortable. "The children's dorms are cool enough, I think. They are built on cement floors, not like the staff rooms."

"I feel like a rich teacher," said Mei Lin.

Little Mei heard Mei Lin's voice and began searching for her.

"Look, she's trying to find you," said Tao.

Mei Lin was pleased. She and Little Mei were going out into

the big world tonight for the first time together. She wanted to be the one to introduce her to the car, the air-conditioner, and the new people in church. Of course, she expected Little Mei to sleep through most of the midnight service.

"Here," said Nurse Bo, interrupting her thoughts. "I filled two thermoses with hot water for you."

"Oh, thank you. What would I do without you?"

"I'm glad you girls are working so well together," said Mother Su. "Mei Lin, this is all I hoped it would be—and more."

"Let's go before we all melt," said Chang. "See you, kids!"

All of the children flocked around them and saw them to the gate. Priscilla clung to Mei Lin's side, and Mei Lin bent down to let the child kiss Little Mei good-bye.

"I wish I could go with you, Little Mei," said Priscilla. "Maybe someday we'll go somewhere together."

"Someday you will," said Mei Lin, smiling. "Mother Su, Priscilla has been a wonderful help with Little Mei. I don't know what I'd do without her."

"I'm glad to hear that, Priscilla. We'll have to arrange an outing just for us girls. What do you think of that?"

"What about us boys?" asked Adam. "We want an outing, too!"

"Well, maybe I could take you boys to the park one day," said Tao. "How about that?"

"The park?" asked Mother Su after they got into the taxi. "Isn't that a little risky, Tao?"

"Ah, it depends on what park, my dear," he answered. There was a gleam in his eye, and Mei Lin knew that Tao had a special place in mind.

By the time they arrived at the marketplace, Little Mei was asleep, so Tao stayed in the air-conditioned cab with her while the women went into the market.

"Look at these baby clothes," said Chang.

Mei Lin walked over to the rack where Chang was browsing. Chang's taste was much more modern than hers, but she looked at the rack of clothing. Chang chose a little pair of blue jean shorts with yellow snaps and a matching yellow ruffled shirt.

"I'll get this one for her," said Chang. "Do you like it?"

"I do." Mei Lin walked over to another rack while Chang paid for her purchase. "This is it," she whispered to herself. She took a lovely red infant gown off the rack and ran her fingers over the shiny Chinese silk.

From a distance it looked like a traditional brocade dress, but up close it had a wider bottom for the baby's leg room. There were beautiful white Shanghai magnolias embroidered on the bodice with frog buttons and a detachable mandarin collar. It was perfect for her Shanghai baby! She took it to Mother Su for her approval.

"Oh, Mei Lin," said Mother Su. "And the collar is detachable! That's good. It's too hot for the collar now, but she can wear it a month from now."

"I don't think she'll outgrow it too soon," said Mei Lin. "Look how long it is. And the sleeves are short."

Just then Chang came up to them. "Ah, traditional but exquisite. Very nice."

Mei Lin smiled. "Thank you, Chang. Look at the magnolias—perfect for a Shanghai baby, don't you think? Did you show your mother what you bought?"

"Yes, she did. You girls will have Little Mei so spoiled—she'll want to stay at the orphanage forever."

Mei Lin shot a quick look at Chang. They still hadn't talked about Little Mei's future. Now she felt more determined than ever to discuss it with Mother Su. Her heart was tied into this baby's life, and Mei Lin couldn't imagine going back to Tanching without her. With all of her heart, she wanted to adopt Little Mei.

"Well, have you finished your shopping?"

Mei Lin turned to see Tao walking toward them—with a baby stroller!

"Sun Tao!" exclaimed Mother Su. "Wherever did you get that stroller?"

Tao grinned. "It is a gift, ladies," he said. His eyes twinkled, and Mei Lin watched Mother Su's reaction. She had her hands on her hips and looked as though she was going to burst.

"Tao?" she asked again.

"*Guanxi,* dear ladies. Connections." He bowed toward the stroller. "The honorable Little Mei must have a carriage, don't you agree?"

Chang squealed with delight. "Father, I love it when you do these things. Wherever did you get the money?"

"Ah, but I didn't do this," he said. "Come, I will show you."

Mei Lin quickly paid for her new baby dress and followed the rest of them to the taxi, where a man stood leaning against the car.

"Brother Tom!" exclaimed Mei Lin. "Why, how did you know we were here?"

Tao answered. "I called Tom on the cell phone while you were shopping. He just happened to be traveling nearby in a taxi, and I invited him to join us."

Mei Lin shook Tom's hand. He stood back, holding her hand at arm's length.

"Look at you, Mei Lin. Are you the same skinny girl who came out of Shanghai Prison No. 14 two years ago? You look wonderful!"

Mei Lin didn't feel embarrassed at all by Tom's compliments. She bowed playfully. "Thank you, honorable Brother Tom, guarder of Chinese secrets and keeper of American *guanxi*!"

Even Chang laughed. "I don't think Father wanted Chinese secrets. He just wants some male company."

"Come on," said Tao. "Everyone into the taxi. Especially you, Be-be."

Mei Lin smiled as Tao unwittingly called Little Mei by her special name. He gently lifted her out of the new stroller and put her in Mei Lin's arms. This time the women rode in the back and Tom and Tao up front.

A half hour later, Tao pulled the taxi into a parking space

near a small park. He led them in prayer over their picnic meal, and then everyone piled out of the car.

"Tomorrow we will take you to our favorite park in Shanghai. For now we will eat here. When the sun sets we will go to the meeting."

Mother Su held Little Mei. Mei Lin watched as the baby's eyes peered over her bottle, trying to focus on the new environment, watching the trees above her.

Mother Su reached into her pocket and pulled out two letters. "This came for you yesterday," she said. "And this one on Thursday. I didn't want to give them to you until you had a moment to yourself to read them."

Mei Lin looked at the return addresses. The first was from Father, the second from Liko. She walked to the bench across from the picnic area and sat down, then opened Liko's first.

My dear Mei Lin,

Old Gray and I hardly know what to do these days. We're both lonely for you but wish you the best in Shanghai. Amah seems to be faring well with Fu Yatou's help. I don't get to see them as often since you left.

The club is doing well. We have been invited to seek higher education from people of higher expertise in our field. Some of the leaders from the other clubs will join us in our new educational opportunity. Hopefully, we will return at the same time you return from Shanghai. I am hoping that our new venture will help me to pass the time more quickly until you return. I wish you could take the courses with us.

I would like to scoop up David and Jonathan and have you cook your mushrooms and vegetables for them. They would surely pack themselves in your suitcase and travel home with you in August.

I miss you.

Liko

Mei Lin closed the letter. Whatever could Liko be talking about? What other church leaders were involved in this higher education? And where was everyone going? Quickly she opened her father's letter.

Dear Mei Lin,

I think about you every day. Amah and Fu Yatou are getting along well. Fu Yatou tries desperately to please. She wants me to tell you that baby Han is well and so are his parents. She misses you and wonders if you will come home early.

Amah is asking if you were able to use the baby blanket she made before you left, and did you take enough clothes for yourself?

The work in the rice field is finished, so our hearts are set on "harvest." Perhaps Liko told you. Our club leaders want to further their education. Some of the finest teachers have been chosen to lead us. Liko is especially excited, but I am concerned for his mother. She does not seem to be as interested.

I was planning to build another room onto our home this summer and surprise you when you return. But I guess that project will have to wait until next year because I plan to take this educational opportunity, as well. Don't worry. It will not hurt us financially. Jade has helped considerably.

You sounded so warm and happy in your letter. I am glad you are living your dream of teaching. Liko will get to pursue his dream of a higher education in our field this summer. Both of you are getting the chance to reach for higher things, and I couldn't be happier. This is good fortune for both of you. We should be back before you return from Shanghai. The Langs will look after Amah. Ping said she would help, too. Don't worry.

Every night before I close my eyes, I think of Mother's

scarf and the red thread that connects us, regardless of time, place, or circumstance.

Give my greetings to Mother Su and her family. Please write to Amah and Yatou while I'm gone. Ping will read it to them.

Yours forever,

Baba

Mei Lin closed her fingers around her father's letter. What did Jade have to do with all this? Suddenly she wished she had brought the scarf. It was really too hot to wear it, but right now she wanted to feel connected again.

Mei Lin looked over the letters again. Father had much more to say than Liko. Was he too embarrassed to say "I love you"? Why hadn't he mentioned Jade's involvement in this?

Mei Lin's head was spinning with questions. Who would have expected such mysterious letters from home?

"Bad news?" asked Chang, sitting down beside her.

Mei Lin looked up. "I'm not sure. Father and Liko say they are taking some kind of higher education this summer. Some sort of Bible training, I am sure. Father says Liko is excited about it, but Liko's mother isn't as happy. And then there's Jade."

"Jade? Who's she?"

Mei Lin looked at her Shanghai friend. "The prettiest girl in Tanching," she said.

"Ah, perhaps the prettiest after you left," said Chang. "Not before."

Mei Lin sighed. "No, she's the prettiest girl no matter who is there. She turns heads everywhere she goes."

Chang patted her on the back. "Come on, Mei Lin. This is a pastor we're talking about here, not some skirt-chasing schoolboy from Shanghai."

"Yes, you're right," said Mei Lin. "I know Liko loves me. But his letter is shorter than Father's and . . ." She couldn't tell

Chang that Liko didn't write *I love you* in his letter. It seemed petty and far too personal.

"And?"

"And ... and Jade is somehow helping Father and Liko finance this new educational opportunity. I don't know what to make of it. They're going away, that's for sure. And Amah will be left at home alone with Yatou."

"Well, I don't think your father would leave unless he felt it was right," said Chang. "Want to pray?"

Mei Lin nodded.

The two of them sat there, eyes wide open, faces tilted to the sky as though they were searching for birds. Mei Lin was searching for the One who made the birds, the One who made the earth and the skies. Something didn't feel right—it was probably her jealousy. Her eyes stared at the sky above, and her heart spoke with their Maker.

Father, forgive me for feeling jealous about Jade. I know you made her, and I should be ashamed for feeling jealous, especially since she's a new Christian. I ask you to bless her and help her become closer to you. I don't know what Father and Liko and Mrs. Chen are doing. It feels strange to be so far away from everyone when this new educational opportunity is happening. I trust you to help me get rid of my jealous feelings. Please help me to love with purity in my heart.

"The picnic is ready, girls," Mother Su called.

"Okay," said Mei Lin. "Ready, Chang?"

"Ready." As Chang stood up she asked, "Did you get anything?"

"Yes," said Mei Lin. "Forgiveness. I got forgiveness."

Chang smiled and patted her on the back again. "Good for you, Mei Lin. Good for you. You know, it almost feels good."

"What's that?"

"Knowing you're human. I mean, you're about as near to perfect as anybody I've ever met. I was beginning to wonder if

Father was right. Maybe you are a saint. A perfect saint."

"Nah, not me," said Mei Lin. She sighed as she folded the letters and stuffed them into her pants pocket. Chang had no idea how imperfect she really was. "Especially not me."

★ ✱ ★

CHAPTER

Twenty

Little Mei's cry wakened Mei Lin. It took her a moment to get her bearings.

Mother Su appeared in the living room and turned on a soft light. "Here, here," she said as she picked up the baby. "Mei Lin, you go to sleep, I'll take care of her."

"What time is it?" whispered Mei Lin.

"Four-thirty. You've only been asleep an hour, and she's up already. I'll get her this time. You sleep."

Mei Lin tried to go back to sleep, but her mind was too busy. She got up to use the bathroom.

The church service had lasted until two-thirty. Everyone was so glad to see her, and they all seemed to know about her work at the orphanage. A woman she barely knew gave her a bag of baby clothes for Little Mei and another bag of clothing for herself! A friend of Brother Tom's squeezed ten yuan into her hand. She felt so loved.

In fact, she felt more love here than from her fiancé in Tanching. Why had he withheld his affection in his letter? Was this a taste of married life with Liko? When out of sight, would she automatically jump out of his affections?

She washed her hands and splashed water on her face. *Think about it tomorrow,* she told herself and walked out to Mother Su. Just looking at Be-be made her feel better.

"I guess I'm getting into her sleep rhythm," she said softly. "I can't seem to go to sleep unless she's settled."

Mother Su smiled. "You're just like a mama, Mei Lin. So tenderhearted and caring. You'll make a great mother one day."

Mei Lin got up and walked away. Right now she couldn't think one more depressing thought. *Think happy,* she told herself. *Now.*

Mei Lin finally drifted to sleep. She wakened with Little Mei at six o'clock.

"Hey, what's this?" she teased. "You're letting me sleep in a half hour this morning?" Mei Lin smiled down at the little face.

Little Mei was squirming a bit, fussing here and there just to let her know she was up. Mei Lin took the last of the warm water from the thermos and made a bottle for her. She sat on the comfortable couch and rested her neck against the cushion. Little Mei's rhythmic sucking sounds nearly lulled her back to sleep.

"Oh!" Her hand jerked back. "Oh my, Little Mei. I nearly let you go, didn't I?"

Mother Su appeared again. "Are you okay?"

Mei Lin smiled sheepishly as she held Little Mei up for a burp. "I'm sorry to waken you. Poor Little Mei nearly rolled to the floor. I'm afraid I fell asleep feeding her. I'm not being motherly anymore, am I?"

Mother Su sat down beside her. "That's motherhood," she said. "I noticed yesterday you looked exhausted. I think we've been working you too hard. You need a break."

"Oh, I love my work. I don't want a break, really."

"Hmmm. When was the last time you slept through the night yourself?"

"Uh . . . three weeks ago?"

"That's what I thought," said Mother Su. "Listen, you take your cot into Chang's room and sleep on her floor. I'll stay up with the baby and take care of her. We aren't going anywhere until this afternoon, so you can sleep straight through until then. Okay?"

The thought of a solid six hours of sleep sounded delicious. Mei Lin yawned and stretched her arms. "Thank you. I can't remember when I've felt so tired."

"You are welcome," said Mother Su. "Now, if you hear this little one crying, don't come out here. I'll have her."

Mei Lin quietly set up her cot in Chang's bedroom. She lifted the blanket over her shoulders and rested her head on the pillow. Even her thoughts couldn't stop her now.

Mei Lin dressed Little Mei in the outfit Chang bought for her the night before. It was cheerful and perfect for the warm weather.

Once again Tao drove all of them, including Brother Tom, to a park for a picnic supper.

Mei Lin breathed deeply. "What is the floral smell?"

"Magnolias," answered Mother Su. "See them over there?"

White magnolias lined interconnected cement walkways, each one somehow leading to a large precipice in the center of the park. The magnolias were encased in luscious green foliage behind cement benches and beautifully carved statues.

"It's beautiful," said Mei Lin.

Tao opened the stroller, while Mother Su and Chang brought baskets of food out of the trunk.

"Are you hungry?" asked Chang.

"I didn't know it till now. This fresh air makes me feel hungry," said Mei Lin.

"Look—your favorite—Mother's chicken and rice dumplings with noodles. And Father's stuffed mushrooms."

Mei Lin smiled. Liko liked stuffed mushrooms, too. She walked ahead of the others, the baby in her arms, wondering where Liko was right now and if he was thinking about her. At the nearest cement bench she sat and pulled a flower close to her face. Its petals felt like Little Mei's skin—silky-smooth and tender to touch.

"Look at this, Little Mei," she said. "Your new red gown has white magnolias on it. You will look like a Shanghai garden."

Little Mei was more interested in sucking her hand.

Mei Lin held the baby's cheek next to hers and pointed up to the trees. "Look!" she called to the others as they neared her bench. "She is taken with the sky and the trees."

"Look who's talking," said Tao. "I remember a girl who preached about the One who made the earth and sky."

"And I have already preached to Little Mei about it, too. I want her to know right away who made her world." She cradled Little Mei in her arms so she could watch the sky above her. "Oh, it's beautiful here."

"Wait until you see our picnic area," said Tao.

They walked past the high cement walls inscribed with dragons to the grove of poplar trees, then turned the corner. There was a bridge surrounded with rock formations and alcoves with flower and plant species of every kind.

"Look at the orchids," said Chang. "Do you like fuchsia?"

"Oh yes," said Mei Lin. "Look at their yellow throats! It's as though they are calling out to us from hearts full of sunshine."

"You are a poet," said Mother Su. "Let's cross the bridge. Then you'll see my favorite garden."

Mei Lin strapped the baby into the stroller, and Brother Tom proudly put the sun visor over her head.

"Oh, this is nice!" said Mei Lin. "Thank you, Brother Tom, for finding this for Little Mei."

"It was my pleasure. Although it is the first baby stroller I've ever acquired."

Mei Lin smiled. "I guess she's too little to read a New Testament?"

"Mei Lin, come see!" There was an edge of excitement in Mother Su's voice.

Mei Lin left Little Mei with Sun Tao and Brother Tom and ran to the opposite side of the bridge to see what Mother Su was so enthused about.

A wall of fragrance filled her head. "Roses!" cried Mei Lin. "I can smell them!"

Mother Su clasped her hands together. "Look, Mei Lin!"

Now Mei Lin saw what the high dragon walls were hiding. There was an array of botanical gardens in traditional Chinese style. A small lake with pedal boats and a family of ducks shimmered behind the gardens. And by the large rocks on the side was a grouping of pastel-colored roses—pale pink, yellow, and peach.

"Oh, Mother Su, these are so lovely! No wonder you love it here."

Mother Su pointed. "Let's eat over there on those benches." Mother Su found a park bench close to the lake with a good view of the roses.

Although the sun was no longer high overhead, Mei Lin could feel the heat coming out of the sidewalk around her legs.

Little Mei seemed to know her part, and she fell right into the day's plans. She drank a full bottle of formula and, after the last burp, fell into a sweet sleep. Mei Lin laid her gently in the stroller and put the visor over her.

Then Mother Su spread a blanket on the grass and everyone gathered around. There were chicken and rice dumplings, noodles, and stuffed mushrooms. Mother Su had made butter and peanut cakes for dessert.

Indulging in Mother Su's cooking was always a pleasurable experience. But to enjoy it in this park was like dining in a land of dreams. A couple drifted quietly on a pedal boat in the center of the pond. Ducks paraded along the banks and then splashed into the pond, rippling the glassy water. A gentle breeze occasionally carried the fragrance of the roses to their blanket.

This would be the perfect place to have a wedding. Of course, Amah would never approve. She would see to it that she had a proper traditional wedding. Mei Lin tried to memorize all of it in her mind so she could tell Ping about it later on.

"What are you smiling about?" asked Chang.

"I am imagining myself telling my friend Ping about this lovely place. She would love it here."

"And?" asked Chang, her eyebrows turned upward.

"And?" Mei Lin repeated. "Okay, you caught me. I was thinking that this would be a lovely place for an outdoor wedding. But Amah would never stand for it."

"Why not?" asked Chang. "It's your wedding."

"Ha! Tell Amah that! She and Ping and Fu Yatou are all making plans while I'm gone."

"What do *you* really want?" asked Chang.

"I haven't thought a lot about it," Mei Lin admitted. "And I really don't mind that Amah wants to plan it. This just seems like the most beautiful place on earth—romantic too."

Chang hugged her knees and rocked back and forth a little. "I've never been to Jiangxi Province. What's it like?"

Mei Lin sat up straight, nearly spilling her water. "You have to come!" she cried. "You and your father and mother must all come to my wedding! Oh, do you think you could?"

"I would love to, and I know my parents would, as well. We will have to try."

Mei Lin could see that Chang was already planning.

"Does Liko have a sister?" she asked.

Mei Lin shook her head. Her mouth was full. "No siblings."

"I thought the rural areas allowed for a second child."

"Not in our village."

"That's too bad. If you have no sister-in-law, then whose shoes will you wear?" asked Chang. "Not to mention who will put the money inside."

"I hadn't thought of that," said Mei Lin. "I guess it's not that important anymore. No one I know is marrying into a big family. Our traditions have had to change with the one-child policy."

"Well, if I come to the wedding, you can change into my shoes!"

"Really?" asked Mei Lin. "What a grand idea. And I do feel

as though you are my sister, Chang, especially now that you are a Christian."

Chang smiled. "I would be honored—as long as Liko and his mother agree to adopt me as the sister-in-law for the day."

Mei Lin laughed at that. "Oh, they are easy to please. Don't feel like you need to put your money in the shoes, though. I can have Liko give you some since you're a pretend sister-in-law."

"Oh, I'll put the money in," said Chang. "I won't have Tanching calling me a cheap sister-in-law!"

Mother Su sat down beside them on the blanket. "Do you want more tea?"

Chang and Mei Lin held out their small teacups, and Mother Su refilled them. "You look so happy over here," she said.

"We're talking about Mei Lin's wedding, Mother. I've invited myself to be her sister-in-law on her wedding day! Mei Lin, we'll have to shop for shoes. What size do you wear?"

Mei Lin smiled. Besides church, shopping was Chang's favorite pastime.

"Maybe you could look for shoes next weekend," said Mother Su.

Mei Lin laughed. "You two are as bad as Amah and Fu Yatou. Liko and I won't be able to marry until he's twenty-two. That's two years from now."

"Well, I don't know if we'll see you again before then," said Chang. "So we'd better go shopping while you're here."

Little Mei stirred in her stroller, and Mei Lin jumped up to check on her. The side of her head was sweaty, but her feet were cool to the touch.

"May I take her for a walk?" asked Chang, coming up behind her. "Baba is walking with Brother Tom, and I thought I'd go with them. Besides, Mother wants to talk to you."

"Sure," said Mei Lin. "She usually sleeps for about three hours in the afternoon."

Chang pushed Little Mei's stroller over the lumpy grass and onto the walkway while Mei Lin turned to help Mother Su clean up the picnic lunch. Then the two of them carried the baskets back to the bench overlooking the lake. Mei Lin sat down and stretched her legs. A breeze blew across the lake and carried the smell of water mixed with floral scents.

"Mei Lin, Joy talked to me last night," said Mother Su. "She presented an interesting proposal."

"Joy? Do I know her?"

"I introduced you to her last night. She's the young woman, quite thin, who testified about her mother being healed of cancer."

"Oh yes," said Mei Lin. "I know who you mean. She gave me a bag of clothing for Little Mei before we left last night. It looked brand-new. Her husband was there, too."

Mother Su leaned forward, studying her hands as though she'd never seen them before.

Mei Lin had never seen her act like this. She put her hand gently on Mother Su's shoulder.

"What is it?" Mei Lin asked. "Does this proposal have you worried? Is it about the orphanage?"

Mother Su looked up at her. "I am concerned about you—how you will feel about it. Mei Lin, Joy wants to adopt Little Mei."

Mei Lin suddenly felt far away from the bench. She inhaled, but her breath was jagged. She felt like someone just pushed her down a high hill and she was still rolling, rolling, down to the bottom.

"Mei Lin?"

Mei Lin looked at Mother Su. Of course Mother Su wanted to find a home for her Be-be.

"Adopt?" she asked.

"Yes. Joy has a relative who thinks they can get the baby an identity card. That way it will be legal. Joy and her husband haven't been able to have children. It would be a blessing for everyone."

Mei Lin looked at Mother Su, her thoughts screaming. *It*

wouldn't be a blessing for me! Not for me! And what about Little Mei?

"What about Little Mei?" she said aloud. She tried to stuff her own desires down, but she knew deep inside that Little Mei was happy with her. They had bonded since she found her in the trash can. How could she just give her away?

"What do you mean?"

"What about Little Mei?" Mei Lin repeated. "What about what she wants?"

"Honey, Little Mei is only three weeks old. She's not old enough to know what she wants—or what is best for her."

"I know," said Mei Lin. She got up and stuffed her hands in her pants pockets. Then she took them out again. She was reacting like Liko, stuffing her hands in her pockets.

She walked to the edge of the walkway and then turned around to face Mother Su. "Little Mei likes being with me. And . . . and I love her."

Mother Su wiped away a tear. "I'm sorry, Mei Lin. I didn't know you felt so strongly. But what will we do with Little Mei when you go back to Tanching?"

Mei Lin heaved a sigh. "I've thought about it," she said. "With all of my heart I want to adopt her."

"You?" asked Mother Su. "But, Mei Lin, if you adopt, you won't be able to have a child of your own. And you would have to wait two years until you and Liko marry. She will be two years old by then."

"I know," said Mei Lin. Then suddenly it dawned on her. This was the most glorious plan imaginable! If she and Liko adopted Little Mei, they wouldn't be *allowed* to have any more children. She wouldn't need to give an excuse for her barrenness to anyone—not even to Liko. Amah wouldn't have to know. She'd never know she was barren or think the gods cursed her. Maybe Amah would even become a Christian!

Mei Lin clapped her hands. "That's it."

Mother Su looked as though Mei Lin had slapped her instead of her hands.

"Really, Mother Su. That's it."

"What is it?"

"Liko and I will adopt Little Mei. It's perfect. Even for Amah."

"Amah?" asked Mother Su. "What does Amah have to do with this?"

When Mei Lin didn't answer, Mother Su stood up and took Mei Lin by the shoulders. "Mei Lin, what is going on that you are not telling me? I know there is trouble because I saw the bear and the dragon in my dream. What is really happening inside of you?"

Mei Lin knew Mother Su was speaking from a heart full of love, but she still didn't want to talk about it. It was too personal, too humiliating. Now she saw the way out of her shame forever—she could adopt. No one would ever have to know. In her heart, it was settled. She looked up at Mother Su.

"I can't tell you. But I want to adopt Little Mei."

CHAPTER

Twenty-One

What was supposed to be a short weekend visit extended into a week of constant teaching. Liko studied hard in between the courtyard classes. When it rained, Teacher Kong taught them in the kitchen and they studied at the table.

They didn't see Mrs. Wen until it was time to leave for their next destination. Before they left the little house, Liko noticed that his companion seemed uncomfortable. He leaned forward and softly asked, "Are you all right, Pastor Wong?"

Pastor Wong turned around, then glanced over his shoulder at Mrs. Wen to see if she was watching. "I do not have words for it, Liko. But inside, in my heart, I know that there is trouble."

"You think something is wrong at the churches?"

"No, not the churches. We are in trouble, but I can't put my finger on it. Teacher Kong seemed to know the Scriptures very well. But it troubles me that he did not begin or end his meetings in prayer."

Liko thought about it. "I guess I didn't notice. Was there anything else?"

"Yes. In the last class he said, 'The period we call grace will soon end and a new kingdom era will begin.' And then he said something about God coming in many forms."

"Maybe he meant that God moves in many ways on the earth," said Liko.

Pastor Wong shrugged. "I don't know, but it made me uncomfortable. And I don't like it that they have not returned our identity cards or my cell phone. My assistants expected me to call two days ago. I'm responsible for several Christians who are in hiding. There are also three evangelists who are depending on me to give them directions this weekend."

At least this time they traveled with the curtains open. The van pulled into a newly graveled driveway that led to a large house nestled neatly in the woods. The men pulled their bags out of the back of the van.

"I'm going to need to do my laundry soon," said Liko. He directed his question to Mrs. Wen. "Do we have time to wash our clothes and hang them before the next session?"

Mrs. Wen smiled. "I'm sure you can do some laundry today." She opened the door and walked in unannounced.

Liko and Pastor Wong walked in behind her and set their bags on the floor.

"Jade!" exclaimed Liko. "What are you doing here?"

Jade sauntered toward Liko, tossing her shiny black hair behind her back. "Aren't you glad to see me, Liko? I thought you would be pleased."

"I'm just surprised," he answered. He glanced over at Pastor Wong. "I didn't know."

Jade left the dining room, and Pastor Wong whispered, "It looks like there's a lot we didn't know."

Liko took a look around. The house was set up very much like the Wens' home, with four bedrooms, a front dining room, and an adjoining teaching room. The only difference was this place had an old stove like those in Tanching. Liko wondered if it had a courtyard out back.

"Where shall we put our bags?" asked Pastor Wong.

"You will each have your own room here," answered Mrs. Wen. "I requested this house. It's too bad you had to suffer through the last one for a few days." She made herself busy at the old stove, setting kindling wood and dry bamboo inside. "I'll light this stove later on so we can make supper. For now, I packed a lunch for us to eat."

Pastor Wong put his head in his hands. "Let's look at the rooms," he said quietly.

"Use the rooms over there on your right," said Mrs. Wen. She was arranging dishes and wiping down tables. "I want to be near the kitchen."

"When are the teachers coming?" asked Pastor Wong.

"Oh, probably not until tomorrow or early next week. Don't worry. I can get you started."

Liko took the room on the far right. He put his bag on the bed and then slipped into Pastor Wong's room, next to his.

"I was thinking—" said Liko.

Pastor Wong put his fingers on his lips and pointed to the light that hung above his bed.

"Thinking is good, Liko," he answered. "Did you unpack yet?"

"Not yet," he answered, catching on to the warning.

Pastor Wong put his finger on Liko's lips, then walked to the bedroom door and shut it quietly. He stood on the bed and pointed to a small knob in the light.

Liko followed Pastor Wong's silent example and stood on the bed beside him. The small knob had a wire going out of it that was snug against the lamp, difficult to see from the floor below.

The room was bugged. Their words were being monitored and probably recorded outside the room.

Liko sat on the bed and hung his head. He rubbed his temples and tried to piece it all together. Why was the room bugged? Why was Jade here?

Pastor Wong took out pen and paper.

I think we are dealing with the Eastern Lightning cult. They have been known to kidnap Christians and try to brainwash them into converting.

How do they brainwash? Liko wrote back.

I've heard that at first they teach the Bible. Then they point out mistakes they think are in the Bible. Then they throw out the Bible and teach that Christ is in China, only this time He came as a woman. They are very dangerous and will harm people who don't believe in EL.

His mother was right. She warned him they shouldn't scatter, and it was better to go home. Why hadn't he listened to her?

My mother is in trouble, Liko wrote. *It's my fault. I wouldn't listen.*

Pastor Wong looked startled. *What do you mean?*

Liko picked up the pen. *She said we should all go home. She quoted a verse. Matthew something.*

Try to remember, wrote Pastor Wong.

Liko bit his lip and tried to think back to what his mother had said the day they were separated. He hadn't responded well, he remembered that. He thought she was just skittish about the attention Jin was giving her. He even felt a little angry, thinking she was spoiling the first exciting thing that had happened to him since Mei Lin returned. Now he was ashamed of his behavior.

Matthew 12, he finally wrote. *It's the verse about scattering.*

Quickly Pastor Wong opened his Bible and traced his finger down the columns of characters till he came to verses 29 and 30.

Liko pointed to the word *scatter* and picked up the pen. *She said we shouldn't scatter. We should stay together.*

Now we must bind the Eastern Lightning strong man.

Liko nodded. *Please pray for my mother,* he wrote.

Pastor Wong nodded. Then he took the piece of paper and folded it until it was tiny and put it in his pocket.

Liko got up to leave. When he opened the door, Jade was right outside. "What are you doing?" he asked.

"Liko!" she said. "I didn't know you were in there. I was just coming to tell you and Pastor Wong that Mrs. Wen spread a picnic lunch for us in the courtyard out back."

Liko looked back at Pastor Wong. "We'll be there shortly."

Liko went to his room and looked at the light above his bed. He wasn't surprised to see the little knob that told him his room was bugged, also. Liko plopped on the bed. He was no longer eager to unpack his bags. He was eager to pray. He dropped to his knees and put his face into the pillow and prayed with all of his heart for his mother.

Just before bedtime, Liko and Pastor Wong walked together around the back courtyard. They spoke softly to each other, barely above a whisper, using as few words as possible.

"They were so nice to us today," Liko said. "Do you still think—"

Pastor Wong nodded. "We must leave as soon as possible. I want to try to find the cell phone first, so we can call for help."

"But we don't know where we are."

"I made a map of our route on the way to both houses. I can find our way back."

Liko's eyebrows winged upward. Pastor Wong was so wise. It made him feel like a little child.

"We must stay together," said Pastor Wong. "And we must bind the strong man and rescue the others. We'll leave at dawn. Bring a water bottle and any money or food you have. Leave everything else."

Liko nodded. He was so glad to have Pastor Wong with him. Jade and Mrs. Wen had treated them like kings that evening. Mrs. Wen even helped him do his laundry. He would never have seen through them without his friend's warning.

"And how do we bind the strong man?" he asked.

"Just one way, Liko. Pray."

Kwan So was troubled. Their new teacher was still as polished and professional as he had appeared the first week. But now he taught without his Bible and even suggested that it is sometimes good to use other books to preach from. So read other literature—that wasn't such a shocking idea—but there was something about this teacher's demeanor, his spirit. He couldn't put his finger on it.

At lunch break, he met Zhang Liang coming out of the bathroom.

Liang put his head close to So's and spoke quickly and quietly. "I'm afraid these people are Eastern Lightning members," he said. "And Shuang and Ke are in their company. These women are debauching and flirting. Be very careful."

So followed his friend back to the classroom, feeling sick inside. The two women sat on either side of them, and the teacher began to speak.

Liang raised his hand. "I must say something," he said. "We Chinese house churches have established rules. The relationships between men and women should be appropriate, and they should not stay too close to each other."

Upon hearing these words, Ke started to weep.

The teacher quickly walked to Liang's chair and leaned close to his face. "Your words are very hurtful. Ke is not even married yet. You are simply not used to overseas people, who are more open."

"Your standards are weak," said Liang. "And your openness will cause trouble for you if you are not careful."

"I agree with Pastor Zhang," said So. "You must establish boundaries so that your people do not fall into infidelities. Adultery is not only sin, it hurts people."

So could feel Shuang looking at him. She needed to hear a Christian tell other Christians that they should be pure and chaste.

Ke stopped weeping and started to massage the neck of the older teacher, who sat in front of her.

How can these people be so forward with their actions? wondered So. He was grateful that Liang had openly stated their position, but it was obvious that they weren't being taken seriously.

That evening So prayed at his desk in his room, with his

Bible open in front of him. He was not only concerned for himself but for the others. Had they realized yet who their "institute teachers" really were? And Chen Li Na . . . he had promised he would watch over her, and now they were hopelessly separated.

Everything was falling into place now—Jin's behavior, Li Na's warning. He flipped his Bible open to Matthew 12 and read the verses again. He determined to bind the strong man that would try to infiltrate his thoughts with Eastern Lightning teachings.

I do not listen to Eastern Lightning. I do not look at Eastern Lightning. I do not think about Eastern Lightning. I do not debate Eastern Lightning. I do not believe Eastern Lightning.

This would be his defense until he could escape.

He heard a knock at his door.

"Come in."

The door opened slightly. Shuang slipped inside and shut the door behind her. She had tea in her hand, which she set on his desk. Without saying a word, she sat down in the chair near the door and stared at him. Kwan So thought about her story and felt sorry for her. He could see the anguish in her eyes.

He sipped the tea and said, "You need to open the door. It is not appropriate for you to be inside my room alone with me with the door shut."

Shuang lifted a skeptical eyebrow, but she leaned toward the door and opened it.

"Thank you for the tea," So said. He leaned forward, his elbows on his knees. "You should influence your husband with the love of the Lord, so that he can repent. Don't lose your mind while you feel empty in your heart, and fall into the scheme of the Devil."

Shuang didn't say much this time. She wiped away a few tears and stared at the floor.

"Jesus will fill up the hole in your heart," said So. "I will keep praying for you."

"Thank you," said Shuang. And with that, she got up and left.

So was distracted. Before, Shuang had seemed very willing to tell him everything she was thinking, but tonight was different. She was clearly overwhelmed in her situation.

He visited the bathroom and dressed for bed. As he lay there in bed, he prayed for Shuang, but his prayers seemed to hit the ceiling and bounce back.

Then he thought of Li Na; he was sorry he had encouraged her to come. He decided to pray for her, and within seconds, his prayers were full of fire, and he could feel their effectiveness launching angels of protection and godly wisdom to Li Na.

He thought of Shan Zu and her scarf. He wondered where Mei Lin was that night and if the red thread still connected them all. He had never felt so far apart from the ones he loved. Loneliness and dark emptiness crept about his bed. His thoughts seemed scrambled, and he fell off to sleep with the light on.

So's dreams were tormented, and he tossed and turned. When he wakened, the light in the room appeared to be blinking on and off. He saw the large light break up into smaller dots of white light. The small dots formed one large light, which blinked on and off again. Lights. Lights of the interrogation room.

"Shan Zu! Let her go!" he yelled, waking himself up. The torment from the dream wouldn't let him go. He kept seeing Shan Zu's face, screaming in pain as the hot irons seared into her fingers.

"Stop," he whispered huskily. "Stop the pictures."

His bedroom door opened. It was Shuang. Her hair was braided down the side, and she was in her nightgown.

"I heard you calling out in your sleep. Are you all right?"

He didn't want to admit it, but he was glad for her company. He couldn't snap out of the dream he was having.

Shuang's hands were wrapped around a tea mug. She walked carefully toward him, carrying the mug as though it were a pot of gold. "Here, I brought you some hot tea. Perhaps it will help."

"Put the tea on the desk," he said. "I'll get it later. Thank you."

"Maybe you need to talk, Kwan So," said Shuang.

"No, you need to leave. If I cannot go back to sleep, I will talk to Zhang Liang."

"The others are not here. They went to a baptism."

"Why didn't they invite me?" He tried to hide his trembling hands.

"They saw you were already asleep," she answered. "It's only you and I in the house. Here, I'll hold the tea for you. Drink the tea from my hands."

"No," he said firmly. "You shouldn't be here in my room in the middle of the night. It's not proper."

"Proper?" she asked. "Kwan So, you said you would be my brother. I heard you crying out with tormented dreams. This tea will help you sleep."

"Will you leave if I drink the tea?" he asked.

"Yes."

"Give it here," he said. He felt suddenly angry with this woman who walked into his room unannounced. He determined to lock his door from now on.

So sat up on his elbows and sipped the tea.

"Are you angry with me?" asked Shuang. She slowly rolled her tongue over her lips. "I can't have you angry with me. I'm just trying to help you."

A burning sensation went down his throat, down his middle, and into his extremities. "What is in this?" he asked.

"How long has it been since you have been with a woman, Kwan So?"

The room started to go around in circles, and So held on to the bedpost. He felt as though he would fly through the air at any moment. "Y-you n-need to leave, n-n-o-ow," he said.

"Here, untie the red bow," said Shuang. She wiggled her braid in front of his face. "Watch my hair fall. I did it just for you."

So turned his head too quickly, and the ceiling came up in his face. "Oh, God, help me!" he cried. "Shuang, you must leave."

Suddenly she was bent over him, kissing his face and hair.

The room was reeling; he was smothering. He grabbed the bedpost at his head with both hands and swung his body off the bed. Both of them crashed to the floor. The hot tea spilled from the desk and onto Shuang.

"Owww!" she cried. "You burned me!"

"You have put something in my tea, woman," said So. "I cannot help you. Get out of here."

Shuang slapped him in the face. "You impudent fool!" She ran out of the room.

So gathered enough strength to crawl to the door and lock it. Then he slid to the floor, and the room went black.

✶ ★ ✶

CHAPTER

Twenty-Two

After class that evening, Law Jin left the room, and Zhang Jun Lee boldly walked up front to Teacher Liu. "Mrs. Chen and I would like to speak to you, Mr. Liu."

He looked up from his pile of papers. "Yes? What can I do for you?"

Jun Lee cleared her throat. "We—Mrs. Chen and I—feel we are ready now to return to our homes."

"What is the matter, Mrs. Zhang?" asked Mr. Liu. "You do not agree with my teaching?"

Jun Lee's eyes widened with surprise. Li Na prayed quietly.

"You are doing a fine job, and we are grateful," replied Jun Lee. "It's just that Mrs. Chen and I did not expect to be separated from the others. We would like our identity cards and whatever is left from our money. We feel it is good for us to return home now."

Mr. Liu's eyebrows scrunched together, and he gripped the chair in front of him. "I have come a long way to bring you this teaching. I cannot return to the prestigious Haggai Institute and tell them that you did not stay for the teaching. Can't you see this will look very bad for me?"

Jun Lee looked flustered, and Li Na came to her rescue. "I think you are overreacting, Mr. Liu. You are still assigned to teach this class all over again to the others, right?"

"That is true."

"Well, then, why don't we agree that we will leave next week? Maybe Wednesday morning. You will be leaving on Friday to teach the others anyway."

"I will talk to Jin about it," said Mr. Liu. "Good night, sisters."

After he left the room, Jun Lee sat in her chair, her head in her hands.

"Jun Lee, what is it?"

"The fish, Li Na. Now the fish are swimming in me, too."

"He seemed offended," said Li Na.

"He's offended? I am offended! Did you hear what he said tonight?"

Li Na looked around before answering. She picked up her tablet and wrote, *Let's write what we feel. The walls may be listening.*

Jun Lee picked up the pen. *He said that God is one God in many forms—he thinks the Bible verses on the Trinity are mistakes. He said the Bible is becoming outdated.*

Li Na looked at Jun Lee. She didn't need to write her next thought; it was etched across her face. *What do we do now?*

Suddenly Jin walked back into the room. "Sisters, I have a surprise for you."

Two women dressed in business suits and black pumps came in behind him. They carried briefcases strapped across their shoulders.

"Zhang Jun Lee and Chen Li Na, I would like you to meet sisters Gu Rong and Foong Qi. Rong and Qi will be joining us for the remainder of your time with us. We thought you would enjoy some more feminine company."

Li Na and Jun Lee shook their hands and greeted them.

Li Na knew she should be relieved that they now had more women than men in the house. But the fish were multiplying inside. She quickly shut her notebook.

"Grandma Zhou has prepared tea in the kitchen," said Jin. "Why don't we meet there."

The four women fell into line behind Jin. Grandma Zhou was bustling back and forth between her leafy green plants on the windowsill and the tea brewing on the stove. Li Na watched her, remembering her first day in this kitchen when she saw the dragon whip its tail behind Grandma Zhou.

After tea, Li Na felt sleepy. "I need to go to bed now," she said.

"Oh yes," said Jin. "Mrs. Chen, I am afraid I do not have another bed for Rong and Qi. They will need to share the beds with you and Mrs. Zhang tonight."

Li Na looked at Jun Lee, startled at this sudden change. For some reason, she felt lightheaded.

"Mr. Law, perhaps your guests would prefer to use my room," said Jun Lee. "I will room with Mrs. Chen. I think that will be more comfortable."

Li Na smiled at her friend, grateful for her quick thinking.

Jun Lee started to get up from her chair, and Jin pulled her back down. Jun Lee gasped. "Mr. Law!"

"I'm sorry, Mrs. Zhang. But, really, it will be better this way."

"I will be back," said Li Na. She smiled weakly. "I need to use our new outhouse. Mrs. Zhang, you'll have to tell Rong and Qi all about it." She stood up and, feeling dizzy, leaned sideways. "I'm not feeling well."

Jun Lee flew out of her chair and was by her side immediately. "I'll walk with you," she said. "I need to use the bathroom, too."

"We'll come with you," said Rong. "I don't want to miss the new outhouse!"

Li Na tried to comment, but the floor came up at her. Everything went black.

Li Na heard someone talking.

Almighty God has come, said the voice. *Believe the Almighty God. All who believe in her will be saved. Mrs. Chen, believe. Mrs. Chen, you must believe.*

The voice was far away, but it was calling her. She tried to answer, but her voice had no power. She drifted into blackness again.

Fire! She saw fire all around her. Liko! Her mouth moved, but no sound would come.

Liko! Get out of the fire! Come here, son! Baio! Baio! Get Liko out of the fire!

Darkness and fire were all around her. Bugs began crawling inside her skin, and she tried to pull them out. Grabbing, slapping, pulling.

Help me! The cry had no voice. No one could hear her. The blackness engulfed her again.

Voices. The voices were calling. *The Almighty God has come. All who believe in her will be saved.*

Suddenly she saw Liko's face. She reached for him, and his form contorted into a monstrous-looking boy and melted in the fire.

"Liko!" she screamed. She sat up. The room was dark, and there was someone beside her.

"Mrs. Chen, you will be all right."

Her body was drenched with sweat. Her sheets were wet, and she feared she had wet the bed. Trembling, she reached for the lantern.

"Lie down," said the voice.

"Who are you?"

"I am Rong, remember? We are sharing the room tonight."

Fear struck the core of her heart. Where was Jun Lee? Surely her friend heard her scream through the paneled wall and would come to rescue her. Li Na forced her feet over the side of the bed. Unsteadily, she leaned forward and again reached for the lantern.

"The lantern needs more oil," said Rong. "We used it up last night. Did you have a bad dream?"

Li Na stood up, then immediately sat down again.

"I wouldn't try to walk, Mrs. Chen," said Rong. "Law Jin gave you medicine to help you sleep."

"Jin?" she said. Her own voice sounded strange to her, as though it were stuck in her throat.

"Lie down," said Rong. "We will talk."

Li Na tried to think. "What happened to me?"

"You weren't feeling well, so Jin gave you some medicine. Don't you remember?"

"No," said Li Na. Suddenly the room was whirling around and she grabbed for the headboard. "I'm going to fall!"

Rong grabbed her arm and pulled her back into the bed. "You need to lie quietly, Mrs. Chen. You will feel better if you lie here quietly."

Having no other choice, Li Na pulled her feet back into bed, and Rong covered them. The change in position made her head hurt, and she felt the spinning sensation return. The terror of the dream came back to her.

Crash! Iron bars dropped around her on all four sides. Flames leaped into the cage, grabbing for her. *Liko!*

She screamed for her son again and again, unsure if she was calling him to rescue her or if she was trying to rescue him. It didn't matter. They belonged together.

Scatter!

No! Don't scatter. Don't scatter! Bind the strong man. Tie him up, Liko, tie him up. Don't scatter, tie him up! Jesus, help me!

The nightmare stopped. Li Na became conscious again. She could hear her own breathing now.

"Mrs. Chen, Almighty God has come," said a voice.

Li Na stiffened. She didn't dare reply. Was she dreaming again?

"Call on Almighty God and she will save you," Rong said. "We are in the era of the kingdom now. Almighty God is on the earth for you."

Rong leaned over her. Li Na knew she was in no shape to defend herself physically. But at least she was sure now that Rong was talking. And she was not talking about Li Na's God.

"Mrs. Chen, your Jesus has sent a woman to the earth," said Rong.

Her mouth was so close that it tickled her ear, but Li Na didn't dare move.

"The age of grace is gone now. As lightning strikes from the east, even so the Almighty God has been raised up in China. She will save you. She will save your Liko."

Li Na lay quietly, pretending to be asleep. Her mind kept going way far away and then coming back. The dizziness made her nauseous, but her stomach did not seem to be very much a part of her. She felt detached somehow from her body.

Jesus! Li Na cried out silently into the darkness. *Save me, Jesus!*

"The Bible was good in Jesus' day," said Rong. "But this is a new day. We have a new kingdom and a new Christ. Chen Li Na will become a believer in our Christ. Chen Li Na will call her Almighty God, you will see."

Li Na trembled, despite her attempts to feign asleep. She prayed silently to Jesus until Rong fell asleep, just before sunrise. Li Na felt the sickness leave her just about the time the green glow from her window lit the room. Then she forced herself to relax and fall asleep after pounding heaven with silent prayers for Liko.

As they circled back around the courtyard toward the house, Pastor Wong spoke in a normal voice about the sunset and said good things about the teaching.

Liko played along. "It's been quite a day," he said with a yawn. "I think I'll turn in."

"Good idea," said Pastor Wong.

"You're not going to bed already, are you?" It was Jade, just coming outside. "I have tea waiting for you in the kitchen. Would you prefer to have it out here?"

"Liko may be interested," said Pastor Wong. "I think I'll go to bed—"

"Oh, please, gentlemen," said Jade. "It's just a little tea. Stay right here, and I'll be back."

"Forceful little thing, isn't she?" said Pastor Wong.

Liko pointed at his ears and laughed. Pastor Wong had forgotten himself.

"Please, don't leave," said Liko. He sat down at a table near the door.

Jade returned with the tea and joined them. "I had no idea we'd end up split up like this," she said. "How's your mother, Liko?"

"I hope she's well," said Liko. "I haven't talked to her since we scattered. Do you have a cell phone that I could use to call her?"

Jade looked uncomfortable. "I'm sorry, I don't. I don't think the phones work way out here, do they? Oh, it's a shame I missed her. Maybe we can all get together back in Tanching. After the Institute, I should have one more week with all of you before I need to go home. Have you enjoyed having me in your house church this summer?"

Liko sputtered, nearly choking on his tea. He was doubly embarrassed that she was so open with her affections in front of Pastor Wong.

"Jade—"

Pastor Wong put up his hand to stop Liko from saying anything further. "We are both grateful that you have paid the way for so many of our pastors to be trained by the Haggai Institute. Thank you, Jade."

Her eyes sparkled at Pastor Wong's affirmation. Liko wondered if the girl was truly that needy. Certainly anyone as beautiful as Jade could easily find affection, especially as open as she was with men.

C. HOPE FLINCHBAUGH

"Let's go, Liko," said Pastor Wong. "It's a long day tomorrow."

The men got up from their seats. Liko used the bathroom and went to bed.

He felt self-conscious zipping and unzipping underneath the microphone in his room, so much so that he decided to sleep in his pants. Between sleeping under a microphone and the prospect of escaping in the morning, he felt jittery. A burning sensation went through his chest and down into his middle. His legs tingled, and then heat went through them. His body felt like it was on fire, but the sensation was not painful.

He turned off the light and lay in bed, his hands behind his head. Liko tried to pray for his mother and Mei Lin.

The door clicked. Liko tried to sit up, but he felt dizzy and collapsed back into bed. "Who is it?"

"It's me, Jade."

"What do you want?"

"I wanted to say good night. Don't you want to say good night to me?"

Before Liko could answer, she was sitting at the end of his bed. She unbuttoned her nightgown from the top and leaned over him.

Liko put his blanket over his face before she exposed herself. "This is wrong, Jade. You must leave now." His words sounded brave, but inside he was trembling.

"Look at me, Liko," she whispered. "The others are all gone."

"What do you mean?" he asked. He wondered if something had happened to Pastor Wong.

"Mrs. Wen asked Wong San Ming to help her with her van. They are taking it for a test drive."

Liko felt panic creep up his back. He was counting on Pastor Wong to protect him—and now he was gone? His mind was reeling, and he couldn't think clearly.

"Liko, look at me," said Jade. "Just one look won't hurt. See, my shoulder has a bruise on it."

The burning sensation shot through his middle, and his mind clouded. Jade put her hands on him over the blanket, and his body tensed.

"Jesus, help me!" he cried. The tea must have had something in it that made him vulnerable, pulling the resistance out of his body. "Deliver me from temptation, Jesus!" he cried.

Instantly, Liko sat up in his bed, still holding the sheet over his head. Jade pulled it down. He nearly toppled sideways. The room was spinning.

Liko squeezed his eyes shut and shouted, "Jade, I am a Christian man with a godly fiancée. You must leave now."

A light flashed.

"What's that?" he cried. Liko jumped off the bed and ran to the door, shielding his eyes as he ran. He flung open the door and stumbled through the classroom and into the bathroom. As soon as he was inside he slammed the door shut and locked it.

"Thank you, God," he said, gripping the sink in front of him. "Thank you, God."

He turned to the toilet and threw up. His stomach was sick, but his heart felt worse. He never dreamed that a woman could be so impudent. Liko washed his face and looked at himself in the mirror. What would Mei Lin say when he told her this?

He washed his face a second time and tried to pull himself back into reality. He was out of breath, his heart still pounding. *Jesus, deliver me from Jade.*

Liko knew he must leave. He was ready to leave now. But where was Pastor Wong?

CHAPTER
Twenty-Three

Rong got up the next morning as though nothing at all had happened the night before. Li Na wanted to question her but thought better of it. Instead, she said, "I felt very sick last night. Do you think Jin would mind if I brought the large tub to this room and took a bath?"

"I think that's a wonderful idea," said Rong. "You stay right here, and I'll go ask the men to carry hot water up for you."

"No, I can carry it myself."

Rong put her fingers to her lips. "I'll arrange it." She disappeared out of the room.

The last thing Li Na wanted was Jin and Mr. Liu in her room. She didn't know exactly what was going on, but after a few hours of good sleep, she knew that it was time to leave. She also knew that she couldn't talk about leaving because it would upset the whole house. And so she played their game.

She steadied herself and stood up. She could feel strength draining out of her legs, and they wobbled a little. She felt as though she'd wrestled with the devil himself last night.

"Jesus," Li Na whispered. "Please tell me what to do next. And help Jun Lee. Oh, God, send your angels to guard Chen Liko and Kwan So. Please tell Pastor Wong and Pastor Zhang we are in trouble here and—"

The door unlatched. Li Na sat down on the bed and covered her legs with the blanket.

Jin carried in a large metal tub, and Mr. Liu was right behind him with hot water.

"Mrs. Chen, are you feeling better this morning?" asked Jin. Li Na looked into his eyes.

"Aren't you talking this morning?" he asked. "Mr. Liu, you can put the water here. Please—go get another bucket of hot and one of cold. We must take care of our guest."

Mr. Liu left without saying a word. Li Na wished she'd have never asked for the water.

Jin walked over to her. She froze. He put his hand on her forehead.

"Oh, I see the fever has left you, Mrs. Chen. That is good. Perhaps you will be well enough to join us this afternoon for teaching."

Li Na could not speak. She felt strange, as though she were slipping off the bed and out of the room.

Bind the strong man and cast him out.

Her lips did not move because they couldn't. Fear had frozen them shut. But her spirit cried out, *I bind the strong man and cast him out.*

Mr. Liu walked into the room and dumped the second bucket of hot water and one cold one into the tub. Rong came behind them with soap and a fresh towel.

All three of them left without a word. Li Na pushed herself back to her feet. She pulled open the small dresser drawer and got out a change of clothes. She held the clothes in her hand and dragged the desk chair toward the tub, leaning on the chair as though it were a walker. She latched the door on the inside.

After catching her breath for a moment, she slipped out of her clothes and into the warm tub. She dunked her head underneath the water, then lathered her hair and body with the soap and dunked down again, rinsing herself clean. The water revived her and she felt fresh again.

Click.

Li Na quickly grabbed the towel and covered herself. She'd latched the door from the inside, but right now it would not surprise her if someone knocked it right down. This house and the people in it were dangerous and strange.

When no one entered, she searched the door, looking for a hole that someone might peep through. She was glad she at least had the presence of mind to put the towel on the chair nearby.

Within seconds she was wrapped up in the towel, her hair dripping water over her shoulders. Now she had but one thought—she had to talk to Jun Lee.

She quickly dressed, then took the opportunity to wash her undergarments and hang them over her bedroom chair to dry. Instinctively, she started to pack her suitcase, pulling all of her clothing out of the drawers. Then she stopped.

All she knew was that she was in trouble. She didn't know why, or who these people were. One thing was for sure—Jin and his friends from the Institute believed that Christ was a woman and the Bible was outdated. They were either deceived Christians or they were not Christians at all.

She put her clothes back into the drawers. She wanted to talk to Jun Lee and plan an escape, but right now she had no ideas to offer. For now, she would pretend to go along with them.

Rong said that Jin had given her medicine, but she didn't remember that. She just drank the tea with everyone else and stood to go to the bathroom. That was the last she remembered.

The tea—maybe it was the tea.

Confusion engulfed her. She felt as though she had a thousand mah-jongg tiles in front of her and none of them matched.

Bind the strong man.

Li Na grabbed her Bible and quickly flipped it open to Matthew 12. She wanted to study the context of the Scripture God gave her that morning at the Wens' house.

Then one was brought to Him who was demon-possessed, blind and mute; and He healed him, so that the blind and mute man both spoke and saw. And all the multitudes were amazed and said, "Could this be the Son of David?"

But when the Pharisees heard it they said, "This fellow does not cast out demons except by Beelzebub, the ruler of the demons."

Now she understood. The strong man in verse 29 was Satan and his demons. A shiver went over her. She pulled her own dry towel from her drawer, wrapped it around her wet hair, and sat down again on her bed to read.

But Jesus knew their thoughts, and said to them: "Every kingdom divided against itself is brought to desolation, and every city or house divided against itself will not stand. And if Satan casts out Satan, he is divided against himself. How then will his kingdom stand? And if I cast out demons by Beelzebub, by whom do your sons cast them out? Therefore they shall be your judges. But if I cast out demons by the Spirit of God, surely the kingdom of God has come upon you."

The kingdom of God—Rong said something about the kingdom of God last night. No—she called it the "era of the kingdom," whatever that meant.

These verses made it clear that the true kingdom of God casts out demons by the Spirit of God. But what demons could God want her to cast out? She remembered the tail of the dragon.

"Oh, Jesus," Li Na sighed quietly. Now she found two mahjongg tiles that matched. God was showing her there was a demon in the house, and somehow it waged part of its war through Grandma Zhou. How thankful she was right now for her Bible. Light began to dawn. One thing she knew for sure—there was a clash of kingdoms going on in this house, and God knew about it. God was telling her that she must discern who was on His side and bind the demons operating here.

Li Na closed her eyes. "Father in heaven, thank you for giving us the warning before we were scattered. I am so glad that you gave me the chance to warn Zhang Liang, Kwan So, and Liko with Matthew 12. Open our eyes to its meaning, and help all of us to hear your voice amid all this clamor about a woman Christ and a kingdom era. I want you to know that I am faithful to you, Jesus. You are the Christ, the only Son of God. Help me to strengthen Jun Lee today. Give us your help and your words to bind this Enemy in Jesus' name."

Now Li Na was anxious to see her friend. She wondered if Jun Lee had also suffered from the tea last night. She brushed her hair and stuffed wads of toilet paper into her pockets, then went to Jun Lee's room. It was empty.

Li Na looked through the glass in the door to the teaching room and saw Jun Lee. She looked a little frightened, but she didn't appear to be suffering physically. Relieved, Li Na went downstairs with the wet towel under her arm.

Grandma Zhou was the only one in the kitchen, washing dishes from breakfast.

"Good morning," said Li Na.

Silence. Li Na felt a brutal coldness coming from the old woman.

She ignored her silence and took her towel outside to hang it over the bamboo wall to dry. She used the bathroom and then, closing her eyes, lifted her face toward the sun.

"Li Na, you are better?"

"Jun Lee! Oh, Jun Lee, how are you?" Li Na embraced her friend.

"I am fine, sister," said Jun Lee. "You looked terrible last night."

"I think I was drugged by the tea we drank, but I'm not sure. All night Rong kept telling me about a Christ who was a female and a new kingdom era and that the Bible was outdated. She insisted that I would come to believe this, too."

"I wanted to check on you, but Qi discouraged me. I prayed for you all night long."

"What has happened this morning while I slept?"

"Mr. Liu taught the first session, and Rong is going to teach now. Qi is to teach us this afternoon. Li Na, I think I know what is going on. I think these people are the Eastern Lightning."

Li Na blinked with surprise. "Oh, Jun Lee!"

"It makes sense. They preach that a woman who is the Christ supposedly came to the East like lightning."

"Is Rong this Christ?" asked Li Na.

"No, I don't think so."

The front door of the house banged.

"The next session begins in five minutes," Jin called. He stood at the front door, watching them.

"You'd better go inside," said Li Na. "We'll talk through the slats."

Jun Lee went inside to use the bathroom. "Li Na," she whispered through the slats. "We must escape."

"I think so, too," said Li Na. "Did you see the bolts on the outside of the bedroom doors?"

"Yes," Jun Lee answered. "I'm coming out. Now you pretend to go inside."

Li Na went inside and pressed her face up against the bamboo to talk to her friend. Jin was still standing at the door, as though he didn't trust them to be together.

"This group is dangerous," Jun Lee whispered. "Pastor Wong told my husband that they beat people and brainwash them."

"Jun Lee, this will probably be the last time we will talk together. We must make a plan quickly. I think we should leave right after lunch. We can ask to go to the bathroom. Be sure to stuff your pockets with toilet paper and, if you can, smuggle out some bread. I'll bring my Bible. The directions are in there."

"Okay," said Jun Lee. "I'll fill my thermos at the courtyard pump and leave it there."

Li Na came out of the bathroom. "We will leave our clothes behind," she said in a low whisper.

Slowly, they walked toward Jin. "Let them think they are still deceiving us," whispered Li Na.

"Yes. But if one of us becomes drugged or injured, the other one must run for help."

"We must stick together," said Li Na. "We can't be scattered."

"But we must escape and tell the police," said Jun Lee. "My husband said it's the only way to stop Eastern Lightning."

They had to stop talking as they reached the door, where Jin was still watching them. He looked especially handsome today in his dark suit and red tie. He had on a gold watch and a new gold chain clasp that held his tie in the front, and looked like an angel of light staring at them from the doorway.

His eyes narrowed with suspicion as they approached. "From now on you will go to the bathroom one at a time."

"One at a time?" asked Li Na as she washed her hands in the basin. Then she laughed. "Why, it will be just like elementary school, Jun Lee."

Jun Lee smiled as she went to the pump to fill her thermos, playing along. "Jin, did we take too much time?"

Jin's angelic smile returned. "Of course not, ladies. It's just that—we must get to our last class."

Li Na sat in the classroom, wondering if listening to Rong would contaminate her thoughts or make her wise to the ways of the Eastern Lightning. Inwardly, she prayed. Outwardly, she listened, taking careful notes about what Rong was saying.

"People are expecting Jesus' second coming," said Rong. "But, actually, Jesus is here."

Li Na found it difficult to comprehend that people really believed this kind of teaching. Rong seemed sincere. She actually believed that Jesus had already come back, and this time He was a woman in China!

They turned in their Bibles to Matthew 24:27.

"Mrs. Chen, will you read this verse?" asked Rong.

Li Na stood and read, "'For as the lightning comes from the east and flashes to the west, so also will the coming of the Son of Man be.'"

"So you see, the first time Jesus came, He came from the west in Israel. The Bible says that the second time He comes He will come from the east to the west. Almighty God plans to begin her work here in China and then expand her glory to the nations of the West. Perhaps you are wondering how this will be accomplished. First, China must be divided so that we can meet the needs of all people. Second, the family needs to be reorganized."

Li Na tapped her pen on the bridge of her nose, appearing to be concentrating. Inside, the fish were swimming. The teachers were moving at a very fast pace now, and she knew that soon she and Jun Lee would be expected to profess belief in their female Christ. When forced to make a choice, Li Na knew she could no longer pretend to be open to their teachings.

"Our country must be divided so that the new kingdom era can begin. The Almighty One is not against families but wants to reorganize them. This new kingdom era does not expect a man and wife to live together and have sex together. The Almighty One will set us free from this confined family. She will bring us into a new lifestyle that expands our family into all who are believers in Almighty One. Under her rule, men and women do not have to marry. They simply have sex with anyone who is a member of the kingdom era. We are one big family and we can reach out to meet one another's needs in this way."

Li Na felt her scalp tingle. No wonder Jin had no scruples about calling her beautiful and holding her hand. And there was something else she hadn't thought of before—why was Jin still single? Now she knew. He believed he was part of a large harem. She wondered if the sex was consensual.

"God is one God, but in many, many forms. Men and women do not need to marry to find family identity. . . ."

Li Na could not listen anymore. She pretended to take notes

as she drew small pictures of the cross, flowers, anything to take her mind off Rong's words. Fear teased her thoughts, tried to grip her mind, and she pushed the fear back, pretending to concentrate on her little drawings while she prayed for wisdom.

The mah-jongg tiles were matching now. Jin and Jade were both in the Eastern Lightning. She hated it that she had encouraged Liko to trust Jade. Her son didn't trust Jade for the same reasons that she herself didn't trust Jin. Why didn't they see it before?

A new realization washed over her, and she sat erect in her chair. *Jade! Was Jade with Liko and Pastor Wong now?*

Jun Lee looked her way.

Li Na quickly pretended to adjust her seating, but her thoughts were pounding against her head. The horses were stampeding again, urging her to get up and run to Liko. She tried to convince herself that it wasn't true, but deep within, she knew it was. Jade had paid their way so that she could be with Liko. Li Na's heart was in her throat, pounding with the horses, and she knew she must think about something else.

Bind the strong man!

Yes! Quietly Li Na prayed. *In Jesus' name I bind the strong man where Liko is staying. I go into that house right now in prayer, and I bind the strong man of Eastern Lightning and I bind the strong man of lust. I tie those demons up in Jesus' name and I take back what is mine. I take back my son, Liko, in Jesus' name. You shall not have him, Satan. In Jesus' name.*

"What do you think of that, Mrs. Chen?"

She looked up. Rong was asking her a question about the lesson, and she had no idea what she had said.

"I don't know," she answered honestly.

Rong leaned over the podium in the front. "We will help you know."

The class was finally over, and everyone filed down the stairs for lunch. Li Na was at the bottom of the steps when she heard a loud thump behind her.

"Jun Lee!" she cried. Quickly she put her Bible and notebook on the stairs and ran back up a few steps to where her friend lay on her back. She put her arms around her neck to help lift her.

Jun Lee whispered in her ear, "Rong pushed me."

CHAPTER

Twenty-Four

Kwan So took his place next to Liang in the first teaching session. He passed him a note he'd written the night before.

Brother Zhang, we must leave—before lunch.

Liang looked over at So and nodded.

Teacher Ye and Teacher Long stood up near the podium together. "Today we would like to talk to you together," said Teacher Long.

So sat up in his chair. He was forming a plan in his mind on how they would escape during their break after the second class.

Teacher Ye said, "We are preachers of the Eastern Lightning."

So felt thunder rumbling from his chest up into his throat. He jumped up, exploding with anger. "You gangsters!" he cried, shaking his fist at them. "You are thieves of the church. You are false Christs and antichrists."

"Pastor Kwan," said Teacher Ye in a patronizing tone of voice. "You have yet to meet our Christ. She is here to reorganize the world, just as your Jesus did two thousand years ago."

"Lies!" So slammed his hand on his desk. "All lies! You are serpents coated in human skin."

Teacher Ye leaned over the podium, his brow wrinkled with vexation, his jaw unyielding. "You will become a believer in the Almighty One."

So stood on top of his chair to make his announcement clear. "I will never give up my genuine faith and give in to your demonic teaching."

Liang stood to his feet. "Jesus is the Christ, the son of the Living God. Only Jesus is called the Almighty One."

"You are the scum and disgrace of China," said So. His chest throbbed with anger.

The two teachers lunged toward them, like two serpents of Satan. Teacher Ye and Teacher Long grabbed So and pulled him down to the ground, jerking his arms roughly behind him until he screamed with pain.

"You will believe what you are told to believe, Kwan So."

Something slammed into his head, and everything went black.

When he wakened, he tried to move his legs, but he couldn't feel them. His hands were tied behind him to a chair in the class-room. Loud music was playing. He had never heard the songs before, but from the lyrics he guessed they were from Eastern Lightning indoctrination. He could barely open his eyes. The teachers were gone. He looked over at Liang's desk. He, too, was tied to his chair, passed out.

So looked around, hoping they were alone. But Shuang was guarding them, watching from the kitchen stove where she was cooking. So turned his head and pretended to be unconscious.

He had to think. *Matthew 12. Bind the strong man. Do not scatter.*

I do not listen to Eastern Lightning. I do not look at Eastern Lightning. I do not think about Eastern Lightning. I do not debate Eastern Lightning. I do not believe Eastern Lightning.

"Liang," he whispered. "Wake up. We must talk."

His friend's face was swollen, and blood was dribbling out of his mouth.

So was suddenly aware that someone was standing behind him. He heard a crack, and pain flashed in his head.

"You will believe, Kwan So." It was Teacher Ye.

So tried to answer, but his stomach heaved and he threw up over his knees.

"Shuang," yelled Teacher Ye. "Get out here and clean them up." He grabbed the front of So's hair and jerked his head backward. "I want you to feel the pain, Kwan So. The pain will help you believe."

So's mouth was full of blood and vomit. The room was reeling. He had no physical power to speak to Teacher Ye, but inside his spirit screamed, *I do not listen to Eastern Lightning. I do not look at Eastern Lightning. I do not think about Eastern Lightning. I do not debate Eastern Lightning. I do not believe Eastern Lightning.*

"Separate them," Teacher Long commanded.

So heard chairs scraping, and he thought of what Li Na said before she left. *"I just know we shouldn't scatter like this."* Matthew 12 rang in his spirit, and he knew she was right—the scattering and separation are part of the plan to ruin the sheep.

Silently he prayed, *Jesus, don't let them divide us. Don't let them scatter your sheep.*

Thwack!

The floor came up at him, and he passed out.

Zhang Jun Lee's face was ashen and her breathing labored.

"Put your arms around my neck," said Li Na.

"I can't," said Jun Lee. "It's my back. I don't think I can walk." Then she whispered, "You must go without me. Find the PSB and bring help. It's the only way."

"Oh my," said Rong. Her tone was mocking as she descended the stairs, her arms laden with books. "I heard her fall, but I didn't see her with all these books in my arms. Are you all right, Mrs. Zhang?"

Hatred spilled into Li Na's heart. It was ugly hatred, the color of the green oil paint on the windows. *I ought to kick you in the shins and send you flying down the steps,* she wanted to say.

Jun Lee must have felt her tense. She whispered, "Forgive, Li Na. Forgive."

Li Na was appalled at her own wicked thoughts. She whispered, "I forgive with Jesus' help." Then more loudly she asked, "What can I do to help you up, Mrs. Zhang?"

"Let me rest here a moment," said Jun Lee. "I must try to get my feet working."

Li Na stepped back and let Jun Lee begin to try to move her body.

Jin appeared at the bottom of the steps. "What's going on here?"

"Mrs. Zhang seems to have tripped down the stairs and hurt herself," Rong replied.

Jin bounded up the stairs. "Can you move?"

"I can't stand up," said Jun Lee. She blew her breath out slowly, and Li Na saw tears well up in her eyes.

She looked at her friend, and her heart screamed, *I can't leave you like this!*

Jun Lee looked back into her eyes, her expression like steel. "I can't move," she said. "You must get help."

Li Na understood the double meaning in her words. Jun Lee was helpless. It was up to her now.

Mr. Liu and Jin helped Jun Lee back up the stairs to her room, and Li Na picked up her Bible. It was her only road map, spiritually and geographically. Her decision was made. It was time to run.

Li Na saw fresh dumplings on the table. As soon as Grandma Zhou had her back turned toward her tea plants, Li Na grabbed four of the dumplings, wrapped them in a napkin, and went outside. She tied the dumplings inside the cloth and stuffed them into her shirt as she walked to the water pump. After picking up Jun Lee's thermos, she pretended to walk casually toward the outhouse. She held her Bible and thermos close to her heart and looked back at the door. No one appeared to be watching, and she was certain no one could see her out of those awful green windows. She walked casually behind the bathroom, then burst into a full run down the old path.

Li Na ran and ran on the path until it veered off, away from the direction of the main road. From that point on, her traveling was slower. She had to force her way through the brush and bamboo. Finally, after she caught her breath, she took a drink of the water and decided to run on the road for a while. Not one car had passed since she'd left—an hour before.

Suddenly she heard a rumbling behind her. A car! She stood rigid with terror. "Jesus," she cried through her sore throat. She found her legs again and made them run into the woods, where she dived behind a clump of brush and lay flat. The roar of the motor grew closer.

The white van! She put her head down as it slowly drove by her location, grinding against the stones as it passed. She kept her head pressed to the dirt beneath her and didn't dare look up. She wondered who was driving and how many were looking for her.

Blood pounded in her temples, and she tried to think of what to do next. She pulled out her Bible and studied the map she'd made on the way to the house. It appeared that the first turn going backward would be to the right. It had taken them fifteen minutes to drive to the house after that turn, so she thought it would perhaps take her another forty-five minutes to walk that far.

She knew that the van would return soon, looking again for her along the road. She walked deeper into the woods until she could barely see the road. She needed to walk as long as there was daylight. She shuddered. She couldn't imagine being alone in the woods after dark. At least the days were long in the summer, and she wouldn't freeze to death after sundown.

Half an hour later, Li Na heard the sound of the van returning. She darted back farther into the woods and fell flat, covering herself with dirt and bamboo.

Adrenaline shot through her back, her heart pounding into the ground. She didn't dare run. *Jesus,* she screamed inside. *Hide me!*

The dumplings! She had forgotten they were there, and now they were squashed flat inside the napkin. She felt them oozing out of the napkin between her shirt and her skin. She covered her head, not daring to move.

Out of nowhere, Li Na remembered the story of Lot in the Bible. Evil men of Sodom wanted to sexually abuse the angels who were visiting Lot. The angels struck the men of the city with blindness so that they stood outside of Lot's house and groped at the door, unable to find the handle.

Oh, Jesus. Do it again—now! Strike these people with blindness so they can't find me. Don't let them abuse me.

Fear gripped her heart as horrible pictures of what her captors might do if they found her flashed through her mind.

"Chen Li Na!" called Jin. "You must return to us. You will get lost out here."

"Mrs. Zhang is calling for you," yelled Qi.

From her hiding place, Li Na could see Mr. Liu walking straight toward her. She was sure he saw her. He stopped about five meters away from where she lay trembling and praying.

"We will torture your friend if you do not return to us!" he screamed, pivoting slowly in every direction. "She will die a thousand deaths, and it will be your fault." He spat on the ground in disgust, turned on his heel, and stalked back to the van.

He doesn't see me!

She could hear the van doors slam, and the sound of the motor gradually faded away.

Li Na's body still trembled, but her faith soared. God was with her, she could feel Him. The thought of His presence with her, hiding her, made her want to sit still for a time. Very softly she sang,

In the cross, in the cross!
Be my glory ever.
'Til my raptured soul shall find
Rest beyond the river.

She sang the chorus again and again until her trembling subsided and strength and courage returned to her spirit. She didn't have much time. She pulled the smashed dumplings off her skin and ate two of them, saving the other two for later. She sipped a little water from the thermos, then opened her Bible and read Matthew 12 one more time.

Slowly it was sinking in that this battle with Eastern Lightning was not against the people themselves but against a belief system that began in the dragon of ancient times—Leviathan, the Devil himself. Eastern Lightning not only had a spiritual agenda, they had a political one—to divide China until it adhered to its own belief system.

"No wonder you said we shouldn't scatter," Li Na whispered in prayer. "Thank you, Father, for keeping me safe. Please help me to move forward and not get lost, in Jesus' name."

Li Na stood to her feet and dusted herself off. From that point forward, she knew she was being watched—by heaven.

Fifteen minutes later she stumbled out of the woods, dirty but unharmed. She was at an intersection. She knew that she was on the right road, and if her memory served her correctly, there should be a village nestled below tiers of rice paddies very soon.

She scrunched her eyes and looked into the western sun. It must be getting close to suppertime. She pulled out her Bible and looked at the map. She would make a right turn and then a left very soon. The wooded area was behind her now. The road was surrounded by fields—the first of medium-sized sugarcane and then others of wheat and rice. There wasn't much room to hide.

Li Na looked to the heavens. "I am trusting you to hide me again, Father, if the van returns. And please give Jun Lee the strength and wisdom from heaven so that she knows how to respond with your heart. Protect her and hide her, even as she sleeps in the lions' den tonight."

She followed the road by the field for a couple more hours. There was no traffic, and she found herself envying the crows that circled above her. They didn't walk or run or hide. They flew with liberty to whatever destination they pleased.

"I envy your freedom," she told them softly.

She heard a rumbling behind her. A red taxicab. *What on earth is a taxi doing way out here?*

Li Na had seen many cabs like this one when she and Baio had gone to Wuhan one time. The cab drew closer, a cloud of dust behind it.

Li Na waved at the driver, and he stopped.

"What are you doing way out here?" he asked.

"I was about to ask you the same question," Li Na shot back at him.

The driver smiled and tipped his hat against the sun shining in his eyes. "Are you all right?"

Li Na saw concern on his face. "Please, sir. Please take me to the next village. My friend and I were kidnapped, and I have to get help."

"Kidnapped?" asked the driver. "Sounds like a wild story to me."

"I know it's unbelievable, but it's true." Li Na suddenly realized she was carrying her Bible openly, and she tucked it underneath her arm.

The cab driver didn't seem to notice.

"Look, I don't have any money to give you, but I could use a ride. Would you trust me to send you the money later if you give me your address?"

"Lady, I've heard a lot of bad-fortune stories in my life, but nobody ever told me they were kidnapped before."

"You don't have to believe me," said Li Na. "Please, just take me to the next village."

The driver sighed. "Well, I'm going there anyway. Come on, get in."

"Oh, thank you!" cried Li Na. She climbed into the backseat, and the driver pulled off before she shut the door.

The driver delivered her to the street of the village cadre and wished her luck, waving off her promise of payment if he would only provide an address.

She quickly tore the map out of her Bible and stuffed it into her pocket. She slipped her Bible into the napkin with the last dumpling and slid it under her belt.

Outside the door of the house, Li Na hesitated. This was a small-village cadre, and she wished she were in a larger village where a proper police report could be filed. After she told her story, the cadre could arrest her for not being a registered Christian. But she had no choice. She had to take a chance.

Li Na rapped on the door. *Please, God, let this cadre be sympathetic and believe my story.*

The door opened. "Yes? How may I help you?"

The man had a baby in his arms, and Li Na couldn't help but smile at the little boy.

"You are Cadre Lu Lok?"

"I am."

"I am Chen Li Na from Tanching Village in southern Jiangxi Province. There is a terrible situation that you must know about."

"Who sent you here?" the cadre asked.

"I took a taxi here," said Li Na. "Jiang Park is the driver, and he brought me to you. Please, Cadre Lu, something terrible is going on and I need your help. I would like to file a report for the police."

"I cannot help you file police reports at this hour," said the cadre. "You will have to come back in the morning."

"No," said Li Na, blocking the door with her foot as he tried to close it. "You don't understand. Some of my friends and I were kidnapped. I am the only one who has escaped. You must help us."

"Kidnapped?"

"Yes," she answered. "I would not be standing outside your door at this hour if it were not urgent, please believe me."

The cadre called back to his wife to come and get the baby. Then he opened the door and said to Li Na, "Please, come in."

CHAPTER

Twenty-Five

After he heard Jade go to her room, Liko stuffed his pockets with toilet paper and tiptoed across the teaching room and dining area. He quietly opened his door and slipped inside, locking the bedroom door from within. He checked his watch every fifteen minutes until he finally decided to sleep with the light on. He dozed off and on and at the crack of dawn got out of bed and dressed quickly, tucking his extra money into his sock.

At least I wasn't foolish enough to give him my last yuan, he thought. *How could we be so stupid? How could we allow our-selves to believe these people were Christians?*

As he prepared to escape, a new realization slowly came to him. *Every one of those thirty-four pastors, including me, has been kidnapped by Eastern Lightning. Oh, Jesus!*

He tried to concentrate on escape, but the guilt was over-whelming. He was the one who had pushed Jade's idea. He was the one who told Pastor Zhang to gather all the pastors. He felt like a little child who had never learned common sense. The more he thought about it, the angrier he became—angrier at Jin and Jade, and even more angry with himself.

Thirty-four house church leaders, including his own mother, were in danger, and it was his fault. His leadership was weak and thoughtless, and he hated himself for dragging others into his own zeal for schooling.

Pride.

Inside, the conviction grew stronger. Most of his anger was because he'd made a fool out of himself. He dropped to his knees and whispered his prayer into his pillow.

"Father, please forgive me for my pride. I feel wounded because I have played the fool and led all of these pastors into the awful clutches of the Eastern Lightning. And worse, my first thought was feeling embarrassed for myself instead of being concerned for the others. Please, God, get us all out of this. And forgive me for being more worried about my reputation than your people's welfare. I ask you to somehow rescue all of us, in Jesus' name."

Liko stood to his feet, quietly unlatched his door, and listened. He opened the door slightly and looked into the dining room and kitchen. There was barely enough light to see. Satisfied that no one was awake, he shut the door and slipped into Pastor Wong's room.

"Pastor Wong!" Liko could hardly believe his eyes. Pastor Wong was gagged and hanging by his wrists from a hook and rope that were attached to the ceiling.

He gave a muffled cry, and his eyes were wild and flashing.

"Wong San Ming doesn't seem to like our facility here," said a nasal voice.

Liko turned to his right and saw a man sitting in the corner. "Who are you?" he asked. "What do you think you're doing? Get him down from there!"

Even as he spoke, Liko pulled a chair underneath Pastor Wong and worked to free his friend's hands.

"I wouldn't do that if I were you."

Liko felt the chair pull out from underneath him, and he lunged forward to grab the rope above Pastor Wong's hands. He swung hard and pulled, yanking the rope with all of his might.

Nasal Voice jumped to his feet. "Stop him!"

Another man charged at Liko from the back corner of the room and tried to grab his feet and pull him down.

Liko kicked him in the face, and the man fell back on the floor, groaning. "You let us go!" Suddenly the rope popped, and Liko pulled himself upward and gave one more yank, throwing his whole body into it.

Crash! He and Pastor Wong fell down together.

"Jesus, help us!" cried Liko.

The man on the floor stood up and came toward Liko head-first. He was tall and stocky and looked like Old Gray in a bull-fight.

Liko moved away from Pastor Wong, who was trying to free his hands. Adrenaline rushed through his body. "Come on, Bull!" he said, exploding with anger. "You want to fight?"

Liko put his right hand up in the air to distract The Bull. He slid his left hand into his pants pocket and pulled out his pocket-knife. He clicked it open and slipped it into Pastor Wong's hands.

Mr. Nasal shouted, "Take the boy! I'll get the other one."

Never taking his eyes off The Bull, Liko ran sideways into Mr. Nasal, knocking him to the wall. *Thwack!* The nasal guy hit his head hard on the wall and slid to the floor.

"Run, Liko!" shouted Pastor Wong. "Run!"

Liko scrambled to his feet. "No! We stay together."

The Bull was in a full run toward him.

Liko jumped in the air and kicked. The kick landed in his assailant's chest, and The Bull was thrown back momentarily.

Pastor Wong was on his feet. Mr. Nasal was trying to get up off the floor, holding his head with one hand.

"Grab the rope," said Liko. He ran to the door and bolted it shut from the inside. He had no idea what other Eastern Lightning members were out there, and he didn't want anyone else in the fray.

"Tie up Mr. Nasal," said Liko. "Gag him."

The Bull charged him again. Liko defended himself, catching his punch and swinging him around. His pushed his knee into The Bull's back, and the man went down. Liko grabbed The

255

Bull's arms and held them tightly behind his back while Pastor Wong tied and gagged him.

Someone was pounding on the door from the outside. "What's going on in there?"

"We have visitors," said Liko. "What do we do?"

Pastor Wong pointed to the window. "That way."

Liko put the chair under the door handle to jam the door shut while Pastor Wong quickly put on his shoes and shirt and grabbed his Bible.

Liko was trying to open the window, but it was jammed shut. He ran back to the door and grabbed the chair, then ran full speed toward the window as Pastor Wong backed out of the way.

Crash!

Pastor Wong used a bath towel to push away the pieces of glass that were still stuck in the windowpane. Liko saw that his wrists were open and bleeding, encased with red and purple rope burns.

"Go!" cried Pastor Wong.

Liko squatted inside the windowsill and jumped. His feet stung, but he was okay. He turned around and put his hand up to help Pastor Wong, who grabbed Liko's hand in midair. His feet hit the ground, and both of them ran full speed toward the woods.

They had almost reached the trees when they heard yelling behind them. Liko glanced back. A small group of people were chasing them, the red van not far behind, rumbling and bumping over the field.

"That way," said Pastor Wong.

Adrenaline shot through him, and Liko could feel the extra push of strength. His heart was pounding from fright and from the intensity of the fight with The Bull. He let Pastor Wong take the lead while keeping an eye on their pursuers. The red van was at the edge of the woods, and people were jumping out.

"There must be twelve of them!" he shouted to Pastor Wong.

"We're faster," Pastor Wong shouted back. "This way!"

Pastor Wong veered left and ran down a steep hill so quickly that Liko thought if he tripped he could easily roll the rest of the way down.

He put his hand on a tree to stop himself and glanced up the hill. About half of the men were still chasing them, just over the knob of the hill.

"We're down to six!"

"Run, Liko!"

They ran as fast as they could down the slope.

Wooooooooooo. Wooooooooo. A train!

"Look!" cried Pastor Wong. "We can beat it! Run!"

Liko and Pastor Wong dashed toward the tracks. The train was coming at full speed.

They were almost at the tracks, and Liko could feel the ground rumble under his feet.

"It's our only chance!" shouted Pastor Wong. "Go!"

"GO!" Liko yelled back.

Both of them leaped like gazelles across the tracks to the other side. Wind whipped behind Liko's back and knocked him sideways to the ground. He rolled into Pastor Wong, whose face was red and sweaty.

"We're faster!" Pastor Wong yelled over the roar of the train and laughed with relief.

Liko laughed with him, gulping for air. He lay on his stomach and looked underneath the tracks. The Eastern Lightning men were at the bottom of the slope, running toward the train.

Kwan So's mouth was full of blood. Inside he heard his own voice screaming, *I do not listen to Eastern Lightning. I do not look at Eastern Lightning. I do not think about Eastern Lightning. I do not debate Eastern Lightning. I do not believe Eastern Lightning.*

He felt water dribble into his mouth. He tried to open his eyes, but he couldn't. The water slid down the side of his throat, and he could barely swallow it. He was outside of the world of the living, locked in the fog.

"You hit him too hard." It was a woman's voice.

"You didn't hit him hard enough!" shouted a man. "If we could have gotten one picture, we wouldn't need to do this."

"Take one now," said the woman.

"Put your clothes on," the man ordered. "I can't take a picture now. Look at his face. Who's going to recognize him this way?"

So tried to breathe more deeply, to connect somehow with his body. Inwardly he screamed. Outwardly he could hear only the voices of the Eastern Lightning members. Then the fog grew thick again and he lost the voices.

Was it hours? Was it days? The fog lifted, but he couldn't tell how long it had been.

No one spoke this time. He tried to move his hand. Then his leg. Nothing.

Oh, God. Am I going to die? Who will take care of my family? Jesus, help me.

Music floated through the fog. Demons were riding on the music. Kwan So saw them, hanging on to little puffs of lyrics like so many dark horses of death.

Stop the music, he screamed.

No one heard him. He couldn't hear himself.

He tried to duck as the demons rode through the fog to torment him. He was trapped, locked in the fog. Nowhere to turn.

Baba! cried a voice.

Mei Lin!

He saw her, tried to get to her—she was too far away! There! She threw something—the wind caught it and lifted it high, carrying it to him—closer, closer. He reached out his hand—stretched toward it.

Catch it, Baba!

The red thread! As soon as he caught the red thread, he saw the cross. The volume of the music dropped slightly. Demons shrank back. A few of the braver ones continued their advance. So lay in the fog, looking at the cross, holding the red thread. He saw Jesus, cut, stabbed, swollen, and bleeding. The music was fading. The puffs disappeared, and demons scampered like little black cockroaches.

The cross! As soon as he thought of the cross, the music lessened.

A voice. A warmth in his ear.

"Have you ever had a tendon taken out of your body? I have the skills to do this, you know. I don't have any pain medicine, but who needs that?"

By dawn Cadre Lu had the legal papers in hand to make the arrests. He loaded four taxis with ten deputies and one doctor. Chen Li Na and Cadre Lu rode with Jiang Park, the driver who had picked Li Na up. The air was warm and dry, and it was difficult to breathe whether the windows were up or down. The taxis sped down the road, leaving puffs of powdery dust in the air behind them.

"Turn left at the next road," said Li Na, referring to the map in her hands. She put her nose inside her shirt so she could breathe. She knew that her first allegiance was to Jun Lee, but her heart yearned to find her son.

"You know, there may be a promotion for you if you capture these criminals," said Park to the cadre. "I've driven for the PSB in Wuhan, and they are bent on finding and stopping the Eastern Lightning cult."

"I saw their names in the paper a few times," said Cadre Lu. "But I never dreamed I would find them in this rural area of Jiangxi."

"I hear they are wealthy," said Park. He looked in his rearview mirror, directing his comment to Li Na.

"I don't know about all of them," said Li Na. "But the people who kidnapped us had two fans in one house."

The cadre turned around in his seat to look at her, an incredulous look on his face.

"Yes, two fans, an electric stove, and indoor bathrooms all in one house. That was the first house they took us to. The house where we are going to now is not nearly as nice. In fact, it's ugly. But the leader of the house where we are going to now, Law Jin, says he has a cell phone business based in Singapore."

"Mrs. Chen, it is important that when we return, we file a formal police report in Shanghai. This is the only way that we will be able to get to the source of the Eastern Lightning in Jiangxi."

Li Na leaned forward. "I will be happy to file the report, but please, Cadre Lu. You have a son. Certainly you must realize how desperate I am to find my Liko. I don't know where they have taken him. We were all scattered."

"Don't worry, Mrs. Chen," said Park. "Cadre Lu will make them talk. He will find your son."

Cadre Lu turned around again to face her and shouted over the crunching tires on the gravel road. "First we must raid the two houses where you know the Eastern Lightning have kidnapped your friends. The county cadres will meet us after this arrest, and then we will look for your son."

Li Na nodded. "Thank you, Cadre. Thank you."

Suddenly she realized that it was the county cadres who had arrested Chen Baio and beat him so mercilessly two years ago. It was their fault that Baio was taken to the county prison and tortured until he died.

Li Na realized that this same cadre could just as easily raid one of her own underground church meetings and "make them talk." She was taking a great risk by reporting the Eastern Lightning, but she saw no other way to rescue the leaders.

Her heart raced. Even though Jun Lee said she should tell the PSB, she wished she could talk to Kwan So or Pastor Wong. How could she be sure she was making the right decision in getting the PSB to handle this? What if it made things worse later on?

Her heart pounded, and she began to tremble. Quietly she prayed, *Jesus, help me. Help me to make the right decisions today. I'm afraid, and I'm so alone.*

A song began to play from far away in the recesses of her spirit.

When light dawns on China
The sound of prayer rises
Prayer brings revival and peace
Prayer brings unity and triumph
Prayer soars over the highest mountains
Prayer melts the ice off the coldest hearts.

Li Na leaned forward. "The house is just around that corner. You can't miss it."

"Stop just before this corner," Cadre Lu commanded.

Park came to a complete stop.

Cadre Lu put his hand out the window and waved downward, then turned on his phone. "Numbers two and three, follow us in and block side entrances left and right. Number four, block the road at this corner. Drivers, stay in the cabs; the rest of you follow me into the house." He turned to Park. "Are you ready?"

Park smiled nervously. "This is about the most excitement I've ever had in my life, Cadre Lu. But I'm ready."

CHAPTER

Twenty-Six

We only have a few minutes before the train passes," Pastor Wong said between deep swallows of air. "Let's go."

Liko's legs felt like rubber, and he wondered if he could run any farther. But he followed Pastor Wong, who veered to the right and went up a hill! *What are you doing?* he wanted to shout. *I can barely run down a hill, much less up one!*

His legs moved like tree trunks. Bamboo was everywhere, and it was difficult to cut a straight path. But Pastor Wong trotted forward, and Liko wondered at the strength of this man who was twice his age.

"Get down, Liko!" he suddenly cried. "The train is almost past—let's hide over there behind the brush."

The two of them dived behind the brush and watched the end of the train pass by. They parted the underbrush until they could see below. Six men ran across the tracks and stood there, talking and pointing to the fields and the hill where they were hiding.

"Are we going to stay here?" Liko whispered.

"We can't run much farther," Pastor Wong softly replied. "I went uphill because I don't think they can run much farther, either. Except for The Bull." Pastor Wong's eyebrows winged upward. "Quite a nickname you chose there."

Liko chuckled. "A bull with horns and legs."

"Yes, well, I think he could run until tomorrow this time. He was like solid rock." Pastor Wong was breathing more evenly now. "I think we should take our chances. God help us."

Liko looked around him. "Let's cover up with some of this," he said. "We'll blend in better."

They threw dust on their pants and grabbed enough loose brush to cover their heads if they needed to. Then they parted the brush once more to peer down at the Eastern Lightning.

"Two of them are headed up here!"

Pastor Wong watched for a moment. "One is headed this way. The other one is going up the other side. Let's stay put."

Liko lay flat, his head pointed downhill. He felt exposed and vulnerable. He prayed, facedown in the dirt.

Ten minutes later, the man was so close Liko could hear the crunch of leaves under his feet. He tensed, his body rigid and flat against the earth.

"Let's go!"

Someone in the distance was calling the man back! Liko didn't dare breathe. He heard the sound of water hitting the ground, and he knew the man was urinating. After the water, the footsteps slowly tramped away.

Neither of them moved for ten minutes. After that, Pastor Wong sat up and looked through the brush again.

Liko didn't move. Relief washed over him, and he began to cry. He remained facedown and wept until he shook, repenting for his pride in trying to impress Pastor Wong and the others, for dishonoring his mother by not listening when she tried to warn him, and for not spending time in fasting and prayer before he left Tanching. He was certain he had never really known the mercy of God until that moment.

Pastor Wong didn't interrupt him, but after a few minutes he put a gentle hand on Liko's shoulder. "We should leave now. They may come back with help or with dogs to search for us."

Liko nodded and scooched up to his knees. He dipped his head inside his shirt and wiped his face. "Which way?"

"They just went over the top of the first hill near the field," said Pastor Wong. "I haven't seen a house for miles. I think we should follow the train tracks. They're sure to lead us to a city where we can get help. Did you bring any money with you?"

"Right here." Liko unfolded his sock. He took off his shoes and banged all of the dirt and leaves out of them, then retied them. "It should be enough for bus tickets home."

"Smart boy," said Pastor Wong as he gave Liko a friendly slap on his back. "Let's go."

Liko and Pastor Wong walked along the train tracks in the opposite direction of the house, keeping a keen lookout for their pursuers. It was easier to walk there, but they were also more in the open.

"Your wrists look awful," said Liko. "And now they're caked with dirt. How long were you hanging there?"

"I don't know. The Bull and the other man came into my room last night. They offered me 150,000 yuan to join the Eastern Lightning, plus the promise of two or three mistresses."

"I've never heard of anything so evil."

"They are very deceptive," said Pastor Wong. "I'm not the first pastor who's been offered sex and money in exchange for conversion to Eastern Lightning. By appealing to greed and lust, they have shipwrecked the faith of some."

Liko kicked a white stone in front of him, sending it flying farther up the track. He felt like an idiot, like a chicken in a house full of wolves.

Pastor Wong put his scarred hand on Liko's shoulder. "Do not hate yourself for being innocent to their ways. Jesus told us to be like little children. It is a good quality."

Liko looked at the older man. How did he know what he was thinking?

"I have led thirty-four pastors to a den of thieves and murderers," said Liko. "I feel like a stupid idiot." He kicked another stone for emphasis.

"The Eastern Lightning has deceived good men much older

than you," said Pastor Wong. "And for a while they deceived me, too."

"But I don't understand. Why do they want Christians? Why don't they evangelize the lost?"

Pastor Wong sighed. "They have a theory that if they convert the leaders of the house churches, then they can convert whole churches at one time instead of evangelizing one by one. In my case, they could convert thousands of house churches, up to thirty million people. That's why the offer was so big."

"Amazing."

"Besides, they see Christians as their most volatile enemy. We are holding to Jesus Christ, the Son of God, and they are holding to the Antichrist, this woman they call the Almighty One. They are evidently quite rich, much more financially prosperous than I realized."

"Imagine all those houses with two fans, indoor bathrooms, electric ovens. I wonder where they get all their money."

"I don't know," said Pastor Wong. "But I intend to find out." He waved his wrists in the air and then blew on them. The dirt didn't budge. "One of their strengths is the money they tempt us with. Your mother was right about plundering the house of the strong man."

Liko smiled. "My mother's verse is exactly what we needed."

"What happened to you last night?" asked Pastor Wong. "I heard you just before I passed out."

Liko told him about Jade's visit. He was embarrassed to tell how she exposed herself.

"Did you see anything flash?"

"Yes, I did! How did you know?"

"I was afraid of that. They probably took pictures."

Liko's jaw dropped. "Pictures? Whatever for? Jade would let them do that?"

"Liko, they are trying to discredit our leadership. If they can get a picture of you and a naked woman in a compromising position, then they can take that picture back to your church as proof of your fornication. Then the Eastern Lightning will try to persuade your church that the Eastern Lightning teachings are right and Christianity is bogus."

Liko clenched his fists. "They are rotten! Imagine Mei Lin seeing this picture they took."

"Were you dressed?" Pastor Wong asked quietly.

Liko looked at him. "Yes—well, I had my pants on but no shirt. But Jade took off her top and kept telling me to look at her. I refused and put the sheet over my head, but then she was all over me. I got up and ran out to the bathroom and locked myself inside."

Pastor Wong laughed. "So that's the slam that I heard. The men were talking to me, and I suddenly passed out. I think there was something in the tea that did that."

"Mine too," said Liko. "It made me . . . it gave me a funny burning feeling."

"And lowered your resistance to Jade?"

Liko looked at the ground and nodded. "Yes."

"Your mother will be very proud of you, Liko," said Pastor Wong. "Your father, too. You've faced the worst temptation for a young man and resisted."

Liko's eyes filled up with tears, and a knot formed in his throat. He missed his father so much right now, he couldn't talk. The responsibility of rescuing his mother weighed heavily upon his mind.

"I have to find my mother," he said.

"Yes, we will have to contact the PSB whenever we get to the next village. Right now we must find some water. I'm hoping that there is a valley beyond that incline—one that has a stream of good water. We're right in between two mountains, so there should be springs coming down somewhere."

Pastor Wong was right. Forty-five minutes later, they both were kneeling in front of a stream, drinking until their stomachs were full. Pastor Wong quickly walked downstream and submerged his wrists in the cool current. Liko couldn't tell from his expression if he was relieved or in agony.

———————

Mei Lin quickly fed Little Mei and then dressed herself. She tried to take her mind off of Mother Su. She knew that her friend was disappointed in her decision to adopt. Well, maybe it wasn't just that. Maybe Mother Su was disappointed that she was hiding her true feelings from her. Deep inside, Mei Lin wanted to please Mother Su, but deeper still was her need to be a mother.

Of course, it was unusual to adopt a child two years before you were married, but she didn't care how odd it looked. She needed Little Mei. If God had allowed her to find this precious little one, surely He wanted her to keep her and take care of her, too. There were details to work out, but she wouldn't concern herself about that now.

She changed the baby's diaper and wiped the sleepy dirt out of her eyes with a warm washcloth. Little Mei was always content to let her do all of this before she ate. Mei Lin wanted to sit and cuddle the baby, but she had promised Elizabeth that she would do her hair this morning and help her get ready for her grandmother's arrival.

Mother Su had arranged for Elizabeth and her grandmother to meet and talk together today at the orphanage. Then Mother Su would come to talk to both of them concerning Elizabeth's custody.

Little Mei gurgled and played with her hands in her drawer while Elizabeth sat in front of Mei Lin on the bed.

"Elizabeth, I prepared a folder of your schoolwork to show your grandmother today," said Mei Lin. "She'll be proud to see your work. You're a fine student."

"Thank you," Elizabeth said softly. She was smiling, and Mei Lin thought she looked as though she might burst at any moment.

"I know!" cried Mei Lin. "Let's give you bangs! You'll look just like your mother! Then your grandmother won't be able to resist you!"

Elizabeth giggled, holding her hand in front of her mouth.

Mei Lin got out the nurse's scissors and wastebasket, and Elizabeth sat on the edge of her bed.

"Hey, your eyes are shining like stars," said Mei Lin. "What are you thinking about?"

Elizabeth smiled up at her, holding her head still so Mei Lin could finish cutting her bangs. "I want her to adopt me," she said.

"Do you know what? I want her to adopt you, too. But I will miss you if that happens."

"I'll miss everybody," said Elizabeth, "but I want to go."

Mei Lin sighed. "I know how you feel, Elizabeth. I felt the same way when I left Tanching Village. I knew I was supposed to come here."

"Are you going to stay here?"

"No, honey. I'm going home the end of August. I live with my grandmother. Did you know that?" Mei Lin pulled Elizabeth's hair back just a little on both sides and put a ribbon in each clip. "Where's your picture of your mother?"

Elizabeth dug the picture out of her pocket and took it out of the plastic pouch. Mei Lin held it up near the light of the window.

"Look at you!" she exclaimed. "Why, you look just like her!"

Elizabeth looked in the mirror and fingered her bangs. "I look different."

Mei Lin hugged her. "You look beautiful, just like your mother."

Elizabeth ran out of the door, banging it as she left. The sound startled Little Mei, who jumped and then burst out crying.

Mei Lin picked her up and held her close. "It's okay, Be-be," she said. "The bad noises won't get you."

Someone banged on the door.

"I wonder who that is at seven o'clock in the morning." She carried Little Mei to the door. "Brother Tom! Good morning!"

Brother Tom looked troubled. "Mei Lin, I have a letter here

269

from Pastor Wong. It was written two weeks ago and hand-carried from person to person. You are on the list of people who are supposed to read it. When you are finished, I am to take it to the house church on the north side."

Mei Lin went outside with Brother Tom and let him hold the baby while she sat on the bench and read the letter. It was well worn and tearing a bit at the creases.

Dear Friends,

A man from Jiangxi Province has offered to bring teachers from the Haggai Institute in Singapore into China. There are about twenty-five pastors so far who are gathering at an undisclosed place to sit under the teachings of these seminary professors. You will need to pay one hundred yuan for the course and the ticket, and they will cover other expenses.

Please pray about this opportunity and consider joining us. You may call me for more details.

PW

Mei Lin folded the paper and stared at the courtyard. Questions paraded through her mind, first about Jade and then about Liko.

"What do you think?" asked Brother Tom.

"My father already told me about this," said Mei Lin. "There is a visitor in Tanching named Jade. I met her briefly before I left. Her cousin set up these classes with the Haggai Institute. It looks like the teachers are coming to China. Liko mentioned it, too. I think they are both going."

"Are you going to join them?"

"No," answered Mei Lin. "I can't leave the orphanage. Are you?"

Brother Tom stared out into the courtyard now. His face remained troubled. "I will not join them," he said. "My place is here. Just in case I'm needed."

Mei Lin understood. Brother Tom was a middleman, a

contact person for Pastor Wong. She gave the letter back to him.

"You look troubled."

He forced a smile. "Perhaps I am too cautious. But with Pastor Wong involved with the Institute, I will be caring for his churches. Thirty million Christians, and the numbers are increasing daily. Three weeks ago they baptized new converts night and day for an entire week straight. All day, all night, lining up at the river to be baptized. The pastors baptized in shifts."

"I never heard of such a revival," said Mei Lin. "How can it be?"

"God continues to do miracles," said Brother Tom. "Evangelists show up in a village and ask to pray for any sick people. God heals the sick people, and the whole village wants to hear the Gospel. The stories are incredible, really. But there are so many new Christians—most of them don't have Bibles, and they need good teaching."

If there was anything that intrigued Mei Lin more than teaching, it was evangelizing. If only people in China knew how good Jesus is, they would want Him to be their God. The idols gave them nothing but fear of their future. Jesus was true hope. He was "good news," as the Bible said.

"It's a noble thing to want to be educated," said Mei Lin. "I'm glad for Liko and Father. But I wonder . . ."

"What?"

"Well, Father told me that Liko's mother has misgivings about the whole thing. He was concerned for her."

"I am having my own misgivings. I can't put my finger on it, but something isn't settling right in here." Brother Tom pointed to his chest.

Little Mei started fussing, so Mei Lin took her from Brother Tom and rocked her back and forth to calm her. "Can you call Pastor Wong?"

"I tried," said Brother Tom. "This letter was sent two weeks ago and carried by hand. Late last night, after I received the letter, I tried to call him. His message center says that the message box is full. He's obviously not taking his calls. He's never done that."

"Maybe he can't get a signal where he is. Do you know where they went?"

"No, and I have no way of contacting him. Does your father or Liko have a phone?"

"No," replied Mei Lin. "There is one member in DuYan who has a phone, but I don't know the number."

At just that moment Little Mei spit up on Mei Lin's shoulder.

"Oooh," said Brother Tom. He stood up to try to find something to clean it up.

"That's okay," said Mei Lin. "I have towels inside."

"Mei Lin, I will go," said Brother Tom. "I have work to do."

"Thank you for bringing the letter," said Mei Lin. "Please keep my father and Liko in your prayers."

The rest of the morning flew by. Cook Chu put Little Mei down for her nap by ten o'clock. Inside the classroom, the students were giddy with excitement for Elizabeth's reunion with her grandmother. Because writing took so much concentration for most of them, Mei Lin decided to play math and Mandarin drill games with them most of the morning to stay within the spirit of the day. Besides, it helped them stay focused on school.

It bothered her that Brother Tom was so troubled about losing contact with Pastor Wong, but she managed to push it from her mind.

"You're dismissed for lunch," she announced. "Don't run!"

Elizabeth appeared at her desk. "Did my hair stay in place?"

Mei Lin refastened one of the loosened clips and straightened her collar. "There, you look wonderful."

"I hope Grandmother doesn't tell Father that I stole the picture." Elizabeth's little eyebrows were furrowed together in worry.

"I think your grandmother will be proud that you took it."

"Proud?" asked Elizabeth. "But I didn't ask Father."

"Honey, you took the picture because you love your mother. She would want it to belong to both you and your father. You couldn't ask him for it, because he was treating you badly."

Tears sprang to Elizabeth's eyes, and Mei Lin pulled her onto her lap.

"I didn't see Grandmother all the time," the girl said. "But we went to see her sometimes."

"Well, Mother Su talked to her, and she is very excited to see you."

"Are you sure?"

"I'm sure," Mei Lin answered. "Now go get your folder and bring it to the staff house. You and your grandmother can eat in my bedroom. I'll turn the fan on."

Elizabeth beamed. "Really? We can talk in your room?"

"Of course. I may need to step in now and then to get something for Little Mei, but I'll move the dresser drawer, and you can use that table to set your lunch on while you talk. How does that sound?"

"Great!"

Elizabeth ran out of the room. Priscilla and Lydia met her at the bottom of the steps, and the three of them ran to Elizabeth's room together to get the folder. Mei Lei knew this reunion was difficult for Lydia and Priscilla. All of the children dreamed of being adopted into a forever family, but Elizabeth was the only one who had a chance for it right now.

Mei Lin opened all of the classroom windows and doors, gathered a few pencils that were on the floor, and left the room. She was surprised to see a woman waiting for her at the bottom of the steps, her back turned as she watched the boys playing ball in the courtyard.

"Hello," said Mei Lin. "Are you—"

The woman turned around. Joy—the one who wanted to adopt Little Mei.

Mei Lin's throat went dry. She extended her hand with the

full intention of greeting her warmly, but no words would come out.

"Mei Lin," said Joy. "Cook Chu told me I could wait here for you. I hope you don't mind."

Mei Lin coughed a bit to clear her throat. "No, not at all. Uh, thank you for the baby clothes for Little Mei. They were all very nice. Is there something I can do for you?"

Joy smiled, her eyes shining. "Did Mother Su tell you? My husband and I want to adopt Little Mei. This morning I was thinking about her, and I just couldn't stay away. I brought some formula for her."

Anger flashed through Mei Lin. She wanted to tell Joy to get out of her orphanage and her life.

The fact that such an uncharitable thought went through her mind terrified her. She didn't remember ever feeling this way toward another Christian. But Joy's timing was awful—she had to go get Little Mei from her nap and help Elizabeth get ready for her grandmother.

"Is something wrong?" asked Joy.

Mei Lin sighed. "I do want to talk to you," she said. She paused for a moment and tried to think merciful thoughts toward Joy. But all she felt was invaded and threatened.

"I have an important meeting to prepare for right now," she finally said. "One of our orphans is meeting her biological grandmother for the first time in months. Maybe we could talk some other time?"

"Oh," said Joy, obviously deflated. "I didn't know. I thought—I was hoping—"

Mei Lin watched her struggle and made no effort to rescue her. She wondered why this woman didn't adopt a baby before. She looked like she was in her thirties. But Mei Lin didn't ask her. She just wanted Joy to leave so she could take care of Little Mei and Elizabeth. She didn't offer to let Joy see the baby, even though she knew that's why she was here.

"Please, call Mother Su and ask her when it would be a good

time for us to meet," said Mei Lin. "I'm sure she will be able to schedule something that will work for everyone."

"All right," said Joy softly. "I'll do that. Thank you."

There was a wounded sound in Joy's voice, and Mei Lin knew she was personally responsible for it. She felt sorry for her, but not sorry enough to let her see Little Mei. She wished she had never taken Little Mei to church.

She led Joy to the gate and then turned her attention to the baby.

"Look, Miss Mei Lin," said Priscilla, coming through the staff door. "Little Mei was crying for you. Cook Chu said I could go get her."

Mei Lin quickly walked toward Priscilla and took Little Mei from her arms. "Okay, Priscilla. Thank you. Now you can go eat lunch."

Priscilla's face fell a little. "Okay, Miss Mei Lin."

Mei Lin hugged Little Mei tightly to her chest. The baby started crying, her little face scrunched up and wrinkled. It seemed she wasn't making anyone happy today.

Elizabeth followed Mei Lin into the staff room, two bowls of noodles in her hands. "I'm going to go get tea," she said, putting her soup on the dresser. "Cook Chu said I can serve Grandmother tea when she comes."

"How lovely," said Mei Lin, raising her voice over the baby's cries.

Mei Lin wished she had set up Elizabeth's meeting elsewhere. She wanted to lie on her bed with Little Mei and rest. Between the news Brother Tom brought and Joy's showing up unannounced, she felt emotionally drained. She laid the howling baby on the bed and placed a rolled blanket on either side of her so she wouldn't roll off if someone sat on the bed. She moved quickly, putting the drawer bed in Nurse Bo's room and then filling the bottle with warm water from the thermos.

The door creaked open. "Mei Lin, Elizabeth's grandmother is at the gate."

"Coming," said Mei Lin. Poor Little Mei was so upset she could hardly catch her breath to take the bottle. Mei Lin cradled her in her arms and went to the gate, Elizabeth at her side.

"Xi-wen!" cried the woman, calling Elizabeth by her given Chinese name.

"Grandmother!"

Mei Lin opened the gate and watched the two of them embrace. The older woman had salt-and-pepper hair, cut short close to her ears. She was petite and very attractive and held a package in her arms.

"Oh, I've missed you, child."

"I've missed you, Grandmother," said Elizabeth. "Thank you for coming."

★

CHAPTER

Twenty-Seven

Pull to the front of the house and stay in the cab," ordered Cadre Lu. "Lock the doors and let no one in until you see me wave."

"Got it," said Jiang Park.

Li Na hung on to the seat in front of her. Tires screeched, and at first all she could see was a cloud of dust.

"Come with me," Cadre Lu yelled back at her.

She jumped out of the car and followed the cadre through the swirling dust toward the front door. Grandma Zhou poked her head out, then quickly ducked inside and slammed the door shut.

"Is there a back door?" asked the cadre.

"I'm not sure," said Li Na. "They didn't use one when we were here."

He motioned to two of his deputies to go to the back of the house.

A bloodcurdling scream pierced the silence.

"Jun Lee!" cried Li Na.

"This is the police," Cadre Lu yelled. "Open up or we'll force entry."

"There are secret doors in the house," said Li Na, suddenly remembering the compartments Jin had shown her. "Perhaps they are escaping."

"Stand back," Cadre Lu commanded. He backed up and shot at the lock, then kicked the door open.

Li Na followed the cadre inside to the deserted kitchen.

"Zhang Jun Lee's room is up the stairs, on the right," said Li Na. Just then she thought of the window with the escape tree that was in the teachers' room.

"There is a window in the teachers' room—"

Crash! A herd of PSB officers ran up the steps and swept past Li Na. She turned to open the door to Jun Lee's room.

"Jun Lee!"

Her dear friend lay unconscious on the bed, blood streaming down the right side of her neck, running into her eye, and soaking her hair.

Oh, God, let her be alive. Li Na turned and screamed down the steps, "Doctor, help! Doctor, come quickly. Upstairs!"

Cadre Lu appeared behind her in the doorway and looked inside. "Is this your friend?"

Li Na held on to the doorframe, her stomach queasy, and nodded.

The doctor brushed by them and rushed to Jun Lee's side. Then he looked back at them, his face thunderstruck. "They cut off her ear."

Li Na screamed and collapsed onto her knees as the cadre recoiled in horror.

She pounded the floor with her fists. "No, no, no!" The madness built inside of her till she thought she would burst. She hugged the Bible hidden under her shirt and rocked on her knees, and her thoughts found a voice. "Jesus! Help us!"

She felt a hand on her shoulder and looked up through a glaze of tears at the doctor.

"Mrs. Chen, your friend is alive, but she needs your help. You must collect yourself and help me."

Li Na looked about. The cadre and his men were gone. "What can I do?"

"Go downstairs and find clean cloths right away. Put water to boil on the stove, and bring me the clean cloths right away. Can you do that?"

Li Na sniffed, her breath jagged with shock and grief. "Yes, I'll do that." The doctor extended his hand to help her up, and she stood, shaking. "Please don't let her die."

"I'll do my best," he answered. "She's losing blood. It's good she's unconscious for now."

Li Na flew down the steps, glad to put her hands to doing something to help her friend. She quickly ran outside to the water pump, where she rinsed out a clean pan, pumped it full of water, and ran back inside to put the water on the stove. She hurriedly pulled out every drawer in the kitchen until she found clean dish towels. She grabbed a stack of them and ran back up the stairs.

The doctor was holding a blood-soaked rag near Jun Lee's head. He took a towel from the pile and held it on the side of her head. "Can you hold this for me?"

Li Na gulped. "My hands aren't clean."

"Use my cleanser," said the doctor. "There."

She pumped the cleanser into her hands and wiped them dry on one towel, then took another and, gritting her teeth, put it over Jun Lee's wound.

"Her back was injured yesterday when one of them pushed her down the steps."

"We'll need boards to carry her out, then," said Dr. Xu.

He had tweezers and a bag. "They left the ear," he said.

Li Na shut her eyes. "I'll do better if you don't show me that," she said.

"Why don't you pray?" he asked. "The cadre is gone."

"Pray?"

"Pray to Jesus." He smiled. "I am a Christian."

"You are?"

"Yes, and I am sure it was Jesus who led you to Cadre Lu's door, out of all the cadres in the world."

"Is he a Christian, too?"

"No, but he is not opposed to them. He allows them to meet in his village as long as they obey the laws and remain good citizens. Out of gratitude, the Christians do all they can to serve him and his wife and son."

"That is amazing," said Li Na.

"So I would be pleased to hear you pray until the cadre returns," said the doctor.

Li Na's scalp tingled. This was something she could pour herself into! She took a clean towel from the stack in front of her to replace the one that was now soaked with blood.

"Father, we ask in Jesus' name that you would guide Dr.—"

"Dr. Xu."

"Please guide Dr. Xu as he cares for Jun Lee. Oh, Jesus, I am so disappointed that Jun Lee was hurt like this. Look down on Jun Lee. Cover her with your healing hands. May the blood from the stripes on your back be applied to her now. Heal her body."

Li Na's voice caught. She had determined not to think of Liko, but how can a mother push her son out of her mind? "And, my God, look down on my son, Liko. Surround him with angels and make a way of escape for him, too."

She turned to Dr. Xu. "Can her ear be saved?"

He glanced up from his bag. "I don't know. We must get her to the hospital right away. It's her best chance."

"You mean she could—"

"Not if you keep praying like that," he said.

His voice was kind, and Li Na repeated his words and the tone of them over and over in her heart. *"Not if you keep praying like that."*

"Father, I ask you to do a great miracle in Jun Lee's recovery. Please don't let her wake up to this pain. Please cover her and keep her until we can get medicine—what is that?"

The doctor pointed a needle toward the ceiling until something squirted out of the tip.

"I have no idea if they drugged her," he explained. "Or what they would have drugged her with. This local anesthetic will help numb the area in case she wakens."

"It's the plant downstairs," said Li Na. "They drugged me with the plant."

The doctor gave Jun Lee the shot in the side of her neck. "I'll hold the cloth," he said. "You go get the pan of boiling water and try to find more rags. And bring that plant up here. I want to see what it is."

The doctor held the cloth with his left hand and jotted notes in a black book with his right. Li Na raced downstairs. She washed her hands in the pump, using the soap from the basin, then ran back inside. The water wasn't boiling yet, so she brought the plant upstairs first and set it on the desk in Jun Lee's room.

She turned to go back downstairs and nearly ran into Cadre Lu in the doorway.

"Mrs. Chen, you must come with me," he said. He was out of breath and his face was flushed. "I think we have them all."

"But the doctor," she said. "The doctor needs me."

"Of course," he said. He turned and yelled down the stairs for one of his men, who came up the steps in a flash.

"Help the doctor with Mrs. Zhang," ordered Cadre Lu.

Li Na looked into the assistant's eyes. He seemed like a good man. "You must go outside to the pump and wash your hands first," she said. "Then bring the doctor more clean dishcloths from the kitchen drawers. Also, he needs the pan of boiling water from the stove."

Li Na looked once more at Jun Lee. "Thank you," she said to the doctor.

"You were a good friend to her," he said. "You may have saved her life by getting us here in time."

Li Na nodded. "I won't forget you," she said, then turned and followed Cadre Lu down the stairs.

The cadre showed her the taxicabs parked side by side, with her Eastern Lightning captors inside. Li Na was trembling, and the cadre put his hand at her back to steady her.

"They refuse to talk," said the cadre. "Tell me their names."

Li Na nodded. "I don't know if they are their real names or

not, Cadre Lu." She bent over and looked inside the car. "This is Teacher Liu, who pretended to be nice at first. That's Law Jin beside him. He is the most deceitful of all. He is the one who tricked all of us into thinking he was from a great school in Singapore, sent here to educate us."

"And this one?" he asked.

There was blood on Rong's right hand, and Li Na felt a wave of hatred rush into her belly. She grabbed the side of the back door until her knuckles turned white.

"You are a snake, the daughter of Satan," she said, leaning her head into the car.

Rong curled her lips and hissed at her.

"Forgive, Li Na." Those were Jun Lee's words on the steps the day before.

Suddenly Li Na had the words to combat the snake. "I forgive you, Rong."

Rong gaped at her, her eyes wide with disbelief.

Li Na raised her voice a little more. "And I bind the strong man of Eastern Lightning, and I plunder his house in Jesus' name." Li Na stood up straight. She had said Jesus' name in front of the doctor, the PSB, and the Eastern Lightning. And she felt good.

"What did you just say?" asked Cadre Lu.

"You would have had to be here before to understand it," said Li Na. "You arrest her body. I arrest her spirit."

Suddenly Rong let out a strangled cry. The driver jumped out of the taxi and slammed the door, visibly shaken.

Rong's mouth was opened like a sepulcher, and she hissed at them as her tongue went in and out like a snake's.

"I thought earlier she was hissing just to be mean," said Li Na.

Cadre Lu stooped over to get a better look. "That woman is crazy," he said.

Rong had fallen over on her side and was writhing like a snake, her hands handcuffed behind her back.

"Look at the blood on her hands." He shouted to another aide, "Officer Chou!"

"Yes, sir."

"Handcuff her feet," the cadre ordered.

The officer ducked down to look inside the taxi. "Yes, sir. With your permission, I may require help."

"Certainly. Mrs. Chen, are these all of the Eastern Lightning members?"

"No, there are two more—Qi and the old woman who stuck her head out of the door when we came—Grandma Zhou. Rong and Qi just came here two days ago. Check the panel in the wall on the left when you go into the teaching room upstairs. It slides. She may be in there."

The cadre's eyebrows rose. "Are there any other secret panels you know of?"

"Not in this house," said Li Na. "But I know of a couple in the first house we went to before we came here."

The front door slammed, and Li Na looked up to see the doctor and the officer carrying Jun Lee downstairs on a stretcher they rigged out of boards and blankets.

"We must take her to the hospital," Dr. Xu called to the cadre. "I've done everything I can for her here."

Li Na looked at Cadre Lu. "I'd like to ride with them."

He frowned. "I'm sorry, Mrs. Chen. I will need your help in locating the other house and filing the reports. We will need to trust the doctor to care for her."

Li Na knew that the cadre was right. Her heart was in so many places at once. The cadre went inside with some men to check the paneled wall, and Li Na followed Dr. Xu to the taxi.

"Please, if she wakes up, tell her that I came, and she is safe. We are going to free her husband now."

"She will probably be in shock," the doctor said. "You've both been through a horrendous ordeal."

Li Na saw pity in his eyes, and she drank in the comfort it brought. A thought came to her. She turned aside and pulled her

283

Bible out of her shirt, then tore out a page—Matthew 12. She folded it up and handed it to the doctor.

"Here," she said. "Give her this. It will help."

The doctor smiled. "Write down your address and a phone number where I can reach you."

"I don't have a phone," said Li Na. "All of our phones and identity cards were stolen from us. But I'll write down Mrs. Zhang's address. Perhaps you can notify her mother-in-law, who lives with her. She will want to know."

"Can she pray like you?"

"Oh yes! Much better than I."

"Then Mrs. Zhang will have to recover."

"Thank you," said Li Na. "I will come to see her as soon as I can." She watched until the taxi turned the corner and was out of view.

Cadre Lu walked out of the house, his officers behind him.

"Officer Fu," he said, "I want you to stay and take pictures. Be sure to get several angles of the bedrooms."

"Yes, sir."

"Mrs. Chen, after seeing this, I think we will need more manpower. We will need to go to Fen Gui, about four hours south of here, to get some more deputies. How long did it take you to get here from the other house?"

"About three hours."

"Very well. We'll meet at my house tonight. We should make it to your friends by tomorrow morning."

"Tomorrow morning?" Li Na was in a daze.

"I'll need to file reports at the station this afternoon and rally a team together."

Li Na had hoped to get to Kwan So today, but she understood Cadre Lu had to follow certain procedures. Besides, she was exhausted.

"You didn't find Grandma Zhou?" she asked.

The cadre shook his head. "I don't know how an old lady

like that can escape from us when the younger ones were captured."

"She did not talk," said Li Na. "But I sensed she was more evil than the rest."

"More evil than Rong?" he asked. "That woman is spooky."

"Yes, I think so," answered Li Na. "In a strange way, it seemed as though she was in charge of a lot of what went on in that house—maybe in charge of what goes on in a lot of places."

"I'll make note of that in the report," said the cadre. "I hope we find her." He wrote several things down in his book, then flipped it shut. "Let's go."

"My things!" exclaimed Li Na. "I need a moment to collect my things and Mrs. Zhang's belongings."

"I'll order my men to do that," said the cadre. "I want them to take pictures first; then they can pack for you and bring your things with them to the house."

"Very well," said Li Na. She suddenly wished she hadn't left her underwear drying over the desk chair, but there was nothing she could do about that now. "I need to use the bathroom."

She quickly pulled the toilet paper out of her pocket and stared at the wad, remembering the day she had warned Jun Lee to travel with toilet paper in her pockets at all times. Sweet Jun Lee had far greater problems to contend with now. Li Na felt as though she'd lived ten years in the last twenty-four hours.

"Did you find the cell phones?" she asked the cadre when she returned. "Jin took Wong San Ming's cell phone and all of our money and identity cards."

"I'll have my men search the prisoners and the house."

"Please, may I call my son's fiancée in Shanghai?" she asked.

"Yes, and ask her to make a formal government report in Shanghai. A family member should report this incident to the authorities. It will give credence to my report last night."

"Thank you for being so caring—and honest," said Li Na. "The Eastern Lightning people have been known to bribe cadres less honorable than you."

While Cadre Lu searched the grounds one more time, Li Na called Mother Su's cell phone. Thankfully, Liko had made her memorize the number before Mei Lin left on her trip.

"Hello, this is Brother Tom."

"Brother Tom? Do you know Mother Su and Mei Lin?"

"Yes, I know them. Who is this?"

"This is Chen Li Na, Liko's mother."

"Oh, hello," said Brother Tom. "Mei Lin told me about you just this morning. I am Pastor Wong's assistant."

"Oh, good. Well, we're in trouble here. . . ."

* ✳ *

CHAPTER

Twenty-Eight

All of the children had gathered at the gate to watch. The boys all said hello to Elizabeth's grandmother and went back to playing. Lydia and Priscilla lingered nearby, watching. Lydia wiped a tear from her cheek.

Mei Lin extended her hand. "My name is Mei Lin. Welcome to our orphanage."

"I am Mrs. Zemin. Are you the one who talked to my granddaughter about finding me?"

"Yes, I am," said Mei Lin. "We are so glad you decided to come."

Mrs. Zemin smiled and drew Elizabeth close to her side. "Oh, after I knew where my girl was, you couldn't have kept me away."

Elizabeth seemed to melt into the woman's side. "I've prepared lunch and tea for you, Grandmother."

"You have? Well, isn't that nice?"

"May I show her now?" asked Elizabeth.

"Certainly," said Mei Lin. "Why don't you introduce your friends to her first? They've been waiting."

Elizabeth looked embarrassed.

"Shall I introduce them?" Mei Lin asked, and Elizabeth nodded. "Mrs. Zemin, these girls are your granddaughter's best friends. This is Priscilla, and this is Lydia. And this little package in my arms is Little Mei. Girls, say hello to Mrs. Zemin."

The girls quietly said hello and bowed politely.

Mrs. Zemin laughed. "I see you are learning traditional manners in your school."

Mei Lin held Little Mei up to her shoulder for a burp.

Mrs. Zemin patted the baby's back. "And it's nice to meet you, too, Little Mei. Is she named after you?"

Mei Lin nodded, pleased that the woman noticed. "She is named Mei after me, and Bo is for the nurse who helped me clean her up after I found her."

"Mother Su told me what happened," said Mrs. Zemin. "I hope you find parents for her soon."

"Thank you," said Mei Lin. "Elizabeth, why don't you take your grandmother to the staff room for lunch. Lydia and Priscilla, did you eat lunch yet?"

The two girls nodded and watched solemnly as Elizabeth led her grandmother away by the hand.

"What do you think she has in that package?" Lydia asked Priscilla.

"I don't know," said Priscilla. "But I know what I'd want if it were me."

"What?"

"A baby. A tiny little baby just like Little Mei."

"Priscilla, you're too young to have a baby like that. Besides, people don't just give away real babies in boxes all wrapped up."

"Where do they come from?" asked Priscilla. "I want to get one."

Mei Lin smiled. "One day soon we'll have to talk about that, girls. Would you like to learn where babies come from?"

Both of them nodded. Then Lydia giggled and ran off, pulling Priscilla behind her. They reminded Mei Lin of her school days with Ping.

Little Mei burped, leaving a little package of her own on Mei Lin's shoulder. She cradled her again to feed her the bottle, trying to keep the sun out of her eyes.

Suddenly tires screeched behind her, and Mei Lin whirled around.

"Mother Su! Brother Tom! What—"

"Mei Lin, you must come with me," said Brother Tom. "It's your father and Liko."

Mother Su quickly came through the gate. "Mrs. Chen just called. There's trouble."

"What kind of trouble?"

"Grab your identity card and pocketbook," said Brother Tom. "I'll tell you on the way."

Mother Su took the baby, and Mei Lin sprang into action. She raced into the staff house and found her purse and identity card.

"I have to go out for a while," she explained as she rushed into the room. "Mother Su is here, and she will come back to talk to both of you."

"All right," said Mrs. Zemin. "I hope everything is all right."

Mei Lin nearly burst into tears. She didn't know what had happened, but she could tell from Brother Tom's urgency that something was terribly wrong. As soon as she was in the car, Brother Tom took off down the alley, turning left at the corner near the garbage cans.

"Mrs. Chen called Mother Su this morning," he said. "It turns out that the leaders weren't meeting with the Haggai Institute after all. The teachers were from Eastern Lightning."

"Eastern Lightning?" Mei Lin repeated. "Pastor Wong told us about them. Why would they go with Eastern Lightning to be taught?"

"They didn't," answered Tom. He stopped at a red light and looked over at her. "They were kidnapped."

"What? Who was kidnapped?"

"I'm not sure yet," answered Tom. "Liko's mother said there were at least thirty leaders who signed up for the course."

"Mrs. Chen escaped?" asked Mei Lin. Her throat was tight.

"She's the only one," said Brother Tom. "She asked us to pray hard. She has reason to believe that your father, Liko, and

Pastor Wong are being held and tortured by them. She is leading the PSB to them."

"Then they should be freed soon."

"It's not that easy," said Brother Tom. "Mrs. Chen said that the Eastern Lightning members posed as Christians from the Haggai Institute, but when they got to the house on a mountain, they staged a police raid and everyone separated into groups of two. Liko is with Pastor Wong. Your father is with Pastor Zhang."

The horror of what happened was just sinking in. "What will we do?" Mei Lin asked. "Are we going to try to find them?"

"No," said Brother Tom. "The local police told Mrs. Chen that a family member must file an official report with the government. That's why I came to get you." He parked the car in the lot in front of a large cement building and jumped out. "I will testify to what Mrs. Chen said. She said the cadre told her it is urgent that we file a proper case. Then the authorities can help us find them. You will need to tell them that you are a guest with Mother Su and Sun Tao."

"But—then they will know we are Christians," said Mei Lin. "They will be able to track our house churches and maybe the orphanage."

"I know," said Brother Tom. "But the pastors may die if we do not file the report. Let's go."

It was after seven o'clock and still daylight when Brother Tom finally dropped Mei Lin off at the orphanage. Neither of them talked much on the way home. Filing the report had taken hours, and they were questioned extensively. By the time they were finished, Mei Lin wasn't sure if they had helped Father and Liko or betrayed them.

"Here," said Brother Tom. He handed her Mother Su's cell phone as she got out of the car. "Mrs. Chen will want to talk to you if she calls again. You can tell her that the report is filed."

Mei Lin nodded. "Thank you. Thank you for all you have done."

"I am going to assemble our members for an all-night prayer-and-fasting vigil. Prayer will bring them home."

"Yes," said Mei Lin. "Prayer. Thank you."

She gently shut the car door and unlocked the gate. As soon as she was inside, Brother Tom sped off down the alley.

The children rushed to her side as soon as she came in.

"Miss Mei Lin! Miss Mei Lin!" David and Jonathan hugged her legs.

"Hello, boys," Mei Lin said softly as she bent down to hug them.

"Elizabeth's grandmother left," said Lydia.

"I helped with Little Mei," said Priscilla. "Mother Su says I was a big help."

"Oh, thank you, Priscilla," said Mei Lin. "You are a great helper with the baby."

"You want to play ball with us, Miss Mei Lin?" asked Mark.

For the first time, Mei Lin smiled. "Oh, Mark, thanks for asking. I haven't eaten since breakfast and I'm quite tired. Maybe later?"

"Okay."

Mother Su appeared in the doorway of the staff house, holding Little Mei.

"Is she asleep?" asked Mei Lin as she stepped inside.

"Oh, she's close to it. I think she's waiting for you to come home. I have a bottle ready for her inside. Look, she turned her head toward your voice to find you."

Mei Lin smiled.

"How did it go?"

Mei Lin sat on her bed and removed her shoes, then slid up to the headboard to rest her back against it. "Here, I'll take Little Mei."

Mother Su handed her the baby.

"It took a long time . . . and I'm still not sure if I helped to

291

rescue Liko and Father and all the others or if my report will get them arrested for being Christians. Brother Tom gave me your cell phone. Is that okay? He thought Liko's mother might call again and want to talk to me."

"Of course," answered Mother Su. She turned the fan on low and pointed it toward the bed, then sat at the foot of her bed. "Is that who that was? Liko's mother? She was a very nice lady, but she was extremely upset."

Little Mei wiggled around, and Mei Lin lifted her for a burp. "How did it go with Elizabeth today?"

"We are working with the grandmother to help her get custody. She's coming to pick her up on Friday."

"For good?"

"Yes," said Mother Su. "I'm sure that Mrs. Zemin will be able to persuade the courts to give her custody—that is, if Elizabeth's father even contests it. That's why we are waiting until Friday. She is going to call Elizabeth's father and ask for custody."

"Wow, that's fast," said Mei Lin. "Where is Elizabeth? I didn't see her with the girls when I came."

"Cook Chu and Elizabeth are talking in the bunkhouse," said Mother Su. "I wanted some time to talk to you, so I asked Cook Chu to stick around and watch the children for me."

"Oh," said Mei Lin. She cradled Little Mei again and looked down into the baby's face. She was so innocent and helpless.

"Joy talked to me today," said Mother Su.

Mei Lin looked up. "Did she tell you I was rude?" she asked. "I am so sorry. I was very unkind. She just—she just showed up out of nowhere. I was stunned."

"Do you remember the dream I had about you, Mei Lin?"

"I was being chased by a bear and a woman riding a dragon. Do you think I'm being chased now?"

"Yes," replied Mother Su. "You were running from two kinds of trouble. There was one thing I didn't tell you."

"What's that?"

"After the woman on the dragon approached you from behind, you climbed higher and used your hands to try to bat her back down the tree. Remember that?"

"Yes. A silly attempt to save myself."

"Well, someone called out in prayer for you. He cried, 'She needs her mother, Lord. I don't know how to help her.'"

"Who—" Mei Lin started to ask.

"Your father," Mother Su answered softly. "Your father knew you needed your mother's help to stop the attacks."

Mei Lin put her hand to her mouth, tears springing to her eyes. "Baba," she whispered. "Here, will you hold her?"

Mei Lin put Little Mei into Mother Su's arms and pulled out the bottom drawer of her dresser. She pulled out the scarf and held it against her face, turning her head away from Mother Su. "Oh, Baba. How did you know? How did you know?"

"I believe God gave me the dream in answer to your father's prayers," Mother Su said softly. "Sometimes a girl needs her mother."

Mei Lin sat down on the bed, covered her face with the scarf, and sobbed. Mother Su laid Little Mei in her drawer bed and walked over to Mei Lin.

Mei Lin cried harder when Mother Su held her. For the first time, she realized the void left inside of her after her mother's death—a void that Amah couldn't reach. Her father gave her the scarf to connect her to her mother, because somehow he knew that she needed her mother right now. She pulled back from Mother Su. She wasn't sure how to receive motherly love. And Father—

How did he know?

"Oh, Baba," she cried.

"Mei Lin, what is troubling you so? Even before the kidnapping you seemed as though you were holding back some terrible secret."

"The bear in front of me?" asked Mei Lin, looking at Mother Su through wavy panels of tears.

Mother Su nodded.

Mei Lin reached into the drawer bed and wrapped Little Mei's fist around her finger, stroking the little one's hand. She sighed deeply. "I cannot have a child."

"How do you know?"

"I stopped my menstrual cycle," said Mei Lin. She looked over at Mother Su, her lips trembling. "No one knows. It stopped after Shanghai Prison. Do you know how hard it is to—to live with this? The beatings are not just a part of my past—they've prophesied my future. I have to forgive the warden every day for the beatings that I took, for the food deprivation, or whatever it was that stopped my cycle. Now Liko will marry only half a woman. And Amah will say that I am cursed by the gods."

Her voice cracked, and she bit her lower lip to keep herself from crying again. She hated hearing the words out loud—*half a woman—cursed by the gods*. She was in the flower of her youth, and every beautiful colored petal had been stolen. She rubbed Little Mei's dimpled knuckles with her fingers.

"I haven't told anyone. I don't know what to do. What if Amah doesn't believe in Jesus because of this? She is so superstitious. And Liko—he deserves his own child. How can I take that from him?"

Mother Su pulled her close and held her again. Mei Lin wept bitterly for the loss of the child she would never conceive and for Liko and for her father, who would never hold his own grandchild. Mei Lin had not cried so hard since she was in prison.

Mother Su held her for some time, stroking her hair and rubbing her back.

"Now I know why the women in the Bible hated barrenness," said Mei Lin, sniffling. "I see why Sarah and Hannah and Elizabeth were tormented. It's a horrible thing not to have children—to never look into the face of your own flesh and blood. Oh, God!"

Mother Su didn't say much; she just held her and whispered the name *Jesus* every once in a while.

Finally Mei Lin pulled a tissue out of her pocket and blew her nose. "Now you know," she said.

The room was quiet for some time, and Mei Lin tuned her ear to the quiet sucking sounds Little Mei was making. She was nearly asleep.

Mei Lin began to breathe more easily. She wiped her tears as they came, but her sobbing had stopped. She heard Cook Chu calling the children to prepare for their snack outside.

"Such a heavy burden to carry all alone," said Mother Su. "No wonder your father was worried."

"I don't know how he knew," said Mei Lin. "But I believe you. He gave me this scarf at my going-away party before I left. It was—it was my mother's." Mei Lin sat up on the bed and smiled a little. "He flung the scarf high into the sky over my head two or three times. There was a soft breeze that night, and it seemed to pick up the scarf and curl it into waves until it landed on my shoulders. Then . . . then he said, 'An invisible red thread connects those who are destined to meet, regardless of time, place, or circumstance. The thread may stretch or tangle . . .'"

"But never break," finished Mother Su.

"Yes," Mei Lin whispered. "It will never break. How did the dream end?"

"Well, I heard your father calling out to God to help you. I started toward you to help you, and then I woke up."

Mei Lin looked down at her knees. "He called out to God to help me. Now he's the one who needs help." She looked up at Mother Su. "I don't know what to do."

"I'll tell you what to do," said Mother Su. "I'll get you some hot tea while you get dressed for bed. I had Cook Chu fill the tub for you—the water is probably still warm enough. Did you have supper?"

"No," said Mei Lin. "I didn't have lunch, either. But I'm not that hungry. Hot tea would be good."

"Hot tea it is. Little Mei is enjoying her sleep, so you should probably do the same. We can talk more about helping your father and Liko tomorrow. You've done your part by filing the report."

Mei Lin yawned. "I am exhausted."

Mother Su left the room to prepare the tea, and Mei Lin took a quick bath. She slipped into a nightgown and sat at the head of her bed, putting her feet underneath the sheet. Her eyes hurt from crying, but her heart felt better.

"Here you are," said Mother Su as she handed her a little white mug of tea and a plate of plum tarts.

"Thank you," said Mei Lin. "And thank you for talking to me. You certainly are tenacious!" She grinned.

Mother Su adjusted her sheet. "I'm not your mother, but I believe God wanted me to stand in for her while you're here in Shanghai."

"You've been wonderful."

Mother Su left to tuck the children into bed. Mei Lin sipped her tea and watched Little Mei sleeping under her tiny sheet. After a time, she slid down inside her sheet and prayed until she drifted off to sleep.

Twenty-Nine

Have you ever had a tendon taken out of your body. . . . I don't have any pain medicine. . . ."

The words swam around Kwan So's mind like swordfish in the fog, needling his soul. Music throbbed in his head like the galloping of demons on dark horses, riding with spears in their fists. Racing, galloping, racing faster, chasing through the fog to find him. He needed to get away, but his legs wouldn't move.

Slam. Footsteps.

"You haven't given him a chance to convert. Why can't you . . ."

So tried to listen, but the voice faded. The horses were galloping on his chest now, down his arm, down his leg. He had to get away. He had to run.

"You can't just dump him in the pond!" someone screamed.

The swordfish were back.

No!

The horses found him.

No!

Dark. A cocoon. He was flying now in a cocoon. A wet cocoon.

Was this what it felt like to die?

Mei Lin! O God, don't let the horses find Mei Lin!

The wind moved then and pushed harder against the deep

fog, swirling it into spiral clouds, around and around. There—in the middle. The red thread!

Kwan So reached for it—his hand would not move. MOVE! His hand was useless, but as he watched, the thread moved toward him anyway, stretching, reaching.

Mei Lin! Mei Lin!

———

"Does this look like the place?" asked Cadre Lu.

"Yes, I think so," said Li Na. Her eyes searched the outside of the house, which was bathed in the glow of the early morning sun. "Oh no. It looks like the vans are gone."

"Maybe the old lady warned them we were coming," said Cadre Lu. "I was afraid of that." He picked up his radio.

"All cars, this is the house. The vans are missing. Approach with caution. Cars two and three, block the road. Cars four and five, take the back. I'll take the front. Now!"

All of the cars sped onto the property at once. Li Na hung on to her seat, barely noticing the speed. Her eyes searched for Kwan So and Pastor Zhang. Nothing moved.

"Stay here!" Cadre Lu yelled back at her. He ran to the front door of the house and opened it easily. Within seconds he ran back outside. "Empty!"

Li Na got out of the car and ran inside. Frantically, she searched the rooms.

So's suitcase lay on the floor in one of the bedrooms. The bed was stripped, but there—on the floor. Blood!

"Noooooooooooooo!" Li Na screamed, her hands at her face. She felt dizzy.

"Mrs. Chen!" Cadre Lu ran to her side. "What is it?"

"There's blood on the floor!" she cried, pointing.

She felt sick and held her stomach. She imagined So with his ear cut off. Cadre Lu helped her to the chair. He bent over and touched the blood.

"It's fresh," he said. He pulled out his radio. "Cars four and five. Anything out back?"

"No, sir," came the reply.

Li Na sat with her face in her hands and quietly prayed. "Oh, Lord, this is fresh blood. And this is So's room. Please tell us what to do to help him."

"Mrs. Chen," said Cadre Lu, "perhaps you would feel better if you went outside and got some fresh air."

Li Na went out back to the patio and walked to the knob of the hill where she had heard the word *scatter* only two weeks before. "Oh, God, you spoke to me then. Will you speak to me now?"

Instantly her mind flashed back to Mother Zhang's dream. *What did she say again? She said that God would pull her out of troubled waters. Then what?* Li Na tried to calm her thoughts and remember her exact words. . . .

"After you were taken out of the water, you turned around and extended your hand to pull Kwan So to safety." Li Na stood up. Troubled waters!

"Kwan So!" she yelled. "Kwan So!"

She ran full speed down the hill, throwing off her shoes when she reached the bottom. She looked back—Cadre Lu and his men were close behind her.

"Look!" she cried. Bubbles were coming up out of the water about ten feet from the edge of the pond.

Li Na dived into the water and swam out to the bubbles. She couldn't touch the bottom! "Help me!" she cried. "He's under here!"

Li Na flipped forward into the water and dived deep. There, through the brown mud, was a sack! Quickly she swam toward it and tried to get underneath to lift it. Her lungs were burning, screaming for air.

Suddenly Cadre Lu was beside her, lifting. Li Na squatted and then pushed upward, moving the sack with Kwan So inside. Slowly his body moved upward through the water, and together they swam to the top. Li Na gasped for air, all the while calling, "Lift him up! Get his head up!"

Four of them pushed the sack to the shore and lifted the body.

Mother Zhang's dream was his only hope now. "You said bring him to safety!" Li Na cried. "Bring him to safety! Don't let him die!"

Cadre Lu stared wildly at her. He probably thought she was talking to him.

Li Na tore open the sack. "Lay him on his side," she said. His face was swollen, and had it not been for Mother Zhang's dream, Li Na would not have recognized him.

As soon as they laid him on his side, water streamed out of his mouth and he sputtered. More water came from his nose and mouth.

"Kwan So! Kwan So! Don't die!"

"They can't be too far ahead of us," said Cadre Lu. He got on his radio again. "Cars four and five, take the southbound road. Car three, take the north. We just pulled a live body out of the pond. They can't be far. Car two, we need a doctor here."

Kwan So sputtered and coughed. Li Na pushed the wet hair back from his forehead. One eye was completely swollen shut— she couldn't see any eyelashes. The other had a thin line of eyelashes protruding through the creases. She kept looking for injuries as she dried his face with the end of her shirt.

"Quickly, go get towels and a blanket!" she said to the officers standing around her. So's left forearm was broken, and she gently moved it by his side.

The doctor appeared and dropped to his knees beside her. He pushed on So's abdomen. After he had worked on him for ten minutes, the choking and coughing subsided.

The doctor ran his hands over So's legs. "His left femur is broken," he said. "And his left arm."

Li Na heaved a jagged sigh. "Is he going to be all right?"

"We'll know more when he regains consciousness."

Suddenly Kwan So opened his eyes. "Li Na?" he said hoarsely.

"Kwan So!" cried Li Na. She took his head in her arms and cradled him. "Yes, it's me, Li Na! You're alive, So! Oh, thank God you're alive!"

Talking threw him into an awful coughing fit.

"Lift him up," said the doctor. "I'll hold his arm."

Li Na lifted his head and back until So was completely in her arms. Immediately, he threw up more water. "Zhang Liang," he muttered.

"Is he in the pond?" asked Li Na.

So shook his head. "I don't know."

Cadre Lu came down the hill. "Is he all right?"

"He talked," said the doctor. "That's a step in the right direction."

"Cadre Lu," said Li Na. "Could Zhang Liang be in the pond, too?"

Cadre Lu ran down to the edge of the pond and searched for bubbles.

"Wait—the secret panel!" Li Na called.

Cadre Lu whirled around. "What secret panel?"

Li Na looked at the doctor, the question in her eyes.

"Go ahead," he said. "I'll hold him up until you get back. Send down one of those officers to help me."

Li Na called, "Cadre Lu, follow me!"

Li Na left the doctor beside So and quickly led Cadre Lu back up the hill and into the main teaching room. She showed him the secret panel hidden in the wall. With the cadre's help, they easily slid the panel door open. A man rolled out.

"Liang!" Li Na cried. "Is he—"

Cadre Lu felt his neck. "He's alive."

Zhang Liang lay unconscious in a rumpled heap on the floor. Li Na knelt beside him and prayed silently over his bloody body. He had cuts and bruises on his face and upper body, but he didn't look as bad as Kwan So. There was a large swelling on the top of his head—he'd obviously taken an awful beating.

"They probably thought he'd die," said Cadre Lu. "These people are monsters!"

Li Na looked up at the cadre, tears in her eyes. "I'm just glad you are here to report this," she said. "This man is the husband to my friend Zhang Jun Lee."

"Ah, the woman whose ear was cut off?"

"Yes," said Li Na. "Shall we take them to the same hospital?"

"We will try to transfer everyone to DuYan hospital. Isn't that the hospital that is closest to all of you?"

"Yes," replied Li Na. "DuYan is the Zhangs' village. Zhang Liang's mother lives there with them. She will want to be with them."

"Go get the doctor," said Cadre Lu. "I need a full report on the condition of both men as soon as possible."

Li Na grabbed another blanket and a pillow and ran back down the hill to So. "They need you inside," she told the doctor.

"The officers are getting a bed for this one," said the doctor. "He's asking for you."

So's arm was wrapped stiff inside a towel that the doctor hung around his neck. His leg had two sticks on either side with cloths holding them together.

"You work quickly, doctor," said Li Na. "Zhang Liang is in the house, the main room."

"Keep his head elevated," the doctor said to the officers. "Take him to the car."

Then he left, his black bag in hand, and the four officers carried So, wrapped in a blanket, to the taxicab. Li Na hurriedly kept pace beside them, trying to get So to talk.

"Kwan So, can you hear me?" asked Li Na. "Wiggle your hand if you can hear me."

He didn't respond. Park slid the front seat of his taxi backward so that it lay flat. "I took a pregnant woman to the hospital one time like this," he said.

The men slid Kwan So into the reclined passenger seat. Li Na slid a board underneath both legs so his broken leg would be supported. Then she laid the pillow under his head. It was warm outside, but his skin was cold to the touch. She covered him with the dry blanket, tucking in the sides so his arms and legs wouldn't fall off the edge.

After she was finished, she opened all the doors of the taxi so they could breathe. Sweat was dripping into her eyes. She wiped it with the back of her sleeve.

"Kwan So, please—can you hear me?"

So coughed a little. His hand moved!

Li Na breathed a sigh of relief. "We found Zhang Liang," she said. "He's alive."

So smiled slightly. His right eye opened just a crack.

"You're going to be okay," said Li Na. She felt the flutter of relief in her stomach. She took his hand and held it to her face. "I'm so glad we found you. So, please—was Liko with you? Did he stay here with you and Liang after we left?"

No answer.

"So, can you hear me? I need to know if Liko was with you. Did he stay here with you?"

So didn't open his eye this time. "No," he whispered hoarsely and then coughed.

"Do you know where they took him?" Li Na asked. She hated to make him talk because she could tell it hurt. But she had to find her son.

"No," he whispered again. "Sorry."

Li Na patted his hand. "It's okay, we will find him."

She covered So with the blanket and made sure his head was propped well, then ran back inside to see Pastor Zhang.

"Is he talking at all?" she asked the doctor.

He looked up at her. "He was badly beaten. Are you his wife?"

"No," Li Na answered. "My—" She put her hand to her mouth and began to tremble. Every dark thought she'd pushed out of her mind for the last three days came forward to torment her. "My—my son was kidnapped by these people. Please, I have to find my son."

Her body trembled. All the swimming fish were on shore now, flipping and jerking and silently screaming for home. Tears streamed down her face. Thoughts marched through her mind. Scenes of Chen Baio and then of Liko—fists, boots, shouts, clubs, more fists . . . She turned and stumbled into the living room and fell to her knees. "Liko, oh, Liko."

After some time, she felt strong arms lifting her to her feet. The cadre handed her a wad of toilet paper. "Here, blow your nose. We will help you find your son."

Li Na went to the bathroom and put water on her face. She used the toilet and then towel-dried her hair, which smelled like the pond.

Cadre Lu knocked at the door. "Let's go."

Li Na quickly dried her ears with the towel and walked out the door. "May I use your cell phone?" she asked.

She tapped in the number Brother Tom had given her the day before. "Brother Tom? We found Kwan So. . . ."

———

"Father!" Mei Lin sat straight up in bed. She was out of breath, her heart thumping. It was nine o'clock already!

Little Mei was gone and a note was left on the bed.

Mei Lin,
   I thought you would need to rest. I have Little Mei with me.
                        Love,
                        Mother Su

Mei Lin jumped to the floor and threw open her drawers and dressed herself.

"I'm coming, Father," she said. "I'm coming."

Mei Lin did not know where she was going, but her dream empowered her to believe that she would find her father. He had called her in her dream. She flung the red thread out toward him. Did he catch it? She didn't know. But she knew she had to find him. *Now.*

She brushed her teeth and then her hair in a fury of strokes, pulling it all back into a ponytail. After using the bathroom and washing up, she carefully tied her mother's scarf to the long shoulder strap on her pocketbook and went outside. Cook Chu was carrying Little Mei on one shoulder while cleaning up from breakfast. Mei Lin ran over and kissed the back of her little head.

"Where is Mother Su?" she asked.

"In there," Cook Chu said, pointing. "Teaching the students."

"Please—tell her—tell her I left. I'll call her later."

Cook Chu stopped working. "Are you all right, Mei Lin?"

"I'll be fine," she said.

Just then the gate swung open, and Brother Tom came running toward her.

"Mei Lin! Good news!"

"What? Is it Father? What happened?"

"Chen Li Na just called my cell phone. Your father—he's alive."

"Alive?" asked Mei Lin. "Is he all right? I was just going to go find him. I had a dream about him, and he was calling me—are you sure he's all right?"

Brother Tom motioned for her to sit down at the bench. He leaned forward, his face intense. "Your father is being transported to DuYan hospital. Mrs. Chen said he was terribly beaten and nearly drowned. Truthfully, he sounds pretty bad."

"Oh no!" cried Mei Lin. "I heard him calling to me this morning in a dream. I knew he was in trouble." She stood up, her hand on the scarf now tied to her purse. "I must go see him."

Brother Tom stood up, his cell phone in hand. "Of course," he said. "I will arrange for you to take a train to WuMa. You can take a taxi from there to the hospital."

Mei Lin stopped him before he made the call. "Did she say they found Liko?"

Brother Tom shook his head. "Liko is with Pastor Wong. They haven't found them yet."

Mei Lin turned her head away, her fist to her mouth.

"Mei Lin, he is with Pastor Wong. If I were in an encounter with Eastern Lightning, I can't think of anyone I'd rather be with than Pastor Wong. Except maybe Jesus!"

Mei Lin smiled at that. "Do you have a number where I can reach Mrs. Chen?"

"Yes, but it's the cadre's cell phone. You have to choose your words wisely."

"I will," said Mei Lin. She took down the number and stuffed it into her pocket. While Brother Tom checked on the time for the next train to WuMa, Mei Lin went to the schoolroom and tapped lightly on the door.

Mother Su poked her head outside the door. "Mei Lin! How are you feeling?"

Mei Lin motioned her outside. Mother Su came out and shut the door behind her.

"I had a dream this morning. Father was calling me, and I threw him the red thread." She fingered her scarf, searching for words as she touched the strands of red that ran through the silk. "I woke up, and I knew he needed me. I didn't know if he caught the thread."

She looked over at Brother Tom. "But then Brother Tom came and said Liko's mother called this morning. Father is badly beaten. He was nearly drowned by Eastern Lightning, and he's going to the DuYan Hospital."

Mother Su gasped. "Oh no! What are you going to do?"

"I would like to go," said Mei Lin. Deep inside she knew she had to go, but out of respect for Mother Su, she did not demand that she leave.

"Of course you must go," said Mother Su.

Mei Lin looked back at Little Mei. "I thought about Little Mei last night. I wanted to keep her for selfish reasons—just so I wouldn't have to face my family. I thought that was okay at first. But now—now I know it's wrong to want a baby just so I don't have to face my family. I mean, I love her. And I do want her—but not for the wrong reasons. Do you know what I mean?"

Mother Su gave her a little hug. "I know what you mean."

"Please, tell Joy that I was rude, and I know she and her husband will be good Christian parents to Little Mei."

"I'll tell her," said Mother Su. "And you know, you were a perfect mother to Little Mei. Everyone says so. Cook Chu and Nurse Bo and even Chang noticed how nurturing you are. I don't think God gave you a mother's heart to take it away. I think there's hope for you to have your own baby."

Mei Lin sighed. "I'm afraid to hope. It will hurt too much if it doesn't happen."

Mother Su patted her back. "Well, don't think about that now, Mei Lin. God has a way of working these things out. I'm just sorry to see you leave. Do you think you'll come back?"

"Maybe," said Mei Lin. "But not for a few months. My father needs me now. Liko probably needs me, too. I wish I knew. After my dream, I know I need to help bring them home."

Mother Su drew Mei Lin into her arms. "Oh, Mei Lin. Every time you walk into our lives you change us. Do you know that?"

Mei Lin allowed Mother Su to hold her. It didn't feel as strange this time.

"I've made a lot of mistakes," said Mei Lin.

Mother Su whispered, "I don't remember any mistakes. I remember love—lots of love. Love for the children, love for my family, and especially love for Little Mei."

Mei Lin turned, searching the courtyard for Cook Chu. She must have taken Little Mei inside for her nap. "I don't know how I'll say good-bye to her." Tears sprang to her eyes, but Mei Lin didn't let Mother Su see them. "Will you tell Chang I said good-bye?"

"Yes, but now you must tell the children," said Mother Su. "I'll wait for Brother Tom."

Mei Lin stood at the bottom of the steps and put her thoughts together. She would tell them her father was in the hospital. Most of all, she would tell them she loved them. She walked up the steps to the schoolroom one last time.

Even though the police were kind to them, just being in the large station made Liko nervous. These were the people who enforced the laws in China—the good laws and the bad laws.

"May I make a long-distance call?" asked Pastor Wong. He leaned over the desk of the head of the Police Station No. 5 in FuZhou County. "There are people who are worried about us."

"Certainly," said the officer. He handed Pastor Wong the phone and then stood right beside him while he called.

Liko grinned. Pastor Wong had the courage of Daniel in the lions' den! After a moment he handed the phone to Liko.

"Liko?" said Mei Lin's voice. "Is it really you?"

"It's me," said Liko. "I'm fine. But I made some stupid mistakes."

"Me too," said Mei Lin. "A lot of mistakes. They're transferring Father to the DuYan Hospital. Will you meet me there? I'll be there by tomorrow morning."

"Yes, as soon as I can." He glanced at the officer, who was still standing beside them, his arms folded. "I love you."

"I love you, too."

Liko hung up the phone.

The officer rolled his eyes and grinned. "Important phone call, huh?" He walked behind the desk and started filing folders.

Pastor Wong picked up the phone and punched the numbers again. "Tom? Have you heard from the others?"

Liko heard Pastor Wong laugh for the first time since the kidnapping—it was a good feeling.

"Why don't you come with Mei Lin to the DuYan Hospital? We need to talk in person." Pastor Wong grabbed a piece of paper and a pen from the desk. "Yes, I'll tell Liko to call her right away. I have it. Thanks."

"Your mother," he said, handing Liko the cell phone and the paper with a phone number on it. "She's all right. And worried about you."

CHAPTER

Thirty

Mei Lin stood in the train station and handed the telephone to Mother Su. Liko said he loved her. That was all she'd wanted to hear for the last month.

"Liko is all right?" asked Mother Su.

Mei Lin smiled. "He's fine. He couldn't tell me much. They were calling from the police station."

She turned at the sound of her name to see Brother Tom coming quickly toward them.

"Ready for some company?" he asked. "Pastor Wong wants me to meet him at the hospital in DuYan."

Little Mei was kicking up a storm in her baby stroller. She looked beautiful in her little red infant gown. Mei Lin bent over the stroller and picked her up. Her dark eyes flashed recognition, and Mei Lin held her close to her face and kissed her soft rose-petal cheek.

"Beautiful Little Mei," she said. "How can I say good-bye?"

She held the infant close and walked away for a few minutes alone with her. Even though Little Mei was tiny, Mei Lin believed that everything she said to her today would go down into her spirit, and her spirit would remember forever. She wanted her good-bye to be right. She found a bench away from all the noise and sat down.

"Be-be," she began. She choked on her words; a sob caught

in her throat. "Little Mei. I love you so much. Do you know that?"

Little Mei wiggled in her arms, moving her legs and arms in a jerking fashion as she did whenever she was excited. Mei Lin closed her eyes for a moment, relishing the weight and feel of the child in her arms, cherishing her gurgles and wiggles.

Lord, help me to remember what this feels like tomorrow when my arms are aching for her. She opened her eyes.

"I love you," she whispered again. "You like to hear that, don't you? Well, I do love you. I believe that Jesus helped me to find you the first day we met. And I want you to know how much you are loved. Now, honey, you're going to be getting a real mama this week. Her name is Joy, but one day you will call her Mama."

A sob racked her chest, and Mei Lin held the baby close and turned her head away from the mainstream of people. This was harder than she thought it would be. She might never have a chance at motherhood again.

"I want you to be a good girl for Joy. And when I come back to Shanghai, you are the first person I'm going to look for. Do you know that? See?" she said, pointing to the white flowers on her dress. "These are white magnolias. You are a daughter of Shanghai. You belong here."

Brother Tom was walking toward her.

Mei Lin held Little Mei close one more time. "Good-bye, Be-be. I will always love you."

She got up before Tom was near. "I'm coming," she called. She didn't want him to see the tears in her eyes.

Mei Lin walked back toward Mother Su. She kissed Little Mei's ear and then her eyelids and once more on the cheek. "Take care, Be-be."

"I'll take your bags and save us a place at the gate," said Brother Tom.

Mei Lin nodded her thanks. She touched Little Mei's tiny fist for the last time, then gave Mother Su a quick hug. Tears streamed down her face as she walked away. She turned around to Mother Su and mouthed the words, "Thank you."

"I love you," Mother Su answered.

Mei Lin stood in line and looked back at Mother Su holding Little Mei. How different her departure was this time. The last time, she left Brother Tom standing at the train station and took home an orphan. This time she was leaving an orphan at the train station and taking Brother Tom home.

He handed her a tissue. The gate banged open and the crowd pushed her forward—forward to DuYan and Tanching—and out of Little Mei's life forever.

———

Li Na clicked off the cell phone and handed it back to Cadre Lu. "My son," she said with relief. "Liko is all right."

"Where is he?" asked Cadre Lu.

"At a police station in FuZhou County."

"Did he file a report?"

"Yes, I think so," said Li Na.

"Good. I will call the station and talk to them. How did he find my number?"

"He called a mutual friend, and they just connected us. Do you know where that police station is?"

"Yes, I can have one of my men take you there if you like."

Li Na smiled. "You have been so kind. A great hero to all of us."

Cadre Lu looked puzzled. "I'm just doing my job. I want to ask you something."

"Yes?"

"How are you connected to these people?"

"The Eastern Lightning?" asked Li Na.

"Yes."

"Cadre Lu, I will admit to you that I am a Christian. These people said they were Christians, and they said they would send us great teachers to help us learn about the Bible. But right after we gathered for their school, they pretended that a PSB raid was coming to this house. We were told to split up—"

"Yes, yes. I know all that. But how did you meet them? Why did you trust them? Are they your friends or relatives?"

Li Na thought about that. She chose her words carefully. "A young girl named Jade came to visit our village over summer break. She was friendly with me and my son. She even pretended to be converted and become a Christian. That's why we trusted her when she said her cousin could get us well-known teachers from Singapore who would teach us and train us. Now I know we were foolish to trust her."

"But—"

The cadre seemed more than puzzled. Li Na sensed an underlying struggle, so she quietly prayed. Did she dare to witness to this officer? Is that where their conversation was leading?

"Mrs. Chen, your Jesus is from the West, and their Jesus is from the East. That puts both of your religions together—East and West. Some people think you Christians are just as dangerous as Eastern Lightning."

The light was dawning. Li Na prayed silently. So much was going on around her, it was difficult to follow this one conversation and answer skillfully.

"Cadre, I spent last night at your house. I spent all day with you. Have I even one time tried to force my faith on you?"

"No," replied Cadre Lu. "I admit I did think of that. But then, I'm wondering if you are being evasive for now until I help you recover your family."

"You are being very honest with me," said Li Na. "I find honesty a very honorable trait."

"Thank you."

"Now I will be honest with you," she said. "You and I both know that there are Christians in your village."

The cadre's eyebrows winged upward in surprise.

"Ah—don't say a thing. But I know they are there, even though I've never met them. Have they even once kidnapped anyone? Do they have houses like the one we are standing in here today? Have they broken the bones or cut off the ears of people who do not agree with them?"

He shook his head.

Li Na smiled. "It is not the Christian way to coerce people to believe. When Jesus was on earth, He walked many miles in Israel to visit with the people. When the people gathered around Him, He healed their sick. He even raised some from the dead. If He were here right now, He would heal Kwan So and He would cast the demon out of Rong."

Cadre Lu laughed. "I think you did a good job of that yourself."

Li Na giggled just a little. "Oh, thank you. It was my pleasure."

The cadre laughed harder. "I have never seen a woman look more like a snake in my life. I can't get that hiss out of my ears."

"Cadre, if Jesus were here He would also talk to you."

"To me?" he asked. "Why?"

"He would shake your hand and tell you that you did a good job rescuing His people. And He would tell you He loves you. He would ask you if you would have Him over to your house for dinner so that the two of you could talk."

"Really?" asked Cadre Lu. "So where is your Jesus?"

"He was killed," said Li Na. "But three days later He rose from the dead. He died a very awful and bloody death to take the punishment for all of the mistakes and sins we do. He wants us to believe in Him. He wants to love us, and He tells us all about himself through the Bible."

"The Bible?" asked Cadre Lu. "But I found a Bible in the Eastern Lightning rooms, not just the rooms where the Christians slept."

Li Na nodded. She understood now why this dear man was so confused. Especially when Eastern Lightning claimed that Christianity and Eastern Lightning were the same basic religion. So she prayed silently, and the answer came.

"Cadre," she said softly, "they study the Bible so they can form lies about it."

"Oh," said the cadre.

Li Na could still see the question in his eyes. She boldly reached under her shirt and pulled out her Bible. Cadre Lu looked surprised, but he didn't say anything. She turned to Matthew 22. "Look at this," she said.

The cadre looked a little scared. He looked over at the doorway. No one was watching, so he peered over her shoulder at the Bible as she pointed and read it out loud. "'Then one of them, a lawyer, asked Him a question, testing Him, and saying, "Teacher, which is the great commandment in the law?" Jesus said to him, "You shall love the Lord your God with all your heart, with all your soul, and with all your mind. This is the first and great commandment. And the second is like it: You shall love your neighbor as yourself. On these two commandments hang all the Law and the Prophets."'"

Li Na let the words sink in for a moment, and then she spoke. "Cadre, Christians believe the Bible is the truth. Eastern Lightning teaches the Bible for a while, and then they throw out the Bible and teach other things. They do it to trick Christians into becoming Eastern Lightning members."

"I see," said the cadre. He looked toward the door and then back at the Bible in her hands.

"Cadre Lu, Jesus said our greatest command is to love. Do the Christians in your village show love to one another and to you and your wife? Are they kind to you or do they run about chopping off ears?"

Cadre Lu stepped back. "I see your point, Mrs. Chen. The authorities over me were told that Eastern Lightning and Christianity are the same religion."

Li Na felt a sweet nudging in her heart.

"Here," she said, handing her Bible to the cadre. She pulled her maps out of her pocket. "And here are the maps I drew on the way to the first house. Why don't you take them as evidence."

At first he looked puzzled. Then a smile creased his face and he reached for the Bible. "Yes, that is a good idea, Mrs. Chen. This is good evidence to present that you were indeed kidnapped and mapping your way so you could find your way out again."

"There is no need to return it," said Li Na. "I can find another one."

"Yes, the bookstores in Shanghai and Beijing carry them now."

Li Na smiled. She played along with his reasoning, knowing it could protect him in offering explanations later on. "I agree," she said. "A friend gave me this Bible about two years ago. I'm sure I can find a replacement—maybe in WuMa. That's near DuYan and Tanching."

"Of course," he said. "One more thing."

"What's that?" she asked.

"Why don't you Christians just register? I like the Christians in my village. But I am putting myself at risk by not reporting their activities. The Religious Affairs Bureau allows Protestant churches. They just want to know where they are."

Li Na sighed. "Cadre, please do not take offense at this, but registering with the RAB is difficult. I just told you that Christians believe all of this Bible, right?"

He nodded.

"Well, we believe we should tell others about Jesus. The RAB tells us we can only talk about Him in church. We want to bring our children with us to church. The RAB says we cannot bring children under eighteen to church because the Bible contaminates their minds. We want to pray for one another if someone is sick or in trouble. The RAB says we cannot pray except once a week on Sundays.

"Many Christians feel that they must either obey the RAB or obey the Bible. We love our government. We love China and we pray for our leaders. We try to be the best citizens that we can be. Only, we must obey God first. Does that make sense?"

Cadre Lu did not answer. Li Na knew that she put her life on the line in talking to him so openly. The cadre could arrest her that moment under a number of charges.

"Thank you for explaining," he answered carefully. "And, yes, I will take this for evidence in the kidnapping. My wife— my wife will be interested in looking at your maps, too, I think."

Li Na understood his meaning. She smiled. "She will be pleased that you confide in her."

"And you . . . do you want to go to your son? Or do you want to see your friend Mrs. Zhang? I can arrange for that."

"Can I ride with Jiang Park to DuYan?"

"Yes," replied Cadre Lu. "That would be the easiest arrangement."

"I will go to the DuYan Hospital," said Li Na. "Then we will arrange to visit Mrs. Zhang and hopefully bring her to DuYan with us."

"I can arrange to have her transferred."

"Oh, would you?" asked Li Na. She felt like jumping up and down. "We are all meeting at DuYan by tomorrow. It would be good if she could be transferred. We've all been scattered apart for so long."

"I will do my best."

Cadre Lu walked to the back of the room and outside into the courtyard. "Finish taking pictures in the house," he called.

He came back inside and walked Li Na to the taxi, giving instructions to the driver and to his officer who drove the squad car with Pastor Zhang inside. Li Na took a few moments to prop Pastor Zhang's head, even though he was unconscious. She put a sheet over him, as his skin was not cool like Kwan So's.

By the time she was finished, the taxi and police car had started their engines. She climbed in the back of the taxi and scooted to the middle to be near Kwan So's head as he stretched backward on the front seat.

Cadre Lu stuck his head inside the front passenger window.

"Take all three of them to DuYan Hospital," he said. He glanced back at Li Na. "Stop and get her something to eat on the way. I'll make sure you are paid well for your trouble."

"Okay, Cadre," said Park. He tipped his hat and smiled.

"Thank you," said Li Na, leaning forward over So toward the window. She extended her hand to Cadre Lu, a gesture of friendship.

He took her hand. "You are a brave woman, Mrs. Chen," he said. "I will make a point of that in my report to the authorities."

Li Na nodded. "Thank you," she said softly. Deep inside, she knew that this kind cadre was offering her his friendship, too.

Kwan So heard vibrations underneath him. He couldn't see. At least the fog and the demons were gone—galloped away on their music.

Mei Lin? He tried to look for her now, but he couldn't see her. She threw him the red thread. Did he catch it? Or did he lose her? He tried to remember.

The red thread—the cross! He saw Jesus—cut, stabbed, swollen, bleeding. How did Mei Lin know? How did she know he needed the red thread?

"Mei Lin," he called. His voice sounded weak to his ears, but his spirit was screaming. He tried again.

"So, Mei Lin is all right."

"Li Na?" His own voice sounded distant and detached from where he lay. He felt a hand on his face and grimaced. *Shuang. Who told her to come back?*

"So, it's me, Li Na. You are in a taxi. We are taking you to DuYan Hospital. Pastor Zhang is in the car following us. You are both going to be all right."

"Li Na—" So tried to pull his thoughts and his words into his body. He felt like he was literally riding beside his own body instead of inside of it. He was not afraid, but he wanted desperately to go back and talk to Li Na.

"It's okay," he heard her whisper. "Everyone is free."

Free? Free.

The words jolted something inside of him. Suddenly he could feel himself sink back into his body. He felt hot tears on his cheeks.

"So, don't cry."

"Li Na?"

"Yes, it's Li Na. Can you hear me now?"

"Free?" he asked. So heard a little sob, and the hand on his forehead trembled.

"We're free, So. All of us. Free."

"Oh—oh, thank God."

More tears fell on his cheeks. His eyes burned, and he tried to wipe them. His arms still weren't moving. There. His fingers moved. He wiggled the tips of his fingers until he could feel his hands. Oh—something was wrong on the left. Pain seared through his shoulder. He felt a cool cloth on his face, gently dabbing the tears—it helped the fire.

"What do you need?" asked Li Na.

"Thirsty," he finally managed.

Moments later So felt water at the corner of his mouth. He opened his mouth slightly. His throat and lungs burned inside, and his eyes were still on fire. Somehow the water touched all of it, and he felt revived.

"More," he mumbled. His mouth felt sticky and polluted.

"Don't struggle so much," said Li Na. "You're going to be fine, So. I called Brother Tom. He went to tell Mei Lin. She is going to meet us at the hospital."

"Mei Lin," he said. "Shanghai."

"Yes, she's coming from Shanghai. She filed a report against the Eastern Lightning for us in Shanghai. She'll be here tomorrow."

"Liko?"

"Liko will meet us there, too. You rest now. Here, take a little more water."

So tried to think. All he could remember was Mei Lin's scarf and the red thread. Did he catch it? He clenched his fist.

Li Na was drizzling more water into his mouth. He opened it and let the water trickle down his throat. It touched the flames, and he wanted more.

"Li Na." There. He said her name. He was so glad she was safe—glad she was here. Darkness gathered around his eyes, and he slipped away from her, sinking into the place she called *free*.

Li Na wiped Kwan So's face with the edge of the blanket. His skin was warming now, and he was asleep or unconscious—she couldn't tell which. When they stopped for lunch, she checked on Zhang Liang. He was still unconscious. She was glad she didn't have to tell him about his wife yet. At least the cadre would have her transferred to DuYan, maybe by tomorrow.

Park pulled into the hospital near the emergency room doors. Men in white jackets hurried out of the doors, pushing a gurney.

"Be careful," she coaxed them. "His left leg and left arm are broken. And there may be other injuries."

The men skillfully lifted So from the taxi and onto the gurney.

Li Na went to the other side of the car. "Thank you, Jiang Park. If you hadn't picked me up two nights ago, none of this would have happened so quickly."

Park smiled. "Mrs. Chen, you have given me a story to tell my grandchildren."

The police car pulled in behind them.

"Good-bye," she said to Park. "And thanks again."

She ran to the police car and leaned in to speak to the driver. "Did he talk at all since we stopped for lunch?"

"No," said the officer. "Groaned quite a bit, though. He might be conscious."

Li Na looked around. As much as she wanted to help Pastor Zhang, she didn't want him to say anything that could get their house church in trouble. She chose her words carefully. "Zhang Liang, this is Chen Li Na. I was with your wife."

"Jun Lee . . ." he murmured.

"She is safe. I will tell her you are here."

"Kwan So . . ."

"You are at DuYan Hospital," said Li Na. "Kwan So and I arrived ahead of you. He has a few broken bones, but he is alive."

The medics were back with their gurney. Liang groaned as they lifted him from the car to the bed on wheels.

"I'm here," said Li Na. "I will visit you after I check on Kwan So." Li Na went inside and to the front desk.

"Kwan So has been taken to the operating room," said the nurse. "They are setting his femur and forearm and looking for other injuries. Are you his wife?"

"Oh—no," said Li Na. "A close friend."

The nurse smiled and closed her folder. "Why don't you sit down over there and wait."

Li Na looked behind her. "This man is my friend, as well. Zhang Liang."

The nurse looked at the new gurney coming in the door and then at her folder. "I don't have anything on this patient yet," she said. "I'll need you to fill out forms if the patients cannot. Don't worry, I will tell you when something new develops."

CHAPTER

Thirty-One

Mrs. Chen, wake up."

Li Na opened her eyes. She was still in the emergency room. She raised her head, which had been resting on Mother Zhang's lap.

"Mother Zhang! I'm so glad you are here."

"The nurse is calling your name, honey."

Li Na slowly sat up and looked in the direction Mother Zhang was pointing. It was dark outside. She pulled her hair behind her ears and smoothed her eyebrows. Her stomach was hollow and her mind felt fuzzy, tired.

"Mrs. Chen?"

Li Na stood and walked toward the nurse.

"Kwan So is out of surgery. He's asking for you."

"Oh, where?" asked Li Na. She looked back at Mother Zhang. Her face was full of pity. "Mother Zhang."

Li Na reached toward her, but the older woman shook her head. "We will talk later. Go with the nurse now."

Li Na followed the nurse back to a room filled with beds, separated only by curtains. So was in the fourth bed on the left. His left eye had stitches, and his right eye was closed. He had a foam collar around his neck and tubes coming out of his nose and arms.

"Oh, Kwan So!" she exclaimed softly. Li Na turned to see a

doctor standing at the foot of the bed, a clipboard in his hand.

"I am Dr. Chow," he said. "Are you his wife?"

"No. He is a widower. I am a close friend of the family."

"Oh—well, he asked for you as he went under anesthesia. I promised I'd get you when he was through. His left leg is broken in three places, and his left forearm is broken. We set the bones. He seems to have dislocated his shoulder somehow, as well. Can you tell me what happened?"

"I . . . I don't know exactly," said Li Na. She looked over at So. "We were with a group. We were kidnapped and separated." She put her hand over her mouth. "I found him in the bottom of a pond tied in a sack." Li Na bowed her head and cried.

The doctor pulled a chair over to the side of the bed. "Here, sit down," he said. "Did this just happen today?"

"Yes, this morning," she said. She wished she hadn't fallen asleep. She felt more vulnerable now than when she first came into the hospital. She wanted to be strong for Kwan So when he woke up.

"Mrs. Chen, I don't know what these people wanted, but they nearly killed your friend."

"Is he going to be all right?" She pulled toilet paper from her pocket and wiped her nose.

"I think so," the doctor replied. "Several teeth were broken or knocked out, and there is an incision on the back of his neck. It didn't look like it was done by a surgeon. It appears they took out a tendon."

Li Na gasped. "Oh no!"

Dr. Chow put his hand on her shoulder. "We were able to stabilize the area for now, but we'll need to do surgery again at a later time, when he's stronger. Was he able to move at all when you were bringing him here?"

Li Na thought a moment. "Yes, he wiggled his fingers—only on the right hand. That's all, I think."

"Good," said the doctor. "And he was talking to me before we took him into surgery. Those are good signs. We will set up a bed for you near him if you like. He should wake up by sunrise."

"They are transferring another one of our friends here tomorrow," said Li Na. "The kidnappers cut off her ear. I hope you will be her doctor while she is here."

"I'll be sure to look in on her."

"And Zhang Liang?" Li Na asked. "That's her husband. He came in with Kwan So this afternoon."

The doctor flipped through his chart. "He's not out of surgery yet," he said. "We will let his mother know when he wakes up. Now let me find a nurse for you."

Li Na followed the nurse to a private room on the same floor. Several men in white coats wheeled Kwan So into the room and pulled the curtain so they could get him settled. She was surprised to see old Mother Zhang when she walked into the room.

"There is a bed here for you," said Mother Zhang. "But wouldn't you like to come to my house and sleep? You won't be able to sleep well in here with all the people in and out of the room checking on Kwan So."

"Thank you, Mother Zhang," said Li Na. "But I should be here when he wakes. He asked for me before surgery. But— could you bring me some clean clothes in the morning? These have been in the pond!"

"Yes, of course. Honey, it was just like the dream of the troubled waters, wasn't it?"

"Yes, it was, Mother Zhang. In fact, we couldn't find him. I stood at the top of the hill, and when I remembered your dream, that's when I knew he was in the pond."

Mother Zhang shuffled to the end of the bed and sat down, patting the middle of the bed beside her. Li Na sat down. She knew she had to tell Mother Zhang about her daughter-in-law.

"Mother Zhang," Li Na started. Images of blood and Jun Lee's swollen face flashed in front of her, and she put her hand to her mouth to cover the gasp that escaped her lips.

"What is it, Mrs. Chen?" asked Mother Zhang. The older

woman patted her hand. "I know you've been through an awful ordeal."

"It's Jun Lee," Li Na finally said. She looked into Mother Zhang's face. "First they pushed her down the steps. Then—" Li Na began to tremble, first in her throat and then her shoulders, down into her arms. She felt as though every nerve in her body stood on end.

Mother Zhang waited patiently.

"I brought the police, but we were too late," said Li Na. "They cut off her ear!" The words rushed out and Li Na sobbed, her head in her hands.

"Lord Jesus," exclaimed Mother Zhang. "Lord Jesus, have mercy." She pulled Li Na close. "Tell me, is she all right?" Her voice was hoarse, choked with emotion.

"She has a Christian doctor," Li Na said. "I helped him care for her, and he told me I could pray. He was kind, Mother Zhang. But Jun Lee didn't wake up. If we'd only been there ten minutes earlier—"

"You can't live in regret," said Mother Zhang. "Don't do that to yourself."

"Dr. Xu said he would send you a letter. That was yesterday. Cadre Lu said he will ask to have Jun Lee transferred here to DuYan Hospital."

"Are you Mother Zhang?" A nurse stood at the doorway. "Your son is out of surgery. The doctor wants to see you."

Mother Zhang squeezed Li Na's hand. "You are a brave woman, Chen Li Na. We will talk again later?"

Li Na nodded. "Of course." She was relieved that she had told Mother Zhang, but she hoped that all of the stress would not be too much on her at her age.

But right now, So needed her attention. Li Na was glad for his sake that he was asleep and couldn't feel anything. He looked so pitiful in all the bandages.

A nurse came in and worked with all the tubes coming out of his body. "He won't be awake for a while," she said. "Why don't you go get some sleep? I'll call you if he wakes up."

"Are you sure?" asked Li Na. She yawned.

"Yes, ma'am. We have a monitor right here that keeps a check on his vital signs and any movement. I'll come get you if he changes."

"Thank you," said Li Na. She slipped off her shoes and curled underneath the white sheet. The nurse dimmed the light above her, and within seconds she was asleep.

Li Na wakened at daybreak and used the bathroom. She couldn't wait to take a bath.

"Li Na."

Li Na poked her head out of the bathroom door. *So?* She tiptoed behind the curtain that divided them. "Kwan So?"

"Li Na," he answered. "I hoped you'd be here."

Li Na felt a rush of warmth go through her middle. "Of course I'm here." She went to his side and instinctively felt his forehead.

"I can't feel my legs," he said softly.

"It's okay," said Li Na. She smoothed his hair back off of his forehead. "The doctor said you did great in surgery last night. Your left arm and left leg are broken." She didn't tell him about the tendon. She just couldn't—not yet.

"What time is it?" he asked hoarsely. "I can only see with one eye, you know."

Li Na smiled. "Joking around, are we?" she asked. "It's five o'clock in the morning."

"I need to know what time it is," said So. "I have to remember."

"Remember?"

"Yes," answered So. "I want to remember what time it was when—"

He coughed a little, and Li Na quickly got a cold cloth and wiped his mouth. His lips were dry and cracking.

"Thank you," he whispered.

"What else do you need?"

"See, I can wiggle my fingers with this hand," said So.

Li Na smiled and touched each finger, pretending to count. "All five of them wiggling away."

"Is it still five o'clock?" he asked.

"Yes," said Li Na. "What—"

"Shhhh," he said. His right eye was barely open, and his left was purple and green, swollen even more since yesterday.

She saw him watching her with that slit in his eye. She didn't move.

"Li Na, I love you."

A wave of shock went down her back. "Excuse me?"

So's smile was crooked. "I thought I'd better tell you now while I'm on all these drugs. I might lose my nerve later on."

"Kwan So!" she said, her voice teasing. "Kwan So, are you sure the drugs aren't talking now?"

His cool fingers reached for her hand and closed around it. It was hard to find expression on his poor banged and bruised face.

"I know it's only been two years since your husband died," he said. He coughed and sputtered a little, and she wiped his mouth again. "It's taken me fourteen years, and I still grieve for Shan Zu. I didn't want to admit it at first, but—I realized the moment I saw Jin drive away with you in that van that I wanted to protect you the rest of my life."

"So," gasped Li Na. "I do care for you. But I don't know if . . . Can God let me love two men?"

His fingers stroked her hand. "He is letting me love two women."

Li Na grew quiet. A rush of emotion swelled within her chest, and she knew. She bent down to kiss his hand, her lips lingering there as she dared to let her heart feel his affection.

"Li Na?"

She lifted her head. "So?"

"Will you marry me?"

On the train, Mei Lin's thoughts had bounced back and forth between Little Mei and her dream of throwing Father the red thread. She kept asking herself the same question—did he catch it?

Now, standing in front of her father lying on a hospital bed, the dream was a blur. She barely recognized him. Her nose burned inside as she forced back tears, afraid he'd wake and see her crying. She wanted to be strong for him, strong as she was in the dream. Her hand trembled a little as she untied the scarf from her purse. She was going to place it in his hand, when she suddenly felt compelled to throw it into the air over his bed.

Mei Lin stood, straightening her back. She stepped sideways a bit and flung it high. The thin material waved above his bed, just as the red thread flew between them in her dream.

"Catch it!" she whispered to Mrs. Chen excitedly.

Mrs. Chen jumped to the opposite side of the bed and caught the scarf as it softly landed. The two of them snapped the ends upward, creating a banner over Father. Again and again they flung it high, watching it curl and land delicately across his middle.

His finger moved! Mei Lin slid the scarf into his hand so that his fist was around its middle.

"The invisible red thread connects us, Baba," Mei Lin whispered.

"Regardless . . ." said Father. He coughed and sputtered a bit. "Regardless of time, place, or circumstance."

"Yes, Baba!" cried Mei Lin. Immediately she thought of her dream. "Yes, it did connect us! Did you see it?"

She wanted to ask him if he caught it, but she didn't—his face looked as though he had caught a fight with someone, not a red thread. His left eye was swollen shut and blackened. Just then a small slit opened in his right eye. Mrs. Chen wiped his mouth with a damp cloth, and Mei Lin moved the scarf inside his fist.

"Can you feel Mother's scarf, Father?"

"Yes," he answered. "Mei Lin, did you see the red thread?"

"Yes," she answered. "Baba, I threw the red thread to you. Did you catch it?"

She stood back again to watch a smile break over his swollen face. A bottom tooth was missing, and a large lump formed in her throat. He looked terrible.

"Come here," he whispered.

Mei Lin bent forward again.

"You saw it?"

"Yes," she said softly near his ear. "I saw it in a dream, and then I threw it to you, like a lifeline for you to hold on to."

"The cross," he said. He cleared his throat, and Mrs. Chen offered him a sip of water. "The red thread is the blood of the cross. The cross chased away the dark horses—demons galloping—Mei Lin, I prayed the horses wouldn't find you."

Mei Lin looked up at Mrs. Chen.

Mrs. Chen shook her head slightly. "He mentioned dark horses this morning. I don't know."

"This—" Father's voice was tight, as if he would choke. "This is a gift to you from your mother and me."

"Yes, Father, she was with us, too." Mei Lin felt helpless— she had never seen her father look so vulnerable, so obviously in pain.

"And now—" He tried to lift his head.

"Can we help him lift his head?" asked Mei Lin.

"Not yet," replied Mrs. Chen.

"Li Na?"

Mrs. Chen walked over and stood beside Mei Lin.

"Thank you," Mei Lin said softly. "Thank you for rescuing him. Mother Zhang told me in the waiting room—you were quite a heroine."

Mrs. Chen gave her a hug. "Mother Zhang's dream helped me realize he was in the bottom of the pond. We made it just in time."

"Just in time," Father repeated.

Mei Lin saw a little smile form on his face.

"Just in time to marry me."

Shock reverberated down Mei Lin's back. "What did he say?"

Mrs. Chen smiled and nervously touched her father's hand. "Your father asked me to marry him this morning."

"Oh!" cried Mei Lin. "Oh, Father! Oh, Mrs. Chen!" Mei Lin hugged Mrs. Chen and then her father and then hugged them both again. "I'm so—so surprised!"

"And happy?" asked Father.

Mei Lin gently squeezed both of their hands. "I'm so very, very happy, Father." She looked up at Mrs. Chen. "You did say yes?"

The three of them broke into laughter, Father sputtering and wheezing until his face changed colors.

"Yes, yes!" said Mrs. Chen. "I said yes!"

It felt good to laugh. Li Na didn't know why she had been so worried about Mei Lin's reaction. Mei Lin seemed truly happy. She only hoped that Liko would feel the same. She knew that Liko loved Kwan So, but he also loved his father. She had questioned whether she could love two men. Would Liko want to love two fathers?

The hospital door slowly opened.

"Liko!" shouted Mei Lin.

Liko swept Mei Lin off her feet and swung her in a circle.

"Oh, this is truly a happy day!" exclaimed Li Na. She clasped her hands in delight as she watched the two of them in each other's arms. She gave them a few moments and then it was her turn. Liko was taller than his father, and hugging him was like reaching for the branches of a ginkgo tree.

"Thank God!" she exclaimed. "Are you truly all right? Did they hurt you?"

"No, Mother," said Liko, smiling at her. "I'm not hurt. And you? Are you okay?"

"Oh yes," Li Na answered. "Just exhausted, really."

Liko held her arms and looked down at her. She saw tears forming.

"I owe you an apology, Mother. You knew we were to go home, and I was angry with you because I thought you were trying to spoil everything. Can you ever forgive me?"

Li Na's heart melted. Liko was not too big to apologize to his mother—even in front of his fiancée and future father-in-law!

"Oh yes, I forgive you," she said immediately. "It all happened so fast, Liko. Don't be too hard on yourself."

"Pastor Wong and I plan to have a meeting next month for all those captured by Eastern Lightning. We want to give everyone time to recover first." He looked beyond her to Kwan So.

Li Na looked up into her son's face. "So collected some battle scars," she said softly.

Liko looked at her quizzically. "Did I hear you laughing in here before I walked in?"

"You don't think we should laugh?" teased So, his voice raspy but bright.

"Pastor Kwan!" exclaimed Liko. "I didn't know you were awake. Can you see through there?"

So grinned. "I can see through a tiny slit in this eye. Your mother punched me in the other one."

"Father!" exclaimed Mei Lin. "You'd better stop teasing her or she might change her mind."

"Change her mind?" asked Liko, looking from So to Mei Lin and finally stopping on Li Na.

Li Na was hoping to tell Liko privately. The mood was so festive now—what if Liko didn't approve? After a moment's hesitation, she spoke. "Kwan So wants to hire me as his nurse."

Mei Lin burst out laughing, and So sputtered and coughed until the bed shook. Li Na felt her face turn red. She looked at Liko—his expression was priceless. His eyebrows were scrunched together and his arms crossed—he looked bemused and bewildered all at the same time.

Li Na put the cloth down and walked back over to him. "I mean—" She looked back at So. "I mean that Kwan So asked me if I would help him permanently. He asked me to marry him."

Liko's eyes widened. "*Marry* you?" He looked past his mother at So and then back at his mother. "Mother—I don't know what to say—I . . . I—did you say yes?"

"Father, don't laugh again," said Mei Lin, holding her hand over her mouth, suppressing giggles. "I'll laugh for both of us."

Li Na smiled back at her and then looked up at Liko. "Do you want me to say yes?"

"Do you want to say yes?" he asked.

Li Na squeezed her son's arm. "I asked Kwan So if it were possible to love two men. He said that God is allowing him to love two women. I will always love your father." She looked back at So. "And So will always love Shan Zu. But God is giving us room in our hearts to love again."

Liko kissed her on the forehead and then pulled her close to him. "Mother, nothing could make me happier."

Li Na felt the sun rise in her heart, warming all the places that were afraid and lonely.

Just then she heard Him—the Holy Spirit. His voice, again, was as still as the beat of a butterfly's wing, but it was there. And she knew . . . God was smiling.

"We're His family now," she said softly. "All of us."

CHAPTER

Thirty-Two

A nurse came in to talk to So. While she and Li Na talked about So's care, Liko pulled Mei Lin close to him. "I missed you."

Her hair was soft against his cheek. He loved to feel her thin arms around his waist and the warmth of her head against his chest. Being with Mei Lin, even in this hospital environment, was intoxicating. Mei Lin had a pure, genuine heart. After Jade's scandalous behavior, he couldn't drink enough of Mei Lin's sweet, innocent spirit.

"Are you Chen Liko?"

Liko turned around to see two PSB officers. He hadn't even seen them walk into the room. Liko quickly stood in front of Mei Lin, putting himself between her and the men in green.

"I need to see your identity card," one officer said.

"I don't have one," Liko answered honestly.

The PSB officer nearly grabbed him by the collar.

"Wait," said Liko. "My card was stolen. But I have a pass from Police Station No. 5 in FuZhou County, Jiangxi Province."

The officer did not look impressed.

Liko reached in his back pocket for his wallet. "May I ask you what this is about, officer?"

"Outside," the other officer said, nodding toward the door.

"You stay here," Liko said to Mei Lin. He looked back at his mother, then stepped into the hallway.

"A Cadre Fang from Tanching Village called our office this morning. It seems there is a situation in your village."

"A situation?" Liko's heart leaped inside, and a wave of panic swept over him. Was it his house church? Had it been raided by the PSB? Fear rushed down his back.

"We are under orders to escort you to Tanching immediately," the first officer said. "Come this way."

"I want to go with you," said a voice.

Liko looked down to see Mei Lin at his side, her eyes pleading.

"Officer," said Mei Lin, "I request your permission to accompany you to Tanching Village."

The officers looked at each other. The first officer answered, "You may come. But stay out of the way."

Liko took Mei Lin's hand and looked down at the ground, following the feet of the officer in front of him. He glanced back. His mother was standing outside So's door. She put her hands together and nodded slightly, a signal that she would be praying. They didn't rough him up or handcuff him, but their command was clear: he was going to Tanching.

Liko did not look around him until he and Mei Lin were in the back of the police car and the two officers had climbed into the front.

He wanted to ask questions, but he thought better of it. The FuZhou County Police Office had probably filed his report with Cadre Fang yesterday, but he couldn't imagine what was in the report that would make Cadre Fang react this way.

"What's this about?" Mei Lin whispered.

Liko shrugged his shoulders. "I don't know. At least we will have some time to talk, if we keep it down."

They remained quiet until the car pulled out of the parking lot.

"You first," said Mei Lin. "I want to hear what happened."

Liko was thankful that the road to Tanching wasn't paved and the car motor was noisy. He told Mei Lin everything up until the escape. He didn't tell her the part about Jade yet. He wanted to be alone with her when he told her that. Liko pondered how awful it would be if the picture Jade had had taken made it appear that he compromised his morals.

Within half an hour they were in Tanching, and Liko directed them to Cadre Fang's office in the center of the village. The three of them got out together.

Cadre Fang met them at the front door.

"Kwan Mei Lin, what a pleasant surprise to see you," said the cadre. He was using his official tone of voice in front of the officers. "Chen Liko, it seems we had a visit by someone who doesn't like you."

"A visit?" asked Liko.

"Gentlemen, I would like you to accompany us," said Cadre Fang to the policemen. "I want to file an official report with your witness."

"Certainly," said the leader of the two.

All five of them climbed back into the police car, and Cadre Fang led them to Mei Lin's house.

Liko tensed. "Is Amah all right?" he asked.

"Amah and Fu Yatou were not here last night," said the cadre. "And it's a good thing they were not."

Liko was agitated by Cadre Fang's evasiveness. He looked down at Mei Lin, his thoughts wildly racing.

The car pulled in to Mei Lin's house, and Liko jumped out and ran into the courtyard. The entire courtyard had been turned upside down—benches, chairs, washtubs. The water pump in the center was smashed, bent off the cement base, its foundation cracked.

"Amah!" Liko yelled. He spun around. If this was some kind of joke the cadre was playing, he didn't like it. "Where are Amah and Yatou?"

"They were at my house for dinner when this happened last night. Ping and I were being good neighbors to them, since Mei Lin and Kwan So abandoned them."

Liko heard Mei Lin gasp. The cadre was pouring on the guilt.

"This," he said, gesturing toward the mess, "is what they came home to afterward."

Jesus, Liko whispered under his breath.

"Cadre, are Fu and Amah at your house now?" asked Mei Lin.

"Of course," he answered. "Ping set up a place for them with us last night. I wouldn't let them come home until the reports were filed and you yourself saw the place. Someone had to take care of them. They were in a state of shock."

"Thank you for taking care of them," said Mei Lin. She turned to Liko. "I have to go to them."

"Go ahead," Liko answered. "I'll be here."

He watched Mei Lin run out of the courtyard. He caught a glimpse of the neighbor, Mrs. Lang, watching them from her window. She was in Kwan So's house church. Maybe she had seen something.

Everything was smashed and scattered all over the floor. The two officers from DuYan moved about, taking notes on their clipboards.

Cadre Fang walked up behind him. "You have made a few enemies while you were gone, Liko? Someone else who sees past your veneer?"

Liko didn't like where this conversation was going, particularly in front of the other two officers. He wondered if this was some kind of perverse joke—it was no secret that he and the cadre did not trust each other.

"This is Kwan So's house," he said carefully. "Why do you insist that I am the one these thieves are looking for?"

"Your water buffalo—"

Liko didn't hear another word. He dashed out of the house and ran toward the old cowshed. He ran inside, kicking the metal bucket across the room. He smelled it before he saw it.

Liko stepped back to the doorway, willing his eyes to adjust to the darkness.

"Old Gray!" he cried.

Old Gray's head hung on the wall in front of a smattering of blood. The rest of his body was in pieces, thrown all about the room.

Liko stared in disbelief.

"I found this note stuck on his horn," said Cadre Fang.

Liko stepped out of the shed and held the paper in front of him.

Liko—
I want to fight—
And you won't win.
The Bull

Liko swung around and punched his fist into the wall of the shed.

"Do you know who this Bull person is?"

Liko looked at Cadre Fang. "I think so," he answered. "Did you check my house?"

"Yes. There's no damage done there. It appears that the Bull person knew that this was your water buffalo. I guess he assumed that Kwan So's home was yours."

Liko wondered if Jade had had something to do with this. She knew he loved Old Gray, and she was probably jealous of Mei Lin, especially after the way he turned down her advances the other night. She may have told The Bull to come here, knowing full well he would destroy everything.

"Did you receive the report from Police Station No. 5 in FuZhou County?" asked Liko. "We were just there yesterday."

"We?" asked Cadre Fang.

"Yes, my friend and I filed reports against an evil cult that kidnapped us."

"Ah, and your Bull friend was one of the kidnappers?"

"That's right," said Liko. He put his arm on the side of the shed and leaned into it. He felt sick.

"And Kwan So—when will he return?" asked the cadre.

"Kwan So is in DuYan hospital."

The cadre's eyebrows winged upward in surprise. "The hospital? These same people kidnapped him?" He fingered his mustache for a moment and then cleared his throat. "I did hear from FuZhou County Police," he said. "They sent me your report. They also said there were as many as thirty-two others who were also kidnapped."

Liko did not flinch under the cadre's icy stare. "That's correct."

"Police Station No. 5 in FuZhou said that every one of them was released after Eastern Lightning received word that the PSB was searching for them. Some of them are injured, but it seems that this Eastern Lightning group has respect for the Chinese Public Security Bureau. It appears that Mei Lin made the official report in Shanghai, and after that the PSB began uncovering their hideouts."

"No one was killed?" asked Liko.

The cadre shook his head. "As far as they know, some were injured like Kwan So, but they all managed to escape."

Liko felt as though a world of evil was lifted from his shoulders. He breathed a prayer of thanks to heaven. With that prayer came the gentle tugging of God's Spirit. He knew he wouldn't feel like thanking the cadre later on, so he made an attempt at it now. "Thank you for taking care of Amah and Fu. And for letting me see all of this before you filed the report."

The other two officers walked up just then and poked their heads inside the cowshed. "Whew!" the first one exclaimed. "What a stench!"

"Here's the note," said Cadre Fang, handing it to the lead officer. "It was stuck on the horns of the water buffalo."

Liko needed to think. The Bull would return, and Kwan So was in no shape to get out of bed, much less wrestle with The Bull. As the cadre talked to the officers, Liko quietly formed a plan. At least until Kwan So was on his feet, he would need to sleep at the Kwans' house. He saw no other way. He couldn't leave them here defenseless.

"Cadre Fang, will you have someone check the Kwans' house tonight?" he asked.

"Yes, I hired one of my assistants to keep watch over the house this evening. But I don't think your Bull friend will be back so quickly."

"One thing about The Bull—he's unpredictable."

While Cadre Fang walked the other two officers to their police car, Liko went down to the Kwans' shed and found his shovel. He found a place about ten meters behind the shed and thrust the shovel into the earth. His muscles tensed when he thought of The Bull taking his revenge out on Old Gray. All he could do now was give his old companion a decent burial.

Each plunge of the shovel was fueled with anger. Sweat poured down his neck and chest. He pulled his T-shirt over his head and threw it aside. The afternoon sun burned his back, but he didn't care. It was his fault that all of his closest friends were hurt. He felt responsible for the awful beatings and—poor Mrs. Zhang! His stomach felt sick every time he thought about her. Grief for his actions consumed his heart.

How could I be so stupid? I led everyone to the slaughter, including Old Gray. And I thought I was such a great help to everyone—what a joke.

He saw dirt fly toward the shed and looked up.

Mei Lin—with a pickax in her hands. She held it over her head and threw its weight into the ground, loosening the soil. Then she saw him watching her, and she stopped and looked at him, the broken earth between them. In the silence, he felt her strength go into his soul. After a few moments, she smiled. She wiped her face with the back of her arm, raised the pickax, and struck the hardened soil.

Mei Lin was bone weary. The dirt seemed to crawl under her skin, between her eyelashes, and into her shoes. It was a fitting service for Old Gray. After the police left, Mrs. Lang brought them a pitcher of water and a meal of vegetables and rice with sweet sauce. They eagerly drank the water but only stopped to eat after Old Gray was covered respectfully.

With the pump broken, they washed as best they could in the rice paddies and then returned to sit on the cool ground in the shade outside the shed wall. The sun would set in a few hours, but neither of them suggested going out to the rock tonight. Ping had arranged for Amah and Fu Yatou to travel to the DuYan Hospital to see Father, so they were truly alone.

Liko spoke first. "When will Amah be home?"

"Ping arranged a taxi to pick her up at eight o'clock." Mei Lin checked her watch. "That's about two hours from now."

"I will sleep on your father's cot tonight," said Liko.

"Thank you," she answered. She felt like a weight was lifted from her. She had pushed back thoughts of The Bull all afternoon; mental pictures of defending Amah or Fu Yatou against attacks from The Bull crowded her mind.

"I made so many mistakes," Liko said quietly. "I pushed everyone to go to the Institute. Then, even though Mother told us she heard from heaven that we should go home, I wouldn't listen. It's really all my fault. And then—then when I realized what I did, I sulked at first because I was afraid I ruined my reputation with the house churches. I had so much pride."

"Then you must humble yourself and receive God's forgiveness," Mei Lin replied.

"That's what Pastor Wong said. I'm working on it. Burying Old Gray brought up those old feelings again."

Mei Lin picked a few blades of grass and made a little pile near her foot. "You shouldn't blame it all on yourself. Brother Tom told me that even Pastor Wong was fooled."

"Pastor Wong knew something was amiss within the first three days. Me? I wouldn't admit it until I walked in the last meeting house and saw Jade standing there."

"Jade?" asked Mei Lin. "What did Jade have to do with it?"

"Everything," Liko answered. "I didn't want to tell you in the police car. Jade was an Eastern Lightning spy, sent to infiltrate our churches. She said this guy named Jin was her cousin and he would connect us with the reputable Haggai Institute. My father wanted to go to the Institute for years, so I jumped at the chance. I was so blind."

"What did Jade say when you saw her?"

"Say?" he asked. "It's more what she did that bothered me."

Mei Lin waited. Liko fidgeted, his hands in and out of his pockets. He finally adjusted his seating and hugged his legs.

"She came into my room two nights ago to try to seduce me."

Mei Lin gasped. "Jade?"

"Yes," he answered. "She put something in our tea before we went to bed. Later, she came into my room and started to undress. I put the sheet over my head so I couldn't see her. I told her to get out, but she wouldn't listen."

Mei Lin was silent. She'd never dreamed Jade could be so brazen.

Liko was suddenly up on his knees right in front of her face. "Mei Lin, I swear to you I did not see anything. I didn't do anything. But someone took a picture."

"A picture?" she asked. Her mind was in a whirl. "Whatever for?"

"Pastor Wong said Eastern Lightning gives a strange tea to lower a man's resistance and then seduces him with a woman. If they can get a picture of a house church leader in a morally compromising position, they will show the picture to all the house church members to convince them that Christianity is false and Eastern Lightning is the true religion."

"How evil," Mei Lin answered quietly. She didn't want to hurt him or sound like she didn't trust him. Still, she had to know. And she had to hear it from him. "Did they get a picture of anything?"

"No," Liko answered emphatically. "I took my shirt off when

I went to bed, but I had my pants on. When she came at me, I couldn't walk at first. The medicine in the tea made me dizzy. It took me a while to steady myself, but when I did, I ran out of the bedroom and made it to the bathroom. I went inside and locked the door until she finally went to bed. The next morning, Pastor Wong and I were supposed to sneak out of the house. I went into his room at the crack of dawn and found him tied by his wrists to the ceiling. That's where I met The Bull."

"Is that his real name?" asked Mei Lin.

Liko grinned. "No, I just called him that because he looked like Old Gray with fists."

Mei Lin listened in astonishment to the story of their escape. When he was finished, she was quiet for a while, gathering her own thoughts.

"I never want to lose your trust, Mei Lin," he said. "You are such a pure, sweet girl. I prayed that you would believe me."

Mei Lin smiled at him. "I believe you, Liko."

Tonight was a night of confessions, and she knew now was the time to tell Liko about her barrenness. She had been wrong to hold it from him for so long.

"I miss Little Mei," she said. That's not what she really wanted to say, but it seemed like a safe place to start.

"Little Mei?" asked Liko. "Who's that?"

"A baby I found in the garbage," Mei Lin answered. She told him the whole story. It warmed her inside to talk about her.

"Then you are honored she's named after you?" he asked when she was finished.

"Honored? I almost adopted her."

"Adopted her?" asked Liko. "How could you do that?"

"I don't know," Mei Lin answered. "But I was determined to do it."

"She really captured your heart, didn't she?"

"Liko, I was going to adopt her to try to hide something."

"Hide?" asked Liko. "What do you need to hide?"

Tears sprang to her eyes. She tried to speak and get it all out, but a lump formed in her throat. She looked away.

"What is it, Mei Lin?"

"You said you made mistakes," she said. "I made mistakes, too. I loved Little Mei. But I wanted to adopt her for selfish reasons. Liko, I . . . I can't have a child."

Liko didn't move. He just stared.

Mei Lin felt bare and vulnerable, her darkest secret uncovered. Her heart was screaming at her, *Get up and run—now!*

Her lower lip trembled, so she sucked it in, tasting the dirt below her bottom lip. "You'll never see our child roll down the hill," she cried, her throat tight. "It's a big stupid dream that will never happen. Well, it's not a stupid dream, but I'm stupid. I can't have children. You can't marry me."

There. She had said it. Mei Lin stood up to run, but Liko stood up with her.

"Wait," he said. "Mei Lin, when did all this happen?"

She put her hand to her face to shield her shame. "After prison," she whispered. "I don't know if it's the beatings or the malnutrition, but . . . I'm barren."

Liko's arms went around her, but she resisted. Despite Mother Su's words, she still felt like half a woman. And Liko deserved more. He held tight, but she was like a stone.

"You can't marry half a woman, Liko. Don't you see? When we can't have children, Amah will think I'm cursed by the gods, and the whole village will wonder if the God who makes the earth and skies is the true God."

"Shhhh, Mei Lin," said Liko. "We have two years. Things may change by then—"

"No!" Mei Lin shouted. She pushed back from Liko. "No! I won't wait two years hoping for something, only to have my dreams dashed to bits like so many scattered tea leaves. It's not fair. It's better not to marry at all. Then no one but you and I will ever know."

"Mei Lin, I love you for who you are, not because you can

carry a child. I want you to be my wife. I don't want anyone else."

"But if we don't marry, no one will ever know. Besides, I was selfish. I thought if I adopted Little Mei, no one would have to know the truth. She could be our one child, and no one would suspect that I was barren. I realized later that I wasn't planning to adopt her because it was the plan of God or it would be the best for Little Mei. I was self-centered, Liko. It was all about what was best for me, not Little Mei. I'm so ashamed of myself."

"But don't you see?" Liko pleaded. "You're doing it all over again. Now you're trying to hide by not marrying at all."

Mei Lin looked at him until tears spilled out of her desolate heart and down her dusty face. She tried to piece together his words, but for some reason they weren't connecting.

"You want to use *me* to hide this time, instead of Little Mei," he said gently. "Don't you see? If we don't marry, it will hurt me. And it will hurt you. You think it will benefit Amah and every other unbeliever in Tanching, but it won't."

She felt jolted by his words. "What do you mean?"

Liko took her hand and pulled her. "Come on, let's walk out to the edge of the field."

Mei Lin wiped her face with the back of her arm and let him lead her to the edge of the field above her house.

Liko looked over the fields of rice and pointed with his free hand.

"Do you see these rice fields, terraced into steps far up that distant hill?"

Mei Lin nodded.

"And the sunshine—do you see how it dances on the waters between the stalks of rice? Mei Lin, the One who made all of this can take care of himself. You don't have to guard His reputation. He's not worried what people think, and you shouldn't be worried, either."

Liko faced her now and tilted her chin upward. "Let's give Him all of our mistakes right now, Mei Lin. And give Him a chance. He may heal you—but even if He doesn't, I want you in my life forever."

The question burned in her heart, and she had to have the answer tonight. "Would you be willing to adopt?" she whispered.

Liko pulled her head to his chest. She felt so loved and wanted. But she longed for a child of her own. She had to know if he would agree to adopt.

He touched her jaw and kissed her cheek. "I will adopt a whole orphanage full of children if it will make you smile."

"A whole orphanage?" she asked. A smile pushed at the corners of her mouth while Liko sweetly kissed the wetness from her face.

A whole orphanage full of children . . . now, that was a dream worth living for.

Liko pulled her close again and held her, his arms around her shoulders and her head against his chest. Together they watched the sunlight dance over the water in sparkling silver shoes, finding new steps as the air brushed past. Young stalks of rice, green and not yet mature, lifted their heads and swayed with the music. Like orphans, they reached for the One who made the earth and skies. Liko rocked a little, and Mei Lin rocked with him until they fell into rhythm with the dance.

AFTERWORD

Across the China Sky **is based on true events as related in this personal interview during my trip to China in October 2002.**

Using a cane, the leader of a vast network of Chinese Christians limped down the hallway and into the hotel room reserved for our secret meeting. Brother Shu (not his real name) was muscular and tall for a Chinese man, flanked with watchful associates. My interpreter told me his leg was injured years ago in prison when he refused to submit to Communist pressure to recant his faith.

Only three months earlier, Brother Shu and his associate pastors escaped a devilish trap he deemed worse than the Communist prison—a cult called Eastern Lightning. In April, thirty-four Chinese house church leaders were kidnapped by Eastern Lightning cult members. The ransom? A promise from the Christian leaders to lead their flock of thirty million to believe that Jesus has already "come again" and in fact lives in China in the form of a woman. The cult's theme verse is Matthew 24:27, "For as lightning cometh out of the east, and shineth even unto the west; so shall also the coming of the Son of man be" (KJV). Believing that the first Jesus was a Western male Jesus, they teach that the Eastern Jesus has now returned to earth and is a Chinese woman who must be followed. Large financial awards and sexual favors are offered to all major leaders who convert to this "Eastern Jesus."

Brother Shu and his associate sat near the hotel window, facing my interpreter, my father, another associate, and me. He looked at us without speaking. He seemed nervous, perhaps suspicious, perhaps just measuring his words.

"I don't want to talk about the kidnapping," he finally said.

I'd hoped for the details of his story, but I assured him I would not pry. He looked at my father, seventy-three years old, and I wondered later if it was the Chinese respect for the elders that made Brother Shu feel comfortable. After telling us about his house church network, he voluntarily began telling us his story.

Cult members infiltrated the churches of the South China Gospel Fellowship. For months they pretended to be Christians to gain the trust of the leadership. They faked conversions and were baptized, gave testimonies, prayed for the sick, gave money to the church, and sang the worship songs. In their hearts, however, the EL wanted to steal the Christian sheep. After EL members gained the leaders' trust, they invited them to study with seminary teachers from Singapore's reputable Haggai Institute.

Believing they were headed for a wonderful underground seminary in rural China, the leaders followed Eastern Lightning members into a vicious trap. After a few days at the "seminary," these powerful men and women of God realized they had been kidnapped. Then the torture and brainwashing began—women seducing men so they could take pictures of pastors in compromising positions, threats of amputating limbs or ears if they did not convert to the cult, threats to harm their families, drug-induced brainwashing where all night long cult members whispered Eastern Lightning teachings into the ears of the pastors as they tried to sleep. All day, all night, the coercion did not let up.

Brother Shu spoke quietly, with great remorse. "Some of our brothers and sisters were caught up by them. The EL broke their legs . . . chopped off their ears, or parts of the ears. They threatened to take a tendon out my body." The thing that caused the most heaviness of heart for Brother Shu is that the EL succeeded so well in deceiving him.

"I would like it if you would tell your President Bush about this Eastern Lightning cult," he said. "Tell people in your country because this cult is already infiltrating the Chinese churches there. And after they convert the Chinese, they plan to go into the American Christian churches."

I hung my head. How could I tell this man who'd suffered so much that I did not have an audience with the president of the United States? He was an eagle in the kingdom, an eagle who'd been broken, wings clipped, and terrorized by a cult he didn't even see attacking him until it was too late. I stood to my feet and shook his hand. "I will tell the American people. I don't have an audience with President Bush, but if God gives that to me I will tell him your story. And I will tell the American people to beware of the Eastern Lightning cult."

Report from Brother Chen*

June 20 we had a denunciation meeting, profoundly exposing and condemning the Eastern Lightning cult. Every one of the kidnapped co-workers talked about his experience during the confinement, disclosing the vile and despicable methods of the EL such as lying, deceit, money, employment opportunities, women, mind-altering drugs, sexual stimulants, dreams, visions, pretending to be ghosts, abuse, spreading division, blackmailing, isolation, spiritual and emotional torments, disrupting families, etc.

Through the sharing and discussions among brothers and sisters, through the denouncing of the EL, we all realized that the reasons why the church had suffered such extreme loss were that we didn't have enough knowledge of and precautions against the EL cult, neither did we have enough legal sense. During the meeting, we agreed on the following strategies against the EL.

1. Put great effort in wide-scale teaching about guarding against the intrusion of the EL false teachers.

2. Root out the EL spies from the church. In every one of our house churches, every believer should curse the EL cult in the name of Jesus Christ.

3. Once anyone is caught spreading the EL teaching, he should be turned over to the police.

4. If someone is kidnapped by the EL, he should shout loudly for help. We'd rather be caught by the police than fall into the evil hands of the EL cult.

5. Once kidnapped, one should guard his heart, be alert and pray constantly, not to listen to, read about, think about, argue with, nor to believe the EL.

6. Those who are released from kidnapping should openly confess their experiences and accept the examination of the body (of Christ). Their ministry should be stopped temporarily. The body should genuinely love and care for their well-being.

7. For those victims who have come back to their sound senses, the body should accept them with trust, so as not to fall into the schemes of the Devil.

8. For those suspected ones who don't seem to have a clear understanding and firm position, the body should try to restore and admonish them in love, faith, and watchfulness.

Let our stumbling be the warning for the future of the church in the rest of the world. May brothers and sisters be alert and watchful, to guard against and resist the schemes of cults and heresies, and to walk in the truth of the Lord.

Brother Chen
July 27, 2002

*This report was presented to Christians in Crisis, a group that is raising up 50,000 houses of prayer for the persecuted church worldwide.